DARIUS HINKS

D0096091

The Ingenious

ANGRY
ROBOT

ANGRY ROBOT
An imprint of Watkins Media Ltd

Unit 11, Shepperton House,
89 Shepperton Road,
London N1 3DF • UK

angryrobotbooks.com
twitter.com/angryrobotbooks
Feed on dreams

An Angry Robot paperback original 2019

Cover by John Coulthart
Set in Meridien by Argh! Nottingham

Distributed in the United States by Penguin Random House, Inc., New York.

ISBN 978 0 85766 789 2
Ebook ISBN 978 0 85766 790 8

Printed in the United States of America

9 8 7 6 5 4 3 2 1

For Kathryn
My heart's a boat in tow

"The excellence of the soul is understanding; for the man who understands is conscious, devoted, and already godlike."

HERMES TRISMEGISTUS

1

Reluctantly, she poured herself from Athanor's innards, floundering through the shit, dribbling through the back streets and brothels. The Sisters of Solace released her with a surprising and beautiful grace, shortening their beards, dropping their skirts and proclaiming her prowess to anyone drunk enough to care. Few women have been so well served by whores as Isten was in the long winter of her grief.

The corpse-light of mandrel-fires picked her out as she hurried towards the banks of the Saraca. They blazed across the filthy water, revealing the fruit of Athanor's latest plague. Corpses, of course, but also bundles of clothes, folded and bound, drifting through the scum in a pitiful flotilla as though destined for a happier world. There was nothing there of any value. This was a plague of the poor. Death, like everything else in Athanor, was unequally shared.

The mandrel-fires were a shocking reminder of how long Isten had been gone – how much she had missed. These were not the ghostly lamps that always lined Athanor's streets, these were heralds of transformation, beacons that were only lit at the time of conjunction; grand, sun-shaped scaffolds of silver and brass that would burn until the Festival of Undying Light. While Isten was embracing the Sisters of Solace, the city had jumped. The sky was an ocean of unfamiliar stars. Life had lurched, blind to her fall, and Athanor had changed. She looked up at a forest of new spires, studying the growth, marvelling at the labyrinthine constructions. With every rebirth, Athanor changed, growing larger, stranger, more bewildering.

She dropped out of sight, moving away from the beacons, hurrying on through the darkness, scouring the quayside for a familiar face. The awnings of Coburg Market had been rolled away leaving only a stink of fish guts and the fine-spun, skeletal facades of warehouses. At this time of night, even the beggars had a better place to be.

She lurched along for an hour, slapping through the blood and the brine, then collapsed on the steps that led down to a jetty. She coughed and spluttered as the cinnabar wormed its way through her skull, oozing painfully through her pores. The Sisters of Solace had blessed her with a particularly potent farewell gift and she lay there for a long time, feeling the city roll beneath her, looking up at its tortuous, seedpod bones. The locals boasted that Athanor's tracery of roads and aqueducts formed a map of the spheres, but to Isten it only ever looked like a cage.

It was nearly dawn when she sobered up enough to realize she was hungry. Her stomach was tight and resentful and she struggled to remember the last time she'd eaten. She hauled herself slowly to her feet, discovering an impressive collection of bruises and sprains. Every inch of her ached. She wanted nothing more than to lie back down again and sleep in the gutter, but she had a date to keep and a memory to honour, so she staggered off down the embankment.

She was leaving the market just as the traders and dock workers started to arrive and, as she hurried past, she heard snatches of their strange argot. Athanor was a city of émigrés and refugees, but the haulers and lightermen of Coburg Street were a particularly mongrel breed, speaking an amalgam of every language that had ever come to the city. They could be half understood by everyone and fully understood by no one. Having no wish to be recognized, she hurried on through the half-light, heading for the Blacknells Road Bridge.

She reached the borders of the Temple District and stooped lower, humbled by the scale of the architecture. Plump, recurved walls swelled out across the river, skimming the water like sails and trailing beautiful, spindle-twisted buttresses. Entrance to the temples was forbidden for commoners like Isten, but a narrow path skirted the walls, running alongside the water's edge, and she soon started to see more people. The Elect would be asleep at this time, but their laborators were abroad, running errands and brokering deals, scurrying like colourful vermin, their turmeric-stained faces hidden deep in lemon-coloured hoods. They were probably too engrossed in their work to acknowledge a wreck like Isten, but she avoided them all the same.

From there she reached the sprawling mounds of the Azorus slums – the ragged, filthy petticoat of the Temple District, steaming in the half-light, hazed by flies and smoke, tumbling down into the river to form a dysenteric slurry of rafts and wharfs, a landslide of rubbish, patched-together tents and wasted scavengers. Here was the city in all its grotesque magnificence – oil-slick wretches wading through filth, shimmering in the half-light, stained rainbow hues by the chemicals that flowed from the temple walls. It was a kaleidoscopic crush, desperate souls picking through the poison that bled from above, risking death and worse as they looked for fragments of wealth. Even the water was transformed as it passed the soaring walls. Chemicals glooped from rusty outlets, threading the Saraca with metal, turning its currents into an eddying, gleaming mirror – the Golden Chain, its links and intersections binding Athanor together, shackling its lost souls.

As Isten forced her way through the crush, she caught glimpses of newcomers. All life was drawn to the Saraca, whether native or foreign. The sacred waters paid no heed to the origins of its supplicants, and Isten saw countless species gnawing at its banks. Many were familiar – the withered husks of cindermen, swimming carelessly past leviathans that could crush them without realizing – hovellers, their pitted carapaces trawling through the shallows like the shells of huge crabs, almost as impressive as the temple walls, trailing storms of salvage nets and flies, their gnarled, bulwark heads plunged deep into the currents. But there were also species that Isten had never seen before – avian creatures that wore their insides as plumage and reptilian things that towered over the humans, looming almost as high as the hovellers. Isten paid no attention to any of it. She could not risk missing an appointment she was already a year late for. She fought her way up to a higher walkway and left the slums behind, heading towards the oldest parts of the city.

The sun had risen by the time she reached the Blacknells Road Bridge, but she was still on time – they were all there, exactly like every previous year, pilgrims, visiting the place where they first set foot in Athanor, huddled like lovers beneath the bridge's whorls and arches.

The sun was rising, and they must have been able to see her face, but they showed no sign of recognition, staring at her as though she were a ghost. They drew cudgels and knives and she faltered, almost turning around.

She wiped some of the vomit from her clothes and tried to smooth down her lunatic hair, but it was pointless – she had taken too much cinnabar. Her eyes were bright red. She stank of piss and sex and she could barely walk. Even by her own pitiful standards, she was a far from inspirational figure. Perhaps now they would see how wrong they had been about her.

"Isten," said someone, she couldn't see who, in a voice that gave nothing away.

She could think of nothing reasonable to say – no way to reassure them that she was sane; no way to reassure herself for that matter. And no way to apologize. She had been gone all this time, without word. She could hardly believe it herself. A painful silence stretched out between them. Then she remembered a bottle of wine she stole from the Sisters of Solace. She lifted it from her coat, wiped the dirt from its neck and held it up to the fading moon.

"My name is Donkey," she said, "and I still know how to do this." She took a few hard gulps and heat exploded in her chest. The wine was better than food – and heavy enough to dull the wildness of the cinnabar. The vivid grey of the dawn grew less intense and her heart finally began to slow. She wondered why she hadn't drunk it earlier.

They straightened their backs and said nothing, still sombre.

Then Lorinc glanced at the others and broke ranks, his massive, stooped frame looming over her. "My name is Goat," he rumbled, lowering his knife and grabbing the bottle, "and I can still do this." He scowled as he drank, making his butcher's slab face even uglier.

Another of them stepped forwards – almost as tall, but ancient, stooped and slow, moving with the precise, considered steps of the brittle-boned. "My name is Worm," said Gombus, "and I always do this." Despite the tremor in his hands, he drank almost a third of the bottle.

One by one, they drank: Feyer, Korlath, Piros and Amoria, until the bottle was almost empty.

Finally, the smallest of them emerged from the shadows. Puthnok's dark, perplexed eyes peered up at Isten from behind her glasses. She reminded Isten of an earnest child, unsure if she should speak in such adult company. Isten had to resist the urge to hug her. "I am the Beast." Puthnok's voice was hesitant, her eyes looking everywhere but at Isten. "And I hope I can still do this." She glugged down some wine and, as she started to splutter, the rest of them could no longer hold back their smiles.

Isten's shame was too raw for smiles, but she grasped each of their hands in turn. Their gaunt faces reminded her of home and she had to fight back tears. Thanks to her, home was further away than ever. She had come so close to losing herself.

"You're an idiot," said Lorinc.

She nodded, unable to disagree, and drank the last of the wine. Then she turned and hurled the bottle into the river, giving it to the flotsam and the dead.

• • •

They called themselves the Exiles, but the Blacknells Road had come to feel like home. They had fought, plotted and dreamed in every one of its coiled ribs. Athanor's soldiery, the hiramites, rarely muddied their boots in that shittiest of pits, the Botanical Quarter, so the people down there made their own rules. There were no gardens anymore, of course, not even the memory of a garden. Isten had never seen so much as a dead weed on the Blacknells Road. But there was privacy, brothels and cheap doss houses, and the knowledge that it was the oldest district in all Athanor. This was the stinking, sewer-less worm that threaded through the whole rotten apple. Even if she had been able to afford better, Isten would not have moved. The Blacknells Road at least had the balls to show its true face. The same could not be said for the rest of the city.

By mid-morning they were sitting in one of their favourite meeting places – just above the tall, eastern gable of the old Alembeck Temple, where its whipcord curls flooded over the equally twisted spires of the Marosa Library. Some of the rafters had collapsed centuries ago, creating a meandering depression from where they could watch the streets below without being seen. In the early days, Puthnok carved the first lines of her manifesto into the timbers and some of the words were still visible – rows of proud, tiny characters, worn and illegible but still resonant. They had become a totem. The Exiles huddled around them when they met, touching the beams with reverence, like supplicants at a shrine.

The streets around the Alembeck were so narrow and winding that they felt more like capillaries than roads, surrounded by buildings that spiralled into each other, entwined like riverweed, keeping the crowds below in a constant, dappled gloom. The building opposite had been boarded up years ago, allegedly after a visit from an Ignorant Man, and no one had dared enter since, so the Exiles were never overlooked.

This high, even the smell wasn't quite so bad. There was a spice market half a mile away, over on Rasbin Street, and the smell of garlic and cinnamon was almost enough to mask the stink of the turd hills drifting through the crowds below.

It had taken Isten hours, but she felt as though she was finally starting to win them over. She had abandoned them for an entire year, without warning, drowning a grief they knew nothing of, so an apology seemed pointless. Even now, the cause of her flight was too painful to share, but she felt the need to atone, so she tried instead to assure them that all was not lost – that it was not too late to begin again. They were far from convinced, and they were as wary of each other as they were of her, but she felt a slight thaw – they were at least answering her questions now.

"What about Colcrow?" she asked, picking cold chicken from her teeth. She had spent the last hour cramming her stomach with anything they could offer and her face was pleasantly slick with grease.

Lorinc grunted. "He left us before you did. He's probably still alive. I'd forgotten that shyster."

Isten shrugged. "I know he was never very reliable, but he used to have the Kardus family in his pocket. He always knew if something was going on. Even if he doesn't want to be associated with us any more, I bet he could give us some kind of steer. We don't need much. Just enough to get us on our feet again. We'd only need enough money to buy a few kilos." She waved vaguely, indicating the crowds squeezing through the streets below. "I'm assuming there's no drop in demand."

"Colcrow has money," said Puthnok, her voice brittle. "That's why people ignore everything else about him."

Puthnok had clearly been trying to develop more of a "persona" since Isten last saw her. The small, circular glasses were new and she was dressed in plain, utilitarian clothes. She had also shaved her head, clearly aiming for something sage-like, but she still reminded Isten of a troubled infant.

"Where's your brother?" asked Isten, suddenly realizing he was missing.

Puthnok's expression darkened.

Lorinc put a hand on Puthnok's shoulder. "The Aroc Brothers took everything, Isten. Ozero ran into a group of them on Caprus Street and they–"

Puthnok gripped Lorinc's arm, giving him a warning look.

Lorinc looked pained and squeezed Puthnok's shoulder. "They've taken everything, Isten."

"Ozero," whispered Isten, dazed by the news of his death. Puthnok's brother had been the strongest of them all.

"If you'd been here," muttered Puthnok, staring at her feet, "perhaps things would have been different."

"Ozero," whispered Isten again, shaking her head.

The cinnabar pulsed back into life, throbbing behind her dry, aching eyes, and the more she studied Puthnok, the stranger the girl looked. Her head swelled until it was larger than the rest of her and transformed her into a grubby foetus, nestling among them like a mystified foundling. Isten struggled to hold down her chicken as an umbilical cord slithered from the folds of Puthnok's coat, snaking across the roof tiles, straining and reaching like a pale serpent. Isten was about to stamp on it when Puthnok's head returned to its normal size and the blood tube dissolved into the roof.

Isten grabbed more chicken and ate furiously.

They all looked at her with doubtful expressions.

Amoria was standing a few feet away with her back to them, looking down over the streets below. Like Puthnok, her head was shaven, but on her the effect was more striking. She had left two tall horns – matted tusks of crimson-dyed hair that jutted up from her skull, adding to her naturally belligerent air. She was leaning on the same bloodstained quarterstaff she had been carrying the last time Isten saw her and she looked as lethal as ever. She glared at Isten. "It's been shit without you here." She stepped away from the roof's edge and waved her staff at the others. "These fuckers would rather starve than actually do anything. The Aroc Brothers killed Ozero and we've done nothing in response. Sayal took him down. And he's still out there. Large as life. He killed Ozero and we did *nothing*."

A couple of the group nodded, but others looked away, ashamed. They looked awful. As Isten ate, she sensed them watching her from the corners of their eyes, trying to gauge what she had become, trying to decide if she could help them.

"The Aroc Brothers have taken *everything* we had," said Amoria. "It got worse after you left. That's why there are so few of us now. It's not just Ozero. The Aroc Brothers killed dozens of our best men. And dozens more left us when we lost control of the river."

"The Aroc Brothers," said Isten, shaking her head. A

cool fury washed through her, tightening her muscles and clearing her head. "That's the first thing we need to deal with." She looked at Puthnok. "Sayal has to die. He's been a thorn in our side since the first day we got here. How much money do we have left?" She looked over at Piros.

Piros was little more than a teenager, a jumble of scrawny limbs lying on his back in the shade, sheltering from the sun. Despite his youth, he looked as grey and haggard as the rest of the Exiles. He said nothing, simply holding up his hand and making a zero with his thumb and forefinger.

Isten used one of the broken rafters to help her stand. The movement ignited the cinnabar again and she almost fell.

Amoria stepped to her side and gripped her arm.

"Colcrow will help us, I'm sure of it," Isten managed to say. "Whatever he's done, he's still an Exile. He swore the oath. And he's got no love for the Aroc Brothers."

"You're a wreck," said Puthnok. "And we're as bad. Why would Colcrow help? He's not interested in what happened to my brother. He's not interested in any of us. We can't pay him and we can't fight. Why would he even speak to us? What could we offer?"

Isten took a deep breath, battling waves of nausea, then nodded. "I can offer him my continued silence. I know the details of his sex life better than he does."

Puthnok frowned and shook her head. "What?"

Isten nodded. "The Sisters of Solace run a very open house. I observed the full, colourful extent of old Colcrow's tastes. He didn't see me, but I certainly saw him. More of him than I would have liked."

"So?" asked Lorinc. "Will he care? He's not known for his high morals."

Isten shrugged. "You'd be surprised. His wife will happily turn a blind eye to most of his exploits, but the poor old witch thinks he's still faithful to her. I don't think Colcrow would want me to reveal the true, exotic nature of his business meetings."

"And why would she believe us over him?" asked Lorinc.

"The Sisters of Solace would tell her themselves if I asked them. They adore me. They treat me like a prophet."

Lorinc raised an eyebrow.

Isten held up her hands. "They take too many of their own drugs. What can I do?"

Lorinc snorted.

"Look," said Isten, gripping Puthnok by the shoulder. "I know *you're* the real prophet, but we can take advantage of the Sisters' confusion. They'll do anything I ask."

"At least now I can understand how you managed to stay with them for so long without any money," said Lorinc.

"Let's do it," said Amoria, spinning her staff around and holding it out to Puthnok, pulling her to her feet. "Sayal's swaggering around Athanor thinking we don't care that he killed your brother."

Puthnok still looked doubtful and she glanced at Gombus. The old man had not spoken since they left the river.

Isten was still squeezing Puthnok's shoulder. "I know what you're thinking. But I haven't forgotten who we are." She nodded to the rotten beams and the faded words. "Your time will come." She looked around at the whole group. "*Our* time will come. We're not destined to die in this shithole. We all know that."

No one spoke and Isten could imagine how hard it was to take a troop-rallying speech from someone who had spent the last year hiding.

"I *won't* fail you," she said, raising her voice, trying to sound as though she believed what she was saying. "I'll get you home. You will see your families. We'll make a new world, just like Puthnok said we would."

They were all looking at her now, but their expressions were hard to read. Amoria was smiling, as was Lorinc, but Isten knew that was only because they'd caught the scent of blood. The rest of them were just staring. They were so gaunt and sunken-eyed that Isten felt like she was in a charnel house. As soon as that thought formed in her mind, the cinnabar made it real. Flesh sloughed from their bones, leaving her surrounded by rotting corpses. She pretended that nothing had happened, trying to keep her words level.

"But until that new world comes, we must find a way to survive *this* one. Which means money. Which means dealing with the Aroc Brothers. We need to make Sayal pay for what he did and then take back what's ours." She was talking with more confidence now, making statements she actually believed in. "We'll get some help from Colcrow, then we'll arm ourselves and pay a visit to the Aroc Brothers." She glanced at Puthnok. "I'm more than happy to deal with Colcrow if it means I can get to Sayal."

One of the cadavers spoke. It was a rotting, worm-threaded lump, but she knew from its raspy voice that it was Gombus. He had finally decided to address her. "And after this deal, Isten? What then? More deals?"

As the corpse spoke, its jaw tumbled down its chest, spilling bluebottles and maggots.

"Only until we're sufficiently well armed to bring the other Exiles to back to our cause," she replied. "We'll buy them with money and violence, but then we'll turn Puthnok's wisdom on them. When they hear what she has to say, they'll start to dream again. We *all* dream of a new homeland. That's our most valuable currency. And then, when we're ready, we'll leave, I promise you. When we have men and arms and money, there's nothing we can't do. We'll go home, Gombus. I'll become the woman you all want me to be, I promise you, but you know what would happen if we went back now, like this. We'd be dead before we saw a familiar face."

"You've said this before." Gombus shook his head, spilling worms from his ruptured neck. "You've spent years doing deals and killing people, Isten. Where has it got us? You can barely stand. And you've soiled your hands doing things I don't want to think about."

Anger cleared Isten's eyes and she saw Gombus properly again. He had an air of gravitas that little Puthnok could only dream of. It wasn't just his weathered, lined skin; there was something venerable about Gombus that was hard to explain. They all sensed it – a calmness that held the Exiles together when they would otherwise have fallen apart. His doubt hurt Isten as much as it always did. And, as always, it brought out the worst in her.

"What else should we do?" she snarled. "Rot up here on this roof, reading Puthnok's manifesto to each other until we die? Let the Aroc Brothers take the city without a fight? Let them murder Ozero without any payback? Stay true to the dream until they sling us in the Saraca with all the other sad fuckers?"

Gombus looked pained but said nothing.

The angrier Isten became, the clearer her thoughts grew.

"There's no deal I won't make, Gombus, if it means we can survive for another year, another *day*. There's no crime I won't commit to keep us alive."

She squared up to him, until her face was level with his chest. "But what about you? Are you still with me, Gombus?"

Isten immediately regretted asking the question. She could see the others watching him closely. He was a relic. A link to the past. A link to Isten's mother and a host of other legends. The loyalty of the group would hinge on what he said.

Gombus shook his head and asked the question none of the others had dared. "Why did you go, Isten? Where have you been all this time?"

"Having fun," she muttered, avoiding his eye.

He gave her a patient stare.

His face was her earliest memory. He was the closest thing she had to family. And his doubt dragged bile into her throat.

"And why did you come back?" he asked.

She nodded to the hollow-eyed faces that surrounded them. "Because they're dying. Because you're dying. And I knew you would be. God help me, I didn't *want* to come back, but not one of you has any sense. Puthnok thinks you're going to topple empires and you can't even feed yourselves."

"Where did you go, Isten?" he said. "You can't have been with the Sisters the whole time. How have you survived a whole year without us to protect you?"

She laughed. "*Protect* me? Can you see yourself, Gombus? How much protection do you think you can offer? Did you protect Ozero?"

Gombus's gaze faltered. He looked wounded and she felt a rush of shame, but that just made her angrier. "You're pathetic," she spat, "all of you. You've forgotten how to *fight*."

"You left for a reason," said Gombus, refusing to let her dodge his question. "I know you've always hated this, but you were never foolish enough to leave us before. What made you go? What did you do?"

Isten felt sick. It horrified her how easily he could read her; how accurately he had pinned her. She was about to insult him again when Amoria held up her hand for silence and pointed her staff.

There was a fox, over on the roof of the library. It was staring at them, its head swaying gently from side to side as it padded backwards and forwards.

"I'll be damned," said Lorinc.

Isten backed away from Gombus, grabbed the last scraps of chicken and threw them onto the other roof.

The fox ignored them, staring directly at her.

"Still alive?" whispered Isten. It was a scrawny, bedraggled runt, with an ear missing, but they had seen it several times when they first arrived in Athanor. In those early days of exile, when they had so few friends, the fox had felt like a symbol of hope, a fellow outlaw. Like all of Athanor's wildlife, it had been transformed by the fumes that spilled from the Saraca. Its nape and back sported a lattice of wire threads that tumbled and spiralled down its flank, encircling its legs, glinting as it moved, making it look more like an invention of the Curious Men than a creation of nature.

"Is it definitely her?" asked Amoria, stepping to Isten's side.

"Look at the ugly fucker," said Lorinc. "It's her."

"How long do foxes live?" asked Isten, looking back at Puthnok, assuming, as always, that she would know.

"We first saw her five years ago. They don't usually survive that long, out of captivity I mean, but here, in Athanor, who knows? I suppose it's possible. It looks like her. I recognize the markings."

The fox watched them for nearly a minute, its head still swaying, then it snatched the meat and scampered off back down the roof, glinting as it vanished into Athanor's bare-boned tangle of domes and spires.

They watched the fox go in silence. So much had happened since they arrived in Athanor. So much had been lost.

Isten's head was briefly clear of cinnabar and she closed her eyes, savouring the breeze whipping through the minarets, bathing her face in the noise and mystery of the city. It felt good to have a purpose. To have a way to help. Sayal had to die. *She* had to kill him.

When she opened her eyes, everyone was watching her, and Gombus's expression had softened.

She said nothing, holding his gaze.

With a trembling hand, he took some coins from his robes and gave them to her. "Of course I'm with you."

2

At night, if she slept too sober, she would see his face, swimming through the dream tide, cold and inhuman. He would smile as he led her to the bed, a ghastly, heartless grimace. Hatred would boil up through her, the hatred she could not risk when she was awake. He could have told her what it meant. He could have stopped her. He could have told her how she would feel. But as the Exiles welcomed her home, and the old life came back, the face in her dreams grew fainter, the anger softer, the darkness kinder. She could almost forget how badly she had betrayed them.

The Zechen baths was the name given to the entire eastern border of the Temple District. There were miles of ancient spas and bathhouses, some were still in regular use, but most were little more than beautiful ruins – a crumbling sprawl of silent fountains and toppled, serpentine arches, suitable only for the musings of poets, dogs and the occasional murderer. Isten barely noticed the architecture, rushing down ribbon-curve walkways with her head down, clinging to the shadows. It had taken nearly a week of discreet questions and whispered threats to pin down Colcrow's movements, but now they were moments away.

Lorinc led the way, hauling his massive bulk over the

ruins with surprising ease. There was a full moon and they made a bold line of silhouettes against the bleached bathhouse walls, but the local cutpurses would all be busy. There were rich pickings to be found half a mile away – in the libraries and colleges on the far side of Anatis Square. The laborators who served the Curious Men wielded none of their masters' power, but they were often to be found carrying the same valuable base metals. The larger colleges were rumoured to be guarded by Ignorant Men, but most of the laborators were left to fend for themselves. Some carried knives beneath their robes, but their only real defence was the reputation of their masters – a defence that worked well on the sane and the sober, but not so well on the majority of Athanor's citizens.

"It's that one," called Amoria, her horned scalp bobbing up and down on the far side of a toppled wall. She was pointing her staff at a bathhouse with lights blinking through its windows.

Lorinc paused, hunched on a headless statue. "This one, surely?" he called back, nodding to another illuminated building in the opposite direction – an impressive dome, surrounded by colonnaded walkways.

They all stopped and looked around for Puthnok. She was way behind the rest of them, clambering awkwardly over the rubble-strewn streets and holding a little lantern before her, despite the blazing moonlight. She had the most peculiar way of walking. She seemed to be in a constant state of falling – scurrying on her tiptoes, leaning forwards, as though battling into a strong wind.

It took her a moment to notice the expectant silence, then she pushed her glasses back up her nose and waved her lantern in the direction of Amoria. "The Varavia baths," she hissed.

Amoria gave Lorinc a triumphant smirk, vaulted a wall and jogged off towards the building.

They rushed down a long portico into a square courtyard with doors on either side and an unused fountain at the centre. Moonlight blazed across the ancient paths and stretched beneath the winding cloisters. Hiding was not an option, so Isten led the others with a confident swagger as they approached the entrance to the baths.

There was no attendant waiting outside. Despite the heat of the day, Athanor's clear skies meant the nights were usually cool. She guessed the attendants would be inside, huddled around a card game. She could hear muffled voices and the rattling of pipes, so the bathhouse was clearly open.

"Do we all go in?" asked Lorinc, trying to peer through a shutter.

Isten had only brought the three of them: Lorinc so that nobody would mess with her, Amoria in case they did mess with her and Puthnok because it was funny to watch her running.

She shook her head. "No, just you and Amoria in case he has Golo with him." She looked at Puthnok. "You can wait out here. If we get our throats slit, tell Gombus he was right to doubt me and that he's permitted to be smug when he sees me in the river."

Puthnok was still breathless from climbing through the ruins, so she just nodded and wandered off to lean against the crooked fountain at the centre of the square.

"What do you have on you?" Isten asked, looking at the other two.

Amoria threw her quarterstaff to Puthnok and pulled out a small, leaf-shaped knife, holding it into the moonlight to proudly show Isten how keen the blade was.

Isten nodded and turned to Lorinc.

He flipped back his jacket to reveal a short, iron crowbar.

"Ok," said Isten. "Don't say anything stupid. I know what Colcrow is, but we're here looking for help, not a fight."

They both nodded, but Isten could see a worrying glint in Amoria's eyes. She stared at her a little longer.

"I understand," she grinned, holding up her palms.

Isten nodded and pushed the door open, unleashing a wall of hot damp air. As she expected, the attendants were waiting inside, but it was clear they would be no problem. Their eyes were blood red and they were slumped in their chairs, staring rapturously at the ceiling with drool glittering in their beards. Most of the bathhouses doubled as cinnabar dens and the staff were usually users who never managed to leave.

The taste of the cinnabar caught in Isten's throat and she froze.

"Come on," muttered Lorinc, his tone sympathetic as he gently shoved her forwards. They had all developed vices over the last few years. Isten's were just more visible. She nodded and carried on, trying to ignore the smell, but even the aroma was enough to unshackle her thoughts. The shadows thrown by candles became more animated, reaching towards her as she headed for the next door.

One of the attendants mumbled and waved to a copper bowl on a table in the corner.

Lorinc dropped a coin in as he passed, knowing that Amoria would remove it again as she passed, along with another two.

They headed to the next room, undressed, wrapped themselves in bathrobes and went on into the steam room.

The heat was wonderful. After hours of skulking through the streets, Isten forgot about Colcrow and revelled in the steam. She closed her eyes and tilted her head back, allowing her muscles to relax. She was still aching from the falls and cuts she had received in the company of the Sisters of Solace, but the steam almost reminded her how it felt to be healthy.

The other two had already moved on, vanishing ghostlike into the steam, so she edged forwards. The first chamber was small and circular, and there were indistinct figures slumped all around her, sat on smooth, tiled benches, their heads hung between their knees. The thick steam made them amorphous and ghostlike – pale, sweltering heaps in the darkness. Isten's mind was still playing tricks on her and she felt as though she was drowning, peacefully, surrounded by shoals of pallid sea creatures, sinking through the floor as the heat pipes rattled and moaned.

Someone coughed, jolting Isten from her trance, and she stepped around the brazier, being careful not to jostle any of the other guests.

It was hard to be sure in the steam, but she did not think any of the ghosts were Colcrow. There would be a very specific crowd of women around him. She opened a door and moved on into the next chamber.

This one was even hotter, and lit by a skylight, so moonlight revealed the slumped figures on the benches in more detail. Lorinc and Amoria had sat down and they watched her approach in silence. Then, when she had almost reached them, they nodded to the bench opposite.

As Isten expected, Colcrow was surrounded by a group of almost identical young women: the same blonde, slender, doll-like waifs he always surrounded himself with. Like everyone else in the baths, Colcrow looked comatose, leant back against the mosaic-tiled wall, his mouth hanging open, his eyes closed and his hands resting palms upwards on his knees. He was not wearing any robes, or even a loincloth, clearly proud of his powerful bulk. In his youth, he had been as impressive as Lorinc, but now he was paunchy and soft, his features hiding in the centre of his jowly head. Since Isten last saw him, he had grown a long, thin goatee and dyed it purple. It spiralled down his gut like a sleeping snake.

Sitting near Colcrow was another large figure. Isten could not see his face, but she could tell by his rigid, upright posture that it was Colcrow's bodyguard, Golo. Golo had been a soldier in the old country, before they were all sent into exile, and he still carried himself with the same brittle pride, despite being almost as old as his master. Like Colcrow, Golo had once been one of the Exiles. A believer. But now he only served Colcrow. And he served for money, not ideals. Isten had no doubt that Golo would be armed.

She gestured for the other two to stay where they were. They were fast enough to help if things went wrong and Isten would rather Colcrow think she was alone.

She picked up a cup of tea from an ice bucket and settled down next to him, waving one of the doe-eyed women away with a glare. Then, after a few seconds of listening to his heavy, relaxed breathing, she whispered into his ear.

"My name is Donkey," she said, "and I still know how to do this." Then she sipped from the teacup and handed it to him.

He did not move, but his breathing changed, speeding up slightly.

Isten thought he was going to ignore her, but after a few seconds he spoke. As always, she was surprised how soft his voice was, purring up from his vast, sagging chest.

"Do you remember," he said, sounding as though he were still half asleep, "the sound of the Stura as it reaches the Narrabo falls? Can you still hear that sound, Isten? I'd forgotten it, but your accent brings it back. The water and the gulls. If I sit here long enough, listening to you with my eyes closed, I could almost be there."

Isten cursed him, inwardly, for taking her back there. She and Colcrow had nothing in common except a homeland, but he had the power to make her heart race with the mention of a river.

"I remember."

He stayed like that for a while, eyes closed and head tilted back, savouring the memory. Then he opened his eyes and gave her a nauseating smile, taking the tea.

"My name is Duck," he said, sipping from the cup, his voice husky with loss and sleep. "And I can at least do this."

He studied the eerie, wraithlike figures that surrounded them, as though only now realizing where he was.

"You should be careful," he said. "I hear there are agents looking for you."

"Agents?"

"So I'm told." He laughed. "Come on. You're not as dim as your friends. Did you think we were forgotten out here? We remember our home, Isten, and home remembers us. Your name in particular has been mentioned, along with that grim little radical you love so much."

He was an inveterate liar, but this had a worrying ring of truth to it. "Puthnok?"

Colcrow nodded, looking eagerly around the chamber, staring into the steam. "Is she here?" He moistened his plump lips. "The grumpy child-woman? I hear she's worth money."

"No," muttered Isten, thrown by his unexpected talk of agents. "No, she is not." Anger boiled through her chest, fuelled by the cinnabar. She sniffed the steam. There was an underlying sweetness.

Colcrow smiled and closed his eyes again, sliding his palm slowly down the thigh of the girl next to him, wiping the sweat from her skin. "One can truly *breathe* in here."

Isten looked across the room, trying to make out the shapes of Lorinc and Amoria, but the dream-state was taking hold again. The forms in the mist had begun to stretch, elongating into something blind and foetal, drifting through the heat, clutching at the air. The clanging of the heat pipes became an arterial thud. The walls pulsed and contracted, sweating, dripping, pressing down.

Colcrow shook his head. "You look worse every time I see you." His eyes sparkled with amusement. "And I hear you've deserted our little family. Where have you been hiding yourself?"

Isten took the cup and finished the tea, trying to fix her thoughts in the moment. She struggled to remember what she was doing there, then she caught a glimpse of Amoria, leaning forwards, staring at her through the steam, her face human once more.

"With the Sisters of Solace," she said, calmed by the memory that she knew things he did not.

His smile faltered, then returned. "The beautiful changelings. I thought you had more class."

"I go there to see who else is visiting."

His expression hardened. "What do you want?"

Isten moved her face so close they could have kissed. "Are we still friends, Colcrow?"

"What do you want?"

She leant back for breath, unable to bear his heat. "A little news. A chance to earn some money." She looked him in the eye. "You know me, I won't dog your heels. I just need some capital."

His expression remained fixed. "And if I don't help you?"

"We don't have to discuss that." Isten was conscious of the poor girls sat around her, caught in the thrall of this vile predator. She felt dirty even talking to Colcrow, so she pictured Puthnok's round, earnest little face, reminding herself why she was lowering herself to this.

He leant back and stared into the steam. "I'll help you, Isten, but not because you crawled in here with some sordid threat in mind. And not for the Exiles, either. I'll help because your voice reminded me of the River Stura, and that is worth something."

He tilted his head back against the mosaic and closed his eyes. He thought for a while, mouthing names and numbers, stroking his goatee like it was a pet. When he spoke again, his voice was so low she had to lean in close to hear.

"We're all struggling, Isten. But our old friends, the Aroc Brothers, have been incredibly lucky. Money and drugs seem to be falling into their hands with shocking ease since they drove us out of business. Every week I hear news of some incredible stroke of luck that has befallen our lumpen friends. And they'll soon be in receipt of one of the largest drug shipments to get through the city walls since we arrived at," he waved vaguely, "whatever wretched hole we've landed in this time. I don't know the nature of the drugs, other than that they're very valuable, but they're currently waiting in a warehouse near the Azof embassy, south of the docks. The Aroc boys won't send anyone there until midnight tomorrow, but I happen to know that the shipment arrived early, a few days ago, so it's already in the warehouse. And the strange thing is that no one seems to be guarding it. I suppose whoever smuggled the drugs this far doesn't want to be associated with them, but it's still odd that there's *no one* watching them." He paused, shuffling his weight slightly. "I could give you the address. Imagine what a blow it would be if someone arrived tonight and stole from those poor Aroc boys."

Isten nodded, unable to hide her pleasure at the idea.

Colcrow smiled. "You'd love to hurt them, wouldn't you? Your glorious reign ended when they decided that south of the Saraca wasn't enough for them, isn't that right?" He gave her a look of mock sympathy. "I suppose that's when it all started to go wrong for you. All those madams and procurers paying somcone else for protection. Such a shame that the brothers decided to put us out of business." Bitterness crept into his voice. "Such a shame that you weren't better able to fight our corner."

"If the drugs are so valuable, why aren't *you* down at that warehouse?"

He shrugged. "I'm not as desperate as you. There's something odd going on with the whole deal. Something smells bad. I've had the place watched at all hours and there's no sign of guards. A shipment like that with no guards? It makes no sense. I'm missing something. If I was in as much of a mess as you, perhaps I'd take a risk, but I'm not, so I won't."

"And if I go, what would your cut of the profits be? What's the split?"

"Fifty-fifty."

She laughed out loud, causing a few people to look up.

Colcrow raised a finger to his lips, stroking it gently from side to side in an obscenely sensuous way.

"Isten, I'm taking a risk, telling you this. That kind of haul would warrant a death sentence, you know that, for anyone involved. And how will you shift it once you have it? You've been gone too long, Isten. All of your old friends work for the Aroc Brothers now. I hardly think you can ask them to sell it, can you?"

Isten shook her head, guessing what was coming next. "But you'll be prepared to take it off our hands at a cut down price."

He rested an arm over her shoulder and pulled her close, filling her nose with the heady scent of his perfume. "A *reasonable* price. We're friends, remember."

3

As she lay there, accepting their solace, the Sisters shared stories with her – the dreams and secrets of their most enraptured clients, intoned at the height of passion with all the urgency of prayer. In the darkness of their ecstasy, bewildered lovers whispered stories of Curious Men, so lost in happiness that they dared speak of the unspeakable. Faith is the lie we wish to be told and, in the early days of her grief, with death at her side, Isten took comfort in every untruth. The Curious Men are no more than stokers of the mandrel-fire, said the Sisters, easing her away from the grave. They will never truly be Athanor's regents. They're a lie. Another fire breathes life into the city. The animatis. The lungs, the blood and the heart. The Ingenious.

Gombus welcomed them with sleep still in his eyes, stepping back from the door and ushering them into a gloomy entrance hall. He lived in one of the lodging houses that crowded the streets around the Blacknells Road. It was called the Rookery and it was slightly more reputable than some of the other establishments. The street was crammed with slums, doss houses and brothels and there was no time, night or day, that the sound of fighting did not reverberate through the thin walls. Gombus led them up piss-reeking stairs, past rubbish and sleeping whores and on into his room. There was just enough space for the four of them to squeeze in next to him.

He nodded for them to sit on his bunk and turned to the only other piece of furniture in the room – a crooked, waist-high cupboard that had a bottle of wine and some cups on top of it. He gave them all a drink and sat on the cupboard, eyeing them over the top of his cup. In such a confined space, he seemed less fragile, looming over them as they shifted awkwardly on his bunk. Even surrounded by so much poverty, there was something regal about him. He looked like a carving of a hollow-cheeked king: proud, hook-nosed and tragic. He ran a hand across his silver stubble and sipped the wine, haloed by a blade of moonlight.

"Did Colcrow help?"

Isten nodded, feeling even more uncomfortable as she told him the pitiful nature of the agreement.

He nodded and finished his drink. Then he fetched the bottle and refilled the cups.

"I wish we could kill him when all this is done," said Amoria. Her face twisted into a snarl. "He makes me sick."

Gombus shook his head. "We all swore the same oath. We do not take the life of an Exile – whatever else we do, we'll never sink that low."

Isten nodded. "Whatever he is, he's one of us. We don't kill our own. I know he's a–"

Isten was interrupted by an explosion of noise from outside. A fight had spilled out onto the street.

Gombus leant over them and snapped a shutter across his single, tiny window. "Colcrow always was devious, even as a child. I'll be amazed if he even sticks to fifty-fifty."

Isten shook her head. "He'll stick to his word. We're a reminder of home." She frowned, remembering what he had said about Puthnok. "He gave me a warning."

"About what?"

She had not mentioned this to the other three and they looked at her in surprise.

"He said there are agents in the city, looking for us."

Gombus frowned, his drink hovering an inch from his lips. "Agents?"

"From home. He said that Emperor Rakus knows we're here, in Athanor. Colcrow said the emperor has people *in* the city."

"Why would they care about us after all this time?" asked Amoria.

Gombus nodded at Isten. "Some of us are not very good at being discreet. Maybe someone has heard the name Isten and put two and two together."

As always, Isten felt nauseous at the mention of her ancestry. She shook her head. "Even if that were true, how would they be in touch with Rakus?" She remembered that the city had undergone conjunction while she was with the Sisters of Solace. She felt an absurd hope. "Where are we now?"

Amoria rolled her eyes and laughed. "Yes. Athanor has taken us back home to Rukon. The revolution begins today. We've already beheaded the emperor, we just forgot to mention it to you."

"We're not sure *where* we've come yet," said Gombus. "But the new arrivals are definitely not from Rukon. You'll see them soon enough. Savage creatures. Headhunters."

Isten frowned, feeling foolish. "Then how could anyone

be in contact with Rakus?"

Gombus shrugged. "Ask Colcrow."

Puthnok was looking even more anxious than usual. "Do they know about the manifesto?"

Gombus shook his head. "I doubt it. It's the name 'Isten' that would bring Rakus after us. Especially if they work out she's the right age to be *the* Isten."

"Who knows what they've heard," said Puthnok. "If they're in Athanor, and they're in touch with home, we might all be in trouble."

Amoria laughed and waved at their pitiful surroundings. "I love the fact that you only think we *might* be in trouble."

Puthnok blushed and glared at the floor. "*More* trouble. We should keep our heads down."

"We should arm ourselves," said Isten. "We're powerless like this. It doesn't matter if it's agents from home or the Aroc Brothers, we're sitting ducks for anyone who wants to get rid of us." She waved at Gombus's filthy, sagging room. "Most of us don't even have this level of privacy. The whole of Athanor probably knows our business. Where do Feyer and Korlath and Piros sleep? On the streets?"

Gombus shook his head and waved his cup at the floorboards. "Here, usually, if they sleep at all."

"We're living like animals," said Isten. "But let's not die like animals. There'll be no glorious uprising if we die in these hovels."

Amoria nodded. "The embassy is only an hour from here. If we move fast we could be there and gone before dawn."

"Where are the other three?" asked Isten.

"They'll be in the Stump if they're anywhere," said Amoria. "But they'll be no use to us at this time of night."

"She's right," said Lorinc. "We'd do better without them. I could carry the bags of red out by myself, if I need to."

"Four it is, then," said Isten, looking at Lorinc, Puthnok and Amoria, knowing Gombus would want no part in it. "Colcrow said the warehouse isn't guarded. The shipment wasn't meant to land until tomorrow. We'll go in quick and then meet back on the roof of the Alembeck."

They all nodded and struggled up from the broken bed. Isten expected to feel some of the old spark, but, as they squeezed back down the stairs, the mood was sombre.

Gombus stood in the doorway, watching them go, sipping his wine, until one of the whores started laughing at him. He shook his head and stepped back into shadow.

The Blacknells Road was full of noise and drunks, even at this hour, but by the time they neared the docks the streets were finally quiet and the last mandrel-fires had been extinguished. The Exiles rushed through squares and parks, keeping to the shadows as they neared the embassy and vaulted its spear-tipped railings, dropping lightly into the courtyard beyond.

The embassy was hardly ever used at night and the windows were shuttered. They circled the whole building before finally creeping towards the derelict warehouse – a pitiful, crooked heap, grafted onto the side of its venerable neighbour.

The warehouse was a mesh of wiry, looping spines, silhouetted against the low moon – a bristling mound that looked more like a hawthorn bush than a building. As Isten edged closer to the doors, she drew out a knife and pulled her hood low.

The doors were padlocked, but the lock was a rusted old lump that had clearly not been used for decades. It would crumble with a good hit, but entering from the front of the building would hardly be discreet. She waved for Amoria and Puthnok to scout round one side of the building while she and Lorinc headed in the other direction.

Cats and vermin scattered as they approached, pattering across the piles of rubbish, dislodging rotten timbers heaped against the walls. Isten froze, waiting to see if the noise had alerted anyone to their presence, but there was nothing. The warehouse remained silent, draped in darkness.

Finally, they met the others coming back the other way.

As their faces emerged into the moonlight, Amoria shrugged and shook her head.

Lorinc waved his iron bar at a section of the warehouse that had fallen away, leaving a gaping shadow in the wooden panels. The hole was big enough to climb through and there was a heap of crates stacked beneath it that would work as steps.

Isten looked around to check everyone had their weapons ready, then nodded and padded silently over to the crates.

Before climbing up, she pressed her face to the rotten boards, squinting into the darkness, trying to discern any movement. There was nothing.

She climbed slowly up to the opening, took a last look inside, then dropped down into the darkness.

Isten landed with the silent grace they had all developed over the last few years, stepping quickly into the cavernous space to give the others room to land behind her. Moonlight speared through twisted beams, drawing abstract shapes in the blackness. Isten imagined several figures before realizing they were just shadows thrown by the broken rafters.

As the others landed behind her, Isten's eyes began to adjust and she managed to get a feel for the layout of the building. There were four ceiling-high columns holding up the roof, entwined with the same gossamer-like threads as the rest of the city's architecture, and the floor was covered with shattered crates and pieces of rope. At the opposite end of the main room there was a door. It was hanging at an angle, one of the hinges gone, and Isten could see furniture stacked in the office beyond. The whole place stank of damp, mildew and rat shit. It was like crawling through the bilges of a wreck.

She looked back at the others. They were just shadows amongst shadows, but she saw Amoria's horns catch the light as she nodded to the centre of the room.

Next to a heap of shattered crates there was a single intact box and a trail leading away from it across the muddy floor.

Isten scoured the shadows again, checking that none of them had moved since she last looked but with every second her eyesight grew clearer, and she saw nothing that resembled a person. Colcrow had been telling the truth. There was no one here. The penalty for trafficking cinnabar was death. Perhaps the smugglers who brought the crate had decided it was too risky to wait near such a large shipment until tomorrow night.

Isten stepped slowly forwards, eying the piles of rubbish for anything that might be a trap.

There was nothing and, after an agonizing few seconds, she reached the crate.

It was definitely a recent arrival. It still smelt of the river and the wood was sturdy and securely nailed.

Isten waved Lorinc over and nodded to the crate. He took out his crowbar and slowly, carefully, began to lever the lid off.

The planks were cold and firmly nailed shut. As Lorinc worked at them they protested with a series of petulant shrieks.

He hesitated, giving her a questioning look.

There was still no movement in the darkness, so she nodded for him to continue.

After another shrill creak, the lid opened far enough for Lorinc to slide his fingers underneath and pull it free.

Isten looked inside and grinned.

Amoria hissed with disbelief and Lorinc shook his head.

The crate was crammed with bulging parcels of waxed paper.

Isten grabbed one and pulled back the corner. The heady, sweet smell hit her immediately.

"Red," whispered Lorinc.

Isten frowned, taking another sniff. "But mixed with something else. It smells strange. Good, but strange."

Lorinc shrugged. "Maybe it's come from wherever the city has landed this time? Maybe it's cut with something new?"

Isten shook her head, troubled by the odd aroma, remembering Colcrow's warning. "I can't ever remember–"

"Isten," interrupted Puthnok. She was standing a few feet behind her and made no effort to lower her voice, speaking in an oddly loud, flat tone.

Isten turned, battling a rush of panic.

Puthnok was staring at one of the four columns that held up the roof. She looked terrified.

Isten followed her gaze and saw that the column was moving.

For a moment, she thought it was falling, but then she saw the truth – the strands were curling and reforming, sprouting limbs and fingers. As the column moved slowly into the moonlight, Isten staggered back against the crate, shaking her head and whispering a prayer.

Even before it had left the shadows, Isten knew what it was: an Ignorant Man. It was nearly thirty feet tall and every inch of it was wrought of gleaming, twisted metal. It was roughly human in shape, but draped in a confusing mesh of glinting coils. Only its face was smooth, like a polished tribal mask. It had a wide, horizontal slot for a mouth, a smaller, vertical slot for a nose and two empty, perfect circles for eyes, both set on the same side of the nose, one above the other. As it stepped towards Isten, she heard a furnace, roaring deep inside its chest.

It must have weighed several tonnes but it moved with an eerie, fluid grace. Isten was so horrified that it took her a moment to realize that it was holding out its hand towards her, fingers splayed. There was a glowing circle engraved into its palm, trailing tendrils of smoke.

"Isten!" howled Amoria, sprinting forwards and shoving her aside.

Something flashed, silently, in the dark.

Amoria screamed. Her pain was terrible to hear and it sliced through the quiet of the warehouse. Then it stopped, abruptly silenced.

Amoria had pushed Isten with such force that Isten fell to the ground, rolling through shards of broken wood and landing a few feet away.

Isten leapt to her feet and saw Amoria standing motionless in front of the crate, frozen in an unnatural pose. She was balanced on one leg, her hands outstretched. Her mouth open in a silent scream. Then she fell forwards, still locked in the same pose, hitting the floor with a muffled clang. Rather than slumping onto the floor, she bounced and clattered, still frozen in the same position, like a toppled statue.

"Isten!" cried Lorinc as the towering shape turned to face her and slowly extended its hand.

Isten jumped aside as the giant's palm flashed.

There was no explosion. No impact. And she felt no pain, so she sprinted in the opposite direction, back past the giant towards the front doors of the warehouse.

The metal giant transformed again, spiralling and tumbling down to human proportions, as though it were melting. Freed from its monstrous bulk, it raced after Isten, moving with sickening speed, holding its palm towards her.

She weaved and ducked, threw a feint, then barrelled through the locked door, smashing easily through the rotten wood and the rusted lock.

She heard the clang of metal footfalls behind her and ran on, hoping that the others would be safe if she led the Ignorant Man away.

She dashed into the network of alleyways leading down to the docks. She had navigated those steep, winding lanes in various mental states and knew them as well as anyone in the city.

The footfalls came closer but she dared not look back. She cursed Colcrow one last time and leapt over a low wall, tumbling headlong into the void.

The streets that snaked down to the docks were cut into the side of a steep hill and she had thrown herself down a forty-foot drop, easily enough to kill her if she had misjudged the fall.

She landed with a resonant splat in a fast-flowing open sewer. Then she lay back in the filth and looked up at the distant silhouette of the Ignorant Man. It watched her in silence from the road above, its metal frame seething with fine, tumbling strands. Then it turned and walked away, vanishing into the night.

Isten closed her eyes, sank back into the faeces, and hurtled away, carried on towards the blessed waters of the Saraca.

4

Before the towers and the roads, the gold and the mystery, there was the Lamp of Trismegistus, the cradle of Astral Flame, the font of all power and the seed of the city. But even as the lamp did its work, severing the bonds of time and nature, the first Curious Man felt a shadow of doubt. What had he plucked from the crucible? What was this ember he had cast into the stars? What had he willed on his sons?

As Rasnik approached the end of his life, he began to dream of the beginning. He ran towards a mountain of winding, resplendent spires, his parents chasing after him, confused and afraid, calling him back, dazed by pulses of light, witnessing the arrival of paradise. Wherever he had been born, wherever he was running from, he was one of the lucky few, summoned into the city by the Elect and offered a new life. He opened his eyes and stared at the low, smoke-stained ceiling of his room, followed by echoes of the dream. He remembered the look of wonder in his mother's eyes during their first days in the city, surrounded by fly-harried crowds and serpentine walkways, tumbling ever deeper into the labyrinth.

He smiled, forgetting his ravaged flesh as delirium

painted his childhood across the mouldering walls. Dawn seeped through the window, gilding the cracked paint and igniting dust motes, and he murmured to himself, reciting the names of childhood friends. He spent his last morning feeling happier than he had done for months, and when the landlady tapped at the door, he managed to invite her in with a clear voice.

Abdua's face was hidden behind a leather bag, her eyes peering out through two crudely stitched holes. The old fool still thought she might escape the plague, even though it had taken everyone else on the street. "You have a visitor," she said, bustling over to the window and looking down into the street.

"A visitor?" Rasnik laughed. "No one knows I'm here."

"Not just any visitor," whispered Abdua, and he noticed how odd her voice sounded. She was shaking. "A Curious Man."

Rasnik was so shocked he sat up. "What are you talking about? You old idiot. The Elect would never come here, not to this *pit*. And what would they want with me if they did." His anger grew as he realized she had robbed him of the first pleasant thoughts to visit him in months.

"Idiot, am I?" she snapped, clearly in a state of panic. She forgot her fear of the plague and waved him over to the window. "Come and look. See for yourself."

He was so irritated with her that he managed to haul his wasted legs off the bed and place his feet on the rug. His legs trembled as he rose, but managed to hold him, and he staggered over to the filthy window, peering out into the sun-drenched dust. His rooms were in the northern reaches of the Azorus, on Barduli Street, where the slums

sloped down towards the wealthier quarters of the city,
looming over their affluent neighbours like a warning.
It was one of the most plague-ravaged areas in Athanor.
Nobody came to Barduli Street and yet, swarming beneath
his window, there was a crowd – hundreds of beggars and
traders, jostling each other, climbing onto door frames
and walls, trying to get a better glimpse of the incredible
vision approaching Rasnik's lodgings. It was a wire-framed
dome, an egg-shaped confection of golden threads, a
palankeen, flashing and glinting as it swayed and lurched
down the street. Rather than being pulled by horses or
carried by slaves, it was carried on a nest of spindle-thin
limbs, glinting, jointed needles, forged of the same golden
alloy as the cage, not welded to the dome but juggling it,
tossing and catching the carriage as they scuttled through
the crowds. Rasnik felt as though he were slipping back
into his dream. The palankeen looked like a gilded insect,
approaching him with a series of slow, drunken lunges.
Through the slender bars he saw a nobleman dressed more
richly than anyone he had ever seen in Athanor. He was
enveloped in voluminous, full-length robes, the cloth dyed
a vivid, wonderful yellow and glittering with ceremonial
chains. He held a short staff in one hand, a filigreed, golden
sceptre worked to resemble a serpent wrapped around a
sword, and he wore an equally beautiful crown, a single
sheet of gold, tall and twisted, hammered into the shape
of a flame. The crown enveloped his entire head and was
fronted with a mask of flat, polished metal. The mask's
design was simpler than the rest of his finery – just thin,
rectangular holes for the mouth and nose and two circles
for eyes, both on the same side of the mask.

Abdua gave Rasnik a triumphant glare. "What is *that*," she said, "if not a Curious Man?"

Rasnik shook his head, unable to answer. He had lived in Athanor for eighty years without seeing one of its rulers, without even meeting someone who had seen one of its rulers. And now he was faced with this incredible vision. "Why did you say he was looking for me?" The anger was gone from his voice, replaced with shock and fear.

The Curious Man's carriage halted in the middle of the street. Its bowl of needle limbs gently lowered the domed cage to the ground and yellow-robed attendants bustled around it, driving back the crowds to clear a space.

"He's been visiting everyone who's dying," whispered Abdua, still staring through the window. "Everyone took by the plague but not yet dead. He's been tending to them. Praying with them. Easing their passing."

"Dying?" snapped Rasnik, as he watched the cage unfurl its strands. It looked like a metal bud opening its petals, revealing the regal figure sitting inside. "I'm not dying."

Abdua gave him an incredulous look. "I'm amazed you've lasted this long." She nodded at the window. "But not many of us will speak to one of the Elect before we pass."

Rasnik stared in amazement as the Curious Man stepped from his mechanical carriage and nodded at the crowds. The morning light seemed to be radiating from him rather than the sun, burning in his lemon robes, shimmering across his crown, spinning in his wake like the tail of a comet.

His attendants gripped the knives at their belts and scowled, and the crowd fell to its knees, staring at the road as the glorious figure strode past, heading for Rasnik's lodgings.

"He *is* coming here," whispered Rasnik. He reeled from the window, falling, but managing to direct his fall so he landed on the bed. A violent cough ripped through his scrawny chest, painting strands of crimson across the sheets.

Abdua backed away, pressing her hands to her mask.

"I'll send him up," she said, heading for the door, her voice muffled.

Rasnik wiped his face on the sheets, scrubbing at the blood and pus and running his fingers through his hair. A Curious Man. From their first days in Athanor, his parents had told him tales of the Elect – visionary seers, ruling the city from the hidden vaults of their temples, nurturing it like gardeners, creating power and growth and light with their secret arts. Fusing the force of the sun with the power of the elements. Never, in all those years, had his parents dreamt that their son would meet one of them.

A few minutes later there was a polite knock at his door.

"Come in," gasped Rasnik, "please".

And there he was, the Curious Man, sweeping into Rasnik's lodgings on a shimmer of flame-bright robes, illuminating the room like a saint in a fresco. He removed his helmet and his face was shockingly human – kind, smiling and careworn, clean-shaven and framed by blond, shoulder-length hair. He rushed to the bedside and gently took Rasnik's hand, showing no fear or revulsion, only concern.

"Forgive me for arriving unannounced." His voice was soft and full of good humour. "I'm Phrater Alzen."

"Rasnik," he replied, trying to rise so he could bow.

"Please," said Alzen, shaking his head. "Save your strength. You are about to become a traveller. You have a journey ahead of you."

He turned to Abdua who was loitering in the doorway, her mask removed and her hair greased back. She clutched her hands together and rushed forwards, an eager expression on her face.

"Please take a message to my servants," he said. "No one is to enter the building while we are praying. I sense the moment is close and I intend to stay with Rasnik until the end."

She nodded and was about to rush from the room when he held up a hand and smiled. "If you could wait downstairs too, please, Abdua. Rasnik and I have much to discuss. We will need complete privacy."

"Of course, Your Holiness." She looked horrified by the suggestion she might interrupt anything. "I'll wait downstairs until you ask for me." She hesitated at the threshold, looking at Rasnik with almost as much awe as she had looked at the Curious Man, then she hurried away.

Alzen crossed to the door, closed it and turned the lock. Then he pulled the shutters and plunged the room into darkness. The darkness was only brief. There was a rustling sound as he took something from his robes, then a warm glow flooded from his hand, splaying golden beams between his fingers and making the room feel as though it were lit by a flickering fire.

He walked back to the bed and placed the source of the light on the sheets. It was a silver egg, about the size of a man's fist and covered in golden filigree. The filigree was formed into a fine, winding network, designed to resemble hairline cracks. Light was bleeding through the metal coils. Mandrel-fire. Undying Light. The magic of the Elect.

Rasnik stared at the egg. It was probably more valuable

than anything he had ever seen in his life.

"Beautiful, isn't it?" said Alzen. "Alchymia of the purest, most ancient kind. The Old King gave it to me as gift, many years ago."

"Is it my time, Your Holiness?" asked Rasnik, ashamed to think how terrible he must look to this noble being.

Alzen nodded. "Indeed. Time to rejoin the Prima Materia. Time to let the cosmos conceive of you again." He picked up the egg and examined its filigreed cracks, as though looking for something. "You will see wonders that even the most devout seeker has never glimpsed."

Rasnik noticed something new in Alzen's voice. Something just beneath his genial tone.

"This will ease your pain," said Alzen, taking a small pipe from his robes and blowing into it, filling the air with sweet-smelling spices.

Rasnik took a deep breath and his pain did indeed fade. He lay back on the bed with a sigh of relief. He tried to thank Alzen, but he found that his muscles had relaxed to such an extent that he could not move his tongue. All that emerged was a faint groan.

Alzen smiled and held a finger to his lips, shushing him like a restless baby.

As Alzen shuffled closer, Rasnik realized what Alzen's tone of voice reminded him of. It was like the eager hunger of a cinnabar addict. After years of addiction, Rasnik could recognize the sound of desperation. His awe began to be replaced by fear. Why had Alzen sedated him?

Rasnik tried to move away from him, but the strength had completely gone from his limbs. His fear grew.

"Time is of the essence," said Alzen, sounding less

cheerful, "so I've had to find ways to expedite my work." He stopped fiddling with the egg to give Rasnik a gentle pat on the arm. "I'm sure you would have died soon, old friend, whether I arrived or not. Very few people survive the later stages of the plague." Something clicked and he looked back at the egg. "Ah, found it." He rose from the bed and returned to the door, checking it was still locked, then came back towards Rasnik, light spilling from his hands and flashing in his eyes.

"You're destined for something greater, Rasnik," he whispered, gazing at the metal egg. He was talking to himself now, seeming to have forgotten Rasnik. "Phrater Ostan guesses the truth, perhaps, maybe even Phrater Zimos, but none of the others. There's only one true catalyst. They struggle with their petty acts of transfiguration, dreaming that they could regain the powers we lost, but they don't know where to start. They have no idea." He sat next to Rasnik again. "They see me getting closer, but they think my success stems only from the purity of my spirit."

Rasnik watched with a mixture of horror and fascination as the egg began to change. The golden cracks parted, fracturing its surface and revealing something inside.

"Coagulus," said Alzen, his voice full of pride.

The egg folded itself away with the same, jerky, clockwork movements as Alzen's palankeen, revealing a neat, square piece of cloth. It was folded carefully and patterned with a tracery of faint blue lines.

"The Old King didn't understand the gift he was giving me," said Alzen, gently stroking the folded sheet. "And, even if he had, he would never have dared use it. As desperate as my brethren are to revive the glories of the past, they would place your life above the requirements of the Art. I understand, of course, but that's why we've been growing weaker, century after century."

Rasnik moaned again, trying to call out for help, trying to lift his arms to defend himself, but it was useless. All he could do was watch in terrified silence as Alzen unfolded the sheet.

Alzen took one corner and stood up, allowing it to unfurl. It was gossamer fine, rippling from his fingers like smoke.

Only when it had fully unfolded did Rasnik realize what it was: the flayed skin of a man, complete with arms, legs and puckered holes where the eyes would have been. It was pale and diaphanous and, he realized with dawning horror, still alive. The faint blue lines were veins, and there was movement in them – blood, pulsing through the billowing sheet.

Alzen draped the skin over the bottom of the bed, like a second blanket, then stepped back into the shadows.

Rasnik moaned again as the skin began to move, rippling like silt on a riverbed, undulating in little waves and flowing across his body, moving towards his face. His moans grew shriller but no louder as the creature's face settled over his own. He was paralyzed, but he could feel everything. Coagulus stretched out in every direction, pressing over his chest and limbs, folding around him, embracing him, merging with him.

"If you died, unattended," said Alzen, as the skin tightened itself around Rasnik, "your quintessence would be lost, the very spark of your being, the thing some call a soul, would simply die. But Coagulus will preserve your essence. And it is no *ordinary* essence. Your soul has been ennobled, Rasnik – ennobled by me, even though you did not know it. The cinnabar you bought from the Aroc Brothers came from me, you see, and it was laced with potent elements: flores, mercurius sublimatus, aurichalcum and minerals so rare I have spent a lifetime gathering them. But with you as a crucible they will produce something glorious. And for that, I think the crime of hastening your death seems a small price to pay."

Agony exploded across Rasnik's body as Coagulus melted into him, scorching like acid.

"It will be quick," said Alzen, smiling again.

5

Even the Sisters could not give Isten what she sought. They cradled her head, wept tears on her cheeks and sang of her beauty, but she knew what she was. The word dragged at her heels and echoed in her sleep. Unworthy. She was the lesser now of a greater then.

Isten was rocked by a grating cough as she leant over the table and picked up a pile of polished bones. She was shivering violently and her vision was split by torrents of sweat. There was a mandrel-fire somewhere behind her, and the light hurt her eyes and tightened her skull. If she moved too fast, she would fall from her chair. It felt like she was on fire. Things that had been pleasure had turned to pain. Cinnabar would indulge its devotees for a while, circling in their guts, waiting patiently to be fed, but when it sensed abandonment, it raged like a cuckold, flaying nerves it had previously caressed.

She looked around the table at a circle of unfamiliar faces. She panicked, unable, for the moment, to remember where she was. Athanor was not a city in which a lone woman, crippled by addiction, could survive for long. Then she remembered the warehouse and the Ignorant Men. And the death of Amoria. She stared at the bones in her hand. They had once been a rat, she thought, snaking down the banks of the Saraca, climbing the Golden Chain with all the other scavengers; now they were a game. A game. Of course. She remembered where she was. She had come to Brast's house. He used to be one of the Exiles, and he was one of the city's few citizens who wouldn't leave her headless in the river. No lover ever remembered Isten with fondness, but Brast at least would not see her dead. When she arrived and showed him Gombus's coins he had smirked in disbelief, but let her in, helped her wash, given her new clothes and let her join a game. Now he was sat in a corner drawing her, documenting her decline with the same mock disdain he always affected in her presence.

"Throw," said one of the other players, speaking in a dry whisper. She was so confused, and the room was so gloomy, that she had thought her fellow gamblers were all human, but as the speaker moved into light she saw that it was a weazen. She had never seen one so close before. From certain angles, it might have been mistaken for a gaunt man, but as it turned, the light splashed over its strings of flat, leaf-shaped planes. It was like a puppet made of razor-edged shells, shimmering and iridescent in some places, rough and encrusted with dried muck in others. It looked incredibly fragile, and so flat it barely seemed to inhabit three dimensions, but Isten had heard weazens were harder than iron and sharper than a falcata. This was one of the wingless types, but she could see small, vestigial pinions fidgeting on its shoulders as it grew more annoyed by the delay.

"Brast," it hissed, turning to look back at him, clicking and clattering as it moved spilling flies into the air. "The girl.

Send her away." The weazen glared at Isten and raised the jumble of bladed plates that passed for its hand, scraping them together like knives.

Isten sneered at the creature but she knew she was in danger. The other players looked as irritated by her erratic behaviour as the weazen. Brast would not be able to help her if the whole table turned against her. She gripped the knife in her belt and threw the bones across the table. Then she laughed, despite the agony lancing through her temples. It was a high score. She reached carefully across the table and slid piles of coins towards her lap. After what had happened, she could not return to the Exiles empty-handed. It was her fault. Amoria died because of her. But if she could return to the others with enough money to buy arms and men, they still might listen to her. They could still begin again. She could find a way to help them. It was a faint hope, but it was all she had to cling to. The thought of Amoria, clattering onto the floor of the warehouse, caused her mind to slip away again. She stared into the grain of the table. Whorls and spirals. The armour of the Ignorant Man, sprouting and transforming, reaching towards her.

The weazen watched her closely with the one eye that was facing her, studying her shaking hands and the sweat dripping from her nose.

"I have cinnabar," it said, leaning back in its chair, causing its plates to grind and click. There was a revolting smell coming from it, and fly larvae bubbling in its joints. "Back in my rooms."

"I can buy my own," she muttered, snapping back into the moment and counting the coins. "Another round?" She found herself revelling in the thrill of a winning streak.

A few of the players muttered and shook their heads, but the weazen was still glaring at her and it nodded.

The others were slightly more reluctant, but as Isten pushed the rat bones back towards them, they reached into their robes and placed coins on the wine-stained table.

She caught the look of wry amusement on Brast's face but refused to acknowledge it.

The first player threw the bones and grunted in disgust. He left the table and went to sit beside Brast, studying the picture he was drawing.

The next player threw and, again, it was a low score. Isten recognized him. He was one of the spice traders from Rasbin Street – a tanned, leathery lump with eyes as yellow as his teeth. He shook his head, taking the loss more philosophically than his friend. He lit an oil lamp and heated up a beautiful jade tar-pipe, taking a drag and leaning back in his chair, staring at the ceiling and muttering to himself, filling the room with the sweet, heady scent of burning flowers.

The next player to throw had more luck and he leant forwards, his sweaty face lit up by the glow of the oil lamp. "Antinomie. You should have taken it while you could," he said, eyeing the pile of coins on Isten's lap.

She picked one up, looking at the design on its face. A circle of flames around a smaller, solid circle. The symbol of Athanor. The symbol of the Curious Men. She said nothing to the sweaty man, placing the coin back on her lap and turning to face the weazen.

It extended its segmented arm with a screech of grinding joints, still staring at Isten as it lifted the bones and sent them rattling across the table. "Amphiarae," whispered the creature. It was the highest score so far.

Isten could sense that Brast had set down his drawing and walked over to the table to watch, but she refused to meet his eye as she picked up the bones and threw them.

"Olum," said Brast, sounding, to his credit, more disappointed than amused.

Isten thought she might slide from her chair, but she would not make such a fool of herself in front of Brast.

As she shoved the pile of coins across the table towards the weazen, she saw, rather than the city emblem, the faces of Gombus and Puthnok, cast into the coins, their eyes as dull and lifeless as the scratched metal.

"One last game," she gasped, grabbing the creature's arm.

She hissed and snatched her hand back, blood flying from her fingers.

The weazen laughed. "With what?"

Isten's pulse was hammering and the fire in her skin was so fierce she could barely breathe. Sweat was pooling beneath her on her seat and the shadows were starting to collapse, fragmented by the flickering oil lamp and the heavy, perfumed scent of the tar smoke. The only thing she could see clearly was the pile of coins. Several of which had been given to her by Gombus – the mark of his forgiveness. At the very least, she *had* to return with those.

"There must be something," she gasped, hands trembling as she wiped the sweat from her eyes.

"Time to go, gentlemen," said Brast, stepping to her side and placing a hand on her shoulder. "My friend needs to rest."

"No!" she gasped, trying to stand.

Brast pressed down on her shoulder, keeping her in her seat.

She glared up at him. His face looked like a skull in the lamplight, pale and angular.

"No more," he said, speaking to her as though she were a tiresome child.

"Let me go," she warned, gripping the handle of her knife.

The others laughed and Brast raised an eyebrow. "You can barely walk."

"We'll take care of her," murmured the man smoking the pipe, a lecherous smirk on his face.

Isten managed to shove Brast away and stand, waving her knife at the circle of rippling faces.

"Go," muttered Brast, shaking his head in disbelief.

With a chorus of laughter, the players gathered their things and staggered out into the night.

Isten was still gripping her knife as Brast closed the door and turned to face her.

She could sense him drawing her, adoring her, even now, with her cinnabar-wasted face and her bone-jangling tremors. For all his pretence of disapproval, she knew he was obsessed with her. Such absurd devotion made her recoil. He was like a net, encircling her, weighing her down.

"Those coins were all I had," she said.

"And you gambled them. Clever."

She strode across the room, grabbed his easel and hurled it at him.

He stepped aside and it smashed against the door. The paper tore as it fell to the floor and she was left facing a shredded portrait of her gaunt, desperate face. She looked like a wounded animal, looming from the darkness, moments from death. She stared at the portrait in shock. Even in tatters, she could see how accurate it was. Brast was a liar, except when he had a pen in his hand.

He held up his hands in a defensive gesture. "If you really want to stick a knife in me, do it in the morning. If you try now I'll have to steady the blade for you." He waved at the door leading to the stairs. "Let's get some sleep. Maybe in the morning you'll remember that I saved your life."

She could only just hear what he was saying. Her thoughts were fixed on the dreadful portrait. "I'm *important*," she said, knowing how ridiculous she sounded, not even sure what she meant.

He shook his head. "Only to the Exiles. And you don't believe in any of that stuff."

"What do you mean?" she snapped, managing to focus on his face. "What stuff?"

"Revolutions. Politics. Ideals. That *stuff*. The things that get in the way of your endless party. Have you forgotten everything you told me when you loved me, Isten?" He came closer, a wraith in the dark, eyes full of bitter love. "You don't believe we can *ever* get home. You think Puthnok is a hopeless, naive fool – that they're all deluded. That there's no way back to Rukon and that Puthnok will never start her revolution. You just play along with them through guilt. I know you, Isten, better than any of them. Why do you think I left?"

Isten felt a rush of guilt. She probably *had* told him those things, while in the grip of a cinnabar binge. She had shared truths with Brast that she had not fully shared with herself.

He looked away and she saw that he regretted his words. However cloying she found him, at least he still felt something for her. She needed all the help she could get. For once, she had made a good decision. This was probably the only safe place for her in the city outside of the Sisters' seraglio, and she could never have made it that far tonight.

Brast waved her to the stairs. "Don't worry, you can have the bed to yourself. You still smell like shit."

Isten had to hold back a smile. He'd want her even if she was still in the sewer, but for once she managed to hold her tongue and not ridicule him. She nodded in grateful silence and let him take her upstairs.

She woke with a cry of fear, picturing the expressionless face of an Ignorant Man, looming towards her from the darkness. For a moment, she could not remember where she was, then Brast rose from a mattress on the floor and placed a hand on her arm. The lamps had all been extinguished but there were a few fingers of moonlight slicing through the shutters of his bedroom. She was shaking, drenched in sweat, picturing metal faces in the shadows.

"What have you done to yourself?" asked Brast.

She gripped his hand, feeling a growing sense of panic. "It's not me, Brast." She pictured Gombus's proud, tired face, and the grotesque shape of Amoria as she died in the warehouse. "What have I done to the Exiles?"

He sat next to her on the bed, shaking his head, speaking quickly. "Whatever happened, they brought it on themselves. They're deluded. You said it yourself. They're killing you with all these absurd dreams. One woman can't stop the world and make it work again. They expect you to get them home and reclaim their past. Is it any wonder you've ended up like this? It's madness. That's why I left. I couldn't bear to watch them any more. What happened this time? What did they ask you to do?"

"I spoke to Colcrow," she said, "and he–"

"Colcrow? Why would you listen to him? He doesn't have an honest bone in his body. He deserted you even sooner than I did. Why would you trust him?"

"He told me about a shipment. I thought it would be a chance to get us back on our feet again. But there was something odd going on." She gripped her head, trying to rid it of visions, trying to think clearly. "There was an Ignorant Man there, waiting for us. Either Colcrow betrayed me or something weird is happening. Why would Ignorant Men be anywhere near a drugs shipment?"

Brast shook his head, frowning. "Ignorant Men? Are you sure that's what you saw?"

"No, of course I'm not sure. I'd never seen anything like it. But it looked exactly how I imagine an Ignorant Man would look. And even if it wasn't, it was definitely something to do with the Curious Men. Some product of the Art." She whispered, as though they might be overheard. "It was alchymia, I'm sure. It wasn't a living creature. It was a machine. An automaton. Wrapped in golden threads and lit up with mandrel-fire. It took one look at us and tried to kill us. Amoria died. I think the others got away, because I led the Ignorant Man away, but Amoria is dead."

Brast looked shocked. "Dead? What is all this? What have you got yourself mixed up in?"

"Not just Amoria. The Aroc Brothers killed Ozero too. They control the shipments into the Caris Docks now, they run the fights on Erkle Street and every brothel near the river is working for them. The city's theirs. We've lost it all."

Brast nodded, his eyes clouding over. "I heard about Ozero. Poor sod. Sayal cut his throat while two other Aroc

Brothers held him down. Then he–"

Isten held up a hand. "I'm going to deal with Sayal."

She looked around for her clothes and spotted them, folded neatly on a chair. They reminded her of the corpse bundles she had seen floating down the river. She pulled away from Brast. "I have to get back to the Exiles."

"They're killing you."

"I saw Amoria die, but I don't know what happened after that." She shook her head and reached for the clothes. "The others should have got away, but I have to make sure."

"At least wait until the morning," he said. "Let me give you some food." He managed a tentative smile. "I'm sure you remember the quality of my cooking."

For a moment, she forgot everything and laughed, caught unawares by his unexpected joke, imagining the burnt fish and glutinous rice he would give her if she stayed. "No," she said, getting dressed. She felt less panicked, but no less certain. Her face was tight with pain, but she forced it into something resembling a smile. "Thanks for not letting me kill you."

His expression darkened and she saw that, without even trying, she had hurt him again. She had such a knack for doing that. The warmth faded from his voice.

"You won't make it to the Blacknells Road. You're half dead. You'll end up back in the sewers."

She nodded, still struggling to get dressed, her arms shaking badly. The clothes he had given her were actually hers: a black short-sleeved coat of padded leather, weathered and scarred, but still intact; black hooded robes; leather vambraces, breeches and knee-length sandals. He must have kept them for all these months. "My knife?" she asked.

He nodded to a pile of sketches on a table. The knife was on top of the drawings.

Isten grabbed the weapon and managed to stuff it in her belt but, as she tried to leave, she almost fell and had to steady herself against the doorframe.

"Do you have any cinnabar?" she asked.

He shook his head, not looking at her. Then, as she nodded and opened the door, he came after her.

"You've got no money. What will you do? Let me give you enough to buy–"

"I'm going back to the Sisters of Solace," she said, interrupting him, determined to have no more of his charity. "They'll give me help even if I have no money. Once I'm straight, I'll make it back to the Blacknells Road."

He shook his head, but took her arm, helping her down the stairs. He grabbed a falcata from the wall and stuffed it in his belt. "Let me at least get you there," he muttered. "If you're going to kill yourself, I don't want it to be tonight."

"I feel the same way," she said, as they headed out into the night. She managed a faint smile. "Or I would have accepted your offer of a meal."

6

Phrater Alzen rushed through the Giberim Temple, his robes snapping behind him. The chamber was a vast sun-drenched octagon, topped with a magnificent ribbed dome. The emerald-green walls were clad in a storm of copper lattice work, crashing and soaring around columns that reached hundreds of feet to cradle an undulating honeycomb vault, an ocean of glass tiles, each facet staining the sunlight a different colour, spilling a profusion of reds, golds and blues that flashed across balustrades and walkways before igniting the gilded mosaic floor, a circle of ceramic flames framing a polished onyx sun.

Another Curious Man rushed to his side, dressed in identical finery and looking equally harassed. It was his old friend, Phrater Ostan. "For God and the Temple," whispered Alzen.

"God and the Temple," Ostan replied.

"Did you know about this?" asked Alzen.

Ostan shook his head. He was shorter and stockier than Alzen with far less heroic features – wary eyes, jowly face and an expression of perpetual bafflement. Even draped in yellow robes and hung with golden baubles, he looked more like a harried cleric than a skilled practitioner. "I was on the other side of the temple. I had to summon a contrivance to get here so quickly." He dabbed his face, looking furious and exhausted. "Most inconvenient."

"I was on the other side of the *city*," muttered Alzen.

Ostan nodded and glanced at him. "I know. You're an example to us all, Phrater Alzen. Mixing with the vulgar like that. So selfless. Everyone has been talking of it – how bravely you tend to those wretched souls." He shook his head. "If only my heart were even half as pure as yours..."

Alzen was not listening to his friend. He was watching the crowd gather on the dais up ahead, a rainbow-drenched multitude milling around the black sun. There were dozens of Curious Men, surrounded by a small army of scribes, secretaries and laborators. The entire fraternity had been summoned. Whoever was to be dragged across the coals, the Old King clearly wished the humiliation to be as public as possible.

"If a crime is worthy of a such a gathering," said Alzen, "surely it's worthy of some deliberation beforehand. I can't believe that nobody knew this was happening. There must be a reason we were given no advance warning."

Ostan nodded, but they were too close to the crowd to continue the conversation. Allegiances amongst the Elect were always uncertain, and it was never wise to be heard openly criticizing the Old King.

They climbed the steps of the black dais and joined the crush of figures, nodding in greeting to their brethren and heading towards the circle of chairs at the centre of the mosaic.

The other phraters were already taking their seats, but several of them rushed over to Alzen, bowing as if *he* were the Old King and stumbling over their words as they praised him for his recent successes. Alzen took the compliments with a dismissive wave of his hand, outwardly playing down their significance, inwardly rejoicing.

It was unusual for the whole fraternity to be gathered at once, and the clamour continued for a few more minutes as the phraters shared news and greetings while their attendants adjusted robes and crowns, fussing around their masters like bees at pollen, until finally being shooed away. Then everyone fell quiet as a distant door clanged open and the Old King entered the hall.

He was preceded by another legion of attendants, some carrying standards, metal-forged images of the Athanorian sun – stylized flames surrounding a black circle. Seleucus was riding in a palankeen like Alzen's, a dome of gilded tracery, cradled by a mass of needle-like limbs, but the Old King's carriage was large enough to carry both his throne and the enormous bulk of Seleucus himself. He was a giant, like every previous Old King, transfigured by alchymia reserved only for the regent. The palankeen climbed the steps of the dais with a rattle of oiled joints and a hiss of escaping steam, before disgorging Seleucus in a torrent of golden threads, placing his throne in a gap in the circle of chairs.

Alzen had avoided Seleucus since his coronation and his breath faltered as he saw how the regent had changed. As well as being over ten feet tall, most of the Old King's skin had vanished, enveloped by a tangle of burnished coils. He was clad in ornate golden armour that was engraved with heliacal symbols, but it was hard to see what was armour and what was flesh. His face resembled the armature of an enormous sculpture. No skin, just a mask of glittering filaments woven in the likeness of a man's face. He carried a ceremonial bronze staff that was nearly as tall as he was and his throne was flanked by an armour-clad honour guard, but Seleucus's real protection came from the creature that padded up the steps and lay down before his throne: Mapourak, the emerald lion, twice as tall as a man and blessed with a calm, human intelligence. It surveyed the circle of phraters with disdain, its eyes half-lidded and its faceted body glinting as it moved.

Alzen was no longer looking at the Old King or the lion. He had noticed something that caused his pulse to race. At the side of the throne some of Seleucus's guards were holding a chained man. He was not one of the Elect; not even one of their attendants. He was one of the verminous little crooks from the Azorus slums. Alzen did not recognize his face, but he knew from the man's grotesque mutations that he was one of the Aroc Brothers. Alzen prayed that the prisoner did not recognize him. Associating with criminals was expressly forbidden. If the Old King had learned of their connection, Alzen would soon be getting a closer look at the lion.

Seleucus sat in silence for a few minutes, looking down at his expectant audience. His breath emerged from his threaded mask as slow, heavy tendrils of smoke. The fumes drifted away from his crown, serpent-like, catching colours from the honeycomb vault as they writhed above the dais, moving towards the circle of phraters, seeming to sniff at them.

Alzen endured the attentions of the smoke with all the calm he could muster, knowing that it was an extension of the Old King's thought, knowing that he was being examined.

"What is the greatest secret of the Art?" said the Old King. His words spilled more fumes into the air. Like the first, they were opaque and leaden, flowing purposefully across the chamber and showing no sign of dissipating.

"Purity of heart," murmured the phraters, sounding awkward and uncomfortable as the smoke surrounded them. They were all conscious that Mapourak was Seleucus's executioner.

"Purity of heart," agreed Seleucus. His voice was as inhuman as the rest of him, deep, musical and resonant. "To be curious, of course, is essential, there is never any doubt on that score. But purity... purity is harder to define." His words had birthed another sinuous cloud and he paused for a moment, letting the shapes roll around the phraters, brushing against their robes and faces.

"There was an incident last night," he continued, "in a warehouse next to the Azof embassy." He reached down and stroked Mapourak, his metal fingers clinking along the lion's crystalline mane.

To Alzen's horror, more of the smoke tendrils drifted his way, circling his crown like carrion crows over a corpse.

If Seleucus noticed, he gave no sign. "There was a shipment of cinnabar in the warehouse." He glanced at the shivering chained wretch next to his throne. The man was covered in lesions and bruises and his fingertips were dripping blood onto the tiled floor. "I have learned that the cinnabar belongs to criminals who call themselves the Aroc Brothers. They intended to move it today, but a rival gang arrived at the warehouse and tried to steal the shipment."

Alzen was still reciting his incantation and, to his relief, the fumes drifted away from him, settling on another phrater.

The Old King leant forwards in his throne, staring down at each of them in turn. "Now, why would I drag you all away from your work to discuss such a matter? To our shame, Athanor is rife with criminality, but I would not summon you here to discuss the death of a few..." He glanced at his prisoner. "Misguided souls."

The Old King sat back and fell silent again as the vapours caused by his speech rolled across the gathering.

"When the Aroc Brothers arrived to discover the attempted theft, they also found something else."

Seleucus waved to his guards and they carried an object into the centre of the dais. It was covered in a black cloth, and at a nod from the Old King they unveiled it.

There was a chorus of gasps as the phraters saw the lifeless, metal corpse of Amoria, frozen in the position she had been in when she died.

"Transfiguration," said Seleucus, the music fading from his voice, replaced by an edge of fury. "This low-born thief was killed by alchymia." He tapped his staff on the floor, clearly struggling to remain seated, so great was his anger. "The glorious subtleties of the Great Art have been deployed in defence of a squalid, illegal drugs deal. And the only souls in Athanor capable of wielding such power are seated in this room."

Alzen recited his incantation with even more urgency, trying to stifle the rage that was burning in his chest. No one should have known about the shipment. He had left the Ignorant Man there as a warning to the Aroc Brothers, an example of what he could do, nothing more. There should have been no deaths. Someone had betrayed him.

"Can anyone explain this to me?" asked the Old King.

No one spoke. The only sound came from Seleucus's metal mask as the fumes hissed through his mouth grille.

He nodded. "Return to your cells. I will visit each of you in turn until I discover the truth."

He watched them for a few more seconds, then he returned to his carriage and left the chamber.

When the doors had closed behind Seleucus, Phrater Ostan turned to Alzen. "What kind of fool would get mixed up with gangs?"

Alzen shook his head, still staring at the contorted metal corpse on the dais, wondering which of the Aroc Brothers he would kill first.

7

"How do they drink this shit?" Sermo grimaced at his tea, clanging the cup back down on the metal table he was seated at. It was still early but, behind him, the Valeria Bazaar was stirring into life. Traders were bustling through foliage-draped colonnades, filling the square with noise and dust as they prepared for another day of business. The vast bulk of a hoveller was being herded through an archway into the square. The hunched creature was the size of a small house and its owners were yelling curses and wielding sticks as they steered it through the stalls, tearing awnings and smashing trellises as it refused to acknowledge their blows. Its barnacled, lice-infested carapace was laden with sacks of turmeric and saffron and every time it thudded against a wall, it filled the air with an explosion of colour and insects. Sermo watched the scene for a while, amused by the traders' increasingly irate attempts to direct the enormous creature.

From what Sermo had seen of the city so far, the place was a chaotic farce, played out by the inebriated and the half-human, with no apparent logic or purpose. It seemed to Sermo that Athanor had absorbed so many cultures and races that it had no idea what it was anymore. There was no way to know who stood where in the hierarchy – the

Curious Men were allegedly the city's rulers, but they were not like any rulers he had encountered before, hiding in their laboratories, manipulating the city in ways only they understood, and beneath the Elect, there was just this slovenly jumble of emigres, none of whom even seemed interested in where the city was. It moved and changed every few years, but the crowds thronging its streets were so absorbed in their own petty intrigues that they never appeared to care what was happening beyond the city walls.

He tried his tea again, finding it no more palatable on the second attempt, and returned his gaze to the streets below. The bazaar was one of the highest points of the city, and from here he felt as though he was *almost* able to understand Athanor's bizarre, skeletal structure. The street that led from the market square intersected with several others, all of which turned and looped down towards the rest of the city, creating a bewildering mesh of roads, domes and viaducts. Far below, flashing gold in the morning light, was the river, already busy with crowds of fly-shrouded scavengers. From this distance, it was possible to see the arc of the river as it reached up to swallow its tail. The river devoured itself endlessly like the ouroboros, the mythical serpent that was wrought in high relief around so many of the minarets that filled this part of the city. He had tried to comprehend the cyclical nature of the Saraca, but it only made his head hurt. Somehow, the ruling priesthood of Athanor had bound physics to their will, creating a confluence with no beginning and no end, girdling their absurd city with its burnished, binding currents.

Sermo's face was distorted by a mass of angry, red scar tissue. It covered most of his head, a souvenir from his journey to the city. The scars had left his features in a constant, brutal snarl and there were only a few bristle-like tufts of hair sticking up from his pink, heat-rippled scalp. Traders stared in surprise as they passed his table, taken aback by his brutalized face, but Sermo tried to ignore them, doing his best to hide his injuries under the hood of his cloak. He was meant to be a spy and he caused a stir wherever he went. The whole thing was a farce.

He shoved his cup away with a muttered curse and was about to move on, when he saw a familiar face rushing through the market stalls. The man was scrawny and stooped, swathed in filthy black robes, and his face was just as scarred and tormented as Sermo's. The burned man weaved through the bazaar, keeping clear of the hoveller, which was now thudding its low-hanging head into a column, eliciting more furious insults from its owners.

"Vola," said Sermo, as the man reached his table, gasping and grinning.

"He's here," said Vola, bent double with his hands on his knees, trying to catch his breath. He nodded back through the archway that led from the square to a street running on the other side of the bazaar.

"Who?"

"The artist. The one who used to live with Isten. I saw him coming out of a brothel on Crassus Street." Vola's eyes were wide with excitement. "I'm sure it's him."

Sermo nodded and rose from the table. Vola was a moron, but after weeks of enduring Athanor, he was happy for any kind of distraction. He dropped a coin on the table and sauntered off through the colonnades, waving for Vola to follow.

They forced their way through the bazaar, emerged into a sun-drenched avenue on the far side and looked around.

"He went that way, down Dacia Street, towards the park," said Vola, heading in that direction. They walked past the facades of several grand townhouses and entered a shady arboretum, crowded with shrubs and frankincense trees surrounding a grassy hill with a tomb at its summit.

"There," whispered Vola, pointing to a man who was walking through the trees, heading towards the tomb. He was as thin as Vola but, where Vola was stooped and stunted, this man was tall and proud-looking, wearing elegant blue robes and carrying rolls of paper under his arm.

"That's him," said Sermo, shocked. They had spent weeks scouring Athanor, crossing countless regions and districts, but this was the first sign of progress. "Brast. He knows her. He's one of them." He wiped some of the sweat from his eyes, dusted down his heavy, Athanorian-style robes and pulled his hood forward, trying to hide his scars.

They strolled around between the trees, pretending they were chatting and enjoying the shade, as the artist stopped outside the tomb, sat down against a tree, spread his paper on the grass and began to draw.

"Of all the places in this city," said Vola, "the best thing he can find to draw is this."

Sermo nodded. It did seem a strange choice. The tomb was one of the few structures in Athanor that had not been transformed by the chemicals that spilled into the river. The stones had remained resolutely square and unadorned, not sporting any of the organic shapes that had sprouted from other parts of the city. It was a simple pagoda-style heap of tiered grey stone, shattered and crumbling in several places and leaning slightly to one side. Whatever Sermo thought of Athanor, its architecture was spectacular, but this place was decidedly ugly.

"What do we do now?" asked Vola.

"Where was he when you first saw him?"

"He was leaving a brothel."

Sermo looked at Vola with a disgusted expression.

"I was waiting outside," said Vola, scowling back at him.

Sermo rolled his eyes. "Are you sure that's where he came from?"

"Absolutely."

"Then we're starting to learn a bit about our artist friend. He likes to visit brothels and draw the only ugly building in Athanor. Now we just need to bide our time and see where he heads next. If we can find out where he lives we might even find Isten waiting there."

Vola's eyes glinted.

Sermo nodded. "We'll be as rich as–"

Vola gripped Sermo's arm and looked around the arboretum.

Sermo cursed as he realized Brast had vanished. The papers were still scattered at the top of the hill, but the artist was gone.

They sprinted up the hill, peering into the shadows beneath the trees, but there was no sign of him.

"You idiot," muttered Sermo as he grabbed a piece of paper and studied it. It wasn't a sketch of the ruin, it was a sketch of Vola's burned face. "He saw you."

Sermo folded the drawing and tucked it beneath his robes, grimacing. "Well, whatever we might have learned about him, it's meaningless now. He won't come this way again if he thinks people are after him."

They headed down the hill and walked back under the stooped trees, heading for the archway that led back out onto the street.

"Not my best work," said a voice in Sermo's ear as an arm wrapped around his shoulders and a blade came to rest against his throat. "But you're not much of a model."

He tensed, but had the sense not to pull away.

Vola turned to look back at him. He cursed and drew his knife, but backed away as he saw the falcata Brast was holding to Sermo's throat.

"I still think it's a reasonable likeness though," continued Brast, fishing the drawing from Sermo's robes. "Good enough to pay me for at least." He nodded at Vola. "How much have you got?"

Vola snarled but, before he could say anything, Sermo said: "Just give him what you have."

Vola fished some coins from his robes and tossed them on the path.

"Good start," said Brast.

Vola shook his head and threw a dozen more coins to the ground.

"And your friend's," said Brast.

"Careful," Brast warned, as Vola approached Sermo. "You don't want me to slip."

"On the left," muttered Sermo, directing Vola to the coins.

"Now let me go," said Sermo, when there was an impressive pile of money lying on the grass.

"Perhaps," said Brast, sounding quite amused by the situation. "Perhaps not."

"That's all we have," said Sermo.

"Why were you following me?"

Sermo met Vola's eye, giving him a silent warning.

Neither of the men answered the question.

"Then maybe it's a no," said Brast, tightening his grip on Sermo's shoulders.

"Hiramites!" gasped Vola.

There was a clatter of armour as a group of soldiers entered the park. They wore tall conical silver helmets of a peculiar design, forged to give the impression that the soldiers' faces were upside down, with a hooked nose and snarling mouth above the eyeholes. The effect was as disturbing as it was intended to be. Hiramites acted as Athanor's standing army, but also as its law enforcers and, when they saw what Brast was doing, they began hurrying across the grass, drawing their swords.

"Wait," said Sermo. "We can get you…" His words trailed off as he realized the blade had gone from his throat. He reached up, expecting to find blood pouring from his jugular, but his neck was intact.

He dragged Vola from the coins and they sprinted through the trees, making for the other exit as the soldiers raced after them, ordering them to halt.

8

Phrater Alzen cursed as he entered Verulum Square. He had forgotten that tomorrow night was the last night of the celebrations. The Festival of Undying Light would take place under the stern gaze of one of the Curious Men and Athanor would formally welcome its new citizens and settle into its new life. As a result, the square was swarming with people. Banners were being draped from the arms of veiled statues and scaffolding was being erected across the facades of crumbling mausoleums. Alzen had arrived alone, on foot and divested of his ceremonial gown, not wishing to draw attention to himself, but now, faced with legions of commoners, he wondered how he would find anyone. Verulum Square was a beautiful ghost – a memory of the time when this corner of the city had been the most popular burial place for Athanor's nobility. The architecture was in a different style to much of Athanor, but no less grand, colonnaded tombs topped with cinerary urns, fragments of age-worn friezes and huge, spiral columns supporting shattered statues, but everything was crumbling into disrepair and only used by families that were too poor to be buried in newer, more vibrant parts of the city. With every conjunction, Athanor grew, sprouting new streets and

absorbing new cultures and, with each new limb, a part of
the city's core was abandoned, like the rotten trunk of a tree
pushing all its strength into new growth. But this crumbling
necropolis had hosted the Festival of Undying Light since
before records began. However sad it seemed this morning,
tomorrow night it would be reborn, as glorious as it had
been when the city first tore itself free.

Expecting the square to be empty, Alzen's message to
the Aroc Brothers had been a vague order to meet him
near the fountain at its centre. As he stepped out into the
crowds, Alzen could barely see the fountain. As well as the
workmen erecting marquees and hanging lanterns, there
were already hundreds of celebrants, arrived early to find
a good vantage point. Alzen made his way through the
stinking crowds, peering at the fountain and trying to spot
one of the Aroc Brothers. They were not brothers at all,
not even all male. The name of their organization was one
of the hallmarks of stupidity that had led Alzen to choose
them out of all the gangs he might have employed. But he
assumed they would at least have the wit to send someone
that he would recognize. His message had made it clear that
he was furious.

Alzen spent an angry few minutes circling the fountain,
keeping his face hidden in his hood, until he finally saw
someone he knew. Sayal was the leader of the brothers and
he was accompanied by four of his men – glowering, low-
browed brutes, clutching weapons Alzen had helped them
acquire: gleaming, bulky crossbows.

Sayal nodded in recognition but remained seated on
the steps of the fountain. The man's nonchalance shocked
Alzen. Sayal may have been the gang's leader but he had

never shown such blatant disrespect. No one else in the square knew who Alzen was, but Sayal did. He should at least have risen and performed a discreet bow. Alzen glanced at the crossbows, feeling a premonition of danger. He had a knife under his robes, but he was not armed in any alchymical sense. He shook his head, irritated by his own nervousness. What possible threat could the Aroc Brothers be to him? The meeting with the Old King had spooked him, that was all.

He strode over to Sayal and glared down at him.

"Rise, when greeting one of the Elect."

Sayal remained where he was for a moment, leant back on his elbows, smirking at his men. Then he stood and dusted himself down.

As Sayal sauntered towards him, Alzen had to resist the urge to strike. His whole demeanour was disgraceful.

"We expected to hear from you sooner," said Sayal.

The Aroc Brothers belonged to some nondescript, sub-human species that Alzen could not even name. Sayal and his guards were humanoid, but grotesquely gelatinous and protean. Sayal's head was pale, translucent and rippling, like the pulsing umbrella of a jellyfish. Alzen could see his brain, bulging and reforming beneath the surface, like quicksilver melting in a crucible. His skin was moist and he had the eyes of a fish, huge and unblinking with no irises, just large, misshapen pupils, suspended in a metallic soup. All of the brothers were big, nearly seven feet tall and hunched over by the weight of their bullish, muscled shoulders and long, powerful arms. All the Aroc Brothers wore their hair in the same bizarre fashion: thin plaited strands, so thick with grease it stuck to their scalps like rivulets of black oil, pouring from the crown of their misshapen heads. They were freakish, ugly-looking things, but they understood their place and had never shown him such disrespect before.

"Not here," snapped Alzen, glancing at the people rushing past. He nodded to one of the gloomy avenues that led off the square.

Once they had found a quiet spot, in the doorway of a crumbling mausoleum, Alzen pushed Sayal back against the frame and glared, ignoring the crossbows that were pointed at him.

"What happened?"

Sayal's body shifted and reformed beneath his palm. It was like pressing into cold porridge. He snatched his hand away but continued scowling.

"It was a fuckup." Sayal was still wearing the same infuriating smirk.

"No one should have known the shipment was there." Alzen was still battling the urge to hit the man, but he sensed Sayal was about to share some news with him.

"Agreed," said Sayal, "but that's not really your biggest concern." Sayal lowered his voice, even though they were alone. "Your metal man was seen."

Alzen clenched his fists as Sayal took obvious delight in sharing what he thought was a surprise.

"It smashed half the warehouse down, by all accounts, then danced through the streets. We killed most of the witnesses."

"I know what happened," said Alzen. "What do you mean you only killed *most* of the witnesses?"

Sayal looked disappointed that he hadn't surprised Alzen. "Well, we killed all of them bar Isten."

"Isten?"

Sayal laughed. "You don't need to worry about her. One of the Exiles. She's a wreck. I heard she's gone to the Sisters of Solace looking like a corpse. And if she comes out of there alive no one would listen to her anyway."

Alzen shook his head, but before he could say more on the matter, Sayal continued.

"I've been considering the terms of our deal, Phrater Alzen."

Alzen's shock was almost as great as his fury. "How dare you," he whispered, pleased to see a flash of fear in Sayal's eyes. "It's thanks to my cinnabar that you've dominated half the city. I could kill you in your sleep. And I could do it without even entering that ridiculous palace you're polluting. I could fill your veins with silver and turn your heart to iron."

Sayal shook his head. "Your Holiness. What do you think will happen if I suddenly die by your hand? You know how many brothers I have. And they all know your name. And they can all sing like birds. People already know alchymia has been used to protect drugs. And then used to kill me as well? I'm sure your fellow phraters are keen to know exactly who was responsible. Isn't your whole doctrine based on 'purity of spirit'? Devotion to your Art?"

Alzen gripped the knife handle tighter. "You know nothing of the Art. And if one of your blubber-faced siblings tried to enter the Temple District they would be killed for sacrilege before they breathed a word of slander against me."

"Of course. But we would not be so stupid as to try and approach your noble brethren." He glanced at the crowds in the square. "We have more lowly friends, Phrater Alzen, but they are numerous. Some are even the laborators who buy your metals and work in your temples. They would all be fascinated to learn that one of their august masters was our chief supplier of cinnabar."

"Spread your rumours. Laborators would not *dare* speak against me, and if they did, no phrater would listen."

Sayal gave him a concerned smile. "Can you be *sure*? Can you be sure such a salacious rumour would never reach the ears of the Old King? From what you said, you and he are not exactly the best of friends as it is."

Sayal held up his hands and smiled. "But there's no need for any of this, Your Holiness. There's no reason for our agreement to end so acrimoniously. We're not asking much. And I have no desire to see you executed."

"What *do* you desire?"

"You've already been so generous," said Sayal. "There are no gangs who would dare threaten us now. We're so well armed and we've stockpiled so much cinnabar that we could feed the market for years even if you never gave us another ounce of the stuff."

"Stockpiled? You were meant to flood the market. To ensure that there wasn't an addict in the slums who went without."

"Exactly. And now we're getting to the nub of the issue, Your Holiness. The market is indeed flooded. The Azorus slums are awash with drugs, as you requested." He coughed and the effect was disturbing, causing his flesh to ripple and bulge. "Which is why prices are so low."

"Prices? What do prices matter to you? I've given you everything you need."

"Wealth is what we need. And not the pocket change you give us, Your Holiness. *Real* wealth. The kind of wealth that comes from charging the proper price for things."

"You've been holding drugs back?"

"Yes. And we intend to keep doing so, Phrater Alzen. In fact, we mean to tighten our grip. Supply and demand. You must understand, Your Holiness. We have our families to think of." Sayal gripped Alzen's arm, darkening the sleeve of his robe with gummy fluid. "But we'll still need your cinnabar, Your Holiness. We need to keep a steady supply."

Alzen was trembling with rage, but he already felt as though he had said too much. He needed to think in the privacy of his cell and then decide how to deal with this treacherous worm.

"Just one last thing, Your Holiness," said Sayal. "After tomorrow night's job at the festival, I think it's best if *I* decide what happens next. I'll send you a message. I'll decide the time and place of the next meeting."

Alzen was dazed by the man's presumption, but Sayal was already sauntering off down the avenue with his guards, heading back to the crowded square.

Alzen wanted to hurl his knife into the man's back, but he took a deep breath and leant against the doorframe, shaking his head, shocked by the whole encounter. Sayal could no longer be trusted. He would need to deal with him, but he had to think carefully about how. The disaster in the warehouse had already put him in danger.

Thinking of the warehouse reminded him of something else. He was not happy that a witness had been left alive to roam the city. Sayal said she was with the Sisters of Solace, but what was her name? He gripped his head, trying to squeeze the memory from his skull. "Isten," he hissed, after a few seconds. Then he rushed down the alleyway, whispering her name as he went.

9

Numberless and fearless, the pilgrims came, washed up on the riverbank like shells, heavy with memories and scars and hoping for a new world. Athanor crushed them under its heel, brutally indifferent, leaving the fragments lapping in the shallows. But a few broke the surface, fighting the current, reaching for hope.

Brast had left Isten on a columned veranda that surrounded Alabri House. He stayed with her for a while, cursing her for dragging him to such an out of the way place. He'd sounded furious, but she knew he was really just worried. Her convulsions had been growing worse on the way back through Coburg Market, and she was so weak that Brast had practically carried her the last half a mile. Alabri House was beautiful, a sprawling, single-storey building built entirely of driftwood. It looked like a graceful wave, whitecaps frozen in the act of cleansing the filth of the city. Its gnarled, sun-bleached curves always filled Isten with a sense of calm before she'd even entered. As soon as she heard movement in the house, she ordered Brast away, keen to be rid of his hangdog face. He'd hesitated, but she'd summoned the last of her strength and warned him off, explaining that the Sisters would not be pleased to see him. Once he was gone she'd leant back against one of the columns, hidden from the rising sun, and fallen asleep.

When she awoke, she was being carried down a high-ceilinged hallway, decorated with shimmering, white tiles and punctuated by dome-shaped archways, all screened with billowing, gossamer-thin curtains. She could remember the hallway clearly enough from her previous visits, but everything through the archways was harder to recall – a dreamlike collage of unrelated scenes and faces.

She was being carried by Naos, the Sister who nursed her last time. She was as Isten remembered: powerfully built and heavily muscled with a short, grey beard and sad, drowsy eyes. Isten had guessed long ago that the Sisters were something other than they appeared to be, but even their mask was wonderful: a beautiful, perfect vision of androgyny.

"I'm unwell again," said Isten, finding it surprisingly hard to speak. Her vision was failing, obscured by a blizzard of silver lights, making it impossible to see anything clearly. She was aware that Naos was smiling at her, but she could only see her face by not looking directly at her.

"You're dying," said Naos, pausing by one of the archways.

There were two old men seated to one side of the curtains. They were on small, wooden stools and locked in an embrace, looking at the floor with their foreheads pressed together and their arms thrown over each other's shoulders. They were whispering urgently but talking over each other, rather than conversing. There was a copper bowl on the floor between them and, every few seconds, a drop of blood would fall from one of their faces and hit the bowl, making it ring like a ceremonial bell. The blood vanished as soon as it touched the metal.

As Naos approached, the men fell silent and the blood ceased falling.

"He's on his way," they said, speaking in unison. They spoke in such a strange, heavy accent that Isten could barely understand the words. "He knows she's here."

Naos nodded, then pushed through the curtains and carried Isten inside.

The room was full of scented smoke that enveloped Isten, easing her pain and returning a little strength to her limbs.

Naos placed her back on the floor and Isten found that she was able to stand.

There were shapes moving through the fumes and, as Isten's eyes adjusted, she saw that they were not in a room, as she had thought, but on the shores of a small, foggy beach. She laughed. Naos had brought her home. This was the stretch of coast she had played on as a child, before Gombus smuggled her out of the country. She dropped to her knees and plunged her hands into the cold, wet sand, letting it tumble through her fingers as she inhaled the mist-filled air. Somewhere, in the distance, she could hear her mother, speaking to a crowd of followers, eliciting roars of approval, describing glorious changes that she would never live to achieve. The scene was both lie and truth, like everything in Alabri House, but Isten did not question it. She lay back and looked at the grey sky, the sky of a world with fixed seasons and constant stars; a world that was nothing like Athanor.

Naos had vanished but Isten was not alone on the sand. Gombus was at her side. Not Gombus as he was now, old and weary, but Gombus as he had been in the old country, when Isten was still a child.

"She loves them," said Isten, listening to the delight of the crowd as they cheered her mother's every word.

"She loves everyone," replied Gombus, smiling, not realizing how his words knifed into her.

Gombus handed her some bread and, as Isten took it, she guessed that, back in the house, Naos was giving her something more powerful than bread. She took the illusory food and swallowed it.

The beach faded as Isten ate, swallowed by a fast-growing dusk that turned the waves to iron peaks and flooded her joints with cold. Stars blinked into view and her mother's voice began to fade.

"No," she begged, wanting to hold the memory a little longer, wanting to hear a few more of her mother's words. Even if they weren't directed at her, they were still a treasure.

It was no use. The darkness spread until Gombus was little more than a silhouette. The last echoes of her mother's voice vanished, replaced by groans and whispered prayers. Other shapes appeared in the darkness, other silhouettes, and the stars became cracks in a distant ceiling, spilling shards of light onto a sea of upturned faces, children mostly, like herself. Their faces were anguished and afraid and, instead of damp sand beneath her, Isten felt hard, dry metal, lurching and swaying as though the world had been cut adrift.

"Did she live?" she asked, looking up at Gombus, already knowing the answer.

He looked down at her, his eyes full of tears but also full of pride. "More than any of us," he said.

Isten pressed her face into his side. He knew that wasn't what she meant.

Gombus held her as moans turned into howls. People were dying.

"Will we make it?" she said into his robes, relishing the briny smell of the cloth.

"Some of us." He handed her another piece of bread.

She ate, and the scene changed again.

There was a little more light now, and Isten was in a small, filthy bedroom. The window was boarded shut, but there was dry, harsh light breaking through the cracks and she knew she was back in Athanor. There was rubbish piled on the floor – scraps of food, empty bottles and the flat, desiccated remains of a rat, staring up at her with one bright, accusing eye.

A shadow loomed over her, but it was neither Gombus nor Naos. It was the man whose smile framed her nightmares. He led her gently to the bed and told her to lie down and remove her top. Then he turned away and stooped over a metal bowl. After a few minutes, flames filled the crucible, lighting the man's face from beneath, stretching his features into a fiendish mask. He placed a knife in the hot coals, muttering a prayer. Then he returned to the bed. In one hand he was holding the glowing knife and, in the other hand, he had a small bottle.

"To ease the pain," he said, giving her the bottle, still smiling.

Isten hesitated. This was the past. The decision was already made. But still she hesitated. Could she undo everything, here in the Sisters' house? No, she knew she could not. She took the bottle and drank, closing her eyes, wishing her past away, waiting for the pain to begin.

When she opened her eyes she was back at Alabri House, lying on the warm grass of a trellised garden, bathed in sunlight and surrounded by the strange, contorted trunks of juniper trees. The trees rolled and turned across the garden in such a wild profusion of shapes that they looked like ecstatic dancers, their gnarled limbs frozen at the climax of a sacred rite. Isten could imagine them springing to life and sweeping her along with their frenzied devotions.

The garden was surrounded by verandas and there were other people sprawled on the grass. Some were entwined, lost in passion, and others were insensate, dazed by whatever delights the Sisters had shared with them, but others were simply talking quietly in the sunshine. Most of the figures were as solid as the trees, but others were like an afterimage, translucent and faint, moving through the others like ghosts. There was none of the frantic mania that characterized much of Athanor. A sense of calm filled the garden, carried on the heady, woody fragrance of the juniper trees. Back inside the house, someone was playing a kora and the sound filtered through the garden, shimmering in time with the dappled light.

"There are quicker ways to kill yourself than cinnabar," said Naos.

She was sitting behind Isten, cross-legged in the shade, heating the bowl of a tar pipe.

Isten sat up, feeling much better than she had done for days. There were breadcrumbs on her jacket and she realized that Naos had given her food rather than cinnabar. She patted down her limbs. They were painfully thin but intact and they had finally stopped shaking.

Naos nodded, her eyes closed as she smoked the pipe. "And you can't stay here, revisiting the same scenes, living in the past."

Isten shook her head. "I don't want to stay. I just needed

to recover." She gripped the knife at her belt. "I have a debt to repay. One of my countrymen lied to me, Naos, one of my own people. He sent me into a trap and Amoria died."

"Colcrow." Naos seemed, as always, to know what Isten was thinking.

"Amoria died because of him." Even the tranquillity of the garden could not dampen Isten's pain. "He must have known what was waiting in that warehouse. I think he sold us out to the Aroc Brothers."

Naos took another slow drag from the pipe, keeping her languid gaze on Isten. "You think that Colcrow knows the plans of the Curious Men?"

Isten was about reply when she realized how unlikely that was. The Elect did not share their schemes with lowlifes like Colcrow.

"And was it the Aroc Brothers who were waiting for you in the warehouse?"

Isten shook her head, confused.

Naos extinguished the pipe and dusted ash from her robes. "You have a visitor." She stood and held out a hand towards Isten.

"A visitor?" Isten frowned as she let Naos pull her to her feet. "I told Brast to go home. I don't want–"

"Not him." Naos led her back across the veranda and into the house.

They returned through the long, tall hallway that Naos had originally led her down. The two old men were still seated outside the curtains with their copper bowl, but they were both asleep, slumped back against the faded tiles, snoring and muttering into their beards.

Naos led Isten down the hallway, past several more

archways, until she came to one that was smaller than the others and framed a door. The door had been left ajar.

They entered a library. Pale, diffuse light was radiating through screens at the far end of the room, washing across walls decorated with the same glazed tiles as the hallway outside. The library was lined on all four sides by alcoves, each of which was crowded with books. All of the folios were bound in identical white calfskin and decorated with gold leaf. The sound of the kora was drifting through the screen and the library had the same calm atmosphere as the garden outside.

There were cushions on a rug in the centre of the room and Naos waved Isten to one of them, then she turned to leave. She hesitated in the doorway, looking back at Isten, seeming unsure whether to speak.

"What?" asked Isten, sinking into the cushion.

"The past is fixed."

Isten frowned. "Of course."

"Even here."

Isten shook her head. "I didn't come here to undo my past. I just needed a rest." She pictured Gombus, Puthnok, Lorinc and all the other Exiles. "So I can find a way to help my friends."

Naos nodded. "You'll be at peace for a while. We've given you a remedy. If you stay away from cinnabar you'll continue to recover. But…" She shrugged.

Isten was about to reply when she heard the sound of footsteps approaching.

"Consider the choices that lie ahead," said Naos. "The future is *not* fixed."

Isten was about to reply, but Naos was already smiling in

DARIUS HINKS   99

greeting to whoever was nearing the door. She ushered him into the library and left, closing the door behind her.

The man was handsome in a dignified, aristocratic kind of way and looked decidedly out of place in the plain, threadbare robe he was wearing.

"You poor thing," he said, crossing the room and taking her hand. "You look exhausted."

"Do I know you?"

"Forgive me," he said. "My name is Phrater Alzen. I belong to the Fraternity of the Elect."

He took a small, silver egg from his robes and placed it on the table in front of her. "I have come to help," he said, smiling warmly.

10

There was a father, just out of sight, hovering at the edge of her memory. No one would speak of him but she knew he was there. She could feel the bristles on his chin and the pain in his laugh, and, when she closed her eyes, she could almost picture his face, painted in blood across her lids, daring her to remember his name.

Isten stared at Alzen in surprise. Even in a house this strange, he was an oddity. There was a faint metallic sheen to his face, as though his skin was impregnated with fragments of gold, and his irises sparkled the same way, glinting as he smiled. Beneath his tatty dark robes, she caught a glimpse of finery, folds of luxurious amber-coloured cloth.

"You're one of the Elect?" She felt a mixture of revulsion and fascination. The Curious Men were an extreme example of everything the Exiles despised: privileged, unelected, remote, feeding off the sweat of their starving subjects and hiding behind a smokescreen of mystery and ritual. The Exiles had no interest in changing Athanor, even Puthnok was not that ambitious, their battle was far from here, but Isten still felt a flash of rage as Alzen beamed at her.

He nodded, still gripping her hand, and laughed. "My disguise is not a particularly inventive one."

The Curious Men were a mystery even to the oldest citizens of Athanor. Isten felt dazed to be talking to one. "Disguise?" she said. "Why would you need to hide your identity?"

He loosed her hand and dropped down into the cushions, starting to fiddle with the metal egg he had placed on the table. "We're a cloistered bunch, Isten. The Art demands it – focus and purity, purity and focus, nothing else." He nodded at the screen separating them from the garden. "Not for us the pleasures of the flesh. My fraternity would not approve of me visiting Alabri House, even if they knew I had only come to nurse the sick."

Isten shook her head, wanting no help from such a man. "I'm not sick any more. The Sisters have treated me. I was about to leave."

Alzen nodded, still adjusting the egg's delicate mechanisms. "I understand." He took a small ivory pipe from his robes and breathed a cloud of dust into the air. It was beautifully scented, and Isten felt a wonderful sense of relaxation wash through her limbs. The feeling blossomed in her chest and she lay back across the cushions, staring at the floral plasterwork on the ceiling. The moulded petals moved in response to her gaze, growing and twisting, furling and unfurling.

"Leaving to go where?" asked Alzen, in the same cheerful tone as he clicked the egg open.

"I have to kill someone," she said. As the words left her mouth, she felt a flash of alarm. Why had she said such a thing out loud? Especially to a man like this?

Alzen leant over her and she saw that he had taken something from the egg. It looked like a delicate, folded sheet. "And whom do you intend to kill?"

"Sayal," she said, finding, to her dismay, that she was powerless to hold back her words. "He leads a gang. The Aroc Brothers. They stole our money and our businesses. They killed my countrymen. I have to ruin them."

Alzen faltered, clearly shocked by the mention of Sayal. He had been about to unfurl the folded sheet, but he stopped and lowered it onto his lap. "How?"

Isten was feeling increasingly dazed. She could no longer move her limbs or sit up and her words were slurred, but the whole experience was so pleasant that she made no effort to fight the drowsiness. "I'll raise funds and re-arm the Exiles. I've done it before and I'll do it again..." Isten was about to say more but, to her relief, her mouth would not obey, mumbling gibberish.

Alzen was studying her closely. His smile had faded. "The Exiles? That's the name of a gang?"

She nodded.

"*Your* gang?"

She nodded again.

Alzen muttered and shook his head, a puzzled expression on his face. Then he lifted another pipe from his robes. It looked like a penny whistle. He took a box, like a snuffbox, pressed powder into the pipe and blew it into Isten's face.

A delightful euphoria rushed through her. She was still too weak to sit, but her mouth was once again able to form speech.

"We've lost dozens of men at their hands," she said, still finding it impossible to hold back the truth. "I was absent for a whole year, and without me to hold the Exiles together, people just lost faith and fell away. But we still have Lorinc, Feyer, Korlath and Piros, and maybe Puthnok and Gombus.

And there will be others I can round up. I think maybe I could convince Brast to come back. Maybe even Colcrow."

"Not enough," said Alzen. "The Aroc Brothers have forged an *empire* over the last year. They control everything illegal that happens along both sides of the river: whores, drugs, gambling, pit fighting. And they have an army of heavily armed thugs at their disposal."

Even in her confused state, Isten found it strange that a Curious Man would know so much about a criminal gang.

"But Sayal is still an idiot," she said. "All I need is a tip-off – some details of whatever they're planning next, and I could pull the rug from under their feet. We never had any problems dealing with them before, but then they got their hands on the best weapons in the city and suddenly have a limitless supply of cinnabar to sell."

Alzen looked away from her, staring at the ceiling. For a while he said nothing, obviously lost in thought. Then he stuffed another lump of powder into his pipe and filled the air with a new aroma.

Isten felt strength returning to her limbs and managed to sit up. She also found that she could think without blurting out every thought that crossed her mind.

"The Sisters of Solace are very skilled, but I have hastened your recovery," said Alzen. "I realize the effects may have felt a little strange, but you should now feel quite reinvigorated."

Isten found that she did, indeed, feel better than she had done for a long time. But whether Alzen had helped her or not, she still felt like she was conversing with a serpent.

She nodded to the small folded sheet that was still lying on his lap. "Were you going to do something with that?"

He gave a dismissive wave of his hand. "Just another remedy. It won't be needed now. You have recovered so well." He placed the cloth carefully back in the metal egg.

When he had closed the egg, Alzen rose and stood next to Isten. "The Aroc Brothers are a scourge."

As Isten's head began to clear she tried to connect the events of the last couple of days, sensing that this conversation could be far more important than she at first guessed. The drugs in the warehouse were the property of the Aroc Brothers but they were guarded by alchymia. Alchymia could only be produced by a Curious Man. That in itself was peculiar. The Elect never mixed with the city's lower orders, and they expressly forbade the use of drugs, executing anyone caught dealing them. And now here was a Curious Man who knew of the Aroc Brothers' dealings and seemed angry at them. There had to be a connection.

"I'm surprised you've heard of the Aroc Brothers," she said, speaking more carefully now that she had regained control of her words.

Anger flashed in his eyes. "I've heard of them. Would you really like to see them ruined?"

"Would you?"

He did not reply, but she saw from his expression that he would.

"But you can't be seen to move openly against them," she suggested.

He glanced at the metal egg, seeming to debate whether to start fiddling with it again.

"Perhaps we could work together," she said, feeling that she was pushing on a door with no idea of what lay beyond.

Alzen looked back at her with a mixture of wariness and excitement.

She shrugged. "Look, I don't know what connection you have with those lowlifes, but if you told me, and I didn't keep it secret, you'd just kill me. It would be as easy for you as crushing a fly, wouldn't it? Or is everything I've heard about Curious Men wrong? So what do you have to lose by talking to me?"

The doubt was still in his eyes but she could see that he was intrigued. She realized that, for some reason, he was as desperate as she was.

"If I were to do something as unpleasant as killing you," he said, "the rest of your gang would spread rumours. They'd try to smear my reputation."

Isten laughed, genuinely amused. "You think I'd tell the Exiles I was working with you? They hate me as it is; if they thought I was getting help from a Curious Man, *they'd* want to kill me." Her smile faded. "They certainly wouldn't consider me fit to lead them any more." She shook her head, realizing how dangerous this whole conversation was and wondering if the cinnabar was still messing with her judgment. The Exiles despised Athanor's ruling elite. It would be the end of everything if they found out she had even *considered* working with Alzen. "Perhaps it's not such a good idea," she muttered, looking away from him, suddenly feeling very uncomfortable in his presence. She rose and looked at the door.

"Wait," said Alzen, gripping her arm.

She reached for the knife Brast had given her and grabbed the handle, glaring at him.

He gave her the same kind smile he had shown when he

first entered the room. The doubt had gone from his eyes. "Perhaps we *might* be of use to each other."

She said nothing but didn't pull away, still enticed by the idea of overthrowing the Aroc Brothers.

"I see fear in your face," he said. "Fear that your friends would learn of your dealings with me. And I certainly couldn't have it known that I was dealing with someone like you. So it would seem we'd have a mutual need for secrecy. In that respect, at least, we would be ideal partners."

Isten nodded, her thoughts racing. He was right. And if she played along with Alzen for a period of time, she could benefit from his help. Then, later, if she wanted to be rid of him, she could find some way to reveal his deviant behaviour without exposing her connection to him.

"Partners in what?" she asked, shrugging off his grip, but also letting go of her knife. "What exactly are we discussing?"

Alzen locked the door. Then he checked the window and sat back down on the cushions, waving for her to do the same.

When she was seated, he took a small paper-wrapped parcel out of his robes and looked at it. Again he hesitated, mouthing something and frowning. It was clear he was unsure whether to proceed.

Isten's pulse hammered in her temples. She didn't know if it was the Sisters' house playing with her mind, but she felt as though something momentous was about to happen; something that could finally turn her fortunes around.

Finally, Alzen nodded and folded back a corner of the paper parcel.

The smell hit her immediately. Cinnabar. And not just any cinnabar. It was peculiarly potent. Just like the shipment she had seen in the warehouse.

Alzen held the parcel towards her.

Isten licked her fingertip and reached out, then hesitated, remembering Naos's warning. The smell was already causing her vision to change and her heart to slow but she did not *have* to taste it, she told herself. She had a chance, here in the Sisters' house, to change, to resist, to rethink who she was and make her future better than her past. Then she remembered who she was, remembered every wrong choice she had made in her life, and realized she was kidding herself. She had never resisted anything. She never would. Sadness gripped her as she realized that, for her, there was no way to really change, even here. She stroked her finger across the crimson block and tasted it.

"It's good," she said, leaning back in the cushions, watching the room melt around her, letting the cinnabar drown her shame. "Very good."

Alzen nodded. "And I can supply you with a lot. For free."

"Free?" Isten was busy watching the plasterwork bloom, but she could still hear how unlikely that sounded.

"*Free.* All I'd ask is that you sell it cheap and to anyone who needs it. I want it spread across the whole city, particularly the Azorus Slums. I have my own reasons."

"And what about the Aroc Brothers?"

"Well, there are two things we can do about them. You would be selling cinnabar so cheaply that no one would be interested in buying any more from the Aroc Brothers. That will quickly bring them down to earth. But, before that, I could help you achieve your plan of killing Sayal. I know his movements. I can give you enough information to hit him when he's at his most vulnerable. I know, for example, that tomorrow night, he'll be at the Festival of Undying Fire.

He'll be in a certain catacomb beneath the necropolis while the celebrations are in full flow."

"Grave robbing?" Isten sat up and tried to clear her thoughts again. "There are no corpses in those tombs. They were plundered centuries ago."

"Not all. He has learned the location of a tomb that is still intact. The tomb of one my ancestors – one of the original Curious Men. There will be all sorts of–"

"And he learned of this tomb from you?" interrupted Isten.

Alzen gave her a warning look and ignored her question.

"The tomb will be full of precious metals," he said, "which he will use to acquire even more men and weapons. But, if I give you the location of the tomb, you could give him a surprise. There will be no soldiers down there, because no one will expect anyone to be digging around beneath the square."

"For good reason," muttered Isten. At the Festival of Undying Fire, the boundaries between the living and the dead were said to become less clear. People dismissed the legends as nonsense, but no one liked to stray too near the crypts' gaping mouths.

"It's not the dead who've wronged you," said Alzen. "It's the Aroc Brothers. And I can give you a chance to strike back at Sayal when he least expects it. He thinks you're dead, or as good as. He won't expect to see you coming at him with a knife."

Isten nodded, excited by the idea, but then she shook her head. "But it'll *only* be me. I'll never be able to convince the other Exiles to follow me after what happened last time – not until I can show them I've actually done something good. Can you give me some soldiers from your temples?"

"The whole point is that I must have no hand in this. Is there no one who could help you?"

Isten pictured the desperate, unshakeable devotion she had seen in Brast's eyes. "There is one friend. Someone I might be able to convince." The thought made her skin crawl, but there was no one else who would come near her. "But that still wouldn't be enough for us to take on the Aroc Brothers if they arrive in a large group."

"Two might be enough. You won't need to fight them."

"What do you mean?"

"The catacombs are only opened during the night of the festival. All you need to do is follow Sayal down there and make sure only you come out. There are doors all through the catacombs. Doors with locks. They're ancient, but some of them still work and I can teach you how to work the mechanisms. If you follow the Aroc Brothers until they are a few levels below the square, you would just need to let them go ahead, then lock the doors. As you head back up, you could lock the others too, in case they managed to make it through the first one."

"Leaving Sayal stuck down there."

Alzen nodded. "Until the next festival. By which point he will be as dead as everyone else in the crypts."

Isten started pacing around the library. She looked at the packet of drugs that was still on the table. "And the cinnabar?"

"Kill Sayal, and I'll know I can do business with you. You will have your first shipment within the week."

Isten stopped by the screen and closed her eyes, letting the sunlight warm her face, relishing the pleasant dizziness that the cinnabar had left her with. The kora player was playing faster and Isten could see the music filtering into the room – a blizzard of crystalline notes, weaving around her. She smiled. This was it. Finally, after years of waiting, years of promising, she was going to lift the Exiles from the gutter. She couldn't get them back to Rukon, but she could make them the lords of their new home. She pictured Gombus's face. Finally, she would show him that she was worth something.

"We have a deal," she whispered.

"Hold out your hand," he said.

She did as he asked, thinking he was going to shake it, but, instead, he pressed his fingertip against her bicep, leaving a faint orange stain, like faded henna.

Isten was about to ask what the mark meant, but he held up a warning hand. "A mark of trust. Don't wash it away." Then he reached into his robes and took out a purse containing more money than Isten had seen for years. He dropped the purse into her hand. "Get yourself some food and decent lodgings. You're no use to me dead."

11

Ghosts stretched under the city like knotted roots, gossiping and muttering, talking constantly, content with their own company, until the day when they finally saw through the lie. Then they spread up through seams of rock and bled through Athanor's walls, desperate to share what they had learned. They encircled the living and screamed the truth at them. No one is above death, they cried, not even the Elect. The living walked on, oblivious, and the dead fell back in despair, forgetting what they had learned, sinking into darkness.

Crowds flooded into Verulum Square, a golden tide, drowning the mausoleums in yellow cotton and catching the light of its mandrel-fires. Tradition dictated that the celebrants wore yellow robes and wooden masks, painted gold in tribute to the Curious Men and in thanks for another successful conjunction. The people of Athanor revelled in this chance to mimic their enigmatic lords. Some were pushing huge, wheeled, wicker sculptures made in imitation of the Elect's automata – domed, spider-legged chariots and winged skeletal serpents, all woven by hand and painted gold. Everything was in motion, dancing and leaping, apart from the regiments of hiramites mustered at the back of the square, watching the proceedings in silence from behind their tall, silver helmets, swords drawn and legs apart, ready to march on the crowds at the first sign of trouble.

It was almost midnight and the square's crumbling architecture was as black as the sky, silhouetted by the fires, adding to the theatrical feel of the festival. It seemed as though the whole necropolis was a stage peopled with teetering, wicker titans. At one end, there was a stage, a huge, tiered platform, dozens of intersecting metal circles raised high above the crowd on a latticework of curling struts. The struts were made of polished metal and, as the lights flashed across them, they seemed to burn, giving the impression that the stage was held aloft by a raging furnace.

As the crowds surged between the ruins, the Curious Men were walking onto the stage, dressed in the splendour that the crowds were trying to emulate: plush, yellow robes, tall, flame-shaped helmets, rods of office and, in some cases, ceremonial swords so long they had to be carried by scrums of stooped, shuffling attendants.

Isten and Brast were crouched on the empty pedestal of a long-gone statue, looking down over the crowds and sharing a bottle of wine.

"What if he's not there?" asked Brast.

Isten did not really register his question. She leant back against the shattered masonry, thinking of her glorious return to the Blacknells Road, imagining the Exiles' faces when she told them she had robbed the Aroc Brothers of their leader and gained a free supply of cinnabar. After Alzen left she had spent another blissful hour with the Sisters, satisfying a lust more potent than anything she had felt in years. When she was done, they had bathed and clothed her and made her look almost human. "What?" she muttered, turning away from the crowds to focus on Brast's yellow mask. She had made both the masks and deliberately given his a jolly grin, amused by the idea of his wry, bitter eyes glowering at her through such a juvenile face.

"What if Sayal isn't in the catacombs?"

"Then my informant lied and we'll leave." Isten's voice echoed strangely through her own mask. She had given hers a thoughtful, wise-looking expression, finding that contrast almost as amusing as Brast's grin.

"No, I don't mean that. I mean, what if Sayal sends his men down there, but hasn't bothered to come himself? What if it's just his grunts?"

"That's not his style. And, from what I've been told, this job is particularly important to him. He'll be there." She stood up, adjusted her mask and checked she had everything. She was wearing the same leather armour Brast had given her the night before and she had the knife tucked into her belt. In her trouser pocket she had the note Alzen had given her. It described the entrance they needed and the route through the catacombs, and it also explained the door mechanisms. "Let's go," she said, heading for the pedestal's steps.

Brast took a moment to fold away the picture he had been sketching, so Isten stood for a moment, looking out over the crowds, feeling as though *she* were on a stage, surrounded by thousands of devoted followers. It occurred to her that this must be how her mother had felt, back in Rukon, when she addressed the huge audiences that came to hear her in the final months of her life.

"Ready," said Brast, dragging Isten back into the present. They climbed down the slumped steps and entered the crowd, swallowed by the noise and stink. The majority of the celebrants were human, but the city's other races were represented too. Isten had to fight through towering carapaces and charred, smouldering haunches as well as red-faced drunkards.

"We've got plenty of time," she said, glancing back at Brast. "Sayal's not planning to make his move until the end of the ceremony when all the fireworks start going off. They're hoping the fireworks will drown out any noise they make getting in."

"Noise? But the gates to the crypts are open on festival night."

"But none of those passages are used any more. Apparently, their plan is to wait for the noise to start – in case they need to smash through collapsed walls or broken railings."

They clambered up onto roofs and balconies and managed to cross the square reasonably quickly. Everyone else was too busy celebrating to notice the two slender figures who slipped past them.

"You've changed," said Brast, as they dropped from a broken portico and landed back in the mob.

"What?" she yelled, struggling to hear him over the noise of the crowd.

"You've never kept secrets from me before," he said in her ear, as they passed the stage, where the Curious Men were performing one of their obscure rituals, preparing to address the crowd. "But you looked furious when I tried to find out who your informant is."

She halted and glared at him, wondering if she'd made a mistake asking him along.

"Don't worry!" he said, his mocking tone sounding absurd through his cheerful mask. "I'm just intrigued to know who you could feel so protective over."

She realized, to her relief, that he had no inkling of who she had been talking to. Incredibly, even now, even here, he was just jealous.

She took another swig from her wine bottle and hurried on. "It's not important who it is." She nodded to the teardrop-shaped archways looming up ahead of them. "We're almost there."

On this side of the platform, there were hardly any celebrants. Only those who had arrived too early and were now too inebriated to realize that the festival was about to begin, slumped across the ruins like landed fish, belching and mouthing gibberish into the moonlight. There were also a few groups huddled in the shadows, making deals or threats or trying to sell things that weren't theirs to sell.

Isten and Brast rushed on until they stood before the row of arches. They were each over thirty feet tall and too deep to be penetrated by the glow of the mandrel-fires. They looked like gaping mouths, locked in a silent scream, and their breath was a cold, damp breeze, quite unlike the dry heat that was still radiating up from the stones in the rest of the square.

Isten hesitated as she looked up at the towering shapes.

"Scared of ghosts?" laughed Brast.

She ignored him and waved to a toppled statue a few feet away. "Sayal isn't due for another couple of hours, but we should hide just in case. They might send a scout over here early."

They climbed over the rubble and found a comfortable

vantage point from where they could watch the arches without being seen.

"Which arch is it?" asked Brast as he squeezed in next to her.

She pointed. "Third from the right. The one with the crack up the side."

"Tell me again how much you're paying me for this?" he whispered.

"Still nothing," she replied.

He laughed, quietly. "I can't believe you're listening to another tip-off after what happened at the embassy."

"This is different."

"Let's hope so."

He finally fell quiet and the two of them waited, watching the occasional drunk stagger past and waiting to see if Isten's luck really was on the up.

Behind them, they heard the sounds of the festival. One of the Curious Men was addressing the crowd, using alchymia to project his voice across the square. It was the usual rubbish. He was explaining how grateful they should all be. The Elect had used their noble, glorious Art to once again steer Athanor to a place of safety and bounty. Over the last few months, he said, their diplomats had brokered deals with their new neighbours, ensuring that Athanorians would want for nothing. Isten had to stifle a curse as she thought of the poor souls in the Azorus slums or the doss houses on the Blacknells Road. Most of the crowd knew they were being duped, but they loved their golden lords all the same, howling in delight, drunk on the pageantry and mysticism. Isten could picture the scene – the Curious Men would be performing some parlour trick, summoning shadows from flames or blessing statues with speech, anything to keep the mob entertained and stop them asking why so many people were starving when a single phrater wore enough gold to buy a lifetime's food. Then there would be a parade, as representatives of the new immigrants fawned to the Old King and swore allegiance. And after that, the mandrel-fires would die and the fireworks would begin. Isten had avoided the festival for years, sickened by the hypocrisy. At least from behind the platform she would not have to watch the farcical performance. Alzen would be up there, she realized, with a jolt. He would be nodding and smiling and endorsing the lies. Suddenly, she felt the urge to tell Brast what she had done, tell him about Alzen and ask him if she was doing the right thing. She gripped the knife in her belt and kept her mouth shut. It was too late for that. Brast would despise her. As would all the others.

They were so tightly crushed together that Brast felt her tense and looked at her. "What?"

"Nothing," she muttered.

He was about to say something else when she nodded through the hole that was acting as their window on the arches.

A group of men had emerged from the shadows and were moving towards the arch with the cracked wall. They were walking in a way that made it clear they were not just escaping the sycophancy in the square. They were gripping brutal-looking metal crossbows that Isten had only ever seen in the hands of the Aroc Brothers, and they were looking all around as they approached the arch, scouring the shadows for any sign that they were being watched.

Isten carefully raised her mask and leant forwards, staring into the darkness, trying to see if Sayal was there. There were six of the lumbering brutes and they were all wearing the same wooden masks as the rest of the crowd, but their bulbous heads meant the masks were crooked and only half-attached.

Isten gripped Brast's arm as one of the brothers looked back their way. Like all of them, his hair was a mass of thin black braids, oiled and plastered to his head in coils and loops, as though black tar had been poured down the back of his pallid head. Unlike the others though, he was wearing a thick band of silver around his head, studded with gems, marking him out as the leader.

"That's him," she whispered.

Sayal stared at the toppled statue for a few long seconds and Isten thought he must have somehow heard her whisper, even over the roaring of the crowd, but then he waved his crossbow at the archway and lumbered off in that direction with the others swaggering after him.

Quickly, the Aroc Brothers vanished from sight and Brast turned to face Isten. "What do we do now?" he whispered. "There are no fireworks. There's still another hour of drivel before that happens."

"They might just be waiting inside the arch. Keeping out of sight. Getting ready."

"What if they're not? What if they're heading down into the catacombs?"

"I have a map of the route. It's fine. As long as we don't see them come out, we know they've gone down. Then all we need to do is go in, lock a few doors and come back out again."

As the minutes rolled on, however, Isten began to grow restless. It worried her not to follow the brothers. She wanted to be sure they were taking the route Alzen had drawn.

After another ten minutes of anxious waiting, she looked at Brast. "They might recognize me, even with the mask, but they wouldn't know you."

"What?" he hissed. "What are you asking?"

"Just wander over there, looking like you're drunk. You wouldn't have to get too close to see if they're all still hiding in the archway. And if you can't see them we'll know they've gone down and we're safe to follow."

"Wander over there? Did you see those crossbows?"

"They're not going to start shooting random passers-by. They're trying to be discreet. Just don't walk too close."

He muttered a curse but, as she guessed, he could not refuse her. He climbed out of the rubble, staggering off in the direction of the arches.

Isten could see him weaving in and out of view for a while, then she lost sight of him.

She began to worry, and after a few minutes she wondered if she should head out and look for him.

"They're gone," said a voice in her ear.

She whirled around with her knife in her hand and only just managed to stop herself gutting Brast.

He backed away, hands raised.

"Don't do that," she muttered, pacing off towards the arch and waving for him to follow.

Athanor was hot in the day and cool at night, whatever the date and wherever the latest conjunction had left it. Some artifice of the Curious Men maintained the ideal weather for whatever it was they claimed to do all day but, even at night, Isten had rarely experienced the damp chill that met her as she approached the door to the catacombs. The entrance was clearly ancient, its shape deformed by time and the strangeness of Athanor. The frame had been engulfed, long ago, by a slow-growing explosion of metal latticework that knifed through the porous rock in spirals and curls, glinting in the moonlight like a metal waterfall. The arch looked more like a huge, natural grotto than a manmade structure.

Isten crept into the darkness, knife in one hand, wine bottle in the other, glancing back to check Brast was with her.

He nodded in his ridiculous mask, gripping his falcata.

The archway led into a long portico and Isten hesitated at the sight of the columns. They were deformed by the same torrents of filigree that had consumed the entrance and they reminded her of the Ignorant Man that killed Amoria.

Brast reached her side. "What is it?"

She stared at the nearest column, imagining faces and hands, but finally shook her head and waved him on.

The entrance to the catacombs was a smaller affair. An oval-shaped door, usually barred and locked, but left open tonight so that the dead could "partake" of the festivities. No one in Athanor believed that revenants actually lumbered from the crypts, but it was a long-held tradition. Two small mandrel-fires had been placed either side of the doorway, glass, liquid-filled orbs on slender pedestals, their pale light washing over the rubbish gathered at the foot of the door. The air was ripe with the smell of piss and fox shit and the place had a generally unloved air. Only the most confused drunks ever came near the catacombs. The graves had been robbed countless centuries ago and this whole area of Athanor was unsafe after dark.

Isten carefully picked up one of the mandrel-fires, keeping it in its metal cradle and being careful not to spill any of the liquid from the glass. No one knew how the Curious Men produced the viscous, metallic slop that illuminated the city, but everyone knew what happened if it got into your bloodstream – tremors, madness and then death.

She stepped carefully through the doorway and the light revealed a long, straight passageway that descended at a steep incline, plunging down under the square. It was collapsed in some places and enveloped by metal strands in others, but still passable. There was no sign of the Aroc Brothers, but Isten fancied that she could hear noises, echoing back down the chamber.

She hurried through the gloom with the light held before her, glancing repeatedly back at the portico to make sure none of the columns had moved.

The passageway led through another doorway into a broad, circular hall, with four doors dotted around the circumference. The ceiling must once have been a dome, but it was so crumbled now that the original shape was hard to make out. Monstrous talons of stone reached down, like bloated stalactites, dripping dust and water onto Isten as she strode out into the centre of the floor, raising her light to take in the scale of the place.

"Look," whispered Brast, nodding to a pale shape at the foot of one of the columns reaching down from the square above.

She tensed, thinking he might have seen one of the Aroc Brothers, but it was a corpse, seated in a regal pose in an alcove at the base of the column.

"How can that still be here?" asked Brast, heading over for a better look and waving for Isten to follow. "After all these centuries."

They needed to keep moving, but Isten was as fascinated as Brast and crossed the chamber, pointing the light at the corpse.

"Did you never listen to Gombus when you were a child?" she said. "These catacombs were built for the first Curious Men. He said they preserved their flesh somehow." She tapped the glass containing the mandrel-fire. "With the same chemicals that light the streets, I think he said."

As they neared the corpse, they saw that much of it had gone – the whole lower half in fact, but the chest, arms and head remained in the same position, seeming to levitate above the seat. The corpse looked more like a rusted, metal sculpture than a body. It was holding an ornate, serpent-entwined rod in one hand, and a small crucible in the other. Its eyes were closed and its expression blissful.

"Is it a statue?" asked Brast, staring at it in wonder, raising his sword to tap the thing's face.

Isten shook her head. "I think it's one of them. The Elect." She looked up into the darkness. "These columns must be the foundations for those massive statues up in the square." She looked back at the corpse. "Gombus said this is what Curious Men become when they finally die of old age – consumed and preserved by their magic. That's probably why no one's dared take it, even after all these years. From what Gombus said, they're toxic. Besides, I imagine the Curious Men have specific forms of execution for people who tamper with their ancestors' corpses."

Brast lowered his sword and took a step back.

Isten stared at the body for a moment longer. It had been sitting here for thousands of years, watched over by the statue up in the square, but its beatific smile was identical to the one she saw on Alzen's face – the smile of a smug, satisfied tyrant, equally unafraid of life and death. She shook her head. The sooner this was over with, the sooner she could forget she ever met Alzen.

"Let's go," she said, nodding to one of the doorways. "My map says they'll be headed that way." As they rushed into another passageway, she said: "All we need to do is check they're down here, then we can look for a door and lock them in."

The passageway was another steep incline, taking them even lower, and the air was now almost icy. The sickly light of the mandrel-fire gave no warmth and Isten wished she'd thought to bring a cloak. They passed through one of the doors Alzen had described, then two more, before Isten heard voices ahead.

She opened the valve on her lamp and killed the light. She and Brast both stumbled to a halt as they found themselves in absolute darkness.

"Follow the walls," said Isten, reaching out and placing her palm on damp, shattered tiles. The dark reminded her of her childhood voyage to Athanor, hearing her friends dying all around her, but she kept walking, trying to sound more confident than she felt. "The ground's pretty even."

They stumbled along like that for a while, until the passageway bent round to the right and they saw a light. Not mandrel-fire, but the flickering, smoky warmth of a real torch. It plucked silhouettes from the darkness. The hulking shapes of the Aroc Brothers were unmistakable, and Isten grinned.

"They're down here," she whispered. "We just need to head back and lock those doors we passed."

"Which one?" replied Brast.

Isten felt like hitting him. The idiot had spoken loudly enough for the brothers to hear. Then her stomach tightened as she realized it wasn't Brast who had spoken.

She stood and whirled around, raising her knife just in time to parry the blade that flashed through the dark towards her.

The force of the blow sent her flying back through the air and she cracked her head against the stone, dazed and bleeding as her attacker lunged into the light.

Sayal had removed his mask and his face bubbled into a grin as he drew back his falcata for another thrust.

His blade collided with Brast's and the two men began exchanging furious blows, filling the darkness with sparks.

Sayal was massive but Brast was quicker. They circled each other, lunging and slashing as the other brothers began pounding back up the slope towards them.

"Isten!" laughed Sayal as he fought. "What the fuck are you doing here?" He launched a savage flurry of sword strikes at Brast's head, causing him to stagger back towards the approaching brothers. "We won. You lost. Just fucking die."

Isten wiped the blood from her eyes and launched herself from the wall, slamming into Sayal's side. His body was strangely elastic, and his bulk enveloped her. They tumbled through the air and slammed into the opposite wall.

"I heard you creeping around up there," he said, crushing her in a suffocating bear hug. "I thought it would be a stupid drunk." He laughed. "Looks like I was right."

Sayal gasped and loosed his grip as Isten smashed the wine bottle on the wall and jammed it up beneath his rib cage.

He fell back against the wall, cursing and picking out the broken glass, trying to stem the blood.

Isten grabbed Brast and hauled him back up the passageway.

"Get to the door," she gasped.

As they sprinted through the half-light, the air came alive with movement. Crossbow bolts whistled past them, pinging off the walls and clattering across the floor.

They had almost reached the next door when Sayal barrelled into Isten and sent her sprawling across the floor.

She rolled clear and leapt to her feet, knife in hand, ready for his attack.

He lashed out with his falcata, but she sidestepped and dived, plunging her knife into his chest.

His flesh swallowed not just the knife but her hand too, and she found herself trapped, wrist-deep in his chest.

Sayal laughed and pulled her closer, his bulbous, inhuman eyes rolling.

She let go of the knife, wrenching her hand free in a shower of blood.

Brast attacked, forcing Sayal to defend himself as Isten rushed to the door and checked the mechanism. It matched Alzen's description.

"Brast!" she cried, her hand hovering over the lock. "Back here."

He was still fighting furiously, circling and lunging at Sayal.

The other brothers had stopped firing for fear of hitting

Sayal, but they had almost reached the door.

In a few seconds the brothers would reach them and it would all be over.

Isten cursed, looking from the lock to Brast and Sayal. If she locked it now, the Exiles would be victorious, but Brast would be left down here to die.

She shook her head, wishing she had enough steel to leave Brast behind, then rushed back through the doorway and leapt at Sayal, landing a solid punch on the side of his head.

He fell away from Brast, staggered, then ran up the slope, through the doorway. "This way!" he cried, waving his men on. "The bitch is trying to trap us down here."

Isten and Brast ran towards him, but he backed away, laughing.

Isten was about to race after him, when she had a better idea. She checked Brast had also made it through the doorway, then turned the door's lock, following the complex pattern Alzen had described, and backed away.

For a horrible moment, nothing happened. Then, just as the brothers were about to reach the door, a wall of bars rattled down from the ceiling and slammed into the floor.

The full weight of five Aroc Brothers smashed into the door, but the metal bars were thicker than a man's arm. They barely juddered.

The brothers fell back, shock and outrage visible through the eyeholes of their happy yellow masks.

Isten turned away from them and looked back up the corridor.

The smile dropped from Sayal's face.

"You're going to open that door!" he bellowed, charging back down towards her.

Brast stepped from the shadows, swinging his sword at Sayal's face in a fast, backhanded slash.

Sayal parried, but he had no time to stop Isten slamming her fist into his face again and he fell back, hitting his head on the wall and falling to the floor. His falcata slipped from his hand and clanged across the tiles.

As Isten grabbed the discarded sword, Brast leapt forwards, swinging his sword at Sayal's face.

Sayal rolled aside and sent Brast flying with a kick to the stomach.

By the time Isten had got the sword and turned to attack, Sayal was backing away from them again, heading up the passageway and vanishing into the darkness.

He reached the next doorway and struggled with the lock for a moment, cursing and spitting as Isten and Brast watched in amused silence. Then he turned and glared back at them. The humour was gone from his face, replaced by a fury so savage his features had become unhinged, rippling and flowing into each other, spiralling around a hard, blood-filled snarl. He was unarmed and bleeding heavily from his chest. Sayal's anatomy was not like a normal man's but Isten guessed that even he must be close to death, or at least unconsciousness.

The other Aroc Brothers were looking up at them through the lower door, dazed and unable to fire their crossbows safely, and unable to get through the door.

"I was happy to let you die in the gutter," growled Sayal, his words muddied by the blood in his mouth. "But now I'll have to find a way to make you *suffer*."

She strode towards him, drawing back the falcata, with Brast at her side, doing the same.

"You won't be finding ways to do anything," she grinned as they rushed at him.

He turned and sprinted up the slope.

He ran with surprising speed and, as they left his brothers behind, the light faded until Isten was running through absolute darkness, following him only by the sound of his grunting, laboured breathing.

Isten could hear Brast at her side, swearing and hissing as he tripped and lurched through the darkness.

"Are you hurt?" she asked.

"You thought about leaving me, didn't you?" he said, ignoring her question.

"No!" she said, but she knew he was right and it gave her an oddly cold feeling.

They reached another doorway and Isten grabbed Brast by the arm. "Wait!"

She fiddled around in the dark, struggling to find the mechanism, then finally triggered it and brought another wall of bars slamming down into the ground. "Just in case they ever got past the other door," she said.

"It was Sayal we were trying to kill," he muttered. "Those poor bastards were just grunts."

"Grunts who killed our kin," she snapped, but the strange chill grew in her chest as she realized she hadn't considered letting them out. They would die a slow death down there.

They carried on climbing back up through the darkness and the sound of their footfalls started to change, echoing round a larger space.

"We're almost back at the antechamber," she said. "Slow down. I can't hear Sayal's breathing anymore."

Faint light stretched down the slope towards them as they entered the domed hall, coming from the entrance to the catacombs.

"Where is he?" muttered Isten, turning on her heel, knife held out before her, staring into the shadows.

After the utter dark of the lower levels, she found she could see reasonably well in this gloom. She looked at each of the four doorways in turn, and then peered at the alcoves and their rusted, crooked cadavers.

"Did he sneak back down?" Brast looked back at the doorway they had just come through. "Perhaps he's going to try and reach his men?"

Isten shook her head. "He must be in here somewhere. And we'll never get a chance like this again – him, on his own, wounded and unarmed." She strode into the centre of the chamber and howled. "Sayal! Face me, you coward!"

The only answer was the echo of her words.

Isten cursed and rushed across the chamber, heading back towards the entrance to the catacombs, still gripping the sword she had taken from Sayal.

They rushed through the colonnaded portico and back out into the square. The sound they had heard in the crypts was deafening out here, and the night sky had been torn open by fireworks. The Curious Men knew how to keep the mob happy, and the display was as impressive as ever – a dazzling, coruscating storm of light, exploding over the crowds, showering embers on their upturned masks and drowning out their cheers with screams and bangs.

Isten staggered out into the night, pieces of firework landing all around her, clattering on the ruins and sparking in the dark. "We lost him," she muttered, coming to a halt and shaking her head, looking at the silhouettes of mausoleums and revellers.

Brast ran to her side, breathing heavily. "Maybe." He nodded at the flagstones beneath their feet. There was a large pool of fresh blood where Sayal must have paused to bind his wounds. "Maybe not."

12

After leaving the festival, Isten stayed in the north of the city and headed to the Alcazar – a circular network of narrow, shady streets, surrounded by a high, vine-swamped wall. Like many of Athanor's districts, Alcazar had once been a kingdom in its own right, a fortified city, and, as Isten and Brast walked through the old Eastern Gate, it was like entering a different country. The sun, rising behind them, threw long shadows down the main street, leading them into Alcazar's dusty maze. The buildings were low and blocky, slabs of sunbaked sandstone and terracotta, so parched and ancient that they looked like they could be dissolved by a decent downpour of rain. Balconies and vine-draped pergolas stretched overhead, so that the streets seemed more like tunnels than open roads, but there was none of the intricate, metal tracery that covered much of the city. Athanor had never quite managed to conquer this web of quiet, thyme-carpeted alleys and looping, poppy-filled thoroughfares.

Most of the locals were asleep as Isten and Brast trudged through the dust, still clutching their bloody falcatas and covered in cuts and bruises. Isten made her way to the street Alzen had chosen for their rendezvous and looked around at the various teahouses that lined it. Even at this time, many of them had put out awnings and tables. She laughed quietly when she recognized one of the owners, recalling how she had once enraged him. He scowled at her but she took a seat all the same and, after a few minutes, he wandered out and clanged a samovar and some cups on the table without a word of greeting.

They sat there for a while, sipping the spiced tea and massaging their various wounds. As they drank, a few shutters started to open in the walls around them as the Alcazar started to stir. A group of children appeared, chasing cats through the streets, kicking up dust and laughing as they fought with sticks.

"So, what next?" asked Brast eventually.

Isten's head was pounding. She was already regretting sampling Alzen's cinnabar in the Sisters' house. She would need to ask him for more when he arrived later or the shakes would start again. She shrugged. "I'll need to find out if Sayal survived or not. Maybe Colcrow will be able to tell me."

Brast grimaced at the mention of Colcrow. "And then? If Sayal *is* dead?"

The owner of the teahouse had emerged to scowl at her again. Isten gave him a mocking smile, then, when he sneered and shuffled back inside, she answered Brast. "I need to speak with my contact again. We arranged to meet on this street. He's offered to give me more help."

Brast viewed her closely over the rim of his teacup. "He sounds like a helpful soul."

She ignored his attempts at trying to wheedle the name out of her. "He might be. It depends how successful we were last night."

"What game are you playing, Isten? You abandoned the Exiles for a year, sick of the sight of them, half killing yourself with cinnabar, now you're back trying to help them again and you're getting information from someone so disreputable you won't even tell me their name. Who could be more disreputable than *me*? What are you hiding?"

He was speaking in the mocking tone he used when trying to disguise how desperate he was to please her. She started to remember why she had avoided him for so long. She felt like she had returned to the scene of a crime. "It doesn't matter," she muttered. "I have a new source of information and one of his conditions is anonymity." She fished out one of the coins Alzen had given her and placed it on the table. "Here, have some money. And get back to whatever you spend your time doing."

He looked offended, but took the coin. Then he leant across the table. "At least tell me this. Why did you leave them for a whole year? What made you run away like that? They all know you're a wreck, so it can't be that." He was staring at her. "What did you do that was so bad?"

Isten tightened her hands into fists and glared at the table. None of the Exiles must ever know. Especially now, after she had compounded her treachery by consorting with one of the Elect.

"If I need you again, I'll find you," she said.

He leant back in his chair. "Oh, will you? And then will you tell me what's going on?"

She said nothing.

He shrugged, finished his tea and stood, looking back down the blazing, coral-coloured avenue. "Then don't bother finding me." He turned his gaze back on her. "You've plumbed new depths, Isten, I can smell it. I can't imagine what can be so bad that even you won't speak of it." He frowned, about to ask a question, then shook his head. "Thanks for the tea." He sauntered off, heading towards the old city gates, giving the dust a few desultory slashes of his sword as he went.

Isten watched him go, missing the chance to share her burden. If anyone could hear the truth and not want to kill her, it was Brast.

The owner of the teahouse dragged himself out into the sunlight and glared at her.

She held up her cup with a smile.

He grimaced, took the samovar and shuffled off to fill it again.

Isten spent the next couple of hours sat in the shade of the teahouse, tracing shapes in the dust with her foot and watching the Alcazar fill with people. Many of them were staggering, hungover revellers from the square, still wearing their yellow masks. The paint was smeared now and covered in blood-red wine stains. As she sipped her tea, Isten felt as though she was watching the return of a defeated army, round-faced and grinning, weary and demented, their features disfigured by fire. The yellow faces began to stretch and mutate, coming alive, bloated heads staring at her with excited grins. Suddenly, she felt as though everyone on the street had come looking for her.

She shook her head and looked away. It was the cinnabar. Whatever Alzen gave her must have been powerful stuff. She was starting to hallucinate. The hallucinations always became more vivid as cinnabar left one's system, and more threatening.

She listened to a rattling sound for a while before she realized that it was her cup, dancing on the metal table. Her hand was shaking. She gripped it with her other hand and looked around. Still no sign of Alzen. Her anxiety grew. She needed to find some more cinnabar soon. Or at least something to dull the madness and the tremors. She kept her gaze locked on the table, but she could still sense the yellow, grinning faces, pressing closer, hungry and desperate.

"Torus," she said, trying to keep her voice level as she rose from the table and entered the teahouse, pushing through curtains into the gloomy interior.

The old man was just inside, hunched over a table, writing something. He leapt up at the sight of her, horrified.

"What do you want?"

She held up a placating hand. "I know you remember me, Torus," she said, looking round the room. It was a small, rough-hewn chamber, lined with rows of shelves, crowded with tins of tea and gleaming samovars. The only light came from an arrow-slit window, and after the glare of the street, Isten found it hard to see clearly. "I need something."

"Tea?" he asked, backing away from her. "I'll bring it to your table."

"Not tea," she said, leaning against the doorframe to steady herself, giving him a pointed look.

He stepped forwards and the single shaft of light fell across his face. His gaunt, grey, stubbly features were twisted into a snarl. "I don't sell anything else."

Isten's head was spinning more violently than it should have been. What had Alzen given her?

She reached beneath her jerkin and grabbed a coin from the purse Alzen had given her. "Are you sure?" She held the coin up so that it glinted.

He glared at her in silence, but she saw a telltale twitch in the corner of his mouth.

She took another coin out.

He looked anguished now, rubbing his hands together and glancing at a doorway at the back of the room. "I can't," he whispered. "I don't."

Isten held the coins out for a few more seconds, trying to keep her hand steady. Then she cursed and took out a third.

Torus's eyes widened.

"What have you got?" she asked.

"Seeds," he whispered, staring past her to the street outside, checking no one was near.

"Vistula?"

He nodded, looking disgusted with himself.

She nodded.

He gestured for her to follow him into the next room.

This one was darker and more cluttered – a storeroom, piled with crates and jars. Rats scattered as they entered and someone stirred upstairs.

"Torus?" came a voice from the room above. It was a thin, scared-sounding croak.

"Yes," he called back. "Just getting more tea."

He moved some boxes and fished out a pewter bowl with its lid tied securely in place. He removed the lid and revealed the contents. Isten knew what they were, but they really *did* look like small, black seeds, like onion seeds. They filled the storeroom with a pungent, medicinal aroma.

He snatched a mortar and pestle from a shelf, then hesitated.

"Give me the money," he said, not meeting her eye.

She felt a sinking feeling. Why had she offered him *three* coins? That was almost everything Alzen had given her. Waves of nausea were washing through her and she had no option but to hand them over.

He looked at them in shock for a moment, then stashed them under his robes.

He put all of the seeds in the mortar, along with a selection of powders that he took from a wooden cabinet. He gently pressed the ingredients with the pestle, releasing more of the smell. Then he grabbed a jug and poured a few drops of water into the powder.

He gave the mortar to Isten, went back into the larger room, peered out into the blazing street, then hurriedly returned to her and snatched the mortar back.

They both stooped over it, peering at the contents, wondering if such old seeds would work.

It took a few seconds, but then the paste began to coagulate, bubbling and clumping together, as though moulded by invisible fingers. As it moved, the paste grew paler, turning grey and then translucent white as it formed into a small, writhing grub – a fine, segmented worm, like a tapeworm, coiling and tumbling across the black metal of the mortar, reaching up into the air, trying to escape.

Despite his earlier reluctance, the old man seemed pleased with himself as he gently plucked the worm from the mortar and held it up in front of Isten.

He nodded at her and she knew what to do, pulling her lower eyelid down and looking up, exposing the underside of her left eye.

He leant close, so close that his garlic breath filled her nostrils.

He placed the writhing worm under her eyeball.

She closed her eye and the grub shifted under her lid, cold and frenetic, trying to escape. It felt like a muscle spasm, fidgeting and tickly against her retina.

Isten felt no revulsion, knowing what came next.

The worm burst, exploding across her eye, dissolved by her tears, spreading its juice.

Torus checked the door again, then repeated the process, producing another pale worm and dropping it in Isten's other eye.

For a few minutes she sat there in the dark, wondering if nothing had happened, blinking away tears, but then the drug started to take effect. One by one, her muscles relaxed and the tremors vanished. She slumped back against the wall with a sigh of relief, causing Torus to hiss a curse and move the jars she had nearly dislodged. Everything Isten had been tormenting herself over – her betrayal of the Exiles, her pact with Alzen, even the way she tormented Brast, suddenly seemed delightfully absurd. None of it mattered, she realized. She laughed, grabbing Torus's shoulder.

For a moment his wariness vanished and she saw pride in his eyes, the pride of a skilled artisan who rarely gets to practice his craft.

Then he looked panicked. "Outside," he whispered, helping her to her feet.

"I have to wait here," she said as he bundled her out into the daylight and tried to steer her past the table.

He hesitated and she dropped back into her chair. "More tea," she said.

Torus looked furious again, but he was obviously keen to avoid a scene. "Be normal," he hissed in her ear, leaving her at the table and going back inside.

Isten sprawled happily in her chair, watching the sunlit crowds jostle through the alley. Her eyes were now dry, but the world still looked as though it had been refracted by tears, painted in shifting dabs of colour, beautiful and pointillistic, tumbling past her like breeze-snatched blossom. The hallucination was only a side-effect – the *true* wonder of vistula was its power to dissolve fear and pain, but Isten enjoyed the display all the same. The yellow masks that had so disturbed her a few minutes earlier now seemed like blissful friends, smiling at her in greeting rather than leering like predators.

Isten spent the rest of the morning this way, enjoying the colours and sounds of the Alcazar and forgetting her troubles. The sun had almost reached its zenith when she recognized a tattered black gown. Alzen was wearing a battered wooden mask, just like everyone else pouring into the Alcazar.

Alzen nodded as he sat down.

"Sayal is still alive," he said.

Isten knew she should be angry and disappointed, but the vistula made that impossible. She sat up in her chair and was about to answer when the teahouse owner came out again, carrying a cup for Alzen.

She waited until the old man was gone before speaking.

"He heard us and doubled back," she said, sipping her tea. "But don't worry. I can do this."

He smiled and held up his hands, as calm as she was. "Of course you can. It's fine. Don't worry. This was just one chance. There will be others." He looked thoroughly pleased. "The men you locked in the catacombs were his most trusted brothers. You've caused him a big problem. Sayal is furious." He laughed. "And not at all well, from what I've heard." He sipped his tea, still smiling. "We've dealt him a serious blow. The metal in that crypt would have bought him even more men and weapons, but now he's on the back foot, wounded and trying to work out which of his simpletons he can trust to lead his various operations."

Isten laughed. She had half expected Alzen not to arrive, or to arrive in a rage and say the deal was off, but he seemed delighted.

"He has no inkling that we're connected," said Alzen, speaking to himself as much as to Isten. "So I can keep informing you of his plans until his whole organization collapses."

Isten looked around to make sure no one could be listening in on their conversation. The Alcazar was now crowded with people, as noisy as any of Athanor's bazaars, but the din was so great that none of the passers-by would be able to hear their discussion.

"What next, then?" she said, trying to focus on his eyes, despite the way the vistula was making his mask ripple and flash. "What about the cinnabar you promised? Do you have it here?"

"Let's deal with Sayal first. We've wounded the oaf, but we're not rid of him. He's got a burgeoning rebellion on his hands so he's called a meeting, tonight. He's gathering all the brothers he thinks he can trust and he's going to promise them positions of power if they swear to back him and talk down all his doubters. He's bringing them over to his house in Gamala."

"Gamala?" Isten was shocked. Gamala was one of the

wealthiest quarters of the city. Only the Elect's most senior diplomats and officials lived there; or so she had thought.

Alzen's tone soured. He clearly found the idea as repulsive as Isten found it surprising. "Yes. He bought the Bethsan Palace and filled it with blubber." He shook his head. "No matter. By tomorrow we can be rid of him."

Isten shook her head. "I have no men. My friend from last night…" She hesitated, unsure what to say about Brast. "I'm sure I could take on Sayal on his own, but not if he's surrounded by guards."

Alzen moved his chair closer, dragging it through the dust with a shrill scraping sound.

"I saw what you did last night."

Isten's stomach turned at the idea Alzen had been watching her without her knowing. "How?"

Alzen laughed. "The Art. It can do more than move the city, Isten." He nodded to the mark he had made on her arm. "There are many forms of conjunction."

Isten gripped her bicep, as though she could rid herself of Alzen's taint by simply hiding the mark he had left on her.

"You're fearless," he said, tapping her falcata, "and a skilled fighter. I was impressed."

She shrugged. The vistula made even Alzen seem like a trustworthy friend. "I was expected to be a leader one day – in my homeland, I mean. My mother thought I would lead a revolution. My childhood was spent practicing with a sword while she preached to angry crowds."

Alzen made no pretence he was interested in her history. "Whatever the reason, I think you are a worthy partner in my endeavour."

"Endeavour? Killing Sayal?"

"He's just an annoying obstacle. I'm embarked on a far greater work, Isten. A work you could never hope to understand, but yes, you could help me by removing Sayal. And in doing so, you can make your Exiles more powerful than any gang that has ever walked the streets of Athanor."

"But how? Have you got some men you can lend me?"

"No need, Isten. I have been thinking and it occurs to me that I can loan you something far more powerful."

Isten struggled to follow his gist, still enjoying the tumbling petals of light that surrounded everything. She sipped her tea, sat upright again and tried to focus. "What do you mean?"

Alzen looked around to make sure they weren't overheard. "I have pushed the boundaries of the Art, Isten – I have studied an area of the discipline so elevated that my fellow phraters have never even heard of it." His voice trembled with emotion, he was so awed by his own achievement. "I have almost mastered the…" His words trailed off. "Well, let us say, I have developed a form of unshackled magistery, a skill that my brethren cannot even dream of." He reached across the table and took Isten's hand.

Even dazed by the vistula, she was disgusted by his touch, but she forced herself to leave her hand where it was.

"I have almost freed the Art from the laboratory," he whispered, his eyes shining behind his mask. "I can soon practice alchymia without need for all the hindrances and paraphernalia."

Isten shook her head, still unsure what he was trying to

tell her. Like the rest of Athanor, she had no understanding of what the Elect did behind the impregnable walls of the Temple District.

Alzen laughed. "I wouldn't expect you to understand. The point is this: the particular disciplines I am studying will enable me to do something that a Curious Man has never done before. I can channel the Art through the flesh of a vulgar commoner. I can perform alchymia through *you*."

Dazed as she was, Isten knew that this was an incredible statement to make. "That's forbidden," she muttered. "A commoner cannot be... I can't practice the Art. I'd be executed." She laughed at the absurdity. "And I'm not just a commoner, I'm a woman. They would have to invent new ways to torture me."

"Who would believe that you could wield alchymia? No one. Because you can't. Don't you see? That's the beauty of it. That's why it's safe. No one would ever dream that you had channelled my power. No one knows that's possible. Only me. I can work through you, and while I'm destroying Sayal through your hands, I can be miles away in some highly visible place, giving me the perfect alibi."

Of all the things Alzen had said, this seemed the most outlandish, but Isten found herself carried along by his excitement. "So it would be as though I were... As though I were a Curious Man, performing alchymia?"

Alzen waved a dismissive hand. "Of course not. You would only be a conduit. You'd have no understanding of the transfigurative power passing through you." He shrugged and took his hand back. "The point is that I could turn all my power on Sayal, crushing him and his brothers, and neither of us could fall under suspicion. Even if you were seen entering the Bethsan Palace, no one would dream of suggesting you were responsible for the ensuing destruction. And my brothers would never think of accusing me, because I wasn't there."

Isten nodded. The idea was troubling. The thought of Alzen working his sorcery through her was obscene, but obliterating Sayal with arcane powers would give her the victory she needed. She could picture his shocked expression as she transformed him into whatever absurd creation Alzen had decided on. Her excitement was dampened by the memory that the vistula would wear off in a few hours. "What about the cinnabar?"

"We have to deal with Sayal first, but that can happen tonight. With your bravery and my skill, he won't stand a chance. Then, with the Aroc Brothers out of business, the city is yours. I have the first shipment ready and waiting for you. You can start selling it as soon as Sayal is dead."

Isten nodded. "But in the meantime..."

Alzen looked confused for a moment, then laughed. "You want another sample?" He gave her an apologetic smile. "I have none on me. I came straight here from the observances. But you have the money I gave you. There was plenty there to buy some. I'm sure you have friends on the Blacknells Road who could help."

Isten shuffled awkwardly in her seat, until she settled on an appropriate lie. "I lost the purse when we were fighting in the catacombs."

He shook his head like a despairing parent and took out another purse, then hesitated and put it back in his robes. "You look like death. And I don't believe you're going to spend any of this on food."

He called Torus back out and pressed a coin in his hand.

"Bread and wine," said Alzen, blessing Torus with one of his serene smiles. "Before my friend expires at your table."

13

The city wheezed, pulling at the seams, pregnant with promise. Aornos filled the sky with their young, vast, chromatic, seed clouds, banking and billowing, draping the spires of Baphyrus Street, anointing crowds of ecstatic pilgrims and clogging the foetid drains. Tearful ossops dyed their pupae indigo, smothered them in kisses and then hurled them into the Saraca, praying that the weakest would drown in its metallurgical currents, leaving only the strong to return. At the moment of their death, herds of krios set themselves alight, birthing calves from their ashes, not living to see their blinking, canker-clad young. Life crept and bubbled, stirring in doorways, seething through Athanor's limbs, fuelling its hidden fires, sublimated and amalgamated, saltpetre and sand, burned and betrayed, never guessing the truth, never feeling the crucible, never seeing the Curious Men.

Gamala. Garden of Athanor. Emerald cool and hazed by mist. Like much of the city, its foundations had fallen away, leaving a tangled armature of trunks, avenues and bridges; soaring, root-bound limbs, tumbling around each other, cradling its precious ward of parks and palaces – the hidden sanctuaries of the city's elite. Collectively, Athanor's nobility were known as laborators – glorified servants, permitted to enter the outer precincts of the Temple District and even allowed to serve the Curious Men. They were scholars, theorists and diplomats, plucked from the masses at the time of conjunction and spared the brief, messy existence allocated to their less fortunate countrymen.

It was early evening as Isten approached the Bethsan Palace. She passed the distant facades of grand houses, leviathans, half-hidden from the road by groves of olive trees and surrounded by long, ornamental lawns. She had seen Gamala before and instinctively hated the place. It reminded her of the Royal Precincts back in Rukon, where her mother's enemies had plotted her murder over cards and wine. Nothing could seem more absurd than a brute like Sayal living here, acting the part of a high-born noble while his brothers sold sex and addiction to the great unwashed on the Blacknells Road.

But Isten was only half aware of her surroundings. Much of her attention was fixed on the numbness that had overtaken the left-hand side of her skull. Before she left the teahouse in the Alcazar, Alzen placed his hand on her head and performed what he called a "lesser conjunction". At the time, still lost in the blissful embrace of the vistula seeds, Isten had seen no harm in it, dazzled by the prospect of wielding Alzen's power. But now, with her euphoria fading, Isten felt a crushing fear. She had let Alzen into her mind. She could feel him in there, smirking beneath her skull, a malign passenger, watching the city through her eyes. Would he see her thoughts? Would he see her plan to ditch him once she had killed Sayal? She scratched at her thick, tangled hair, wishing she could claw him out.

She reached the edge of the Bethsan estate and headed down a wide, tree-lined road. There was a wall and a gatehouse half a mile away and, even with dusk approaching, she could see movement inside the gatehouse – shapes silhouetted by a fire, passing back and forth behind windows sunk deep in crumbling, stone embrasures.

Isten stayed in the shadow of the trees and sheathed her sword as she edged closer.

"What now?" she whispered as she neared the wall, but she could already feel a strange sensation in her hand. It felt numb, like the side of her head, but it was also tingling and itching. She held it up and spread her fingers. At first, it looked unchanged, but then she noticed that her veins were unusually vivid, as though lit from within, cords of sapphire, throbbing over her finger bones.

Isten.

She whirled around at the sound of the voice, drawing her sword, but there was no one else on the path.

She dropped into a crouch, staring into the gloom.

The voice laughed.

"Alzen?" She lowered her sword, feeling nauseous. The voice was in her head.

He sounded amused. *Were you expecting someone else?*

The last effects of the vistula seeds faded and she tasted the full horror of what she had done.

Is that the gatehouse?

"How long will you be in my mind?" she demanded, ignoring his question, her panic rising.

An hour or two. I'm unable to perform an act of true conjunction on a vulgar mind. So far at least. Who knows? It could be possible, given time, to impregnate your thoughts with–

"Get out!" she hissed, gripping her head and feeling her sanity straining. "I didn't understand. This isn't right. I can't share my *mind.*"

Stay calm. It will seem strange at first, but you will become used to it.

"Get out!" She gripped her skull even tighter. To have his voice in her thoughts was dreadful. It was like feeling a snake twisting in her stomach.

I'm not truly in your thoughts. I don't know what you're thinking. I can't share your memories or see your plans. I can only talk to you and see a shadow of what you see.

Isten took a few deep, slow breaths, leant against one of the trees and took out a wine skin that she had brought with her from the Alcazar. She drank what was left, gulping it down, not pausing for breath until the skin was empty. Dizzying warmth flooded her head, dulling her fear. She waited a few moments, feeling the alcohol rush through her veins, then she opened her eyes and looked around. She was insane. There was no other way to describe the sensation. She was sharing her head.

"Never again," she whispered, her voice trembling.

If that's what you wish. We'll kill Sayal and then communicate by more normal methods.

Isten was still taking deep, slow breaths. Her heart had slowed a little and the thought that all this would soon be over went some way to calming her nerves.

"Tell me then," she said, glancing back at the gatehouse. "What do I do?"

She could feel Alzen's excitement in his reply. *Draw your sword and knock on the door. When you attack I'll channel my alchymia through your blade.*

"Knock on the door?"

Trust me, Isten. Purity and devotion are the hallmarks of my creed. I would not lie to you. This will work.

Whatever the Curious Men were, Isten doubted they were honest. They promised too much and gave too little for that to be the case. But, he *was* speaking directly into her mind. He clearly did wield power. And the city was littered with signs that the Curious Men's alchymia was real. She grimaced and edged closer to the gatehouse, taking another cautious look through the windows. Now that she was closer, she saw that there were only two guards waiting inside. Even if Alzen's claims came to nothing she could still probably take them on. She was shaking from lack of cinnabar, but the wine had dulled the tremors and the food she ate in the Alcazar had brought back some of the vigour she felt with the Sisters of Solace.

"Fine," she muttered, gripping the falcata tightly and striding out onto the path.

She heard alarmed voices coming from the gatehouse before she even reached the door, but she hammered her sword hilt on it all the same.

The door flew open and she backed away, sword raised as the two Aroc Brothers emerged. They were as hulking as the ones she had left in the catacombs and they were sporting the same ridiculous, greasy kiss-curls. They wore no festival masks and Isten grimaced at the sight of their translucent faces. They stepped onto the path, loading bolts into iron-plated crossbows.

"Is that her?" said one of them, frowning.

"Who?" grunted the other one.

"The Exile."

Isten raised her falcata and the tingling in her palm became an explosion of heat. She gasped, almost dropping the blade, feeling as though fire was coursing from her skull, down her arm and into the sword.

"What's that?" grunted one of the Aroc Brothers. They were both staring at her in surprise.

Isten looked down and gasped in shock. Her arm was sheathed in metal strands, interlaced like the delicate openwork of an incense burner. The filaments were stretching and curling, enveloping the sword handle.

"What are you?" muttered one of the Aroc Brothers, backing away, his crossbow hanging forgotten in his grip.

The wine in Isten's veins merged with a new, even more exhilarating intoxication. She felt like a torch, kindled into flame, charged with furious energy.

She laughed and dived forwards, swinging her sword.

The falcata disintegrated, exploding into a shower of metal strands. They ripped through the air and smashed into the guards.

As the guards fell away from her, light flashed in her eyes, blinding her, but she could still feel the inferno blasting through her bones. It was like no high she had ever experienced.

She closed her eyes, savouring the power jolting through her body as the sword bucked and kicked in her hand.

Then, as suddenly as it came, it was gone.

The storm passed and she staggered backwards, trailing smoke and coughing, her nostrils clogged with a sulphurous stink.

As the alchymia left her veins her laughter faded. She felt hollow and inert.

The smoke cleared and she saw what she had done to the guards. They were sprawled on the floor, contorted, frozen in their death throes, so swamped in metal tracery that they were barely recognizable. Their faces were fixed in silent screams and their metal shrouds were glowing and smoking, as though newly forged.

Dazed, Isten looked down at her arm. The metal tracery had vanished and her skin was normal again. The falcata had also regained its usual form, with only a few wisps of smoke revealing what had just passed through it.

Isten reached for the wineskin, then cursed as she remembered it was empty. The heat had gone from her veins, but she could still feel the numbness in her skull.

"Alzen?" she whispered.

Did it work? Even disembodied, she could hear the breathless excitement in his voice.

"What was meant to happen?" She stared at the smouldering corpses.

Transfiguration. My alchymia should have transmuted your opponents into a different element.

"They're like Amoria." She felt a mixture of excitement and horror at what she had just done.

Amoria?

"My friend. She died in the warehouse by the Azof embassy, turned to metal."

Then it worked. Alzen sounded even more excited.

"You sound surprised. You said I could trust you. Weren't you sure if this would work?"

I knew. But you must understand, no phrater has ever managed to channel alchymia through the mind of a vulgar commoner before. My skills have–

"Fine. You've managed to dilute your essence with my pondwater blood. What now?"

You don't have long. Sayal has summoned his brothers and they'll start arriving soon. It won't take long for someone to discover what you've done. Even with my help you'd be wise to kill Sayal before everyone else arrives.

Isten rushed through the gatehouse and began running up the road. "Will it work the same way?" she whispered. "When I attack?"

It will work better. The alchymia is growing accustomed to your quintessence. I will be able to channel even greater power through you this time.

Isten felt a rush of excitement as she ran, imagining how that would feel. The wine was affecting her balance though. She was lightheaded and clumsy, weaving across the path.

"What about those crossbows? Even if his guests haven't arrived, Sayal will be well guarded. It won't matter how much metal I make if everyone fires at once."

True. Alzen thought for a moment. *Wait here. Let me try something.*

Isten stopped and leant against the nearest tree. There was a bend in the road up ahead but still no sign of the palace.

As she stood there, beneath the boughs of the tree, heat blossomed in her skull again. This time, rather than horror, she felt excitement and a strange kind of hunger. She closed her eyes, willing the power to consume her, delighting in its molten heat.

Rather than pulsing through her arm into the sword, the alchymia radiated out through her skin, bristling and rippling over her body, making her feel as though she were caught in a summer storm. The sensation grew so delightful and intense that Isten began to laugh again.

After a few seconds, she realized it was not going to stop. She opened her eyes and beheld a glorious transformation. Her whole body was encased in a living, golden mesh – the same shapes that had enveloped the guards. She raised her arm, staring in wonder as the strands rolled and reformed, accommodating her movement with a shimmering, tumbling dance. She looked like Athanor. Alzen had clad her in the skin of the city.

"What is this?" she whispered. "What am I?"

Alzen sounded as awed as she did. *The Ingenious.*

"The what?"

Nothing. Alzen's excitement quickly faded. He sounded annoyed that he had used that word. *You are a glimpse of what I will become – of what I have been working towards all these years. Soon, I will...* He sounded guarded. *I've armoured you with alchymia. That's all you need to know. You are like one of the Ignorant Men. You're tempered by sacred fire.*

Isten walked away from the tree, grinning, unable to contain her delight. She felt spring-heeled and full of vigour. She felt weightless, as though she could have leapt from the ground and soared across the treetops. She lashed out with her sword and burnished tendrils spiralled through the air, engulfing a tree and turning it into a beautiful, lifeless sculpture, veined with copper, gold and silver.

Wait! snapped Alzen. *There is a limit to how much of myself I can share. I am currently surrounded by the rest of my fraternity. Conserve the power until you need it.*

She nodded, still grinning as she sprinted down the avenue of trees, heading for the bend in the road.

As it turned, the road fell down into a valley, trailing up to the Bethsan Palace like a streamer hurled from its gate.

The palace was an incredible sight, suspended hundreds of feet above the ground by an elaborate pedestal of stone fronds with the road snaking up through the centre. The building was like a colossal crucible with a vast, circular structure rising from its centre, a flat disc of architecture, its circumference punctuated by hundreds of star-shaped windows. It looked like a goblet holding an enormous coin. The circular part of the palace seemed to be the main living area, with lights glittering in dozens of the star-shaped windows. At its centre was a huge window, built of thousands of panes of glass. From the side of the valley, where Isten was standing, the palace looked like the eye of a cyclopean titan, peering over a hill, speckled with embers and staring at her through the darkness.

Isten hesitated, wondering how many guards Sayal would have installed in such a colossal building, but then she felt the vigour pulsing through her limbs and realized she didn't care. She felt godlike. The metalwork responded to her excitement, orbiting her muscles as she jogged down the road into the valley, her gaze locked on the monstrous eye.

"Do you know the layout?" she asked as she ran.

I do. I can direct you to a discreet entrance.

It took another half an hour for Isten to reach the foot of the palace. The road soared up into the darkness, surrounded by the palace's winding mass of buttresses and pilings. At the base of the house's "crucible" there was a broad, double staircase, sweeping up to a set of mountainous doors. The doors were open and she could see lights inside – not mandrel-fire, but the shifting glow of real fires, spilling out through leaded windows and splashing across the upper steps.

Ignore the staircase, said Alzen. *Go left, round to the side of the house.*

Isten nodded, and when she reached the end of the road, she skirted round the walls, stooping low behind the hedges that bordered the gardens.

She heard voices coming from inside the house, echoing out into the dusk, but there were no sentries visible. Sayal had no one to fear, she realized. The Aroc Brothers ruled all the districts around the Saraca. No one would dare challenge them – certainly not here.

Her heart was racing as she reached an archway that led into a different part of the gardens and she saw another staircase, leading up to a smaller door.

"Here?" she asked.

Yes.

Isten dashed up the steps, checking the moonlit gardens as she went, but seeing no one else around.

The door was locked.

She drew back her falcata, about to smash the lock with the sword handle.

No, said Alzen. *Too noisy.*

Isten looked around for another way in, but the lower half of the palace was curiously devoid of windows. There were a few, but they were too small to crawl through.

Place your hand against the lock, said Alzen, sounding excited again.

She did so, and as her skin touched the cold metal, her shroud of metal coils splashed across the door, rippling over its surface like liquid.

Some of the wires spiralled through the keyhole and Isten was thrilled to find that she could feel the mechanism, as though she had reached through the hole with her fingers, touching the springs and pins. Life on the Blacknells Road had taught her many skills her teachers in Rukon never expected she'd need, and picking a lock was delightfully easy when one could reach inside the mechanism.

The door clicked open and the cords of metal peeled away from the door, wrapping themselves back around Isten. She looked at her hand in wonder, then shook her head, turned the handle and pushed the door open.

She was in a long, rectangular storeroom. There was no illumination, apart from the moonlight she had let in through the open door, so it took a moment for her eyes to rationalize the shapes. What she took at first to be sleeping men, turned out to be sacks of grain and seeds, heaped on the floor beneath shelves holding urns, wheels of cheese and bottles of oil. The room had clearly not been used for a long time. The sacks were covered in dust and the smell of rotting food rushed out to greet her.

"Sayal doesn't know what to do with a house like this," she sneered.

Perhaps you could put it to better use? said Alzen.

"What?"

We can talk about it when he's dead. There's a servants' dining room through that door. I doubt that's in use either. The door at the far end leads to a hallway and then a staircase. The staircase leads up to the main house.

Isten crossed the storeroom and opened the door slightly, peering into the gloom beyond. The dining room was even darker, but she could just about see a low table surrounded by mouldering cushions and cabinets full of dusty crockery. It had the air of a tomb and Isten made no attempt to hide as she entered, confident that no one had eaten in there for months, perhaps even years.

At the far end she found the door and made her way to the bottom of the stairs.

Light was washing down from above, falling in shafts through the spindles of the staircase, and she could hear voices, drunken, slurred, raised in anger.

She gripped her falcata and started creeping slowly up the stairs, conscious that, as the light played over her, she was glittering like a jewellery box.

Remember, said Alzen. *Be quick. The rest of his brothers will be arriving any time now.*

Isten was not really listening. She was picturing Ozero's face. Remembering him as he was when she last saw him, his arm around Puthnok, blushing with pride as his sister read the latest drafts of her manifesto. "Not long now," she whispered.

The stairs led up to a long gallery, with a vast, concave window at the far end. The glass was stained blue at the centre, around a black circle: the eye of the cyclops.

She peered over the top step and counted around a dozen Aroc Brothers. Some were sprawled in chairs, drinking wine or smoking tar pipes, and the rest were standing in a group next to the window, locked in a furious argument. The largest of them was wearing a golden band around his head.

"Sayal," whispered Isten. "I can see him."

Get as close as you can before you attack.

Isten nodded. She climbed the last few steps and began

walking calmly across the room, passing through the pools of light thrown by tall windows that lined the gallery, her expression serene and amused, a faint smile playing around her lips.

None of the seated guards paid any attention to her, either too inebriated or simply fooled by her nonchalant air.

Isten was only a few feet from Sayal when he broke from his argument and stared at her in shock.

"For Ozero," she said, speaking clearly and calmly.

Sayal reached for a knife.

Isten levelled her sword at him and gold tore through the air, hitting his head and kicking him backwards.

He smashed through the domed window and fell, pinwheeling into the darkness, surrounded by a blizzard of shattered glass.

A few seconds later, everyone in the gallery heard his body thud onto the courtyard, hundreds of feet below.

The other Aroc Brothers stared at Isten in shock, then grabbed knives and crossbows and leapt to attack.

Isten was laughing as she brought her falcata round in a wide, lazy swipe. Tongues of metal rippled through the air, slicing through the brothers and flaying the skin from their faces.

They fell like coins from a purse, clattering across the floor and gouging channels in the walls.

Isten heard footsteps behind her and whirled around.

The other guards had lurched drunkenly from their seats, their bulbous, fish-like eyes full of dazed horror.

One of them fired his crossbow, but the bolt clanged harmlessly against Isten's chest and bounced back across the floor.

The others struggled to load their weapons, panicked by the golden vision striding towards them.

Isten slashed the air with her falcata, unleashing another gout of metal.

The gold ripped through her attackers, sending them clanging back across the gallery, but it also lashed across the walls, smashing pictures, enveloping furniture and tearing a forest of spikes from the floor.

She staggered backwards, unbalanced by the ferocity of the power blasting through her, struggling to keep hold of the sword as the room exploded, transformed into a labyrinth of weaving, golden branches. She felt an intoxication more potent than anything she had experienced before. She forgot everything but the heady, glorious thrill of the power.

Finally, the violence was too much and the sword fell from her grip. She fell backwards onto the nest of brittle shapes and the power ceased, snuffed like a flame, leaving her gasping and exultant, half-blinded by the afterimages of the blast.

Isten?

She could hear Alzen in her thoughts, but she was unable, for the moment, to reply, too dazed by what had just happened. The gallery was a smoking beautiful mess of golden twine. She had transformed it, turning it into something wonderful. No, she realized, Alzen had transformed it. She was no more than a vessel for his power. Her euphoria started to fade, until she remembered that she had killed Sayal.

She staggered to her feet and climbed through the convoluted shapes back towards the window. She leant out through the damaged glass and saw Sayal's broken remains far below, chunks of fractured metal, surrounded by a fast-growing pool of blood.

"For you, Ozero," she whispered but, in truth, her mind was elsewhere. She was thinking of how it felt to wield such power.

Isten? repeated Alzen.

"Sayal's dead," she replied, trying to calm herself, remembering why she was there. "You said once he was gone you would supply me with cinnabar." She hesitated to repeat his promise, feeling as though she might shatter the dream by speaking it aloud. "You said you would give it to me for free."

It worked, said Alzen, sounding dazed, not seeming to hear her question. *How did it feel? To have that sacred fire in your heart?*

She shook her head, looking back at the gilded chaos she had wrought, unable to explain. "The cinnabar," she demanded. "Will you keep your promise?"

It was hard to tell, but she had the strange impression that Alzen was weeping. *Of course,* he said. She heard the same wonder in his voice that she was feeling. He was as surprised as her. *Tell me where to send the first shipment,* he said, sounding a little calmer, *and it will be there by this evening. The city is yours, Isten of the Exiles. The city is yours.*

14

She fell through the streets, propelled down Athanor's loops and arches, drunk on victory, lost in the wine-reeking mess. Finally, power. Finally, a way out. It was dizzying. Glorious. And yet, as the city flashed by, a quiet, familiar voice whispered in her ear: You're falling, Isten. You're falling.

The Stump punched through the Botanical Quarter, rising like a righteous fist, trailing veins of rock and a skin of crumbling, lichen-clad outbuildings. It was the largest structure on the Blacknells Road and it seemed entirely appropriate that an alehouse should be the terminus of every street in the district. It was even older than the Alembeck Temple, whose warped facade watched it disapprovingly from the far end of the road. Both were sites of worship, but the Stump was the only one that still drew a congregation.

As Isten barged her way down the Blacknells Road, the sun was rising behind the Stump, turning the building into a smouldering silhouette. It looked like the shoulder of a black mountain, caged by the city, but the locals claimed that it had once been a living creature, enveloped during one of Athanor's earliest conjunctions – the head of a basalt-browed colossus that survived imprisonment for weeks, howling and straining to free its entombed limbs until, finally, the Curious Men filled its heart with cords of iron, silenced its cries and left this cavernous maze of grotto-like chambers.

Isten had her falcata in one hand and a grain sack in the other and she was carrying herself with the proud, triumphant air of a victorious general. She battled through the crowds outside and crossed the bridge that led into the Stump. Supposedly, the bridge was what remained of the giant's tongue and the entrance at the top was its gaping mouth.

Even at this time of day, the Stump was an explosion of noise. Drinkers crowded every one of its windows, laughing and singing over the sound of erratic drums. The entrance was a single permanently open doorway that led into a huge, barrel-shaped atrium. The atrium reached right up to an opening in the distant roof, and a column of sunlight fell down through the middle of the building, revealing hundreds of ravelled, intestinal stone balconies. The shape of the amphitheatre amplified the sounds of revelry, creating an oceanic roar. In the circular space at the bottom of the atrium was the bar, a jagged lump of limbs and spurs that was supposedly the top vertebra of the fossil's spine.

Isten still had some of Alzen's money left, so she bought a wine skin and headed up one of the staircases that spiralled the walls. As she fought through the crowds, she was pleased to see looks of surprise on the faces of people who recognized her. Everyone had thought she was dead, ruined by Sayal, but here she was, swaggering through the Stump with a skin-full of expensive wine. No one challenged her, but some rushed off to spread word of her return and, for once, she was pleased to think she would be the talk of the Blacknells Road.

As she headed away from the atrium, out into the warren of tunnels and lounges, Isten enjoyed sinking back into the Stump's womblike murk. There were no mandrel-fires in the Stump because the clientele enjoyed the privacy of its shadows, but the tunnels were faintly lit by needles of daylight. The light fell through holes in the walls, reaching down from the roof and creating a network of fine columns, spearing dust motes and rippling across the rough-hewn walls.

Away from the atrium, the noise of the crowds took on a muffled, subterranean quality that combined with the falling lights to give the Stump a beguiling, dreamlike atmosphere. As one grew more drunk, the Stump became less real, and time became increasingly elastic. Drinkers often lost themselves for days, sunk in a fever dream of smoky, shadowy figures and whirling lights. It was not unusual for drinkers to find that the taciturn stranger they were drinking next to was actually a corpse, mouldering quietly in the corner with rats nestling in their chest.

Unlike most of the Stump's guests, Isten moved with purpose, following a familiar route through the maze, shoving past the lecherous and the belligerent as she made for one of the deepest, largest lounges. She was not ready to face Gombus yet, not after what had happened to Amoria, but some of the other Exiles would be in their usual place, and she could not stop grinning as she considered the news she had for them.

The lounge was crowded with a roaring, heckling mob, all waving scraps of paper and hurling insults at the two figures in the centre of the room. Two blood-drenched men lurched through the crowd, staggering across the beer-slick, uneven floor, landing listless punches on each other.

Isten shouldered her way to the middle of the room and shook her head as she saw that one of the fighters was Lorinc. Lorinc was big, and powerfully built, but his opponent was bigger and clearly about to win. As Isten grimaced, the man landed a flurry of savage blows on Lorinc's head, sending him flying back into the crowd.

"What are you doing?" she muttered, furious at Lorinc's stupidity. Isten used to run pit fights in the Stump every week, and Lorinc was often doing the punching, but the fights were all rigged. Without her guidance, the Exiles had a worrying weakness for honesty.

She tried to move round the circle and get closer, but she couldn't fight through the crush and, as Lorinc tried to rise, his opponent leapt forwards and kicked him, hard, in the face.

Lorinc's head jolted back, spraying blood across the delighted crowd.

Lorinc landed heavily and lay still.

Half of the crowd roared, waving their scraps of paper.

As the crowd moved away, Lorinc was left alone on the floor and Isten rushed towards him. She tried to stem the blood rushing from his nose. He was dazed but conscious, groaning as he tried to focus on her.

"Isten?" said someone. She looked up to see Exiles staring at her in shock: Feyer, Korlath and Piros, shaking their heads in disbelief.

This time she met them without shame. She knew she was going to save them. "Let's talk," she said, hauling Lorinc to his feet and nodding to a gloomy chamber.

"You're a fucking disaster," said Lorinc, avoiding Isten's gaze as he wiped blood from his face and tried to hold himself as though he wasn't in agony. It was only a week since the incident in the warehouse and the death of Amoria, but the Exiles were even more wary than when she met them under the Blacknells Road Bridge.

Isten nodded, taking the abuse with good grace and resisting the urge to point out the irony of him saying that as he bled all over the table. She could not quite manage to hold back her smile.

"You think it's funny?" Lorinc's brutal features flushed with colour and he gripped the table. Lorinc was a head taller than anyone else in the alcove and his ape-like bulk meant the other four were squeezed uncomfortably around him on the bench. As he leant towards Isten, the table tipped and everyone had to grab their drinks.

"Amoria's dead. And you come back here with a fucking smirk? I stood up for you, Isten. I told Gombus Amoria's death wasn't your fault. That we couldn't have known the Aroc Brothers would be guarding the warehouse with… with whatever that thing was."

"It *was* my fault. And I don't think it's funny."

"You did smile, though," said Piros. Isten had never seen the ashen-faced teenager without a pipe in his mouth. He was so pale and wasted that he seemed to hang from it, as though the pipe were the only thing holding him off the floor. His eyes were perpetually bloodshot and his hair hung around his face in lank, greasy strands. "Are we funny?"

"You look different," said Lorinc, still trying to catch his breath from the fight. He frowned. "Not quite so shit."

She nodded. "I have news."

Lorinc glanced at the grain sack Isten had taken from the Bethsan Palace. It was lying at her feet, tied securely with rope.

Isten smiled, not hiding it this time. "I want to see Gombus and Puthnok."

"Well they won't want to see you," said Piros, taking another drag on his pipe. "After what–" his skeletal body was shaken by a violent coughing fit. His face turned a worrying shade of purple and Isten glanced at Lorinc, who grimaced and shook his head.

When Piros managed to stop coughing, he wiped some spit from his jaw and, with a determined expression, took another drag on the pipe. His eyes strained and filled with tears, but he managed not to cough. "Gombus isn't angry with you any more," he said in a hoarse voice. "He just thinks you're bad news."

She nodded, her eyes glinting with amusement. "He's wrong."

Her cheerful demeanour had made them all curious.

"What is that?" asked Lorinc, looking at the bag. Some of the anger had gone from his voice and she could see a hopeful glint in his eye.

She nodded at the entrance to the alcove and Lorinc rose from the table, blocking it with his bulk.

When she was sure they weren't being watched, Isten took the sack, placed it on the table and untied it, pulling it open to reveal the contents.

The Exiles looked shocked, disgusted and then delighted as they recognized Sayal Aroc's severed head. Isten had performed some minor butchery on it before bringing it to the Stump, cutting away the strands of gold where her blast had sliced through his neck, hiding any evidence of alchymia.

"How?" whispered Lorinc, as Isten closed the bag again and hid the head.

They were all staring at her in amazement and Isten cherished the moment. After so many years of being a disappointment, she had finally shocked them in a good way.

"I couldn't come back without good news," she said, "after what happened in the warehouse. So I came up with a plan and got Brast to help me."

"Brast?" Piros laughed, shaking his head. He waved his pipe around in a flamboyant gesture with an exaggerated grimace. "The spectre! Wasn't he too tortured by his art to leave his house?"

"Too tortured by Isten, you mean," laughed Lorinc.

Isten ignored their jokes. "I got a tip-off that Sayal was going down into the catacombs beneath Verulum Square, on the night of the festival. While he was down there, we managed to jump him. He got away but," she grinned, "I trapped his most trusted heavies down there. They're still there now, rotting, with no way to get out."

Lorinc laughed – the kind of deep, genuine belly laugh that she had not heard from him in years. He leant back in his chair, eying her with wonder. "You're one fucking surprise after another. Just when I think I've wasted all these years trusting you, you turn up with Sayal Aroc's head."

She smiled at him. Even as a child he had followed her into every scrape, shouting down anyone who doubted her. "When I was with the Sisters of Solace I learned where Sayal lived, so, once I'd robbed him of his heavies, it was an easy enough job to turn up unannounced and do to him what he did to Ozero."

She dropped her smile and looked around the group. "And I made sure that he understood why I came for him. It wasn't about turf wars or money; it was about Ozero."

"So now what?" asked Lorinc.

"The Aroc Brothers are over," she said. "At least for now. Sayal was the only thing that stopped them turning on each other. They'll be busy fighting each other for a few weeks at least. By which time we'll have supplied every pusher in the Botanical Quarter with cinnabar at half the price they were paying the Aroc Brothers. If they do manage to get their shit together, they'll find out that they have no customers anymore."

"At which point they'll come looking for us," said Piros. He tried to laugh but it turned into another wracking cough and he had to calm himself by drawing on his pipe again. "They'll use those shiny crossbows to turn us into wall decorations."

Isten shook her head. "The money we make from the cinnabar will buy us our own crossbows. Bigger, better ones. And, if the Aroc Brothers do want to take us on, they might have another surprise. We're going to tell every Exile in the city that we're back in business. They can stop grubbing around in the gutter for scraps and join an army." Isten's words were tumbling from her mouth as her excitement grew. "We'll rule this city. And once we have it by the balls,

I'll find a way to get us out of here. Money is power. When we have power, we'll be able to do anything. The Curious Men decide where each conjunction will take Athanor. And when we rule their city, I'll tell them where they need to land its rotting carcass. I'll demand that they take us back to Rukon."

Her outburst left them looking even more shocked than when she showed them the head.

For a moment, no one spoke. The only sound was the distant roar of the crowds in the atrium and Piros's wheezing breath.

"You're insane," whispered Lorinc. "*Tell* the Elect to take us home? How would we even speak to them?"

"I have new contacts," said Isten. "The Sisters of Solace have given me ways to do things you can't imagine. Once we've sewn up the cinnabar trade and taken back the brothels and the fights and all the other businesses we pissed away, we'll be ready to go home."

It was obvious that they all agreed with Lorinc about the state of her mind, but, along with the incredulous looks, she could see the stirrings of hope in their eyes.

Piros raised an eyebrow. "And all we have to do to start this great adventure is sell vast amounts of cinnabar at a cut-down price, you say?"

Isten nodded.

"Cinnabar that we don't have," said Piros, scratching at his long, greasy hair with an exaggerated frown, pretending to consider a tricky puzzle.

"And if I show you the cinnabar, will you wipe that stupid expression off your face?"

Piros sneered, ready to give her a sarcastic reply, but then he hesitated, thrown by the certainty in her voice.

"Meet me out the front of the Alembeck Temple tomorrow tonight," she said, rising from the table. "Drag Puthnok and Gombus along. Tell them I've killed Sayal and found a way to dig us out of this shit."

"Isten," cried Lorinc as she turned to leave.

She smiled. "I'll be there."

15

For God and the Temple they cried, as the city ate their young. The plague reached into everything, twisting and corrupting. Hearts burst like sores and the river swelled with dead. Deeper still, beneath the clamour of the prayers, Athanor wept, weightless and afraid, dreaming of home, remembering the ballast of rock.

Alzen held the young man's hand as he took his last breath. Coagulus was wrapped tightly around his face and body, a living winding-sheet that muffled the man's final rattle. Alzen closed his eyes as Coagulus fed, absorbing the man's soul with a barely perceptible tremor and passing it through Alzen's fingers. He sighed as a wave of memories flooded his thoughts. Since channelling his power through Isten, Alzen had felt his spiritual growth accelerate. He was so close to becoming the Ingenious that he could almost feel it, Absolute Reason, simmering at the edge of his consciousness, ready to reveal its final secrets. The alchymia he loaned to Isten had been created with all the usual charms, philtres and paraphernalia but, when he passed the Divine Light on to her, when he hurled it through her limbs, it shone freely, giving him revelation after revelation. As Isten killed the Aroc Brothers, answers that had eluded

Alzen for months suddenly became clear. He was haunted by it – by the sensation of transmitting his power through her flesh. He could not stop thinking about the glorious sense of ascendancy he felt when he joined his mind with hers. And he kept picturing her dark, gaunt face, staring at him, troubled and wary, unreadable thoughts in her eyes. He shook his head, annoyed by his lack of focus.

He rose from the corpse and backed away from the bed, leaning against the wall of the squalid, fly-infested room. There had been so many of these tragic hovels; he had debased himself for years, placing his hands on these vulgar commoners, but now he sensed that he was only weeks away from mastering the Art. It would all be worth it when he showed the other phraters what true power was and sent the Old King snivelling from his throne.

The man on the bed had not been suffering from the plague. Alzen had seen that as soon as he entered. He had some kind of virus. He would have recovered in a day or two. But Alzen had played along with the confused family, telling them their son was beyond saving and that he would ensure his final moments were painless, both of which were untruths. There was no time to be patient. He had to master the Art soon. The Old King was suspicious. There were still Aroc Brothers out there who could spread rumours. If he did not move fast, everything could be ruined.

He heard movement outside the one-room hovel and went back to the bed, peeling Coagulus off the body with a moist *pop*.

He cursed as he saw that the man's face was locked in an agonized grimace. That would not really fit with his description of events, so he tried to massage the corpse's face into a more serene expression. To his annoyance, the face remained resolutely tormented.

"Is it over?" said a tremulous voice at the door.

Alzen muttered a curse and quickly folded Coagulus back into the egg without even pausing to wipe the creature clean. The whole situation infuriated him. All this absurd pretence was beneath him. He was trying to solve the mysteries of the universe and he had to act like a common charlatan.

He took a small copper bowl from his robes and crushed a cube of blue powder into it. He placed his finger in the corpse's mouth, caught some spit on his finger and pressed it into the bowl with the powder. Then he took a glass vial, about the size of his index finger and poured scented oil into the mixture.

He placed his hand over the bowl and shook it, muttering a few words. The bowl burned hot beneath his palm and then, with the heat still on his skin, he pushed the corpse's face again, repeating the same phrase. The face relaxed, looking slack-jawed rather than at peace, but at least not tormented.

Alzen shook his head as he secreted the bowl back in his robes, muttering another curse as he spilled some of the mixture on the cloth. Once he had become the Ingenious, there would be no need for any of this. He would harness elements with a thought, bending nature to his will with the ease of a god. He smiled at the thought. In the tongue of the ancients, the word for God was the same as the word for the Ingenious.

"Your Holiness?" came the tearful voice at the door.

Alzen swapped his smile for a sad, concerned expression and let the anguished family in. As they bustled past him, wailing and sobbing, Alzen's mind was elsewhere, picturing the day when he would ascend the throne, drenched in divine light, steering Athanor with a casual wave of his hand as his brethren begged him for forgiveness. Then they would realize how wrong they had been in their choice of Old King.

As the man's grieving relatives pawed at him and pressed their ugly faces into his robes, Alzen felt a jolt of alarm. The Old King! Today was the day on which Seleucus intended to visit his cell. The young man Alzen had just murdered had been strong and had taken much longer to die than Alzen had hoped. The whole morning had already gone. The Old King would be there within the hour.

He tried to sound sincere as he gave the weeping family his best wishes and then he hurried away from the gloomy, stinking hut, striding out into the midday sun.

The Azorus slums were particularly rank at this time of the day, and Alzen donned his ceremonial helmet as waded off up the muddy riverbank, heading away from the Saraca back towards the Temple District. His attendants went ahead of him, barging a path through beggars and salvage crews and brandishing knives at anyone who tried to approach him.

When he reached the road above the embankment, his attendants rushed up to one of the temple gates and opened them, admitting Alzen into a long, colonnaded avenue that led into the blessed, cloistered, most secret realms of the Elect. Gates clanged shut behind him and the din of the slums faded, replaced by the gentle sound of flowing water. Laborators bowed as Alzen passed, but he ignored them, striding through a series of courtyards, avenues and gardens, all of which were networked by a complex series of copper-lined channels and gullies cut into the flagstones. Some were as slender as a man's arm and some were as wide as a small river, and crossed with bridges, but all of them ran with the same, shimmering liquid. It flowed over the copper, and tumbled into ornamental pools, clear and colourless, but too viscous to be water.

As Alzen approached a large octagonal court, he reached the point of confluence at which all the streams and rivulets met. At the centre of the court there was a golden cage, roughly egg-shaped and wrought of thousands of woven metal threads: the Microcosm. It towered over Alzen, nearly a hundred feet tall, and as the streams of liquid converged at its base, they formed a blaze of light that filtered through every one of the strands. Gathered around the Microcosm were dozens of robed, hooded laborators, standing at braziers, tending the flames and mumbling a low, droning chant.

Through force of habit, Alzen paused before the cage to whisper a prayer. He was close enough to see the outer strands growing and curling like the shoots of a metal plant. The cage was Athanor in miniature – a perfect replica of the Elect's great masterpiece, showing every baffling detail of its design. Snaking through it all like a bullion serpent was the Saraca, endlessly circling, with the Temple District trapped in its dislocated jaws.

It was only ten minutes until his meeting with the Old King, so Alzen kept his prayer brief and hurried across the court, through more avenues and gardens, until he neared the building that housed his own cell.

He hissed in annoyance as he saw the squat, lumpy form

of Phrater Ostan. He was scurrying towards him from a doorway, his expression anxious.

"Alzen!" he cried.

Alzen pretended not to see him and kept rushing towards his cell.

Ostan blocked his way.

Alzen halted with a sigh. "Phrater Ostan," he said, giving him a slight nod and a forced smile. "I'm afraid I can't talk. Seleucus is coming to my chambers to discuss the incident in the warehouse."

"It's more than that now." Ostan leant close and lowered his voice to a conspiratorial whisper. "Have you heard about what happened in Gamala, in Bethsan Palace?"

Alzen shook his head, his pulse quickening.

"It's happened again. Someone used alchymia as a murder weapon. Some hallucinogen peddlers from the Botanical Quarter had taken possession of the Bethsan Palace and they have been transfigured by some crude, violent form of alchymia."

"A crude form?" Alzen struggled to hide amusement. None of his brothers understood the incredible significance of what he was doing.

Ostan nodded, looking horrified. Then he gripped Alzen's arm and smiled. "But there's good news too."

Alzen gently removed Ostan's hand. "Really?"

"Yes. When the murders took place, you and I were attending the observances in Anatis Square. We are above suspicion."

"Weren't we always?"

"Of course." Ostan blushed, looking flustered and embarrassed. "But now the Old King can be doubly sure that we had nothing to do with these disgraceful acts. He saw us, plain as day, at the observances when the criminals were being murdered."

Alzen smiled. "I'll be late, Phrater Ostan."

"Of course. Forgive me. Go. You may find that the Old King doesn't even arrive though. What possible reason could he have for interrogating you now?"

Alzen managed to maintain his smile until he had broken away from Ostan and was striding towards his cell.

His attendants had already opened the door in readiness and his housekeeper rushed out to meet him, looking distressed.

"His Majesty is already here," he said, bowing and fawning as Alzen entered the building.

"Here?" Alzen stopped and glared at him. "Where? Where have you left him?" He looked around the entrance hall, seeing no sign of the Old King's attendants.

The housekeeper was pale with anguish. "He insisted I admit him to your laboratory, Your Holiness. I left him in the antechamber but he did not wish to wait there."

Alzen stared at him.

The man looked terrified.

"No matter," said Alzen, finally, with a shrug. "I have nothing to be ashamed of. I'm sure the Old King will be fascinated to learn what I have been doing while he attends to matters of court. Have you offered him any wine or food?"

The housekeeper shook his head, his eyes wide.

Alzen laughed. "Fetch some, Bucra! Seleucus wears a heavy crown. The least we can do is greet him with some civility."

Bucra bowed and rushed away, calling out to other attendants as he went.

Alzen's brief moment of panic had faded as he strode across the entrance hall of his chambers. What did he have to fear? When Isten killed the Aroc Brothers, he had been standing just a few feet away from Seleucus, surrounded by his fellow phraters. There could be no suggestion that he was to blame. He remembered how close he was to success, and as he headed down the steps towards his laboratories, he was beaming.

The steps led down into a long, barrel-vaulted antechamber that led in turn to the laboratory. These lower chambers were all lit by pale, lifeless mandrel-fires, fixed in sconces on the walls, and the air was much cooler than the rooms above, cut deep into the rock and decorated with polished hexagonal tiles that gleamed and shimmered as Alzen rushed across them. He was still dressed in his ceremonial finery and felt more than ready to face Seleucus. He had removed his golden helmet upon entering the house, and his blond tresses tumbled freely down his chest, mingling with the yellow folds of his gown. He had his rod of office in one hand, he was using the other to brush away the dust of the slums.

The door to the laboratories was a circle of polished basalt, built in the shape of the black Athanorian sun, surrounded by a vast mosaic depicting circles of fire stretching out into the heavens. At the centre of the door was single hole and, as he reached it, Alzen opened the lock with a key and pushed the door open.

The chamber beyond was crowded with the Old King's attendants and they bowed as Alzen entered, but there was no sign of Seleucus himself. Alzen rushed through more rooms, ignoring the greetings of his laborators, until he found Seleucus.

The Old King was waiting for him in the large, rectangular room where Alzen did most of his work. The gleaming colossus was looming over a crowd of anxious-looking laborators who were struggling to answer his questions. The room was filled with stone tables, on which dozens of corpses were lying in various states of dismemberment and decay. The chamber was lit by a single mandrel-fire, a ball of light encased in a glass dome in the centre of the ceiling, burning so bright that the room had a slightly surreal, dreamlike quality. Every surface in the chamber was clad in white polished marble and the mouldering, bruise-dark flesh of the cadavers was shocking against the flawless sheen. The walls were lined with shelves holding plump, globular bottles, filled with powders and tinctures. At the far end of the room there was an ancient-looking brazier, ten feet in diameter, wrought of rusting iron and filled with gently smouldering coals.

Seleucus was dressed as he had been when Alzen last saw him – wearing the same elaborately embellished gold armour and carrying his tall, bronze staff. He looked up as Alzen entered and the harsh light revealed the strangeness of his face. As Alzen had guessed in the Giberim Temple, Seleucus's face was now made entirely of golden filigree – a beautiful, inert mesh locked in a regal scowl. Looming behind him, almost as tall as the giant regent, was his lion, Mapourak.

"Phrater Alzen," said Seleucus. Despite the cold rigidity of his face, his voice was deep, mellifluous and full of warmth.

Alzen crossed the room and halted a few feet from the Old King with a deep bow. "Your Majesty."

"Call me Seleucus, for goodness' sake," laughed the Old King. "Surely down here I can be a simple phrater again? A man can only bear so much pomp."

Alzen laughed. "Attending functions and diplomatic dinners is not all that you hoped for?"

"Alzen, you don't know the half of it. If I so much as break wind there has to be twelve formal dinners and a royal portrait to celebrate the occasion."

Alzen smiled, but there was something peculiar about hearing jokes spilling from such an inhuman mask.

Seleucus looked around at the corpses and bottles. "Whereas you have been working in uninterrupted peace. All I hear is how much progress you're making, Alzen, but you never come to discuss it with me."

"I would not presume to bore you with my minor successes."

"Spare me the false modesty, Alzen, we know each other too well. I've heard that you are performing acts of transfiguration that no one has seen since..." He laughed. "Well, that no one has seen before at all."

"You are too kind."

As the king spoke, his words had filled the air with tendrils of heavy, slow-moving smoke and Alzen was conscious of them circling above his head, watching him. However innocent the conversation sounded, Alzen knew what it really was: a series of carefully placed traps. He was being baited and studied. There was no way Seleucus could have guessed he was behind the murders, but he would be wary of him all the same. There was never an

Old King who enjoyed hearing his subjects sing the praises of another phrater. It delighted Alzen to think how jealous and frustrated Seleucus must be every time he heard how Phrater Alzen was becoming the greatest ever practitioner of the Art.

"And your techniques revolve around the study of the dead?" asked Seleucus.

Another barbed snare. Necromancy was utterly forbidden.

"The study of *anatomy*, Your Majesty. The spirit leaves its mark upon the flesh. By examining the mechanisms of material life, I learn more about the Sacred Light." He shrugged. "But, to be honest, I have learned more in the slums than I have in our temples."

"Ah, yes, of course." Seleucus nodded and began strolling around the corpses, with his lion padding after him. "I have heard much of your work with the depraved and the vulgar." He paused, near to Alzen, enveloping him in questing strands of smoke. "Our brethren tell me that this is the cause of your success – your humility."

Alzen shrugged, blinking as the fumes caressed his face. "I do what I do because it feels right. It feels right to ease the suffering of those poor souls as they pass from one realm to the next. But, I have to admit, every one of my breakthroughs follows an expedition into the city."

Seleucus leant over one of the corpses. It was an inkworm, one of the creatures that lived in the silt of the river – a giant, rotting cephalopod, larger than a man, with one long tentacle and a bloated sac for a head.

"Strangely human faces, the bezerin," said Seleucus, running a finger across the worm's face. The creature had black, oily skin and, as the Old King said, its eyes and mouth had an oddly human aspect.

"Some of the salvage crews have learned to speak with them," said Alzen. "They feed them fish in return for directions to metal deposits. Apparently, they are quite sociable animals. They prefer to live near the slums and boats than in the deeps of the river." He grimaced. "Their young play with the vulgar children."

Seleucus nodded. Then fell quiet, stroking the creature's face as though he were petting a living animal, ignoring the black blood that oozed from its wounds.

"We live in strange times," he said after a while, still looking at the corpse.

"Majesty?"

"For all these centuries we have kept the secrets of the Art to ourselves. The city has grown more wonderful and complex, but never before has someone outside of the fraternity harnessed our power."

Alzen tried to keep his tone relaxed and cheerful. "Ah, yes. I see. Yes, it's a troubling situation. I have only just returned from the slums, but Phrater Ostan informed me of the deaths in Gamala. Something needs to be done." Alzen's face was completely shrouded in fumes, but he gave no sign that they were bothering him. "Have your interviews with the other phraters shed any light on the problem?"

"Not yet." Seleucus stared at him. He was now so close that Alzen realized he had made a mistake. Not all of the old Seleucus had vanished. His human eyes still stared out from behind the mask, clear, blue and intense, peering at Alzen's face.

"Gamala is full of laborators," said Alzen, waving at the servants that surrounded them, their yellow-painted faces hidden in their deep hoods. "Could it be that a low-born has somehow found a way to mimic our techniques?"

"No." Seleucus shook his head. "Impossible. Only someone of noble blood could even attempt the rudiments of the Art. It has to be a member of our fraternity."

Alzen nodded. He knew that as well as Seleucus but felt the need to pretend he was at least thinking about the problem.

"I'm wasting your time," said the Old King, suddenly sounding cheerful again. He backed away from Alzen and the strands of smoke dissipated. "You know I would never suspect you, old friend. I came here mainly because you have been avoiding me since the coronation." He turned away and stroked Mapourak. "I wanted to check there were no hard feelings."

"Hard feelings?"

"It could easily have been you who was given this crown, Alzen. We both know it. The vote was very close."

Alzen felt a rush of anger as he recalled the day of the conclave. It took an immense effort for him to keep his reply cheerful. "I had a lucky escape. I doubt I would have progressed this far if I had to spend my time attending formal dinners and celebrating my bowel movements."

Seleucus did not laugh and he kept his back to Alzen. "Your progress is impressive, Alzen. Many of the other phraters are trying to imitate your success, visiting the poorest areas of the city and tending to the sick, hoping that such virtuous deeds will elevate their souls to the level of yours."

Alzen had to stifle a laugh at the thought of his poor, misguided brethren, nursing plague-rotten idiots and thinking it was the key to mastering the Art. "That makes me happy," he replied.

The Old King turned to face him and, as the mandrel-fire flashed over his mask, Alzen caught a glimpse of something unexpected in Seleucus's eyes. It seemed, for a moment, that the Old King was amused by him – laughing at him. Then it was gone and he looked as stern and regal as before.

"I won't waste any more of your time, Alzen," he said. "Continue with your work. I will let you know when I have news on these strange occurrences."

With that, he nodded and headed for the door.

Alzen was thrown by the Old King's sudden departure. He had expected a long interview, and questions about his techniques, but the meeting had actually felt like a formality.

"Your Majesty," he said, sounding a little confused.

As Seleucus neared the door, Alzen's housekeeper entered, looking flustered and leading a phalanx of servants, all carrying trays laden with food and drink.

They had to scatter as the Old King and his attendants stormed out of the room.

"Too late," snapped Alzen, taking a bottle of wine and a glass and sending his servants away again. Then he ordered everyone else to leave the room and headed over to the crucible. He stared into its embers, sipping his wine, considering everything that had happened over the last few days: the death in the warehouse, the treachery of Sayal and the Aroc Brothers, his luck in finding Isten and his conversation with Seleucus. As heat rippled through the embers he pictured Isten's face again. It merged and flowed, shimmering in the smoke. That morning, before he headed out to the slums, he had stood at this crucible and performed an act of transfiguration beyond anything he had achieved before. With just a few ingredients he had summoned the cadaver Seleucus had just been stroking. What had she done to him? With a few words and tinctures he had dragged the dead creature from its murky grave and landed it here in his laboratory. Never, in all his years of study, had power come so easily to him. He felt closer than ever before to mastery of the Great Work. Soon, he would achieve something his brothers had not even dreamt was possible: the ability to wield power using only his mind. But why had his research leapt forwards at such speed? He pictured Isten in the embers again. His progress was linked to her somehow, he was sure of it. When he channelled his power through her body, his understanding tripled. He held his hand over the embers, feeling the heat, remembering how it felt to be in her mind.

He felt his thoughts slipping away again. Something about that scrawny, vulgar woman was confusing him. He considered the facts. The first breakthrough had been using human souls as his base material. By being present at the moment of death he could use Coagulus to capture souls and harness their potency. The next step had been realizing that it was not enough to wait for the occasional windfall – he needed to kill those who were not going to die of their own accord. Now, there was another revelation. By channelling his power through Isten, he had seen facets that had previously eluded him. She acted as a catalyst.

As he turned to go, he hesitated. From another angle, the embers looked more like Seleucus's face than Isten's. The

Old King looked up at him with the same peculiar, mocking expression Alzen noticed when Seleucus was about to leave. The face was only in Alzen's imagination but, as he left the laboratory, it stayed with him, making him feel inexplicably troubled.

16

As the city grew, demons came to feed, boiling in the wake of the riverboats, invading Athanor's sewers like the serpent of sin, rising into agonized throats to become tongues, eager to announce their rule. But when the clouds broke they screamed, outraged and confused, confronted by an Eden with no God.

She waited for them by the front doors of the Alembeck Temple. It was dusk, and the crowds were thinning out, leaving the narrow, sheer-sided street to the rats and the shadows. The temple doors had been boarded up for decades and the warped frame was ripe with the smell of urine, but Isten stood proudly on the top step, arms folded, legs apart, as the Exiles trudged towards her through the dusty gloom. Gombus was there, she saw with relief, the gaunt mahogany of his face reminding her of another world. With his high, sharp cheekbones and long, hooked nose, he was the epitome of a Rukoner but he was horribly wasted. His shoulders knifed up through his robes like shards of wood and he was leaning on Puthnok for support. The darkness turned Puthnok's spectacles into black, featureless circles, but Isten could imagine her solemn, humourless eyes staring through the lenses at her, cold and disapproving.

Lorinc was there too, loitering at the rear of the group next to Colcrow and his crowd of golden-haired teenagers. Her surprise grew as more Exiles gathered at the foot of the steps, faces she hadn't seen for years in some cases, looking up at her with a mixture of suspicion and fascination. Now that she had a steady supply of cinnabar from Alzen, Isten was wonderfully calm and clear-sighted. The shadows were rolling and tumbling around her countrymen, but she had the delirium under control. She held up a bottle of wine and smiled.

"My name is Donkey," she said, taking a swig. "And I can do this."

She walked down the steps and handed the bottle over and the Exiles passed it round, enacting a ritual none of them knew the origins of.

A few passers-by stopped to gawp at the strange scene so Isten went back up the steps and waved for the others to follow.

They looked puzzled as she approached the huge, rotten doors of the temple. The route up onto the roof was round the back of the building.

Isten shoved the doors. They fell open, revealing a candlelit interior none of them had ever seen before. Isten waved again and stepped inside.

The Exiles hesitated at the threshold as they saw rows of men waiting in the antechamber – large, bare-chested warriors with fierce, scarified faces. They were heavily muscled and carrying brutal, two-handed axes. The warriors' bodies were deformed by what looked like huge tumours or growths. It was only upon closer inspection that the lumps were recognizable as shrivelled, smoked human heads, sewn into the warriors' flesh as grisly battle trophies. The shrunken heads had stitched-up eyes, but it was still possible to see the agony of their final moments, their disembodied faces howling, silently, from the warriors' chests and arms.

They saluted Isten as she passed them, causing the grimacing heads to stretch and thud together. Isten had used some of Alzen's money to hire herself an honour guard.

"What is this, Isten?" asked Gombus, freeing himself of Puthnok's grip and approaching her, staring at the hulking warriors in shock.

She was pleased to see that he was as intrigued as everyone else. Finally, there was something other than disappointment in his eyes.

"Headhunters," she replied. "Newly arrived in Athanor and seeking someone to serve."

She nodded to one of the headhunters and he closed the door, then she raised her voice, talking to the whole gathering.

"You told me years ago, Gombus, that I would one day lead us to victory. You pointed out the birthmark on my arm and told me what it signified: the fox of the Rukon – the symbol that would prove I was my mother's daughter; the symbol of hope that would be a rallying cry to every oppressed soul in the homeland I can barely remember. You said that, one day, I would be the one to stop the executions. To give our people the chance to live in peace. I was only a child, but even then I understood the burden you were putting on me – the importance of it." For the first time in her life, Isten heard power in her voice – not the power of Alzen, but the power of conviction; the strength of will. She could hear *faith* in her voice. It was the voice she heard in her dreams. The voice of her mother.

The Exiles were staring at her in shocked silence, waiting to hear what she said next. "It terrified me," she said, staring at Gombus. "I had no idea what to do. How could I carry that kind of weight? I had no idea how to be who you thought I was. I have struggled..." Her voice faltered and Gombus shook his head, about to speak. She held up a warning hand, glad to finally share a pain she had hidden for so many years. "It is not your fault, but I did things I am ashamed of. And then, when I could take it no more, I did something so awful I had to leave." She rolled up her left sleeve and revealed her upper arm. Where there should have been a birthmark, there was an ugly mass of scar tissue.

The Exiles finally found their voices, gasping and cursing and looking at each other in shock.

"Isten!" cried Puthnok, her voice shrill with anger.

Gombus was shaking his head still and his face looked grey, but he said nothing.

"How could I atone for this?" asked Isten, raising her voice over the din and gripping her mutilated arm. "I was so angry. So scared and confused. So *stupid* that I tried to cut my past from my skin. How could I come back to you after that?"

She looked up, tears in her eyes, wondering what they would do, now that she had finally revealed the betrayal.

Even now, they stayed quiet, waiting to hear what came next.

She wiped away her tears. "But the Sisters of Solace nursed my wounds. They mended my soul. And in their beauty, I saw that there is always hope. If they could believe in me, perhaps I could believe in myself. But they did more than nurse my spirit. They put me in touch with new contacts, new sources of information." She gave Colcrow a pointed look. "Reliable information."

She gave the headhunters a nod and they lit more torches, lighting up the nave and revealing a crate at the far end.

She waved for the Exiles to gather round and opened the chest to reveal the sacks of cinnabar Alzen had sent her.

The Exiles looked even more shocked. Then Lorinc started to laugh and, quickly, the laughter spread through the group. Even Puthnok was shaking her head, dazed by the size of the haul.

"How?" she demanded, when the laughter had died down. "How did you pay for it?"

"My contact gave it to me for free," she said.

"Free?" laughed Lorinc. "Why would anyone do that? Who was it?"

"I've sworn to keep his identity secret," she replied. Isten had been worrying about this moment, afraid that the Exiles might guess she was in league with the Curious Men, but now that she came to it, she realized they would never dream of such a connection. It was too absurd to even cross their minds. "That was one of his conditions. The other condition is that we sell the cinnabar at the price he set."

Lorinc shook his head when she explained how cheap that price was. "Why would he want that? We could sell it for three times that."

"Because he's not interested in the money. He wanted Sayal dead and the Aroc Brothers ruined. The cinnabar is my reward for killing Sayal and the low price is to ruin the Aroc Brothers. They won't be able to compete with us.

They'll be out of business within a month."

Colcrow had barged his way through the crowd and he smiled at Isten, speaking in his smug, whispered tones. "And what use is all this cinnabar to us if we have to sell it so cheaply? "It sounds like a lot of work for little gain."

"Look at it, Colcrow," she said. "Look how much there is. Even at that price we'll make enough money to buy whatever we want – tar, weapons, more soldiers like these, anything. We'll own this stretch of the river again."

"We could own half the city," muttered Lorinc, glancing at Colcrow. "All the other gangs will be screwed when we flood the market with this."

"They'll be on us like dogs," said Puthnok. "They'll fight for their lives."

Isten nodded to the rows of headhunters lining the nave. "And they'll find us ready. You always said the revolution would be bloody. Well, let's start it now, here, in Athanor. We can sharpen our blades on the Aroc Brothers' skulls. Then, when we work out how to get home, we'll be ready for anything."

They were all staring at her in amazement as she waved them on, deeper into the temple. Some of the headhunters went ahead, lighting brands on the walls and revealing her next surprise. Each of the chapels off the main room had been furnished with mattresses and blankets and hung with lanterns.

"What is all this?" asked Lorinc, shocked by how she had transformed the place. The floors had been swept and there were piles of clothes and armour next to the beds.

"It's our fortress," she said, speaking loud enough for her voice to carry right back down the nave. "We'll fix the locks and shutters and patch the holes in the roof. We'll be safe."

"Ours?" replied Lorinc. "We own it?"

Isten nodded as she led them towards another chapel. "I bought it."

The headhunters lit more lamps and the Exiles laughed in shock as they saw what the final chapel contained: tables crowded with food and drink and shelves laden with sacks of rice, grains and spices.

"You all look like corpses," she said, turning to face them, her eyes gleaming in the torchlight. "But from now on we will eat like warriors. We will grow strong and healthy again. And it won't stop there. I'm going to arm us properly." She tapped her falcata. "Not like this, but with the modern weapons that the Aroc Brothers used on us. Let's see how they feel when we turn those weapons on them."

As she spoke, most of the Exiles were already pushing past her and gathering around the tables, slapping her on the back before grabbing handfuls of food. The room filled with sounds that had been alien to them for years: relieved laughter and cries of pleasure.

Isten enjoyed the moment, smiling at the sight of her countrymen looking happy. Then she noticed the small group that had remained outside the chapel, watching her in silence from the nave: Gombus and Puthnok, regarding her with troubled expressions, and behind them, Colcrow, shaking his head in confusion.

She headed back over to them.

"Someone gave you the cinnabar for free?" said Colcrow, raising an eyebrow.

"It was payment for killing Sayal," she said, waving at the temple. "Along with the money I used to buy all this."

Colcrow smoothed his robes over his enormous gut, looking no less convinced. "And you won't tell us who this mysterious benefactor is?"

She shook her head. "It was his only condition – along with selling the cinnabar at a cut-down price. He was prepared to pay handsomely for the death of Sayal and, obviously, I wanted him dead too, so I was happy to play along."

Gombus looked at her with concern rather than suspicion. "This seems too good to be true. Are you sure you can trust this stranger?"

"I don't trust him at all. But he paid me, Gombus, and that's all that matters." She looked up at him with more confidence than ever before. "Now we can arm ourselves and drive the other gangs from our territory. We can keep our families safe and we can live in here." She waved her hand at the temple. "Rather than hiding on the roof. You can leave that stinking doss house and be safe here, Gombus."

He smiled, but she sensed he did not mean to stay.

"Aren't you pleased?" she said, looking at all three of them. "We can hope again."

"Hope for what?" asked Puthnok, looking up at her. She seemed nervous and distracted, fiddling with her glasses whilst watching the headhunters in the nave. "To sell more drugs than anyone else? To be more feared than any other gang?"

"Yes! Exactly that." Isten's good humour started to fade. "To grow strong, Puthnok. To finally have a victory."

Puthnok nodded at the feeding frenzy that was continuing behind Isten. "What victory is that, Isten? Growing rich and fat, lounging around this vile city while half of Rukon is dying in servitude. While the Emperor bathes in the blood of our families. Do you call that a victory?"

Isten had never heard Puthnok speak with such vehemence. She still lacked the courage to meet Isten's eye, but her little frame was rigid with anger.

"Puthnok," said Gombus, placing a hand on her shoulder. "Isten is not to blame for the labour camps, any more than she is to blame for our exile."

Puthnok would not meet his gaze either. She was glaring at the floor. "She has cut that mark from her arm. Even if we could get home to Rukon, she would be worthless. How could we prove who she was without that birthmark? She could be anybody. Who will listen to my manifesto now? What use is any of this? What do we care about ruling the criminals of Athanor? We need to get home. We need to burn down the Checny Palace. Not buy ourselves grand houses on the Blacknells Road."

"Grand?" laughed Colcrow, looking at the bowed, rotting rafters.

Gombus ignored him. "We are in Athanor, through no fault of anyone here," he said, looking at Puthnok. "And Isten has found a way to keep us together."

Isten's heart swelled as he defended her. "I don't know how to get us home," she admitted, looking at Puthnok. "But until we can find a way, I swear to keep us all alive. It's the best I can offer." She glanced at Gombus. "I know you hoped for more, but this is all I have. For now, at least."

He nodded but she could still see doubt in his eyes – not the fury of Puthnok, but doubt all the same.

"And what about you?" she said, looking at Colcrow. "Are you with us again? I know you have resources of your own. Will you throw in your lot with us?"

He closed his eyes, smiling, and took a deep breath. Then he enveloped her hand in his sweaty grip. "Remember who set you off again, Isten. Remember who told you about the shipment in the warehouse."

She pulled her hand away, about to remind him that his information led to Amoria's death, but maybe he was right. Everything did start with her jump into the sewers. If she hadn't ended up back at the Sisters of Solace, she never would have met Alzen. She bit back her retort and nodded. "Then bring whatever you have here. I'm going to fix the place up and fortify it. There are more rooms than these. The place is big enough to hold hundreds of us. I want to get every Exile in the city back together."

Colcrow smirked, on the verge of saying something fatuous but, again, the certainty in her voice brooked no dissent. He nodded and looked at his bodyguard, Golo, who was waiting behind the crowd of young girls. "Tell everyone I'm still in touch with. Tell them Isten is marshalling the troops and that I'm signing up for the ride."

Golo nodded and headed off back down the nave towards the temple doors.

Isten could feel that Puthnok was still seething in silence, but decided now was not the time to deal with her. People were coming away from the feast behind her, gathering around, waiting to see what she would say next, so she climbed up into a pulpit and called out, her voice reverberating through the temple. "Eat your fill," she cried. "Rest. Drink. Recover. But, when you are done, there is work to do." She waved at the cinnabar. "Sell as much as you can, as fast as you can. I will be back here tomorrow night at the same time and I want every ounce of it to be gone." She paused, staring at the upturned faces. "Understood?"

They roared at her, like loyal soldiers, holding up wine bottles and knives, grinning and laughing. The sound echoed around the temple and made Isten's heart race. She tried to look serious and stern but found herself smiling. "We're back!" she cried, and they howled again, so loud that even Gombus looked surprised.

As she climbed back down from the pulpit, Lorinc came over to her. "And what will you be doing while we're all shifting this lot?"

"I'm not done," she said as she headed to the door. She waved at the headhunters with their grisly implants and the Exiles, grinning as they ate. "This is just the beginning. I'm going to find us weapons to match anything the Aroc Brothers can throw at us."

"From your mysterious contact?"

She was about to reply when a voice rang out, strong and furious, over the din.

"Where are your fathers?" cried Puthnok, climbing up onto a table and silencing everyone with the rage burning in her eyes. "Where are your mothers? Your brothers and sisters?"

Drinks were lowered and eyes cast awkwardly towards the ground as the Exiles remembered the plight of those they left behind in Rukon.

"How does that food taste?" cried Puthnok, her hands trembling as she waved at the feast. "If you think of your families, wasting in those camps, smashing rocks with broken hands, sleeping in piles like corpses?" She was spitting as she shouted, her eyes full of tears. "Does it taste good?" She stared at Isten. "Does it taste like victory?"

The room was silent apart from Puthnok's fast, uneven breathing. She pointed at Gombus. "There are some here who remember what fighting means. It does not mean murdering pushers. It does not mean feeding every addiction we can think of so that we can grow fat and safe. That's not the fight. We should be fighting against tyranny. Perhaps we can't save our families yet, but there are families here, in this abomination of a city, families that are dying, desperate and afraid with their heads crushed in the gutter by the Elect."

Isten had never heard Puthnok speak with such fervour, with such confidence. She still looked like a timid, bookish child, but her voice sounded like it was coming from someone larger, someone fiercer.

"While we play these games, while we busy ourselves with pointless turf wars, the Elect are free to do whatever they do in those temples that we can never enter. While we sell drugs to the starving masses the Curious Men hide in their towers and laugh, feeding on all this misery like jackals."

For a brief, wonderful moment, Isten had known how it felt to win, how it felt to be triumphant, and now, as Puthnok railed against everything she had just said, she felt the moment souring and slipping away. Anger boiled up through her chest.

"What do you want us to do?" she demanded, striding back towards Puthnok. "Charge the gates of the Temple District? Throw ourselves under the feet of the Ignorant Men?"

"There are ways, Isten," cried Puthnok. She wiped away her tears but her hands were still shaking. "There are things we could do to show the Elect that they have to change, that they have to share their wealth, that they have to feed their people, that they have to fight these plagues. We could burn their ships. We could steal their property. We could deface their statues. Athanor is waiting. This city needs someone to show the way. To rise up and teach them how to really fight. To show them who the real enemy is."

Puthnok paused to catch her breath, staggering slightly on the table.

Isten looked around and saw, to her disbelief, that some of the Exiles were not looking at Puthnok with derision, but with shock, and perhaps even agreement.

"Start your fucking fires," snapped Isten, furious at Puthnok for ruining the moment. "Paint the nose of someone's statue." She glared at the crowd. "But I suggest the rest of you eat and rest and make yourself strong. Whatever dreams Puthnok might have, our first fight is for survival. We can't save anyone here, or at home, if we're dead." She waved at the filthy walls and cracked windows. "Make this place secure. I'll be back in a day or two with the weapons we need to stay alive."

She stormed off towards the doors again. As she reached them, she heard Puthnok addressing the crowd again, quoting from her manifesto, talking about their duty to protect the forgotten and the weak.

Isten paused, her hand on the door, still furious, considering going back to argue again, then she realized it was pointless. Puthnok could preach all she liked. The

Exiles would remember who had filled their bellies and given them a roof again. She shoved the doors open and strode out into the night, dizzy with rage.

17

In Rukon the roads lay flat. They hugged the curves of the earth, rising with the land, climbing through forests and meadows but never aspiring to the sky, never pining for the deeps. They led children to mines and innocents to their graves, but at least they held their word. They held to the truth. Isten carried them with her like a necklace, cherishing them, recalling every loop and turn, every gravity-bound stone.

She waited for Alzen on Coburg Street, as they had arranged when she left Bethsan Palace. It was early morning and she had spent a sleepless night prowling the streets. She was too angry at Puthnok to rest, but she also wanted to make sure no one was following her. Some of the Exiles would be fascinated to know who her contact was and she couldn't risk them blundering in and ruining everything. The fish market was already crowded and noisy but she had chosen a warehouse so dilapidated that no trader ever used it. She sat at the back, perched on shattered crates, hidden in the darkness, her hood pulled low as she looked out into the dazzling sun. Dozens of riverboats were moored at the jetties and hovellers were wading through the shallows, hauling cargo from the boats up into the street, haloed by screaming gulls as they hurled sacks under the awnings.

As she waited, Isten's mind slipped back to the events at Bethsan Palace. She could not stop thinking about how it felt to have alchymia pouring through her body. She had been an addict long enough to recognize the symptoms. She was *craving* the power she felt that day. She was hungry to taste it again. When she first met Alzen she felt nothing but revulsion but now, if she pictured his pompous face, there was something else mixed with the loathing: a kind of need. Of all the addictions Isten had battled, this one seemed the most perverse, and the most dangerous. Alzen was a monster but, to her shame, she felt excited about the prospect of seeing him again. It was obscene. Shameful. She felt a wave of self-loathing and stood, preparing to leave the warehouse.

She had only taken a few steps when Alzen arrived, strolling into the darkness dressed in his scruffy disguise, pretending he was just stumbling through the market.

He peered in her direction as he entered the shadows, momentarily blind from the brightness outside.

"Are you there?" he said, feeling his way along the wall.

"Here," she muttered, sitting back down with a mixture of fear and excitement.

He shuffled over and sat down next to her. He looked different. Rather than imperious and self-satisfied, he looked hesitant, troubled even. She felt, again, how grotesque their partnership was but, now that she had seen him, the hunger was even stronger. She remembered how it felt to have the alchymia playing across her skin, glittering and rolling, responding to her every movement.

"Has the cinnabar been sold?" he asked.

"It's happening as we speak," she said. "We're going to shift it all by the end of the week."

He nodded, recovering some of his usual smug demeanour, looking into the middle distance with a half smile. "At the price I specified?"

"Everything is being done as you requested. They know the price and I've told them to spread the cinnabar as far as they can across the slums. If they–" She paused, hearing something near the entrance to the warehouse.

Alzen heard it too and stood up, squinting into the daylight.

Isten's falcata flashed as she drew it and padded over to the door. There was no one there. She peered outside, blinking and struggling to see. People were thronging past but no one seemed interested in her. All the same, she felt troubled as she headed back over to Alzen.

"This is dangerous," she muttered. "If the other Exiles knew about you everything would be ruined." She thought of the way the Exiles had looked at Puthnok, and how much more weight Puthnok's words would carry if everyone knew their feast had come from a Curious Man.

"There's another way," said Alzen, his voice sounding oddly hesitant again. "A way we could speak without being together."

Again, she felt that peculiar mix of nausea and excitement. If she let him into her thoughts again, it would be possible for him to work his sorcery through her body. But it also meant he would see what she saw, even if, as he claimed, only dimly.

He sensed her hesitation and shook his head. "Only as a temporary measure. You told me you want to seize some of the weapons the Aroc Brothers use. If we combine forces again, I can direct you to the right place, loan you my strength, as I did before, and then you could simply wipe my mark from your arm and be as you were."

Loan you my strength. The words gave her a shameful rush of excitement. She tried to hide her feelings, speaking in a gruff voice. "How long would it take? How far are the weapons from here?"

He nodded to the riverboats outside.

Isten was so shocked she laughed. "Here?"

"Yes. There's been trouble at the city walls. A problem with the conjunction. It happens sometimes. People do not always welcome Athanor with open arms. I don't know the details, but the phrater in charge has ordered reinforcements and supplies."

"But I can't board those boats. I'm a commoner. I'm, what would you call me? 'vulgar.' I'd be arrested before I set foot on the deck."

"If you wandered up dressed as you are, yes. But I can make you look like a laborator. I could give you robes, chains of office, keys and directions. No one would question you then."

"You're one of the Elect. You have all this power. Why not just channel it through me and spirit me on there?"

He raised an eyebrow. "Spirit you? You do not understand the Art. I cannot simply summon things from the air. Transfiguration is a subtle, complex process that requires hours of preparation." Excitement flashed in his eyes. "At least, it is until I have completed my great work. I'm close to something wonderful, Isten." He was speaking with more candour than she had heard before. "I'm close to mastering a new *kind* of alchymia. And then, once I have transformed myself, once I have been elevated, I *will* be able to wield power in the way you describe. I and the power will become one. I will become alchymia." He shook his head, his eyes straining. "I will become the Ingenious."

"The Ingenious?"

He nodded, but he was looking into the middle distance, seeming to have forgotten her. Then he shook his head. "Besides, even if I did the necessary work to 'spirit' you onto the boat, you would still be in danger dressed as you are. Subtlety is what we need, and discretion. If you appear to be a laborator, you can simply board the boat and reach the weapons. That will be quicker and easier and I can spend my time preparing for the theft."

"So what are you proposing? If you're not going to use me as a weapon, as you did in the palace, will you need to channel your power through me at all?" She immediately regretted asking him the question, afraid that she was right.

His voice regained its smooth, unctuous tone. "Picture the scene: I've got you on the boat. You wait until the weapons are unguarded, then approach the crates, which are as tall as you. How will you get the weapons home?"

"Ah, I see."

"But, if I return to my cell, and prepare, I will be able to perform an act of transfiguration *through* you. If you can place your hands on the crates, it will be as though I am there, in the hold. I will be able to use my alchymia to transport the weapons to wherever you need them to be."

She thought for a moment. "So it would not be like before, in the palace, when I... When I killed Sayal."

"Not exactly. There would be no need to fight, but there

will still be need for our minds to coalesce. I will still need to work through you. If you can reach the hold, and place your hands on the weapons, I can transmute their molecules with sacred fire and…" He hesitated. "It is hard to explain to–"

"To a *vulgar* person?" Isten was more amused than annoyed. Alzen clearly considered her to be barely human, but here he was, having to work with her to achieve whatever end he was striving for.

He stared at her, his expression unreadable.

"We use the word vulgar in a different way," he said. "To us it simply means one who is not versed in the Art."

"And 'commoner'? What meaning does that word have for you?"

He shook his head.

"It doesn't matter," she said, looking at the door to the warehouse again. "We should leave. If you put your mark on my arm again, you can get me on the boat, lead me to the weapons and send them elsewhere. Is that what you're saying?"

He nodded. "If I mark you again, we can part company and still speak by telepathic means. My preparations will take the rest of the day, but I can have everything ready by midnight. Come to this exact spot and your disguise will be waiting for you."

She laughed as she considered the risk she was taking. "If I'm discovered pretending to be a laborator, I'll be executed."

"You won't be discovered."

"Where would the weapons appear?"

"Where do you want them?"

"The Alembeck Temple, up on the Blacknells Road."

He nodded.

She held out her hand, her heart quickening in anticipation, then she hesitated. "Why are you helping me do this? We're already selling the cinnabar you gave me. I've killed Sayal. Why are you taking such a risk to get me those weapons?"

He laughed, and tried to sound blasé, but she sensed he was holding something back. "We've barely started, Isten. I want the slums to be awash with my cinnabar. And I want to be sure that no one else is dealing the stuff. We're rid of Sayal, but there are still hundreds of Aroc Brothers. I want them gone, as much as you do, and if you can't match their weapons, you'll have a hard battle on your hands."

She still hesitated. Clearly, he had been in league with the Aroc Brothers and then fallen out with them; she had guessed that within minutes of meeting him, but there was something else, something he wasn't telling her. She thought of her shameful hunger – her desire to be bonded with him again. Could it be that he was feeling a similar desire? She must be as repulsive to him as he was to her, but perhaps, somehow, he wanted what she wanted? Perhaps that was why he seemed hesitant?

"If your power is growing," she asked. "Do we even *need* weapons? Why not channel your sorcery through me, like you did at the palace? You could just cut them down with your magic."

"Because no one must know of our partnership," he snapped, revealing a flash of rage before quickly regaining control and softening his voice. "Because we must be discreet. I will not join you in some running battle through the slums, with all of Athanor watching, but I'll help you arm yourself and supply you with so much cinnabar that every criminal in the city has to kneel to you."

She nodded. His explanation made sense. She still sensed he was holding something back, but she decided the rewards were worth the risk. "So, when I'm dressed as a laborator, I simply stroll up to the boat?"

He nodded. "If you look like a laborator, you'll have no difficulty buying passage, and if anyone speaks to you during the journey, I can prompt your answers."

"Only men can be laborators."

"Your face will be painted yellow and you'll be wearing a hooded robe." He lowered his gaze, looking at her wiry, muscle-knotted body. "And you're not particularly..." He waved his hand, searching for the right word.

"I look like a man?" she prompted.

He laughed awkwardly.

She nodded and held out her arm.

As soon as he had drawn the sigil on her skin, she felt that strange numbness at the back of her skull, and the same wash of revulsion. It was disgusting. She could feel Alzen lurking in her thoughts like an unwelcome houseguest, but she also felt thrilled, already imagining how it would feel when his sorcery blazed through her skinny arms, transforming the elements, moulding reality.

"Midnight?" she said, rising to leave.

Midnight, he said, leaning back into the shadows to watch her, speaking directly into her thoughts.

18

When the Exiles arrived in Athanor, Isten could only sleep in Gombus's lap, unable to close her eyes without the lullaby of his rattling chest. As his lungs wheezed a mournful berceuse, she gripped his arm and pictured home – tyrants, riots and burnt remains. We all carry ghosts, said Gombus, but you carry a nation's dead. Don't forget them, he whispered as she drifted into dreams. Don't forget who you are.

Isten had crossed the river many times, but always on foot, hurrying over the contorted bridges that spanned its harlequin currents, never on a boat. She had not paid for a cabin, so she was up on the deck with the crew, watching the light of the mandrel-fires dancing in their wake, caught in the oily wash. The boat was called the *Sign of the Sun* and its crew were a ragged mix of races and species. They paid no attention to her as they worked, singing and swearing in their peculiar argot as they barged past, manning the rigging and stashing cargo in the hold. Most trade went from the walls into the city, but Isten had been surprised to learn that they also took things back *to* the walls. Among the cargo she saw crates and sacks branded with the black Athanorian sun – a sign that they were from the Temple District. These must be the supplies for the men at the walls that Alzen mentioned, and maybe exports, headed beyond the walls, to whatever kingdom's skies Athanor was currently filling. As well as the cargo, a regiment of hiramites had boarded, marching up the ramp in silence, their faces hidden behind the upside-down masks of their conical helmets. They were now sat, still silent, in small groups, polishing their falcatas and checking the fastenings on their armour.

From the river, Isten could see huge swathes of the city, rising over her like the crown of a leafless tree, spurs and strands, silhouetted against the stars. She leant over the gunwale, watching her reflection roll and stretch in the water. She had managed to grease her wild mass of dark hair down so flat that the laborator's hood almost sat normally on her head, and it was strange to see herself looking so unrecognizable. Her face was dyed with turmeric and her robes were made of heavy yellow cloth, stitched with golden thread and draped with keys and slender gilded chains. She looked regal. Important. The thought made her laugh.

Do you hear me even if I only think the words? she thought.

More clearly than if you speak, replied Alzen.

As he replied, the numbness in her head grew and she realized numbness was not quite accurate – it was more like a warmth, like kindling, just starting to catch.

Where are you now? she thought, suddenly intrigued to know more about him.

It doesn't matter. His tone had changed again. When they spoke in the warehouse, she had sensed that he was starting to trust her, to treat her as a confidant, but now he sounded cool and distant.

How will I find the weapons?

Just follow the other laborators when they go below. They'll want to check everything has been stowed safely.

Other laborators? She looked around and saw that Alzen was right. There was a scrum of yellow robes gathered at the stern of the boat, locked in conversation.

What will I say if they speak to me?

I can help with that, but I doubt they'll acknowledge you. They have business of their own to attend to. See that scythe stitched into their robes? That means they work for Phrater Herbrus, one of my brothers. He's the phrater who's out on the wall, watching over the conjunction. He's having difficulties with our new citizens so these laborators are taking him weapons and ingredients. They're busy and nervous about leaving the city. They won't be in the mood to make new friends.

Isten looked down at her own robes and saw the symbol she was wearing: a circle with a dot at its centre, like a simplified version of the Athanorian sun. Which phrater will they think I'm working for. Not you, surely?

No. The sun marks you as a servant of the Elect, nothing more. Not all laborators have a specific master. They'll consider you an inferior and have no interest in you.

Isten laughed but made no comment. She walked the length of the deck to the prow and stared out into the night. They were hurtling down the river at an impressive speed and she could hear engines grumbling and winding beneath her, causing the hull to judder. Athanor's riverboats were owned and powered by the Curious Men. Beneath the water, there was an elaborate tangle of mechanisms, fuelled by barrels of highly combustible mandrel-fire stored in the engine room. There were other boats setting off from the riverbank and Isten could see pale fire beneath their hulls, shimmering and flickering beneath the surface of the water.

The *Sign of the Sun* had already left the docks and was now passing the slums that surrounded the Temple District. Even at this hour there were hovellers wading through the chemical wash, calling out to each other, filling the night with seismic howls, their shells slopping and booming through the waves. From there, the riverboat steered out into the wider river, skirting Gamala's broad, leafy gardens, then the crumbling domes of the Zechen baths, and then heading so far into the centre of the river that Isten could no longer make out details of the buildings on the shore. Athanor became an abstract glimmer of arcs and loops, but she could still hear sounds, echoing across the bitumen-black water – the clanging of temple bells, the roar of furnaces, even snatches of song, carried for miles on the clear night air, disembodied and truncated, broken up by the tide. It took all of Isten's will not to be impressed by the beauty of the scene. Athanor was her prison. However hard it tried, she refused to let it seduce her.

The *Sign of the Sun* was cutting through the night so fast that within an hour Isten saw districts she had never visited. The further one travelled out from Athanor's centre, the stranger the architecture became. At its heart, in the districts around Verulum Square, the city's original form could still be seen: domes and minarets, maned and robed in golden spines, but essentially unchanged for thousands of years, but the outer reaches of Athanor bore little resemblance to traditional architecture, devolving into a baffling nest of organic shapes. The streets and towers became indistinguishable from each other – wicker-like skeins and thorn-tipped plaits, bound by the will of the Elect. Isten could still hear sounds of life drifting through the night – spectral voices and bestial calls, intriguing and haunting. She knew that, if anything, life out here was even more abundant and strange than on the Blacknells Road. She had met people from the outlying regions of the city and some had never even heard of the Elect, living in their own, isolated communities, blissfully unaware of the tyrants who kept them one meal away from starvation.

How will I get back? she thought, realizing how far she now was from the Blacknells Road. Will you transport me home, along with the weapons?

No, that would be an altogether different matter. You'll have to jump from the boat and swim.

She looked out across the water and frowned. She was a strong swimmer, but the Saraca was wide and cold, and the city already looked a long way off.

She looked back at the laborators. Well, we'll have to move soon then. And there's no sign of them moving.

I thought they would have headed below decks by now to check everything was secure. You're right though. If you don't move soon, you'll leave the city.

What? What are you talking about? What do you mean leave the city?

This boat is headed for the city walls. And it's moving a lot faster than I expected. Phrater Herbrus must be in worse trouble than I thought. I wonder if he–

I can't go to the walls!

Indeed. No. We'll have to try and find the weapons by ourselves. Can you see the entrance to the hold?

Isten's pulse quickened as she realized how vague Alzen's

plan was. She had assumed he knew what he was doing. No, she thought, pacing back across the deck. Then she saw a hatch guarded by some of the hiramites. "Maybe that one," she muttered, heading towards the soldiers.

The soldiers were sitting around the hatch, their heads down, hidden behind their helmets with their cloaks pulled tight around their cuirasses. Their falcatas were lying across their laps, still in their scabbards. They all looked to be asleep, or at least resting.

There are hiramites guarding the hatch, she thought.

Really? The Old King is becoming paranoid.

Not so paranoid, thought Isten. We did come here to steal them.

You're dressed as a laborator. There's no reason you shouldn't go below decks. Walk past them and open the hatch.

Isten shook her head at the ridiculousness of the situation, then strode across the deck, looking as confident as she could, and reached down to open the hatch.

Before she had even touched the handle, the one of the soldiers stood up and barred her way.

"What are you doing?" His voice rang out through his silver mask. She could see his real eyes behind the metal, but she still had the unnerving sensation that she was speaking to an upside-down face.

"I... er..." she floundered, unsure how to reply.

Say you have to check your shipment of minerals, said Alzen.

She did as he suggested but the soldier's eyes narrowed. "I saw you board the boat. You didn't place anything in the hold."

The other hiramites stood and gripped the handles of their swords.

Isten felt a flood of anger as she realized what a mess Alzen had landed her in.

"It was loaded before I arrived," she said, with no idea if that would sound believable.

The soldier looked at his fellow hiramites and then back at Isten. He stepped closer, peering at her face.

"Which phrater sent you here?"

Isten panicked and shook her head.

"Phrater..." Her mind went blank. She could not think of a single name. "I can't remember."

The man took a deep breath and she saw suspicion in his eyes. "No one's going down there. Wait back over by the rails. When we reach the wall I'll take you to Phrater Herbrus and you can explain to him why you're here."

Isten backed away, shaking her head, cursing herself.

Now what? she thought as she reached the prow of the boat and leant against the railing.

This is strange. He should not have challenged you like that.

Well, he did. She looked out at the river. The shore was even further away. I'll need to jump soon or I'll end up drowning.

You need those weapons. There must be another way to get you back. Let me think.

Alzen fell quiet, and Isten resigned herself to watching the city rush by.

Hours seemed to pass and Isten was about to say something when she realized she was finding it harder to distinguish the moonlit surface of the river from the glinting spires of the city. She wondered if there was something wrong with her eyes. Perhaps some remnant of the vistula seeds? She ignored it for a while but, gradually, the flashing of the lights and the swaying of the boat began to make her feel sick.

The lights look strange, she thought. I can't see clearly.

It's the wall.

Isten looked around, confused. What are you talking about? There's no wall here.

As she turned, the lights whirled across her vision, billowing like embers, merging with the lights on the shore. She backed away from the railings, shaking her head. Is this the cinnabar? She sensed that it was not. The splinters of light were nothing like the hallucinations she was used to.

Calm down. You'll draw attention to yourself.

Isten steadied herself by gripping the railing, but her vision was awash with undulating lights. It was as though she were standing behind a waterfall, trying to see through curtains of falling water. She could still hear the sound of the river slapping against the hull, she just couldn't see anything. What is this?

The sublimare, said Alzen. *The outer layer of the walls.*

I don't see any walls.

Athanor's boundaries are metaphysical, Isten, not physical. Alzen sounded amused by her ignorance. *How do you think we maintain the same climate year after year? Conjunction is not a true joining of Athanor to its hosts. There is no actual wall between us and Brauron. The sublimare is a spiritual partition. We seek sanctuary for a while, that's all. The Golden City–*

Brauron? interrupted Isten.

The nation we are currently visiting. Alzen sounded annoyed that she had singled out that word. *A squalid kingdom, full of savages. I pray the Old King doesn't intend to keep us here for more than a year or two. The trade is productive but unseemly.*

Isten was still struggling to follow Alzen's explanation. You said that the walls are guarded by a Curious Man, like you. How can that be possible if the walls don't exist?

The sublimare shields us from the tyranny of physics, but there are other threats. Not every host nation welcomes our arrival. Phrater Herbrus is guarding us against aggression. Beyond here lie Athanor's extremities – the limbs of the city that stretch furthest into the unknown, the newer regions, absorbed from wherever we have arrived – in this case, Brauron. That's what we refer to as the walls – the outer reaches of the city, the areas beyond the sublimare that will eventually become new parts of Athanor.

So the borders of the city are patrolled by Ignorant Men?

Alzen laughed. *Patrolled is the wrong word but, yes, they are present out here, in larger numbers than anywhere else. We greet our new citizens with open arms, but some of them still try to reject us and we react accordingly.*

There was a sinister tone to Alzen's words and Isten was about to ask him to explain what he meant, but then she laughed in disbelief as the world changed around her. The *Sign of the Sun* had sailed into a torrential rainstorm. The starlit spires of Athanor vanished, replaced by a rain-lashed forest and a grey, cloud-draped morning. Isten forgot the danger of her situation for a moment and revelled in the strangeness of what was happening. The Elect rarely allowed it to rain in Athanor, beyond the occasional small shower, but as the *Sign of the Sun* crashed towards a muddy riverbank, a storm slammed into Isten, soaking her robes and filling her eyes, cold and wonderful, reminding her of home. Most of the passengers rushed below deck for shelter, but Isten stayed where she was, savouring the chill and the damp, letting the wind cut into her bones.

She looked back over her shoulder and saw an equally shocking sight: Athanor, seen from outside. A serpentine limb snaked up into the clouds, a vast, coiled bridge channelling the Saraca into whatever alien river the boat was now crossing. Far above, glimmering in the thunderheads, she saw glimpses of Athanor's twisted architecture, suspended in the sky, incredible and terrifying. It took an effort of will for Isten to stop herself cowering. She was only seeing a fraction of the city's enormity, but it was still astonishing.

This is how Athanor grows, she thought.

Yes, and this river is only one point of conjunction. There are roads, walkways and other tributaries of the Saraca reaching down all along this coast, linking us to Brauron. And when it's time for the next conjunction, and Athanor moves on, we shall retain those new extremities, adding to the glory of our creation, as we have done for thousands of years.

Isten looked back at the forest, still delighted by the sight of such violently miserable weather. The *Sign of the Sun* had almost reached the riverbank and she could see buildings half a mile inland, nestling in the trees. They were tall, slender towers, ghostlike against the colourless sky, half-hidden by the mist.

Look at the riverbank, said Alzen. *You can see the city growing.*

It took a few seconds for Isten to see what he meant, but then she saw curving, winding shapes forming from the mud, rising up through the trees like the earthworks of an abandoned fortress.

Those shapes will become streets, said Alzen. *Linking the local architecture to Athanor. When we leave here, a part of this world will come with us. The people of Brauron who are chosen to join us will always have a piece of their home.*

Isten felt a jolt of shock. Did that mean there was a piece of Rukon somewhere in Athanor? A relic of her old life?

What's that? she thought, noticing that the whole coast was littered with dark, contorted lumps. Rocks?

Alzen did not reply, but as the *Sign of the Sun* sailed closer, Isten had her answer. She gripped the railings, feeling suddenly sick. The shoreline was heaped with corpses. They were blackened and smouldering, like the remnants of a fire, but she could see grasping, rigid hands and twisted limbs. In places, the crumbling heaps were shot through with golden seams. The metal flashed in the rain, revealing the cause of the massacre.

You did this? she thought, horrified.

Me?

The Elect. The Curious Men. Did you kill all those people?

When we encounter resistance, we have to protect the city. Phrater Herbrus has defended Athanor, just as I would have done in his place.

Defended? Look at them, Alzen. There are women and children out there. Isten was gripped by a rising sense of panic as she realized the brutality of the Elect – and of the man she had let into her mind.

Alzen sounded irritated. *Do you know how many kingdoms have risen and fallen while Athanor has endured? They are numberless, Isten. Never, in all of mankind's history, has an empire survived like Athanor. This timeless city is our only hope. Is that not worth making sacrifices for?*

"You're insane," whispered Isten, unable to look away from the corpses. They looked like a landslide. There were hundreds, perhaps thousands of them, heaped in the mud and the shallows, butchered for refusing to leave their homes.

Alzen sounded even more enraged. *Insane? And what would that make you, Isten? You knew what I was when you let me into your mind.*

"I didn't," she whispered, but her words faltered in her mouth. Even if she didn't know about this particular horror, she knew Alzen was a monster. He was right. What was wrong with her? How could she have agreed to work with him?

A cold fury gripped her. She could not tell if it was directed at Alzen or herself but as it grew in ferocity the heat in the back of her skull also intensified.

She was gripping the handrails so tightly that it felt like the metal was bending in her fists.

She recoiled in shock. The metal *had* bent. Where she had been holding the rail it had warped and twisted, sprouting a mane of golden filaments.

What is it? demanded Alzen, sensing her shock.

Isten's amazement grew as she realized he had not intended to channel his power through her.

"Nothing," she muttered. She had no reason to lie to him, but she somehow felt it was important that he did not learn what she had just done.

It's just the bodies, she thought. They reminded me of home.

The *Sign of the Sun* juddered as they reached the shore, its hull scraping along pebbles and rocks. There were remnants of previous deliveries scattered amongst the bodies: broken crates and empty sacks sprawled in the rain-hammered grass. And, as the crew dashed about hurling mooring ropes, Isten saw a welcome party hurrying down through the trees – a dozen or so hiramites, sliding and stumbling in the mud as they ran through the meadow, trying to stop their cloaks being snatched by the fierce wind.

How will I get home? she thought. The sight of the bodies had left her feeling desolate. Suddenly, she no longer cared about the weapons. She just wanted to get away. She had some cinnabar hidden beneath her robes and decided to use it as soon as she could be alone.

When you speak to the phrater, just listen to me. Let me tell you what to say. I've no idea why that soldier behaved so oddly, but Phrater Herbrus will be far too busy to concern himself with you. Then, you just need to spot a chance to touch the weapons crates. All I need is for your hands to be pressed against them and I can complete my work. Once I've transported them back to your temple, all you'll need to do is get back on the boat. It will only take an hour or so to unload everything and then the captain will return to the city and you can go with him.

The hiramites on the boat had gathered at a crudely built jetty, and the one who spoke to Isten waved her over, still looking at her with a wary expression.

Dazed, Isten allowed herself to be shepherded onto the shore, and when she climbed up the riverbank into the meadow, she found herself standing with the laborators. As Alzen predicted, they showed no interest in talking to her, or even looking at her, rushing off up the hillside towards the towers, escorted by some of the soldiers. Isten stood motionless, staring at the heaps of dead bodies. This close, the scene was even more horrific, but none of the other passengers even seemed to notice.

"Quick!" yelled the hiramite who was watching over her, noticing that she was hesitating. "It's not safe." He waved at the distant towers, indicating that Isten should follow the other passengers.

She nodded and hurried off through the rain, keeping her robes wrapped tightly around her.

As she climbed up the slippery hillside, Isten peered at the towers, trying to make out their design. There were three of them and they were huge, hundreds of feet tall, ominous shadows in the mist. Then, as the clouds billowed away, Isten saw them clearly for the first time and staggered to a halt, horrified. They were not towers, but metal-clad titans, wreathed in glistening coils and spines, staring out across the forest, motionless and inert. Or, almost inert. Steam was rising from their clenched fists and a faint glow was visible between their fingers.

"Ignorant Men," gasped Isten, recalling the night of Amoria's death. The strength went from her legs and she looked back towards the bodies, realizing what had happened to them.

What are you doing? demanded Alzen.

They'll remember me, she thought, struggling to stay calm. They chased me into the sewers. If they see me here they'll–

They are not the same Ignorant Men. They are sentinels summoned to guard the walls. They have been conjured by Phrater Herbrus, forged here, in this storm. They won't have been anywhere near the warehouse where your friend died.

Isten shook her head, hearing the logic in Alzen's words but unable to overcome her terror as she looked up at the giants. As the rain lashed their limbs, it flowed in rivulets down the metal, coursing over twines and spirals, giving the impression that they were melting and transforming, just as they did when they pursued her from the warehouse.

"Move!" yelled the soldier who spoke to her earlier, his upside-down mask looming out of the rain. He sounded furious.

Go! ordered Alzen.

Isten began trudging slowly up the hillside, but she could not tear her eyes off the Ignorant Men. She felt as though, at any moment, they would turn and reach down towards her, palms blazing.

As she fell beneath the shadow of the metal giants, Isten tried not to look up at their cloud-mantled faces. She could not bear to see those dead, inhuman eyes.

"Over here!" The hiramite waved her on through the storm.

Isten finally saw what Alzen had actually meant when he spoke of buildings. Cowering beneath the Ignorant Men was a low, circular, brick-built watchtower, only two storeys high, topped with crude, thick embrasures and as grey as the sky. It had deep, arrow-slit windows and it was surrounded by a bristling stockade of sharpened posts. There was a column of smoke snaking up into the rain and figures dashing around the watchtower – laborators, hiramites and brutish, half-naked warriors carrying two-handed axes. Even from outside the stockade, Isten could see the faces sewn into their skin, their armour of blackened screams.

Headhunters, she thought, passing through a gate and entering the camp.

Yes. Some locals obviously had the sense not to attack us. You've seen them before?

I employed some. With your money. To protect the Exiles until we are ready to stand alone.

They'll cut your throat if someone offers them better money.

The hiramite was waving to Isten from the doorway of the watchtower and she rushed towards him, starting to shiver from the cold. He stepped aside as she reached the door, waving her inside.

The entrance hall was a wide, low-ceilinged room, with a staircase at the centre, spiralling up to the next level. The narrow windows did not admit much light, and the place had the air of a crypt: cold, dark and hewn from heavy, damp stone. The walls were cracked in some places and covered in blue-grey lichen, and there were patches of moss on the floor. The only furniture was a table and chairs, just inside the door. The rest of the place looked like a warehouse – there were rows of crates, sacks and locked metal chests stacked at the back of the hall, surrounded by piles of falcatas and discarded armour. The laborators had vanished, presumably up to the next floor, but there were a few more soldiers, crouched in the darkness, fiddling with weapons or adjusting their armour. She was excited to see that some of them were loading crossbows, identical to those used by the Aroc Brothers. Behind her, the crew of the *Sign of the Sun* were already arriving, staggering under the weight of more heavy crates, and Isten noticed that they were branded with the same symbol as her robes. The weapons? she thought, but before Alzen could reply, a hiramite wandered over. He had been talking to the soldier who spoke to Isten on the boat.

"The phrater's upstairs," he said, giving her a suspicious look. He removed his disorientating helmet. He was a young man of twenty or so, but his face was thin and drawn and there were dark circles under his eyes. He wore the same metal cuirass as the soldiers that had just arrived, but his was battered and scorched and one of his arms was wrapped in a bloodstained bandage.

Isten panicked, wondering how to reply, but Alzen quickly interceded.

Say you're here to gather minerals and that you just need somewhere to rest after your journey.

Isten did as she was instructed but the soldier looked unconvinced. "Caystrus tells me you need to explain yourself to the phrater, but he's far too busy at the moment, so you can rest. There are beds and food upstairs." He gave her a warning glance. "The headhunters have warned us of another attack any moment, so don't leave the tower."

"I won't."

The hiramite frowned and Isten realized she had made no effort to lower the pitch of her voice.

He stared at her with a puzzled expression. Then he shrugged, yawned and wandered off out into the rain, fixing his silver helmet back in place.

Are the weapons in those chests? she wondered.

Yes, some, but that's not the full load. There are more still on the boat. You need to wait until they've all been carried up here. Go upstairs.

Isten's head was full of the death she had seen outside, so she shuffled over to the steps like a sleepwalker, cursing her own stupidity under her breath.

She shook her rain-sodden robes as she emerged onto the next floor.

The laborators were huddled around a large stone fireplace, talking to another robed figure that she presumed was the phrater. He was wearing the same robes and flame-shaped helmet she had seen Alzen wear, but he was ancient.

Where Alzen was upright and solid-looking, Phrater Herbrus was stooped and frail. He also looked desperate, swaying and gesticulating angrily as he gave his attendants orders.

None of them paid Isten any attention as she approached the fire, reaching out to the flames. Athanor had made a weakling of her – as a child she would have thought nothing of a good soaking, but now she was shivering. The fire was a large one and the heat felt good, dragging steam from her robes.

She could hear the conversation between the phrater and his servants, but none of it made much sense. They were discussing the contents of bags the laborators were holding and he seemed unhappy about something. Isten looked around and saw that there were more hiramites up here and they looked as haggard as the one she spoke to downstairs. They were sleeping on dirty mattresses near the fire, still wearing their armour and looking like they had been asleep before they hit the floor.

There was a window near Isten and she could still see the rain-drenched bodies outside. Do all of the Elect think it's fine to murder innocent women and children? she thought.

Alzen did not reply for a moment, and when he did, she could feel his rage. *You have no idea what sacrifices are made on your behalf, so you can live safely in the city, indulging your habits. How do you think Athanor has survived all these centuries? It is because the Elect are prepared to take on the burden of preserving your way of life. There is nothing we would not do to preserve Athanor.*

To her shame, Isten realized that Alzen's words were almost identical to her own argument when she was talking to Gombus. She was about to ask Alzen something else when a low, mournful sound rang out across the forest. It sounded like the cry of a wounded animal.

"They're here!" said Phrater Herbrus, hobbling past Isten, leaning heavily on a copper sceptre, using it as a walking stick.

"Man the walls," he said, waving at the stairs. His words were stern but his expression was bleak.

The hiramites leapt to obey, kicking the other soldiers awake and clattering down the stairs, drawing their falcatas.

"Over here!" snapped Herbrus, waving for the laborators to follow him as he approached a wide iron brazier at the back of the room. It was a simple iron bowl, a few feet in diameter and perched on a slender pedestal.

As the laborators rushed to his side, Isten hesitated by the fire, looking through the window. The low bellowing sound was growing louder. The whole valley seemed to shake. "What is that?" she whispered.

"You too!" cried Phrater Herbrus, waving his sceptre at her. "Get over here, quickly." The old man's face was twisted in a grimace and Isten wondered what could have scared one of the Elect. She looked back out of the window. The hiramites had formed into lines behind the stockade, their swords drawn, and the ground was definitely shaking now; she could feel it through her feet.

"Now!" howled Phrater Herbrus, and Isten had no option but to obey.

The other laborators had all gripped the edge of the brazier, so Isten did the same, finding a gap in the circle and holding the battered iron in both hands. The metal was cool and full of lifeless ash. Isten wondered what was expected of her.

He's about to perform a transfiguration, said Alzen in her mind. *You just need to steady the brazier. I don't know what he intends to do, but he hasn't prepared sufficiently. The old fool will burn the place down if he's not careful.*

Phrater Herbrus was glancing anxiously at the nearest window, then began taking powders from a row of small pewter boxes arranged around the edge of the brazier. He muttered unintelligible phrases as he scattered the powders across the ash.

Almost immediately, Isten felt the bowl start to move, vibrating and humming like a tuning fork, causing her arms to tremble.

None of the laborators showed any surprise, so she continued gripping the brazier. The others were echoing the phrater's words, droning them like a prayer, so she moved her lips, pretending to join her voice to theirs.

From outside the tower, she heard a tearing, smashing sound. It was shockingly loud, like an avalanche. Isten expected the phrater to react but he remained hunched over the glowing embers, still scattering powders and chanting.

The charcoal in the brazier was now blazing and, to Isten's shock, she saw a shape starting to form. A bubble was rising in the centre of the brazier, hissing and smoking as it neared the phrater's trembling hand.

The was another crash outside and then the clash of swords and the roar of battle cries.

The brazier was growing hot but Isten felt another heat, coursing from her head, down her neck and into her arms. She felt a dizzying rush as Alzen channelled power through her, joining his skill to Herbrus's.

Herbrus gasped in shock, then laughed, looking relieved. "I've managed it!" he cried, staring in delight at the brazier. "One last time!"

The mound of embers shifted and rolled, turning around.

Isten was so enraptured that it took her a moment to realize what the shape was. There was a man trapped in the charcoal, twisted in agony and as charred as the bodies outside, but somehow alive. He tried to scream, but all that emerged from his throat were plumes of smoke. His eyes had burned away, but he reached straight towards Phrater Herbrus, seeming to sense where he was.

Herbrus leant back as the burning man grasped feebly at the air with heat-warped fingers.

What the fuck is that? thought Isten as Alzen's sorcery faded from her body.

An Ignorant Man. Alzen sounded pleased. *Herbrus is spent, he never would have managed this without my help.*

Isten looked at the struggling shape in horror. It was writhing and shivering in agony. That's an Ignorant Man?

Yes. Or, at least, that's the animus of an Ignorant Man. The fuel that drives it. Its soul.

I thought they were machines.

They are. Machines powered by this. Even the Curious Men do not have the power to bestow sentience. But we can capture it. And we can use it to drive our constructs.

Herbrus raised his sceptre and cried out another command. Flames sprang from the brazier, bathing Isten in heat and enveloping the man thrashing at its centre. It was a surreal sight. The bowl of the brazier was only about a foot deep. There was no logical way it could have held a man. Yet there he was, rising from the inferno, visible from the waist up, restrained by flames that had formed into shimmering bonds.

The flames tightened around the man until he was unable to move, spitting embers and trailing fumes, rigid with pain.

"It is done," gasped Herbrus, staggering back from the brazier. He collapsed to the floor and his sceptre slipped from his grip, clanging on the cold stone.

Some laborators rushed to help him, but others rushed over to the wall to peer out through the windows.

Isten did the same but froze in horror at the sight.

The stockade was in ruins, smashed apart and burning, filling the courtyard with waves of black smoke. It was also drenched in blood – gallons of the stuff, far more than could have come from the fight that was taking place. Hiramites were reeling through the carnage, lashing out with their falcatas or lying butchered and bleeding on the ground. It was a confusing scene. The headhunters Isten had seen earlier were fighting alongside the hiramites, swinging their axes with furious oaths, but there were dozens more headhunters leaping through the breach and hacking their kinsmen down, trying to reach the tower.

Isten barely registered the desperate scrum inside the blood-drenched stockade. She was staring in horror at the battle taking place in the trees. One of the Ignorant Men had come to life and strode into the forest, smashing a wide path through the boughs. It was now looming over the valley like a metal god, heat smouldering from its joints and liquid metal spiralling around its chest. After seeing the man in the brazier, Isten finally understood the aura of violence that radiated from the Ignorant Men.

The metal colossus had one arm raised above its head with

its fist locked around a fountain of dark, swirling blood. The blood was lashing and coiling around the Ignorant Man, battering it with thick cords of gore, and Isten realized it was a creature of some kind. The monster was almost as huge as the Ignorant Man and, as it fought, it let out the same, keening howl Isten had heard earlier. She realized that it must be the being that had destroyed the stockade.

A mouth opened in the column of blood and vomited crimson into the Ignorant Man's face. The blast hit with such force that the colossus staggered backwards, toppling trees as it crashed through the rain.

The fist that was locked around the blood monster flashed white and the creature howled again, thrashing wildly in the Ignorant Man's grip.

Phrater Herbrus had joined the laborators at the window and he was leaning against the embrasure, triumph in his eyes.

Isten backed away, not wanting him to notice her. She rushed to another window to keep watching the battle. From this vantage point, she could see the river. She muttered a curse as she saw that the *Sign of the Sun* was preparing to disembark, the crew dashing back and forth on the deck, keen to be away now their cargo had been unloaded.

What is it? asked Alzen.

The boat's about to leave.

Then go! Now's your chance! Everyone is watching the fight.

She looked around. There were no soldiers left in the tower, and Herbrus and his laborators were all staring out of the windows at the giants crashing back and forth through the trees.

She bolted down the stairs and found no one there.

The crates will be branded with a serpent swallowing its tail.

"I see them," gasped Isten, racing across the room and slapping her palms against the sodden wood. "What do I do now?"

Alzen flooded her body with power. It jolted through her with such force that she almost fell, but she managed to keep her hands pressed against the crates as golden ringlets erupted from beneath her hands, tumbling across the wood and splashing up her arms. The heat in the back of her skull flared and Isten laughed as metal billowed across her skin. A storm ripped through her fingers. It was incredible. She could feel the weapons inside the crates, boiling and changing, reforming at her command.

Then it was gone. Alzen extinguished the power and Isten reeled away from the crates, bereft as his sorcery haemorrhaged from her veins.

It's done, he said. *Get to the boat.*

She ran from the tower, straight into the middle of the battle. Hiramites and headhunters were reeling through banks of rain and smoke, lunging and hacking at each other as the Ignorant Man loomed overhead, wrestling with the fountain of blood.

Isten sprinted through the struggling figures, weaving and leaping as she made for the breach in the stockade. The headhunters had all fought their way in towards the tower and the way seemed clear.

She had almost reached the stockade when one of the headhunters turned and charged across the muddy flagstones towards her.

He was just like the men she had hired in Athanor – hulking and savage, his body stretched and misshapen by the heads he had sewn into his skin. He was covered in wounds and drenched in blood, but showed no signs of flagging. As he reached Isten he planted his feet firmly in the gore, rocked back on his heels and hefted his axe at her head.

Isten ducked beneath the blow and rolled across the floor.

The headhunter howled a curse and lunged after her.

Isten thudded into the corpse of a hiramite and, as she leapt to her feet, she grabbed a falcata from the dead man and brought it up in time to parry the next axe blow.

The axe hit with such force that she tumbled back over the corpse, but she managed to cling onto the sword. As the headhunter launched himself after her, she lashed out with a backhanded strike, ripping another scar across his chest.

As he fell back, clutching the wound, she leapt to her feet and continued sprinting towards the break in the stockade, still clutching the falcata.

She glanced back over her shoulder as she ran and saw the headhunter chasing after her.

He pounded across the heaps of bloody wreckage, his face locked in a snarl, but then he halted, confused, as a shadow fell over the courtyard.

The ground shook as the Ignorant Man strode back down the hillside towards the tower. The blood creature was hanging from the giant's fist, trailing like a bundle of intestines, lifeless and silent.

The hiramites cheered and surged forwards, driving the shocked headhunters back towards the stockade.

Isten took her chance and bolted out through the breach and down the hillside towards the river.

The *Sign of the Sun*'s captain was waiting on the riverbank with a few of his crewmen, watching the battle at the tower with a troubled expression.

As he saw the Ignorant Man return from the trees, the captain nodded and made a decision, waving for his crew to board the boat. "The phrater has everything under control," he yelled. "Weigh anchor!"

"Wait!" cried Isten as she stumbled and slid down the muddy hillside.

The captain had already seen her and his crewmen left the boarding ramps in place until she had safely scrambled onto the deck.

"Quick as you like!" he yelled to his crew, ignoring her as she fell gasping onto the boat. "I don't want one scratch on the *Sign*."

Engines rattled into life below the deck and the boat lurched away from the riverbank.

Isten climbed to her feet, staggered over to the railings and looked back at the battle. The headhunters were still howling and lunging but the hiramites were driving them back out of the courtyard, emboldened by the presence of the Ignorant Man, who was striding away from them, hurling gouts of liquid gold into the trees with one of its hands, and still clutching the dead monster in its other.

Isten felt a flood of relief as she realized the headhunters would be driven back. Then she remembered the bodies that littered the hillside and shook her head, ashamed at herself for feeling so victorious.

What about the next attack? she thought. We've stolen their weapons.

There won't be any more attacks. The Ignorant Man has far more power than Herbrus could have given it on his own. Herbrus will use it to make sure there's no one left to be a threat.

The Ignorant Man was wading off through the forest, hurling metal bolts into the trees and clutching its kill.

Isten looked from the giant to the bodies on the shore with a dreadful sinking feeling.

19

She pictured it all burning: towers and trees, streets, everything curling into a brittle husk, the river boiling and the windows melting. She imagined Athanor dying how the people of Brauron had died, eaten by fat barrels of flame that rolled through masonry and wood, filling the sky with soot. It was mesmerizing. She felt the Exiles gathering around her in the dark but couldn't steal her gaze from the flames. She imagined that she had lit the fire, that it was her mind wreaking the destruction. It felt glorious. It felt like Alzen, breathing magic through her skin.

The Botanical Quarter was never quiet. It always seemed to be having a deranged conversation with itself. It was two hours before dawn, and as the Aroc Brothers crept through its narrow, crevasse-like streets, a woman was screaming abuse from an upper window as someone else sang, drunkenly, on one of the walkways. Neither seemed aware of the other, and punctuating the din was the sound of someone sharpening a metal blade in a series of slow, methodical, screeches. Like all of the Botanical Quarter, the street felt like a tunnel, canopied with a mesh of metal, spine-like projections that reached overhead, stretching from lintels and window frames, grasping at the buildings opposite.

At the head of the Aroc Brothers was a particularly massive specimen called Zhoon. He waved the others on with his crossbow, gesturing at a crossroads up ahead, just a few streets from the Alembeck Temple. Zhoon had been forced to kill several of his brothers before he was accepted as a suitable replacement for Sayal, and his clear, amorphous frame was networked with recent scars. Nevertheless, he was grinning as he approached the crossroads. He had made a deal that would make his position unshakeable. By dawn, every one of the Exiles would be dead and his position would be secured.

They reached the crossroads. There was a single mandrel-fire, hanging from a broken shop front, blinking fitfully across the open sewer at the side of the road.

Zhoon waved for the others to wait behind him, keeping in the shadows, as he walked over to the effluence and dropped to one knee, peering into the filth.

For a moment, he saw nothing, and wondered if he had been betrayed. Then, with a slurping sound, a shape began rising from the muck. It looked like a pile of dinner plates, strung together and raised up by an invisible hand, spilling muck and flies as they rotated. Zhoon grimaced at the smell and stepped back.

The jumble of flat shards rose until it was almost as tall as Zhoon, then turned to reveal the vaguely humanoid shape of a weazen.

"Are you Tok?" demanded Zhoon.

"I didn't think you'd come," it said, its voice a dry scrape.

Zhoon struggled to hide his revulsion at speaking to the creature. The weazens ran drugs into the Zechen baths and had been in direct competition with the Aroc Brothers for years. The last time they met, it had been a bloody fight. "Where are the others?" he demanded.

Tok smiled. "I wanted to make sure you were here first." The weazen turned with a series of clicking sounds and gestured at the sewer. The liquid boiled and rolled as dozens of weazens rose from the rank-smelling liquid, dripping muck and moving with the same jerking twitches as Tok. They were surrounded by flies and midges and seemed to vanish every time their plates were turned side on.

Zhoon nodded at the doors of the Alembeck Temple. "My contact has made sure the doors will be unlocked. There will be a few guards, but most of the Exiles will be asleep."

"I hear they're making a mess of everything," said Tok. "They took control of the fights the Kardus family used to run over on Caspingum Street. And when the Kardus family tried to stop them, the Exiles made short work of them." The creature nodded at Zhoon's crossbow. "They have weapons like yours. But they also have an army of psychotic savages who do whatever Isten asks of them. They're supplying people with cinnabar at a fraction of the price you're–"

"I know all this," snapped Zhoon. He tried to control his rage and waved at his brothers, gathered in the gloom behind him. He had brought every last member of the gang, calling in help from every corner of the district. They had taken heavy losses since the death of Sayal, but gathered en masse like this they still numbered nearly a hundred. "With my brothers and your gang combined, it won't matter who's helping Isten."

"You have the money?"

Zhoon waved to one of his brothers, who rushed over with a crate and handed it to the weazen. Tok examined the contents, nodded, then passed the crate to one of its muck-drenched companions.

Zhoon marched across the street towards the temple, waving for everyone else to follow.

"There's a way in round the back that should also be unlocked," he said, looking at Tok.

The weazen nodded and the strange-looking creatures vanished into the shadows at the side of the temple.

Zhoon climbed the steps, and when he reached the doors he paused to look back. His brothers were right behind him, grinning, crossbows raised.

He shoved the doors open and was met by a wall of darkness. He dropped into a crouch and edged inside, crossbow loaded and ready, as his brothers rushed past him, flooding into the shadows.

Zhoon's huge, gelatinous eyes quickly adjusted to the gloom and he dived behind one of the columns that lined the nave, scouring the room for signs of the Exiles. There was nobody there – only his brothers, rushing from column to column, pale and ghostlike.

He waved his crossbow, indicating the doors at the far end of the nave, and they all rushed forwards in silence, swinging their weapons from side to side, looking for the guards.

Zhoon hissed a warning as he saw movement at the far end of the temple. Then he realized it was Tok, leading the weazens in from the back of the building.

Tok looked puzzled by the sight of the empty building, but Zhoon nodded to the doors that led to the chapels, and the whole group gathered outside the first one.

Zhoon looked around, checking that everyone was ready, then booted the door open.

They rushed into the room, ready to open fire, then stumbled to a halt, lowering their weapons in surprise. This chapel was empty too. There were just a few empty crates and a table in the centre of the room.

There was something on the table, and Zhoon rushed over to look. It was a piece of paper. Someone had drawn a smiling fox on it.

Zhoon shook his head, confused, then felt a rush of fury.

"Trap!" he howled, trying to shove the others back towards the door.

The explosion hit, and Zhoon cowered, covering his head. But then he realized the sound was far in the distance.

He looked around in confusion, surprised to be alive, then shoved his way back out into the nave. There was light pouring in through the temple's open doors. He rushed out of the building with everyone else hurrying after him.

There was a column of fire and smoke on the horizon, stretching high up into the clouds. At its base, even from a few miles away, the vast, staring eye of Bethsan Palace was visible as it collapsed in the heat.

"That's coming from Gamala," said Tok, standing next to him at the top of the steps.

Zhoon nodded, feeling cold with shock.

"Where your palace is?"

Zhoon nodded.

"And all of your cinnabar and money?"

The strength had gone from Zhoon's legs and he sat down heavily on the top step, letting his crossbow clang against the stone as his brothers gathered around him, gasping in horror.

Even at such a distance, the explosion made an impressive sight, lighting up the surrounding buildings and sending a low, rolling thunderclap across the city.

"You're ruined," said Tok. The creature's voice was full of disdain.

"Worse than that," said a voice from the street. Isten strode from the shadows, flanked by dozens of the Exiles. All of them were wearing new black leather hauberks and gripping loaded crossbows. They looked stronger and healthier than Zhoon had ever seen them look before. Their wasted frames and sunken cheeks had vanished, replaced by solid muscle and stern, unyielding stares.

One of the Aroc Brothers grabbed his crossbow, but before he could fire, dozens of bolts thudded into him, punching him backwards through the air and leaving him crumpled against the temple doors.

The Exiles stood in silence, smoke trailing from their crossbows.

Another Aroc Brother reached for his weapon.

Projectiles slammed into him and he fell sideways across the steps. They were not crossbow bolts, but iridescent, shell-like discs.

Zhoon cursed and looked at Tok.

The weazen's arm was still extended and missing some of its sharpened plates.

The fallen man cried out in agony as the discs expanded in his flesh, ripping his skin open as they grew and multiplied. It only took a few seconds for him to be sliced apart, collapsing on the steps as pieces of meat.

Zhoon aimed his crossbow at Tok.

"Don't be an idiot," said Tok. "We're screwed, but she's offering us a way out."

Zhoon looked around. Tok was right. They were all lit up by the light on the front of the temple and had no cover. If he tried to fight it would be a massacre.

Isten stepped into the light with a wry smile on her face, looking at Tok. "The Aroc Brothers aren't just ruined, they're hated by every pusher they've driven out of business and every brothel they've been squeezing. When word gets out that they've lost their weapons, their money and all their red, they'll be hunted down like dogs. It's going to be a messy end for them."

Tok looked at Zhoon to see if he would deny any of this, but Zhoon was staring at Isten with a dazed expression on his face.

The Aroc Brothers all began muttering to each other and some of them seemed on the verge of attacking again. Zhoon's shock started to be replaced by fury. If they were all going to die he would take Isten down first. He turned his crossbow on her.

"Mind you..." said Isten, still smiling as she stepped closer, swinging her crossbow back and forth. "We've only burned your weapons. I told my men to remove all of your cinnabar before they lit the fuse."

"What do you want?" His words were a savage growl.

"You know how it is," she said. "I've got all this stuff to shift and not enough people to sell it. I have enough cinnabar to make all of us rich, if only there was some way we could work together."

Zhoon sneered. "Together? You mean work for you."

She shrugged. "It doesn't matter what we call it. If you

work with me to shift all this cinnabar, you can make just as much money as you made working for Sayal. More, I imagine. Sayal probably kept all the cream for himself, didn't he?"

"You hate us. You want us dead."

Isten's smile faltered. "Not so much." She shrugged. "Sayal crossed a line but now he's gone. And I'm starting to lose my appetite for all this killing." She looked down the street. "I've been thinking about something a friend said. While we keep ourselves busy fighting over drugs, the Elect are free to do whatever they like, laughing at us as we kill each other. It's like we're the punchline to a bad joke."

Zhoon searched for the deceit in her voice, but she sounded oddly genuine.

She waved her crossbow at the mountain of flame in the distance. "I had to wipe out half of the Kardus clan and the Voussans wouldn't yield until I'd burned every one of their clubs down. So much endless fucking killing. None of us were born here. None of us will ever be accepted here. We'll always be the outsiders. Maybe we should try being outsiders together?" She shrugged. "Maybe I'm talking rubbish. How about this, though. You've lost. I've won. But that doesn't have to stop you getting rich."

Zhoon shook his head. Of all the outcomes he had expected from tonight, this one had never crossed his mind. It had to be a trick. He looked at the fire in the distance. The palace's eye had almost vanished. He had always thought it looked like Sayal's eye, watching him, even after he died. Seeing it burn down actually felt like ridding himself of a vengeful ghost. He stared at his crossbow for a moment, then lowered it and looked back at Isten. "I didn't think you had it in you."

Isten raised an eyebrow. "That makes two of us."

20

Not me, thought Isten, succumbing to the dream. I alone am awake.

The headhunters formed a circle on the roof of the temple, near where Puthnok carved her manifesto into the rafters. It was late, and in the moonlight they looked like cultists performing an arcane rite, surrounded by Athanor's glittering lights. Sounds of revelry reverberated from the rooms below as Isten lurched across the roof, cursing and laughing as she struggled to keep her balance. The Exiles and their new allies had seized control of every operation in the Botanical Quarter and even extended their reach into the rest of the city. There was no danger anymore, no threat. Nothing left to do but celebrate.

"Is that Lorinc?" slurred Isten. He looked as drunk as she was and wearing an uncharacteristic grin on his face.

As she approached the group, she saw that there were also some of the Aroc Brothers and a weazen sprawled in the eaves, laughing hysterically, tumbling across the slates like leaves in the breeze.

Isten had consumed so much of Alzen's cinnabar that she couldn't be sure she wasn't dreaming the whole scene. The headhunters were jumping up and down and chanting and, as they lurched through the darkness, the shrunken heads in their skin were laughing along with the weazen, bearing their blackened teeth and rolling their eyes behind swollen, stitched-up lids, grotesquely invigorated by their wearers' excitement.

"Lorinc?" she called.

He turned, grinning, his face flushed. "Isten! Over here!" She had never seen him so happy.

Her legs were feeble with drink and she had to tread carefully as she crossed the roof. Earlier in the evening, Athanor had been blessed with one of its rare showers, leaving everything gleaming and wet and even more hazardous than usual.

Lorinc hauled her into the circle and everyone else bellowed their approval, delighted by the arrival of their triumphant leader.

One of the Aroc Brothers was standing in the middle of the circle, drinking furiously. Isten could not recognize the design on the bottle but it smelled like gin. The drinker was balancing on a beam that stretched over a hole in the roof. Isten had thought she'd made the building secure, but it was so old that more of it kept collapsing. As the man drank, everyone else stamped at the broken beams, causing the hole to shudder and spill dust into the rooms below. Isten could see familiar faces in the crowds down there: Exiles, singing and reeling through the temple, revelling in the peace she had bought them.

The man finished the bottle and leapt clear of the hole to a roar of approval. The drop was over thirty feet. If it had fallen, it would have killed him.

"You're insane," muttered Isten.

They hesitated then laughed wildly as she grabbed a bottle and stepped out onto the beam.

The support shifted worryingly beneath her weight. The danger caused her heart to race and, for a moment, her vision became perfectly sharp.

The crowd began chanting and stamping as she drank. The liquor burned delightfully, strong enough to cut through the tar and the cinnabar and give her an exhilarating sense of weightlessness. She didn't care if the beam broke. She was sure she would simply levitate on the spot, laughing, as the roof fell away from her.

The headhunters howled as she glugged the liquid down, and Lorinc roared along with them.

Isten had almost emptied the bottle when the beam began to give.

The headhunters whooped and took a step backwards.

There were only a few dregs left in the bottle so Isten tipped it back and gulped the last of it down, just as the wood gave way.

She tried to jump out of the hole, but there was nothing to push against. The beam fell away from beneath her foot and she dropped.

Her hands slapped against the ragged edges of the hole, struggling to grip rain-slick tiles.

Hands locked around her wrists and lifted her into the air, free of the rubble that tumbled down onto the distant crowds below.

Lorinc had one of her wrists but she was surprised to see that the other was held by Zhoon.

They hauled her back onto the roof and the three of them rolled into a heap, laughing wildly.

"I didn't think you cared," said Isten.

"You're too useful to die," said Zhoon when they had managed to stop laughing.

"I was only trying to save the gin," said Lorinc, with a despairing shake of his head.

She punched him and they started laughing again.

Zhoon climbed unsteadily to his feet, wandering back over to the other Aroc Brothers, but Lorinc and Isten remained where they were, on their backs, looking at the stars.

"You did it," said Lorinc.

"What?"

"The city's ours."

Isten tried to make a joke, but her mouth was unwilling, emitting a confused mumble instead. She massaged her face, trying to rub sense back into her muscles. "Some of the city," she managed to say.

"Enough of the city," replied Lorinc, sounding suddenly serious. "You got rid of Sayal and you made us rich. I knew you'd do it."

As the roof tiles pressed into the back of Isten's head, she remembered the numbness that was loitering at the back of her skull. It had been weeks since she had gone to the city walls with Alzen, weeks since she felt his alchymia pass through her body, but his mark was still on her arm. Unlike the first time, when she had been so desperate to remove him from her thoughts, this time she had baulked at the idea of wiping his sigil away. He had helped her, just as he said he would, supplying her with endless cinnabar and helping her get the weapons she needed, and she had done as she was asked, selling his drugs right across the slums, so there was no need for them to ever cross paths again. Part of her was relieved, especially after the massacre she had seen in Brauron, but another part of her, a larger part, felt panicked by the idea she would never experience his sorcery again.

"What are you thinking?" asked Lorinc.

Isten felt a rush of guilt. She had spent her whole life trying to escape her mother's shadow, sampling every high in the hope of finding peace, but she knew this was different. Alzen's power lifted her out of herself more completely than anything else she had experienced, but the Elect were the enemy. If there had been any doubt about that, it had evaporated when she had seen those bodies on the riverbank. She shook her head and thought of something that wasn't too much of a lie.

"I was just thinking about Gombus. I haven't seen him since I brought you all to the temple."

The humour faded from Lorinc's eyes. He said nothing but his silence was pointed.

Isten sat up. "Have you heard from him?"

"Puthnok still visits him, but she won't say much– beyond the fact that he's ill and disapproves of all this." He waved at the drunken figures lurching past.

"He disapproves of us being alive or of us being in a position of power?" Isten could not keep the hurt from her voice. "Or does he disapprove of the fact that I've managed to win the loyalty of people who previously wanted to kill us?"

Lorinc held up his hands. "Don't shoot the messenger. It's just what Puthnok told me." He shrugged. "To be honest, I think she's probably putting words in the old man's mouth. I think it's more likely *she* doesn't approve. She's become obsessed with the idea of 'fixing' Athanor. She's decided you're never going to get us home to Rukon, so she needs to spread the good word here instead."

Isten looked past the staggering shapes of the headhunters to the rafters Puthnok had carved. "Spread the good word? Who to?"

"She's been turning up at festivals and bazaars, harassing people and telling them how much better their life would be without the Elect."

"And how's that going down?"

"Who knows? You know what the Athanorians are like – even if they harboured any grudges, I bet they'd never have the balls to show it. They're probably too terrified of the hiramites to be seen listening to Puthnok."

The thought of Puthnok's sad, solemn little face threatened to ruin Isten's good humour. "She's so sure I can't get us home, even though Gombus, who she worships like a god, has always said I will."

"Do you think you can? I think you've proven yourself already, but you know what Gombus and Puthnok want."

"*I* fucking want it." She waved at the drunken figures lurching past. Some of the headhunters were swinging axes at each other, slamming blades into beams just a fraction of an inch from each other's faces, laughing and snorting and refusing to flinch. "I don't want this," she muttered. "I don't want to be in this city, Lorinc. I want to go home. I want to topple statues. I want everything Puthnok wants. I want to see Rakus strung from a tree and our people freed. I just don't know how we'd ever achieve that. Only the Elect steer Athanor. Only they control the conjunctions. However powerful I get, I can't–"

"Isten!" cried someone.

She turned to see Brast clambering over the roof. Unlike everyone else, he looked more grim and skeletal than ever. As always, Isten felt a mixture of guilt, irritation and affection at the sight of his sneering face.

"What the fuck is all this?" he demanded, staring at the drunken mayhem.

Isten was about to reply, but he waved his hand dismissively. "It doesn't matter. I need to talk to you."

Isten tried to sober up, sensing, even through her fug of drugs and wine, that Brast had something important to say. She stood and stretched, taking a deep breath, then looked back at him. His long, greasy hair was hanging down over his face, but his expression was not as ironical as usual. He looked worried.

"There are imperial agents in Athanor," he said, leaning close and lowering his voice.

"You're the second person who's told me that," she said, remembering her conversation with Colcrow in the Zechen baths, weeks earlier. "How do you know?"

"Because the fuckers jumped me after I dropped you off at the Sisters of Solace. I was in the arboretum near the Valeria Bazaar. I'd seen one of them earlier, before I left Crassus Street, and I knew he was from Rukon, but I'd never seen him before – not at any of your Exiles gatherings or any other time."

"They jumped you?" she asked. "Trying to do what? Kill you?"

"Not sure. I had a knife to one of their throats and was about to get an answer to that question when the hiramites turned up and we all had to make a run for it."

"Why didn't you come and tell me?"

He scowled. "How the fuck would I find you? I never dreamt you'd be back here. Then tonight someone told me Colcrow has ordered all his lackeys to come here because you've turned it into a palace."

Isten was still struggling to focus on him. "What..." She shook her head, battling to get her words out. "How do you know they were agents?"

"Because they looked exactly like imperial agents. And they were behaving how you'd imagine spies to behave – sneaking around and tailing me."

"We'd better watch our backs," muttered Lorinc, but his eyelids were drooping and he sounded as though he had only half followed what Brast had said.

Isten went and sat next to Brast. "How could they have come here from Rukon?"

He shrugged.

"But you don't think they were from Athanor?"

He shook his head. "I've never seen them before. They've both been badly burned at some point. Their heads were a complete mess of scars. I know there are hundreds of us in this city, but over the years I think I'd remember people who looked like that. And their accents were still strong, like ours were when we first arrived here."

Isten thought for a moment, looking at the now snoring Lorinc, thinking about what he'd said about getting home. "If it was true, and we knew how they'd travelled to Athanor, we could maybe find a way to get home by the same method."

"Maybe they just happened to be in whatever place Athanor has just arrived at. Maybe it was a fluke. They could have been travellers, far from home in some foreign land who just happened to be in the vicinity when Athanor appeared in the sky – and then they could have just got dragged in with all the other new immigrants."

"But, according to Colcrow, they're here deliberately, working for Emperor Rakus, trying to find out if I'm alive. And if they were spying on you, that would seem to fit. That implies Rakus sent them here."

Brast looked away from her, out at the city, at the thousands of glittering lights that surrounded them. From here they could see the river, still busy with lamp-lit barges and tugs. "I suppose..." he muttered.

There was a smash of splintering wood and a howl of pain from over near the hole in the roof. One of the headhunters had managed to sever an ear. The injured savage was laughing as he tried to stem the jet of blood rushing from his head and most of the others were just as hysterical. The axe-wielder was trying to grab the injured man and stop the bleeding. The Aroc Brothers in the group were helpless with laughter. Only the weazen seemed unamused. It was busy trying to walk, drunkenly, along the apex of the roof, without plunging to the Blacknells Road.

Brast stared at them in disbelief.

Isten grimaced, imagining how grotesque and embarrassing this must all look to someone like Brast. She thought of what Gombus would say, or even Puthnok.

"Can you remember the route you took when they followed you?" she asked him.

He was still watching the bloody scene behind her with sneering disbelief. "What?" he said. "What route?"

"Can you remember where you went when the imperial agents were following you?"

"Oh. Yes, but there's nothing to say they'll be there again."

Isten watched as the injured headhunter found his severed ear and began waving it at everyone, shaking with laughter.

"It's worth a try," she muttered, suddenly keen to leave the temple.

21

What is it, she asked, no more than three or four years old, grasping with her fat little fist. Gombus smiled and pulled the ring free. It was made of soft, russet gold, covered in dents and hanging on a chain around his neck. It was your mother's, he said, holding it tight. Isten snatched the memory and buried it, panicked, afraid to let her thoughts catch the light. Why would he have kept her mother's wedding ring?

It took Isten and Brast nearly half an hour to climb down safely from the roof and fight their way through the crowd to the front doors of the temple, but even then, with the first hint of dawn colouring the sky, there was no sign of the celebrations ending. Isten was glad to be away. For the last week or so she had enjoyed the sense of triumph, and freedom from fear, but now, as she staggered back out onto the Blacknells Road, she could feel the falsity of it all. The Exiles might be at the top of the heap, but it was a pitiful heap. True power was as far out of her reach as ever, hidden beyond the curved, impenetrable walls of the Temple District.

Brast was watching her with his usual wry expression, as though sensing her comedown, but he held back from making any comment as they padded off between the arches of twisted metal that covered the street. They made their way through the docks with the sun beginning to glimmer through the city's loops and curls and finally, around an hour later, they reached Crassus Street and, at its far end, the sprawling, driftwood facade of Alabri House. Through the building's arched verandas, Isten could glimpse its peaceful gardens and she felt an overwhelming yearning to enter. But then, as they walked down the street, she had the dreadful feeling that she would not be welcome – that her union with Alzen would be seen as too strange and unwholesome, even for the Sisters of Solace. She remembered her reflection looking back at her from the *Sign of the Sun*, dressed in the saffron-hued finery Alzen had loaned her. She should have burned the robes and discarded the chains and keys – they would be hard to explain if discovered, but something had stopped her. She had stashed them in a chest in her room at the temple, the bright yellow cloth buried beneath sacks and piles of black leather war gear. The Sisters would know, she realized, as they approached the path leading to the front door. They would see her desire for Alzen's grotesque sorcery.

"You're not going in?" Brast looked surprised as she halted at the bottom of the path and turned to face the street.

She shook her head. "If I go in there I could be gone for another year," she said, trying to sound flippant, but she could not hide the worry in her voice.

"Surely you owe them thanks," he replied, speaking with his usual scorn. "Didn't they introduce you to your secret contact? Aren't they responsible for your good fortune?"

Good fortune. The words did not seem to fit how Isten

was feeling. She shook her head. "Where were you when you first spotted the agents?"

He watched her for a moment longer, a curious expression on his face, then he shrugged and nodded to a building opposite. A much humbler structure than Alabri House with a narrow alleyway running down its side. "I saw him there, loitering by the wall. I could see he was one of us at first glance, but I didn't think too much of it." He nodded down the road to a crossroads. Like many of the crossroads in Athanor, it looked more like a petrified explosion than a cross, with roads stretching up and down as well as left and right. "But then, when I headed down towards the Valeria Bazaar, I noticed that he was following me, and doing it in such a ridiculously nonchalant way that it had to be on purpose."

Isten crossed over the road to look at the alleyway. A few lizards scattered at her approach, but there was no sign of anyone lurking in the early morning shadows.

"This leads to Troas Square," she muttered. "He could have come from any direction." She strode back onto the street and headed for the crossroads, taking the road that plunged down into the city. It was a steep incline and she was still drunk, so they linked arms as they walked, like an elderly couple. The sky was cloudless but it was too early to be hot and there was a wonderful clearness to the air that combined with wine and cinnabar to wash away the sadness that gripped her when she saw Alabri House. It was ridiculous, but she suddenly felt certain she was going to find the agents. All these years she had thought it insane that the Exiles might be able to find a way home, but today, with the sun glinting on the walkways overhead and the fresh morning air in her lungs, anything seemed possible.

As she walked, she thought about the Saraca, snaking and rolling through the city, its oily waters crashing against the boats and hovellers. Then she pictured the lean-tos gathered at its banks. She saw a crowd gathering in the junk-strewn mud, with the dawn flashing on the river behind them. She paused. The image was oddly vivid. She wondered why she was daydreaming, with such clarity, about the river.

Brast looked at her, frowning. "What's the matter?"

She shook her head. "That cinnabar we've been selling. It's strange stuff."

"Do you need a rest?"

She shook her head again, but the scene on the riverbank was growing even clearer in her thoughts. It seemed less like a daydream and more like an actual dream. The crowds of scavengers and beggars were forming around a glittering object that was jolting down the beach. It was a palankeen. It was taller than the crowds, its gold, wire-framed, egg-shaped carriage visible over their heads, lurching and swinging from side to side as it approached a hut. As the palankeen neared the ramshackle structure, Isten's viewpoint changed. She was no longer looking at the carriage from afar; she was inside it, looking out, viewing the crowds through the ornate, delicate bars of its cage. The vision seemed more real than the road in front of her. She could smell the unwashed mob that was pressing around the palankeen, wailing prayers and begging for help, and she heard the gulls, screaming overhead, fighting over scraps. Attendants drove back the crowds and the egg-shaped carriage unlaced itself, revealing the marvellous ingenuity of its mechanisms.

She stepped down and waved at the crowds, giving them her blessing, then turned to face an old man who hobbled out of the hut, leaning on a stick. He bowed to her, his eyes full of tears. "It's my son," he said. His voice was trembling with fear, but he still held himself with dignity, even when addressing one of the Elect.

"You've done all you can for him," she heard herself say. It was not her voice, but it was familiar. "I'm Phrater Alzen. I've come to ease his passing."

As she spoke the words "Phrater Alzen", the dream vanished and Isten was left facing Brast. He was staring at her in shock.

"What did you say?"

Panic gripped her. "Nothing. I mean, it's gibberish." She tried to laugh. "This cinnabar is so powerful. I'm still seeing things." She gave him a troubled look. "What *did* I say?"

"You said you were a phrater and that you've come to ease my passing." Brast always wore the same polished veneer of derision and cool, but his mask had slipped. He looked horrified. "Who *is* your contact?"

"A man I met in Alabri House who wanted to shaft Sayal as badly as we did."

They stared at each other.

"Who is Phrater Alzen?" asked Brast, wincing.

"I've no idea."

The lie was so obvious that Brast's grimace grew even more pronounced.

"It's just the cinnabar," she muttered. "I'm talking gibberish."

Brast shook his head and looked at the crossbow strapped to Isten's back. "Only the Elect make these weapons."

"I stole them."

He closed his eyes, massaging his greasy mop of hair, as though battling a headache. "What have you got us mixed up in?"

"Nothing I can't handle." She was growing annoyed with him. "I've armed us and saved us from starvation. Now, if you'll show me the rest of this route, I might even be able to get us all home."

He nodded, loosed his head and began staggering off down the street, but he still had the same anguished expression on his face and he would not meet her eye as she lurched after him.

By the time they reached the Valeria Bazaar, the stallholders had already arrived and begun unloading their wares. Sacks of grain, tea and spices were slammed down onto the paving stones as Isten and Brast made their way past the entrance and carried on down the street.

"I was heading for that park," said Brast. His voice sounded oddly flat and he was still avoiding her gaze.

Isten's mind was racing. What would she do? Would Brast tell the others what she had said? He had no love for the other Exiles, but if he had guessed that she was in league with the Elect he might feel duty-bound to warn the others where all their newfound wealth had come from. She could not let that happen. She imagined the look on Gombus's face if he found out the beloved daughter of the revolution had sunk so low she was working with Athanor's despotic elite. She could not bear for him to learn of this final disgrace.

She nodded for Brast to continue towards the park, wondering what she could do to stop him.

He finally looked at her and she saw fear in his eyes. "The first of them was joined by a second," he said, speaking in the same numbed tones. "I saw him come out of the bazaar."

They entered the arboretum, hit by the scent of the frankincense trees as they approached the tomb on the hill.

Isten stumbled to a halt and leant against one of the trees, her head full of another vision. She was now inside the riverside hut, standing over a youth sleeping on a heap of sacks. The youth was emaciated and his skin was an unwholesome grey, but hope flashed in his eyes as he looked up at her. "Phrater," he said, trying to sit up and bow. She placed a comforting hand on his frail arm and took out a silver, egg-shaped box. Isten remembered it from when she first met Alzen in the library at Alabri House.

"Don't worry," she said, speaking to the youth in Alzen's voice as she opened the egg and lifted out a sheet of cloth. "I've come to help you."

The vision faded and, once again, she was left facing Brast's dazed expression.

He shook his head and backed away. "What have you done?" he whispered.

She reached out but he turned and bolted, weaving unsteadily between the contorted trees and heading back towards the park gates.

Isten was horrified. He was going to tell the others. Everything would be over. No Exile would ever speak to her again.

Without thinking about what she was doing, she whipped the crossbow from her back and aimed it at the fleeing figure of Brast.

The sun had now cleared the rooftops and the arboretum

was empty. She had a clear shot. Her finger hovered over the trigger.

Then she lowered the weapon and watched Brast vanish through the gates.

She threw down the crossbow, dropped onto the grass and slumped against the tree, weak with despair.

As she sat there, she stared at the discarded weapon, considering how close she had come to killing Brast. It was cool in the shade of the tree and she had the unnerving sensation that she was a corpse, that she had died weeks ago and spent the intervening time as some grotesque kind of revenant, masquerading as Isten while actually being just another device employed by the Elect. At the thought of the Elect, she was back in the hovel, draping the sheet of cloth over the confused-looking youth, seeing through Alzen's eyes.

"I have mastered the Art," Alzen said. "I alone have found the way to achieve the ultimate transformation. I alone have learned how to become the Ingenious."

The youth seemed powerless to reply as Alzen spread the cloth over his wasted limbs. To her horror, Isten realized that the cloth was actually skin. She could see the outline of hands and arms, and even a stretched, eyeless face.

"My power is already greater than any phrater within living memory," said Alzen as the skin wrapped itself around the terrified youth. "I learned that the ultimate catalyst is the human soul, captured at the moment of flight. At first, I skulked around for windfalls, waiting for people to approach death, but then I realized that the influx of power is even greater if I simply pluck the apple myself."

The youth managed to groan in horror as the skin settled over his face.

"I understand," said Alzen, sounding sympathetic. "The pain must be a torment, but console yourself with this fact. When you consumed that cinnabar that the Exiles sold you so cheaply, your soul was ennobled, lifted above your vulgar heritage into something wonderful – into fuel for my glorious fire."

The youth was twitching and moaning in agony as the skin melted into him, burning the life from him.

Isten cried out in pain, expressing the anguish the youth could not.

Alzen whirled around, looking at the rest of the hovel. He had heard her cry. "Who's there?" he demanded, rummaging through piles of salvage and scraps of cloth. "I must not be disturbed."

The image fell away and Isten was back in the arboretum, sobbing and gasping, gripping her head. Dreadful realization flooded through her. Alzen's power – the power she had channelled, and still craved – was the fruit of murder. Alzen's power was born of death – from the final, tortured seconds of the innocents that he claimed to be helping. From addicts made ready by the cinnabar *she* had been selling.

Isten wept and curled into a ball, clawing at her scalp where she could still feel the numbness that signified Alzen's presence in her mind. Then she remembered the mark on her arm and sat up. She rolled up her sleeve and spat on the faded sigil, rubbing at it furiously. "Never again," she muttered, as it started to disappear.

Then she halted. It was not enough to erase his mark. Madness and despair were rising in her thoughts, boiling like thunderheads, threatening to blast away what little reason she had left. She had to do more than remove his mark. An idea started to form in her mind. The vision had been reality, she was sure of it. Something unexpected had happened, something Alzen had never foreseen. She had guessed it that day on the *Sign of the Sun,* when her fury warped the handrail. Her bond with Alzen was deeper than he intended. And it now went both ways. She was starting to see things through his eyes. She could use that. She could use it against him. She had to. Alzen could not be left free to murder more defenceless victims.

Isten's breathing calmed a little and she rolled down her sleeve, hiding the mark again. The numbness was still there in her mind, the link unbroken.

She took a deep breath and climbed to her feet, leaning against the tree trunk as she stood. She was about to stoop and grab the crossbow, but she could not bring herself to touch it.

A shadow drifted across the grass as someone approached. She dropped into a crouch, drawing her dagger, remembering that she had come to the arboretum looking for imperial agents.

It was Brast. He was watching her from the other side of the path. He looked wary and troubled. She had never seen him with such naked emotion on his face. He was staring at the dagger she had drawn on him.

She lowered it, embarrassed.

"Don't tell me what it was," he said.

"What?"

"Whatever you did to get those drugs. I never want to know."

She was about to lie, to protest, when he held up a hand for silence and continued.

He nodded to her tear-streaked face. "I don't want to leave you like this." He grimaced and looked at the ground. It was clearly painful for him to speak so openly. "I hate what they've done to you – Gombus and Puthnok and all of them. You never asked to be their saviour." He looked up and his eyes were full of sympathy. "I remember when we were children, Isten, before they got their hooks in you, before they drove us to..." He waved his wine bottle in a vague gesture, signifying all their various vices. "I don't want you to end like this, Isten. I won't talk about what you said. I won't tell the others."

Relief flooded through her and she was about to thank him when he held up his hand again.

"On one condition."

She nodded, dreading whatever he said next. He loved her. He had done since they were teenagers. What did he want in exchange for his silence?

"You have to let me help you," he said.

"Help me what?"

"Help you escape this – whatever mess you're in."

She massaged the back of her head, wondering if such a thing was possible. Yes, she decided, remembering her plan, and the mark on her arm. It had to be possible. And Brast *could* help.

"Get me sober," she said.

Brast's eyes widened. He clearly hadn't expected that.

"Lock me in a room if you have to, but get me sober. I have a plan. I know what to do, but I need to think straight."

He laughed bitterly. "It won't be pretty. After all these years."

"I know."

"What about the agents?"

Isten shook her head. "What was I thinking? Why would they be waiting here, where they were weeks ago? They don't live in this park, hiding in the bushes, just waiting for me to walk past." What had seemed so sure just an hour ago, now seemed absurd. "I was drunk. I wasn't thinking straight."

Brast looked around the park, nodding slowly. Then he noticed the crossbow Isten had thrown on the grass.

He stared it as if it were a serpent. The sight of it seemed to make up his mind. He held out his hand. "A sober Isten. Is the world ready?"

22

Isten lied without compunction or shame, armouring herself in fiction before she learned to walk. She knew, even then, that survival hinged on the speed of her wits, and the strength of her lies.

Alzen ripped Coagulus from the corpse and slumped against the wall of the lean-to, waiting for rapture to arrive. The noise of the scavengers outside faded away as he sank into his own mind, chasing the currents of Sacred Light that Coagulus had leached from the youth. He could see the final point of transfiguration. It was there in the eddies and whorls of his conscience: supreme reason, the Absolute; omnipotence; the Ingenious. So close now he could almost touch it. Absolute mastery of the Art. Freedom from the limitations of his flesh. Ascension. For a second, he thought he had it – that he was going to lock his fist around divinity and rise from this wretched hovel reborn, ablaze with insight and power. Then it slipped away, like every time before.

He cursed and opened his eyes, assailed by the grim reality of his surroundings: filth and flies and, through the packed-earth walls, the wailing, ugly cries of the boy's family and the clamour of the gulls. He felt crushed. He felt the weight of his body like a heavy suit, anchoring him to the temporal world.

"Where is it?" he hissed, glaring at the corpse. Every one of his augurs had told him he would achieve his goal. He had done everything correctly. So why did the moment of ascension still elude him? When he was working with Isten, passing his alchymia through her body, he'd felt as though he was on the cusp of success, but now, if anything, he seemed to be falling back from his goal. Despair threatened to overcome him. Then he shook his head. He would not give up now. Not when he had done so much. He felt a brief chill as he recalled the multitude of corpses he had left behind, just like the twisted wretch lying before him. If he wasn't the Ingenious, he was a simple, sordid murderer. The idea was absurd. He just needed to feed more souls through Coagulus. The final steps were always the hardest. He just needed to increase the volume of Prima Materia. He needed more souls. The thought calmed him. He pushed himself away from the filthy wall and dusted down his ceremonial gown.

He arranged the corpse in a more dignified position and slowly opened the door, allowing the grieving relatives to enter.

"The plague had spread to every part of his body," he said, clasping hands and patting shoulders. "There was nothing I could do except ease his passing."

Dozens of whingeing, malodorous wretches forced their way into the hovel asAlzen pushed his way back outside into the morning light, gasping for fresh air. There was none to be had. It was already getting hot and the slums were hazed by a miasma of flies and steam. The crowds outside were uninterested in the tragedy in the hovel. They were just amazed to see a Curious Man at such close quarters.

They swarmed around him in their dozens, calling out for blessings and dropping to their knees in the mud, full of hope and fear.

Alzen waved vaguely as his attendants led him back to the palankeen, accepting their prayers. The metal carriage unfolded at his approach and he breathed a sigh of relief to have a golden barrier between him and the mob. He settled back in the seat and the machine jolted into life, the spider-like legs raising him up, away from the mud.

As his carriage lurched and swayed along the riverbank, his attendants went ahead, asking for news of people with plague. Thanks to the Exiles, almost everyone in the district had at least sampled the cinnabar he laced with alchymical minerals. It would be easy enough to find someone appropriate.

A scrawny, dark-haired woman ran past, trying to get a glimpse of him, and Alzen was reminded of Isten. He had found himself thinking of her a lot over the recent weeks. Since he returned from the city walls, he had still received the occasional glimpse of her thoughts. She must have decided to leave his mark on her arm. He had only peered into her mind a few times before he tried to pretend the link had been severed. There was something sordid yet enticing about it that troubled him. It was like the vile woman had a hold on him. It would be possible for him to sever the connection himself, but something stopped him. He could not help wondering if his lack of progress stemmed from the fact that he was no longer conveying his power through her. He shook his head, repulsed by the idea of wallowing in her consciousness. More souls. That was all he needed. And the slums were full of them.

Sunlight flashed in his eyes, blinding him for a moment, and when his vision cleared he saw that some of the crowds were rushing away from him, excited about something else – something in the sky.

Alzen leant out of his carriage and saw a dazzling sheet of gold, flipping and tumbling through the clear blue vault, approaching from the direction of the Temple District. It looked like a pillar of flame had fallen from the sun and was dropping towards the Saraca. It was so bright that it took Alzen a few seconds to discern its true shape: an enormous griffin, wrought of the same golden wirework as his palankeen – broad, glimmering wings, the body and tail of a lion and the head of an eagle, all intricately woven from metal strands and coils and ignited by the glory of alchymia.

The crowds on the riverbank were overcome with emotion. To see one Curious Man was a miracle, to see a second was beyond imagining.

The winged carriage looped and banked for several minutes, eliciting cries of delight from the crowd before finally dropping down onto a mud bank, pounding its mighty pinions as it landed, enveloping the crowd in clouds of dust and rubble before finally settling and folding its wings on its back.

Alzen steered his carriage back up the riverbank, weaving between huts and piles of salvage, making for the proud, metal creature.

By the time he reached the mud bank, the griffin's back was unfurling and unthreading, revealing the yellow-robed passenger within.

Even before the Curious Man had climbed out of the cage, Alzen recognized his portly, awkward frame.

"Phrater Ostan," he called, as his palankeen settled next to the griffin. He could never remember seeing Ostan outside of the Temple District. Like most of the Elect, he considered the rest of the city a dangerous, squalid place, best left to the vulgar commoners. Alzen immediately sensed that something was wrong. Only dire news would have dragged Ostan to the slums.

Ostan stepped from his carriage with reluctant, prissy steps, clearly horrified by the idea of walking in the rubbish-strewn mud.

Alzen climbed from his carriage and rushed to help Ostan, and the crowds on the riverbank fell quiet, watching the scene with shocked expressions.

"What are you doing out here?" demanded Alzen as he reached Ostan and grabbed his hand, just in time to stop him tumbling headlong into the filth.

Ostan kept his flame-shaped helmet on, but Alzen could see the panic in his eyes. "We're going to war," he gasped, lowering his voice so that only Alzen would hear.

"War?" Alzen laughed. "What are you talking about?"

Ostan's voice was trembling. "Phrater Herbrus has been killed."

Alzen shook his head, unable to speak for a moment. He had never heard of such a thing. The Elect died of old age, of course. Even the Art could not entirely protect them from the clutches of time, but to be killed? It was unthinkable. "How?"

"Savages, out on the city walls. They attacked his camp in huge numbers." Ostan placed a hand across his chest, as though trying to protect it. "They butchered him, Alzen. They cut off his head."

"Not possible." Alzen shook his head, dazed. "He had summoned Ignorant Men. I saw…" He faltered, remembering that no one knew what he had seen. "I saw him when he left the city," he said, instead. "He was planning to use Ignorant Men to crush any of the headhunters who resisted."

Ostan leant back against the flank of his griffin, looking dejected. "They used monsters, Alzen. Some kind of demonic monsters. They overwhelmed his Ignorant Man and then killed Herbrus."

"What about the hiramites? He had dozens of soldiers with him."

"Apparently, the day before the attack, someone broke into the camp and stole the weapons Herbrus had requested. The hiramites were massacred."

Alzen felt suddenly weak. Killing the vulgar was one thing; causing the death of a Curious Man was another. "Surely the Ignorant Man was more than enough defence?"

Phrater Ostan did not seem to hear him. He was still slumped against his carriage shaking his head. Then he stood up again, grabbing Alzen's arm. "The Old King is sending us to the city walls. He wants us to drive the savages back."

"What?" Alzen's panic grew. "I can't leave the city. My work is progressing. I'm close to something wonderful."

Ostan sounded annoyed. "We all have work, Alzen. I have been–"

"You don't understand!" snapped Alzen. "This is important. I have to be here." He waved his sceptre at the slums. "I can't leave the city."

Ostan's voice was hollow. "It's a royal edict, Alzen. You and I and all the elder phraters are to go. We must finish our work in the temple and ready ourselves for the journey."

Alzen glanced around at the crowds. "Very well, I will finish up here and–"

"No, you don't understand. I have been sent to fetch you. The Old King has summoned us to his private chambers. He wants to speak to us today, to explain what he requires of us. We have to leave now."

Alzen's pulse was rushing in his ears. The sunlight flashing on Ostan's carriage burned into his head, clamping around his temples, causing him to grimace.

Ostan fell silent, staring at the mud and, even through his panic, Alzen pitied the man. Ostan never left his laboratory if he could help it. The idea of leaving the city must have been horrific for him. Alzen placed a reassuring hand on his shoulder.

"Don't worry, Ostan. I'll make Seleucus see sense. It's madness to send men like you and me to do the work of hiramites. We're not soldiers. We should be here, pursuing our studies."

Hope flashed in Ostan's eyes. "Do you think so? Do you think you can reason with him?"

"Of course. This is absurd." Alzen began climbing back into his carriage. "I'll meet you there in an hour. And we'll put a stop to this nonsense."

Ostan nodded, looking slightly less afraid, and climbed back into his own machine. "For God and the Temple," he said.

"God and the Temple," grunted Alzen, as his carriage lurched into movement, scattering peasants and attendants as he powered back up to the road.

• • •

Mightiest of all the domes in the Temple District was the one topping Mosella, the private residence of the Old King. The Specular Adulis was a mountainous, mirrored vault, studded with pearls and rotating constantly, powered by hidden engines of such subtlety and ingenuity that one appeared to be witnessing the revolutions of the heavens. Huge sconces lined the walls, spewing columns of scented smoke that coiled beneath the vault, confounding the eye and adding to the sense that the spinning dome was not the product of human hands, but a glimpse of infinity.

Alzen strode hurriedly across the octagonal hall, his robes hissing behind him over the cool, tiled floor. Other phraters were arriving from dozens of doorways, muttering greetings and looking as anxious as the last time Seleucus had summoned them together.

Beyond the great vault of the Specular Adulis, Mosella became a maze of antechambers and chapels, all constructed of the same polished glass as the dome. Light filtered down through the facets, landing on the monochrome mosaics that snaked across the floors, portraying serpents and dragons devouring their own tails.

Alzen followed the flow of the crowd, acknowledging each greeting with a nod of his head, but refusing to be drawn into conversation. Dozens of hiramites lined the approach to the Old King's private audience chamber. Seleucus's honour guard wore the same upside- down helmets as the soldiers that patrolled the city but, rather than falcatas, they carried tall, barb-tipped spears, like ceremonial harpoons, and their golden armour was worked in mimicry of the spirals that surrounded Ignorant Men.

The guards remained motionless as the phraters flooded into Seleucus's chamber and Alzen barged his way to the front of the crowd, keen to speak with the Old King.

The room was built of the same glass architecture as the rest of the building and diamonds of light splashed across every surface, making it hard to see clearly. It was another octagonal room, but there was no dome, just a low, undulating ceiling of glass planes that gave the impression of water, seen from beneath, shimmering in the light of mandrel-fires that lined the walls. The room was cool and dimly lit and Alzen had the strange sense he was beneath the waves of a restless sea.

Seleucus was seated on a throne at the far end of the long, oval room. In this gloomy, low-ceilinged chamber he looked even more impressive, like a god of the deep, slouched in his abyssal throne, his armour blinking and glittering in the playful light. His lion was at his side and his staff of office lay across his lap. He was paying no attention to the worthies who were gathering before him, listening intently to one of his attendants, an ancient, wraith-thin laborator called Visalta who had served the Elect for as long as Alzen could remember.

Visalta was leaning close to the throne, whispering urgently into Seleucus's ear. The confusing light refracted through the ceiling combined with the wire mesh around the Old King's face to give the impression that the metal was moving, snarling and leering in response to whatever the laborator was telling him.

"Alzen," whispered Phrater Ostan, fighting his way through the crowd.

Alzen nodded and waved him over.

Ostan had removed his helmet and looked even more panicked than he had in the slums.

"What is it?" he hissed, stooping to let Ostan speak in his ear.

"The weapons are in the city!" whispered Ostan.

"Weapons?"

"The weapons stolen from Phrater Herbrus. They're here, in Athanor. They're being used by the gangs in the Botanical Quarter."

Alzen kept his expression blank. "How can anyone know that?"

"They bear the same marks. And they're unmistakable anyway." Ostan shook his head. "Do you realize what this means? The weapons weren't stolen by savages from Brauron. They were taken by someone in the city and brought back somehow." He spoke more quietly. "They were not stolen by natural means. It was alchymia. Whoever was behind the murders in the warehouse and Bethsan Palace was involved in this too."

"Not necessarily. Perhaps the headhunters have some kind of primitive magic of their own. That would explain Phrater Herbrus being killed. He was a powerful practitioner of the Art. It seems strange that even a large army of savages could have overwhelmed him."

Ostan nodded vaguely but looked unconvinced, still grimacing. He was about to speak when the Old King addressed the gathering.

"My brothers," he said, spilling coils of smoke from his mask. "For long centuries, we have been free to focus on our studies, safe in our temples. Safe in the knowledge that our brave legions of hiramites will safeguard each new conjunction." He paused, looking at the light playing across his armour, shaking his head. "But now the unthinkable has happened. One of our own, a member of this court, has been killed."

There was an explosion of gasps and whispers. Clearly, many of the phraters had not heard the news until this moment.

Seleucus held up one of his wire-entangled hands for silence.

"Some crimes are too great to go unpunished. Our rule has been unchallenged for countless centuries, but if it became public knowledge that we are fallible, mortal beings, prey to the same dangers as a vulgar commoner, the status quo we have worked so carefully to secure could be at risk."

Alzen looked round at a sea of shocked, horrified faces. No one doubted the truth of Seleucus's words.

"Phrater Herbrus was a loyal servant of the Temple," continued the Old King, "but we must make no mention of his murder. Word of it must never spread to the city streets. It could have catastrophic consequences."

Alzen wanted to sneer at Seleucus's dramatic tone, but he had to accept that this could be dangerous. Their rule was, in part, secured by the myth of their inhumanity. If it was known that they could be killed like any other man, everything could change.

"But first," said Seleucus, "we must ensure that the savages responsible are crushed. The majority of our new citizens have shown all the gratitude we would expect, but there is a specific faction, a particularly barbaric tribe, who object to our arrival."

"Why, Your Majesty?" cried one of the phraters, his shock

so great that it led him to break protocol and interrupt Seleucus's speech.

Seleucus shrugged. "Religion. The usual stumbling block. They follow some obscure creed that states they, and they alone, can inhabit the stretch of coastline we have arrived at. It is not unusual, as you know, to encounter some resistance, but what is unusual is the power they have harnessed. When they attacked Phrater Herbrus, they were accompanied by beings that seemed more like columns of blood than physical creatures. Herbrus was an experienced and powerful practitioner, but these blood serpents devoured his soldiers and even the Art was not enough to preserve him." He gripped his staff and banged it on the royal dais. "We must act fast. And we cannot leave this matter to the hiramites. I need you to prepare your most powerful distillations and instruments. I will give you a week to ready yourselves."

"We'll leave the city?" asked the same phrater, his fear obvious.

Anger crept into Seleucus's voice and he hammered down his staff again. "You will *crush* these savages. And you will preserve the sanctity of this order. You will make sure that no one ever hears of this atrocity. You will turn the full majesty of the Art on that coast, until there's nothing left but ash and ghosts."

A stunned silence fell over the room. Seleucus's rage had filled the air with a ceiling of smoke, but Alzen's mind was elsewhere. A week? And then he would be battling savages miles from the slums, miles from his laboratory. His breath came in short, shallow gasps and his vision started to darken. This could *not* happen. He could not leave when he was so close. The very next death might be the one to elevate him.

"All of us, Your Majesty?" he asked, breaking the silence. "We all need to leave?"

Seleucus's voice was taut with suppressed rage. "Do you have more important matters to attend to, Phrater Alzen?"

All eyes turned towards Alzen in shock. He wanted to howl at them. They cowered and snivelled before Seleucus as though he really was a god, but if they had shown more sense *he* would be up there on that throne. He managed to stay calm. They would all see, soon enough, what a truly great practitioner was capable of. "Of course not, Your Majesty," he replied, bowing slightly. "I merely wondered if it was wise to send all of us from the city. The Great Work must continue, surely. What horrors could Brauron hold that would require more than a handful of us?"

Seleucus stared at Alzen, fumes snaking round his mask. "Your regent has spoken, Phrater Alzen." His words echoed round the chamber, heavy with power and threat.

Alzen wanted to scream. He wanted to storm up onto the dais and tell Seleucus how important his work was – how close he was to ascending to a state of true power. "Of course, Your Majesty," he said, with a stiff bow.

"One week," said Seleucus, looking out across the gathering and slumping back into his throne. "Prepare miracles, my brothers. Harness the greatest power at your disposal and be ready for my summons. No one must be allowed to kill a phrater and live."

There was a murmur of consent, then, at a wave of Seleucus's hand, the crowd began to disperse.

Alzen forced his way in the opposite direction, heading towards the dais, but before he could reach the throne, a line of hiramites blocked his way, the soldiers glaring at him from behind the masks of their absurd helmets.

"The audience is at an end," said one of them.

Alzen was outraged to be addressed so curtly, but before he could complain, Seleucus strode from the chamber, flanked by his attendants. Mapourak, the lion, remained on the dais and locked its emerald eyes on Alzen, studying him with what seemed to be wry amusement.

Alzen let out an exasperated gasp and stormed from the chamber, hurrying back to his cell.

Ostan was waiting for him under the Specular Adulis, his sweaty, nervous face bathed in splinters of light.

"You said you could make him think again," he said, grabbing Alzen's robes. "You only made him angrier."

Alzen shook his head. "This is absurd. I am so close to completing my experiments. If I leave now, it will be a massive step back. I need to be here. I need to finish what I've started."

Ostan looked shocked by the vehemence of Alzen's words. "What have you started, brother? What is it you're so close to completing?"

Alzen was so furious he answered. "I have nearly mastered a whole new form of alchymia," he hissed, looking around to make sure none of the other phraters could hear. "But if I am dragged away from the slums I can't continue my…" His words trailed off as he remembered how dangerous it could be confiding in anyone, even a loyal moron like Ostan. If the Old King knew what he was on the cusp of, of the incredible power he was about to harness, he would realize he was a threat – a rival for his crown.

"Why the slums?" Ostan frowned. "I thought it was your

laboratory you wanted to be near."

Alzen lied easily and convincingly. "My work in the slums, nursing those poor plague victims, is the fulcrum on which everything else hinges. It is through altruism that I..." His words trailed off as he realized he could not even be bothered to lie to such a slack-jawed lump. "I can't leave," he snapped. "That's all that matters."

"You would not dare challenge the will of the Old King, surely?"

Alzen was rigid with fury. "No. No, of course not. I will simply have to expedite my work." He was talking to the fume-laden air, rather than Ostan, picturing the hovels on the embankment, crowded with the sickly wretches who had consumed his laced cinnabar. "I have a week. I will just have to make sure I have been successful before Seleucus sends us into the wilderness."

"You must prepare for the battle. The Old King said–"

"I will do as I see fit! My duty, like yours, is to serve God and the Temple, and *I* know how best to do that."

Ostan backed away, shocked by Alzen's rage, as other phraters looked their way in surprise.

Alzen lowered his voice. "I will complete my work and then none of this will matter."

Ostan shook his head confused. "Not matter?"

Alzen waved a dismissive hand and began striding off towards the exit, leaving Ostan looking even more flustered than usual.

23

Always different. Always strange. Isten belonged to no one and everyone. No memories of her father, too many memories of her mother. What would she be without wine and smoke and comforting dreams? What would be left?

Isten hurled herself at the door of Brast's bedroom. It rattled against the hinges, spitting splinters, but showed no sign of giving. Even now, after hours of being pummelled and kicked, the frame would not move. The wood was bloodstained and there were scraps of her skin on the floor. Her knuckles were flayed from trying to punch her way out of the room; her hair was plastered to her sweaty face and her fingernails were like broken claws. The room was an explosion of filth. Brast had left food and water when he locked the door, but she'd hurled it at the walls, before tearing the furniture and filling the air with dust and shreds of cloth. She wept and bellowed as she rocked back on her heels and dived at the door again. This time her head slammed against it and, for a moment, she lost consciousness. She found herself sprawled on the floor in a pool of blood and acrid sick.

"Let me out!" she howled, arching her back in pain and rage and slamming her bruised feet against the floorboards.

Brast gave no answer. She could not be sure if he was even in the house anymore. How could he have taken her so seriously? She could not simply stop. Not after all these years. She had not gone a day without alcohol or tar since she was fifteen. And she'd been addicted to cinnabar for almost as long. Perhaps it would have been possible if she'd bought some vistula seeds or carussa sticks, but not like this. Not the raw horror of sobriety.

She was in agony. Her skin felt like it was burning. She rolled and howled, ripping at her clothes, trying to ease the pain. Another wave of nausea surged up from her stomach and she vomited again, hacking bile across the wall as she tried to stand on feeble, shaking legs.

"Let me out!" she howled again.

She could not tell if she had been in there for days or weeks. Nights had come and gone and Brast had replaced the bowls of food and water, so it was definitely more than hours, but time had become elastic. She felt as though she had never been anywhere other than this tiny, filth-splattered room.

"You always blame someone else," said a familiar voice. It was soft and full of gentle humour and Isten's eyes immediately filled with tears. It was her mother's voice.

"You're dead," she gasped, wiping the sick from her mouth and turning around.

The voice had come from the door. The planks had warped and twisted, parting in the middle to reveal a pair of clear, bright, human eyes – her mother's eyes.

"So I'm told," replied the door. "I'd hoped for a more interesting afterlife."

Isten reeled from the wall, trailing spit and shreds of

clothing, staggering into the centre of the room.

"What do you mean, I blame someone else? I have only–" Cramp stabbed through her stomach, doubling her over, dropping her, painfully, to her knees.

"You think all of this is someone else's fault," said the door, looking around the room. "Your addictions, your cruel love affairs, your cowardice."

"Cowardice?" Isten knew her faults but she baulked at that.

"Oh, I know you can run around killing things, Isten. That's not what I mean. That's not bravery. Bravery is exposing yourself to hope, daring to love, daring to believe, to risk failure. Gombus is a good man and Puthnok is far braver than you've ever been, but you sneer at them like they're morons."

"I *love* them." Isten was horrified. "I only ever wanted to save them."

"You sneer at them. You think their dreams are childish and stupid. You think the world is broken and all we can do is survive it. You play along, always at arm's length, always numbing yourself with drugs, forever maintaining your safe, protected distance."

Isten shook her head, incredulous. "Why the fuck did I never hear any of this when you were alive? Where were your fucking pearls of wisdom then?"

The door made a strange approximation of a shrug. "You were seven. And even then you had more control of yourself."

Isten ran at the door, launching herself at the infuriatingly self-satisfied eyes.

This time, rather than rattling under the impact, the wood

swallowed her, glooping like viscous mud. It enveloped her flailing limbs, flooded her mouth and ears, silenced her screams and blinded her. She thrashed and turned, suspended in a wall of thick, resinous pitch.

Panic gripped her. She could not breathe. The door had clogged her airways. Her lungs burned.

With an immense effort, she wrenched herself around and thrust her face back into the room, spitting splinters and snot and slops of liquid timber.

She gulped down a lungful of air but her limbs failed to break free, trapped deep in the door.

"Let me out!" she wailed, straining to free herself. Her skin was burning with even more ferocity. She could feel the rough texture of the wood scraping and scratching at her tormented flesh.

"The truth is," said the door, its voice reverberating through her bones, "that I *did* tell you. I taught you every day. All those speeches and rallies. They were all for you, Isten."

"Liar!" she spat. "You never knew if I was even there. Gombus cared, but only because he thought I was the key to a revolution. You never even made that pretence. While you were basking in adoration, I was forgotten."

"I never forgot you," said the door, but Isten sensed that she had touched a nerve. The cool, amused tone was gone, replaced with hesitance. "Those words were for you."

"One word, to me alone, would have changed everything."

"Don't be a child, Isten. I was teaching you a lesson." The door sounded angry now. "People like you and I are more than just mothers and daughters. We are public property. We are the agents of change. We're kindling – sparks that light fires. My words were for you and they were for everyone. Emperor Rakus is a monster and the time has come to face him down – to face the execution squads down. We can't continue kneeling in subservience while his dungeons grow full and the poor die. We can't continue–"

"You're right," spat Isten. "I *did* hear those speeches. And even as a child I could see through them."

"See through them?" A note of anger entered the door's voice.

"You thought you were a martyr – so fucking selfless, putting the crowds before me, putting the revolution before everything, putting your life on the line for the meek little poor people, but I knew what it was really about. You loved it. The cheers, the fame, the importance. You fed on it. You needed it. I could see it in your eyes, even when I was seven I could see it. And I hated it."

The door fell silent.

Isten realized she was no longer trapped in the wood but staring at it from across the room. The eyes were gone. The planks had regained their usual shape. There was blood and vomit on the frame, but nothing else.

She stumbled back towards it, stroking the wood, horrified, wanting to take her words back. "I don't mean it," she gasped, dropping to her knees and letting her head thud against the boards.

She sat there for a long time, breathing quickly, battling waves of nausea until, unexpectedly, she fell asleep.

When she awoke, she was in bed. It had been put back in place and there were clean sheets pulled up to her painfully thin shoulders. The room had been tidied, the walls cleaned and the furniture put back in place. She reached up to touch her face and found that it had been wiped clean and her tangled mound of hair had been tied back. The shutters had been opened and there was golden light pouring across her face, bathing her in warmth and carrying the sounds of children playing outside.

Brast was bustling about the room, still righting pieces of furniture and wiping away pools of vomit. She watched him in silence, not wanting him to know she was awake, not ready to speak yet. His tall, stooped frame was almost as wasted as hers and his skin was drained of colour. She guessed that he had not left the house while she was battling for life. Unaware of being watched, his face had relaxed. His mask of wry cynicism was gone and she saw the relief in his eyes. Relief that she had survived, she guessed. Something about that made her wince. She cared nothing for her health, or even for her survival, but he did.

He turned to pick up a painting she had torn apart and noticed that she was watching him. He reacted with almost comedic surprise, dropping the paper and backing away, staring at her in shock. Then, within a fraction of a second, his mask was back in place.

"You can clean up after me sometime," he sneered.

She managed a slight nod.

He sauntered over and pressed a cup of water to her mouth. Her lips were cracked and the cool liquid felt wonderful as it trickled down her throat.

"How long?" she managed to croak.

He strolled away from her, affecting disinterest. "Three days and four nights. I thought you weren't going to make it. Lorinc was here on the second day and you tried to kill him."

"Lorinc?" She had no recollection of that at all and the idea unnerved her. Where had she been that she could not remember grappling with a brute like Lorinc? She remembered battling the door, punching her fists into yielding, liquid wood. Had she really been fighting Lorinc? Was it Lorinc she had argued with?

Brast headed downstairs to fetch her some food and she lay there for a moment, feeling the countless pains that covered her body. It felt strangely good. She was experiencing the world as it truly was – unadorned and honest. She felt light and clear-headed. She ran her hands over her bony limbs and chest, gently probing at the cuts and bruises, wincing at the pain. Then her hand reached the mark Alzen had left on her bicep and her good feelings evaporated. In a rush, she recalled what she had seen when she entered his thoughts. He was a murderer and her mind was pregnant with the seed of his crimes. She could feel his power waiting, quietly, at the back of her skull, waiting to be ignited, ominous and alien. How she had desired it – the life force that he had leached from his victims. She had become a monster, a vampire. Along with her disgust, she remembered her purpose – the reason she demanded Brast get her clean. She had to stop Alzen. She had to halt the murders. It was the only way she could think to atone. She nodded, remembering that she also had a plan.

When Brast returned, carrying a bowl of fishy slop, she tried to sit up and leave the bed. The room whirled around her and she nearly fell to the floor.

"Where do you think you're going?" he said, rushing over and helping her lie back down. "You're a wreck."

"I have to get back to the Alembeck."

He laughed. "No chance. Let the Exiles manage without you for a while. You need to rest."

"No, you don't understand, I need to fetch something from my room. It's so I can do what we discussed, when we were in the arboretum."

Brast's face hardened. "So you meant that? You're going to rid yourself of this mysterious 'contact'?"

She nodded, looking at the bed sheets, not wanting to meet his eye. "There's a small wooden chest next to my bunk. I need it."

"Today? Is it really that urgent?"

She nodded and tried to sit up again, but her arms trembled and would not hold her.

"Then let me go," he snapped. "I'll fetch your blessed box if it's so urgent."

"No!" She shook her head, her eyes wide. "Only I can get it."

"Why?" He laughed. "I've done far worse than carry your luggage."

She let her head fall back on the pillow and started at him. "It's private. You mustn't look inside."

He raised an eyebrow, about to make a sarcastic joke, then caught the fear in her eye and shrugged. "Whatever."

"Promise."

He shook his head. "I have no desire to leaf through your diary or steal your love letters."

"Promise."

He held up his hands in defeat. "I promise."

He nodded to the soup he had left next to the bed. "It's nicer than it tastes."

She laughed.

"And if you don't eat something soon, I'll never get my fucking bed back."

She laughed again, enjoying the clear, honest sound. "You're a good man."

He blushed and looked angry, shook his head and turned to go. Then he stopped at the door looked back. "I knew you'd do it," he said. "Get sober, I mean. You're a fighter, Isten. They haven't broken you yet." Then he left.

She flopped back onto the pillow and, a few minutes later, she heard the door slam downstairs. She closed her eyes, enjoying the feeling of the sunlight on her face. She was starting to doze, when she remembered Brast's instruction to eat. She sat up, carefully, still lightheaded, and put the bowl on her lap. The soup was foul and she laughed as she ate, imagining Brast's earnest, angry face as he cooked it, wrestling with spoons and spices, furious at his ingredients for not behaving how he wanted.

She had only taken a few grimacing sips when she heard a sound downstairs. It was a low, heavy thud, as though a piece of furniture had fallen over. She was about to call out, to ask if it was Brast, but she stopped herself, sensing that something was wrong.

She carefully placed the soup back on the table and swung her feet out of the bed and onto the floorboards.

There was another sound, a creaking floorboard. Someone was coming up the stairs, moving slowly and carefully. She grabbed her dagger from the pile of clothes Brast had left her and crept across the room, positioning herself next to the door, so she would be hidden when it opened.

The footsteps came closer and then, very slowly, the door began to open.

Isten relaxed as she recognized the heady, floral perfume that poured into the room. Even before Colcrow's massive bulk swayed into view, she knew it was him.

She was about to step out from behind the door, when she realized he was not alone. There were others coming up behind him.

She waited in the shadows as Colcrow looked around the room, his back still to her, picking up sketches and canvasses and examining the pieces of furniture.

Then he halted next to her pile of clothes and grabbed her leather jerkin. "She *is* staying here," he called out to the people on the stairs.

Two men entered the room, one large and powerfully built, the other small and skinny. They were both wearing filthy, dark robes with the hoods pulled up. They were carrying swords but not Athanorian falcatas: broadswords, more like the weapons of Isten's homeland.

A dreadful realization hit her and, as one of the men threw back his head, her muscles tensed with fury. The man's head was horribly burned. It was the imperial agents. Colcrow had led them to her.

Colcrow turned to face the men, still gripping Isten's jerkin, then recoiled in shock as he saw Isten glaring at him next to the door.

"You're here!" he said, attempting a smile, but only managing an awkward grimace.

"You're working for Emperor Rakus," she hissed, trembling with a mixture of exhaustion and rage. "You've betrayed us." She shook her head, raising her knife. How could even Colcrow could be capable of that?

The agents backed away from her and gripped the handles

of their swords, but Colcrow rushed forwards, standing between them and Isten, holding up his hands.

"Wait!" he gasped. "There's no need for this. Let me explain!"

"Explain? Yes, I'd like to hear that. Tell me why you've led Rakus's murder dogs to Brast's home – and to me. Explain that, you fucker."

His eyes widened in excitement. "We can go home, Isten." He was whispering, as though he could barely believe what he was saying. "You and I. We can return to Rukon. The Emperor has acquired a device. A vehicle." He glanced at the agents for confirmation. "What did you call it? An airship?"

The larger of the two nodded, but neither of them spoke, still gripping their swords and glaring at Isten through their masks of scar tissue.

"We can go home to the Emperor?" She laughed. "What are you talking about? Are you insane? We're only here because Rakus would have executed us all if we'd stayed."

"His Magnificence has offered you a pardon," said the larger agent. His accent was thick and instantly took Isten back to her home. "On the condition that you stand beside him at the gates of Checny Palace and renounce the revolution. If you swear allegiance to the crown he's prepared to offer you a pardon."

Isten reeled under the weight of Colcrow's treachery.

"We can go home," he said, smiling and reaching out to her. "Think of it, Isten – we can leave this wretched city behind."

Colcrow's smile was too much for her. Anger flooded her body with adrenaline and she leapt at him. She grabbed his throat and, as she reached back to punch him, she felt heat explode in the back of her head and rush down her arm.

Her fist slammed into his face with such force that it hammered through his skull.

There was a flash of dazzling light.

Isten and Colcrow thudded onto the floor and the agents staggered back, shielding their eyes.

Isten howled as she felt wonderful, vengeful power rushing through her arm.

Then the light vanished and she gasped. She was straddling Colcrow's corpse with her fist embedded in his skull. But even more horrific than her crime was the nature of Colcrow's death: his head was engulfed in a mesh of golden, spiralling strands. She had killed him with Alzen's sorcery.

She wrenched her fist free, spraying blood and bone as she staggered away from the body. Her fist was a tornado of coils that spiralled through the air towards the two agents.

"Go!" she howled, staring at her hand in horror, holding it up to them in warning.

The agents flinched away from her, one of them dropping his sword, he was so terrified. Then they bolted for the door, their boots thudding down the stairs and out into the street.

Isten slumped back against the wall with golden, bloodstained strands trailing from her arm.

"No!" she groaned, focusing on the heat at the back of her head, trying to dampen it. For a moment, she thought she would be unable to extinguish the inferno, but then her gaze fell back on Colcrow's mutilated corpse and the full horror of it hit her.

The heat died and the tendrils vanished. They whipped back through the air and sliced back into her arm, leaving no trace they had ever existed.

She dropped to the floor beside Colcrow, her tears mingling with the blood rushing from his head.

Isten was still lying next to the corpse when Brast returned. He shouted a hello from downstairs, then halted, staring down at her in horror as he reached the bedroom door, gripping her wooden chest in his hands.

"What...?" he began.

The golden threads had left no trace of sorcery in Colcrow, just a smashed, bloody pulp of bone and grey matter. It looked like his head had exploded.

Brast's face was white as he placed the chest on the floor and stepped closer, staring at the corpse. "Did you...?"

Isten stayed on the floor, still in shock at what she had done. She had murdered an Exile. She had broken their most unbreakable oath. And she had done it with the vile sorcery Alzen had created through murder. "He came here with the agents," she managed to whisper. "He sold us out to them. He led them to your house."

Brast looked confused and doubtful. Then he noticed something lying on the floor near the bed. He stepped around Colcrow's corpse and grabbed the broadsword dropped by one of the fleeing agents.

"The fucker," he whispered, looking at the corpse with new eyes, glaring at the smashed skull.

He helped Isten to her feet. "Then he broke his oath before you did. Selling us out to Rakus is the same as murder." He looked back at the corpse, shaking his head. "How did you do that?"

She leant against him, her breathing laboured and her limbs on the verge of collapse. "I have to rid myself of this," she said, gripping her head. "Quickly."

"What do you need to do?" He nodded at the chest. "Is that the right one?"

"Yes." She stared at it, afraid of what she had to do. But first she needed to be rid of Brast. Perhaps he had half guessed what was going on, but she didn't want him to see the robes and chains of her laborator outfit. She had an idea. "Can you get rid of this?" she asked, nodding at Colcrow's corpse. She winced as she caught sight of his ruined head. "I'm too weak."

He nodded. "I have friends, well, not friends – people who owe me. They'll help me shift it." He led her to a chair. "Sit there. You're still weak."

He rushed downstairs and came back with bread, cheese and water. "You look awful," he said. "Eat something, for God's sake."

She nodded, trying not to look at the bloody mess on the floor as she picked at the food.

While she ate, Brast pulled the sheets from the bed and wrapped Colcrow in a makeshift shroud, grunting as he turned the corpse over, wrapping it several times until it was impossible to see the nature of his death.

"I'll be five, ten minutes at most," he said, hovering near the door, giving her an anxious look. "Will you be ok?"

She nodded, not even attempting a smile.

"Eat all of that before I get back," he said. "Whatever your plan is, I don't think you'll manage it if you can't walk." Then he dashed off down the stairs and left the house again.

Isten stared at the mark on her bicep. It felt like a tumour, eating into her skin. She wanted desperately to wipe it away, to remove the dreadful warm numbness at the back of her head, but she knew she had to bear it for a little longer.

When she had looked out through Alzen's eyes, when she had seen that he was a murderer, she had cried out and he had heard her.

The link between them now went both ways. If she left his mark on her arm, when the time came, she would be able to speak to him, to summon him. She just had to pray he would answer. Somehow, she felt sure he would. She had heard the same hunger in his voice that she felt. When they shared his sorcery, it became something greater than he anticipated. He wanted her the same way she had wanted him. Even now, knowing where his power came from, even now that she had seen the terrified face of his victims, part of her still craved it. Even when she ripped Colcrow's skull apart, there had been delight mixed in with the horror. Such incredible power. It was like nothing she had ever imagined.

She hissed in disgust, horrified at where her mind was going. She had to move fast. She had to sever the tie before she became as monstrous as Alzen. She ate some of the cheese and found, to her surprise, even after all that had just happened, that she was hungry. She sank her teeth into the loaf. With no chemicals washing through her veins, she could actually taste things again. She sat there, next to the sodden, shrouded corpse, enjoying her meal, until she heard Brast calling hello from downstairs.

He rushed into the room, followed by a pair of old burly dockworkers. They both looked at her in surprise, but Brast waved at the corpse. "Quickly. You two get the head end, I'll grab the legs."

They grunted and muttered and hauled the corpse from the room.

Isten waited until she heard the door slam, then ventured downstairs. She edged round Brast's gambling table and opened the shutters on his front window, squinting out into the glare of the street. Brast and the dockers were moving fast and keeping to the shadows. Dead bodies were not uncommon in the Botanical Quarter, but there was always the risk that a hiramite might be passing, and murder, even here, was punishable by death.

When Brast and the others had turned a corner at the bottom of the street and vanished from view, Isten headed back upstairs and opened the chest. She moved her old clothes aside and lifted out the yellow laborator robes. The ceremonial chains and keys were still there, along with the turmeric to stain her face. She almost wished they had vanished so she could abandon her absurd plan. Then she looked at the bloodstained floor and nodded. This was the only way. She had to rid herself of Alzen and rid the city of him at the same time.

She donned the heavy gown, draped herself in the jewellery and dyed her face. Then she slicked back her hair, pulled up the hood and hid her dagger beneath the robes. The food and water had already had an effect. She felt a little stronger and steadier on her feet as she headed back downstairs and walked out into the sunshine.

As she closed Brast's door, she let her hand rest against the sun-blistered paint, thinking of all that he had done for her. A shocking thought hit her. Whatever happened that morning, she could see no likelihood that she would survive. Either she would die, or she and Alzen would both die. She prayed it would be the latter but, either way, she would not see Brast again. "Thank you," she whispered, her hand still pressed against the door. For a moment she could not move, frozen by a sudden sense of loss. Then she rushed off down the dusty street, heading for the river.

24

Alzen cursed as the silver egg slipped from his fingers and bounced across the packed-earth floor. He was clumsy and febrile from lack of sleep and as he dropped to his knees, trying to find the egg, his eyes were too full of sweat to see.

There was a murmur of complaint from the other end of the warehouse but he ignored it. None of them were going anywhere.

"There it is," he muttered, scrabbling across the floor, dirtying his robes. He snatched the egg from the floor and turned back to the row of figures at the other end of the room. There were half a dozen prone shapes lying in the darkness, their terrified faces staring at him from the shadows. He was on Coburg Street, not far from the fish market, in a warehouse owned by the Elect. He had spent the last few days in a frenzy, killing dozens of cinnabar addicts from the slums, taking risks he would never have taken before, sure that he was so close to success that nothing else mattered. With every soul he captured, he felt that he would attain a new state of being, rising from the ranks of the Temple to become their true, omnipotent lord. But with each death, he felt a rising sense of panic. In two days he would be banished from the city – sent to the walls with all the other phraters. And he was sure that if his work was halted now, his progress would evaporate. All that work, all those deaths, for nothing.

Perhaps this time, he thought, heading back towards the row of prone bodies. He had ordered his laborators to gather a whole family of sickly wretches and deliver them to him here, in this warehouse, so he could "help" them. It was dangerous. Questions would be asked when all six of them died in his care. But he had to try something.

He stood over them in the gloom, not even bothering with the pretence of kindness. He glared at them, wondering if it would make a difference what order he killed them in. There were two children, one no more than eight, the other in his early teens. Their souls would probably be the least potent, he decided. The children's parents were also lying on the makeshift beds, a gaunt, leathery-looking sailor from a salvage crew and his wife, who looked even tougher and more weatherbeaten than her husband. Next to them were two more adults – uncles he guessed, by their similarity to the father.

All of them were paralyzed and moaning in fear as he paced around them. He racked his brains, trying to think why he was failing. He had seemed so close, but now, however many lives he took, he seemed unable to cross that final threshold.

He shook his head and opened the metal egg. There was nothing for it. He would keep trying until something happened. Perhaps killing the whole family would be enough.

He stepped towards the father, then hesitated. There was something strange about the man's face. It looked oddly familiar. He stared at him, but the sweat in his eyes was still affecting his vision; the man's face seemed unclear, as though it had been smudged.

He muttered a curse. He had been out here, killing, for three days with no sleep. His mind felt strange, remote and confused, unable to focus. Everything he looked at seemed loaded with a significance he could not explain. Perhaps, in his exhaustion, he was missing something crucial?

He wiped his eyes and stepped closer to the man, staring at his face. Then he gasped and backed away, almost dropping the egg again.

The man's features were flowing into each other as though melting, and when they settled, they formed a new face.

"Isten?" gasped Alzen. There was no mistaking her gaunt, stern face. Her eyes were rolling, unable to focus.

Alzen? she said, speaking directly into his head.

Alzen wondered if he had pushed himself too far. Perhaps he was hallucinating?

I have to see you, she said.

"How are you doing this?" Alzen affected annoyance but, in truth, he was excited. He remembered the thoughts he had had back at the temple. After his moments of conjunction with Isten his powers seemed to lurch forwards. "How are you speaking to me?" he said, staring in confusion at the transformed face. "How is this possible?"

When you passed your power through me, it changed me. She hesitated, sounding almost afraid to speak her hope so clearly. *And I think it changed you, too.*

"You presume to know my mind?" Despite his excitement, Alzen was outraged that Isten seemed to consider herself on an equal footing.

Tell me I'm wrong.

He said nothing.

I felt it, she continued. *When you channelled yourself through me, something happened, didn't it? We could both feel the same thing. Your power was growing. It was changing, wasn't it?*

Alzen was torn between hope and outrage. How dare she tell him what he was thinking? How dare she attempt to wield his power without his permission? "What do you want?" he snapped.

I'm dying, Alzen. But I think that if you were to transfer your alchymia through me, while we are in the same place, while your hand is in mine, I might grow strong again. I might survive.

"Why would I want to help you? We both kept our sides of the deal. I don't owe you anything."

But aren't you intrigued? Can you imagine how it would feel? Think how incredible it was even when we were miles apart. What if we were together when it happened? What would happen then, Alzen? What would it mean?

He paced away from her, trying to calm himself, trying to think clearly. Somehow, he had left a residue of power in her. Somehow she, a vulgar commoner, was managing to perform alchymia none of his brothers could perform – telepathic speech, without the need for equipment or preparation. Even the Old King wasn't capable of that. He shook his head. What had he done? This was far more serious than any of his other crimes. What had he created? He had to see her. He looked at the egg in his fist. He had to stop her. These were the reasons he gave himself, but there was another thought hiding at the back of his mind. What *would* it be like? His hand on hers as they unleashed his power. If she was the catalyst that got him this far, could it be that she was the key to his final transformation?

"Where are you?" he said, his voice uneven.

The abandoned theatre on the corner of Vanitch Street. Do you know it?

His mind whirled. Vanitch Street was only half a mile away, not far from the South Gate of the Temple District. He could be there in ten minutes. "I know it," he said. "I'm on my way."

He dashed from the warehouse, leaving the door banging behind him and his victims flicking in and out of the darkness, blinking in confusion as sunlight flashed across their stricken faces.

25

The Kephali Theatre was a ruin long before it was devoured by Athanor. All that remained was a ripple of stone terraces fanning out from a gloriously ostentatious proscenium arch. The arch was still intact, but buried in a forest of golden, brittle veins. It looked like a burnished coral reef, glinting in the heart of the city.

The sun was at its zenith as Alzen rushed across the terraces. Heat pulsed up through the ancient stone, hurting his feet even through his leather slippers and causing him to pant and curse as he looked around for Isten. There was no sign of her, or anyone else for that matter. The terraces were cluttered with rubble and litter but devoid of people.

He stumbled down one of the aisles, feeling as though he might collapse at any moment. The combination of heat, exhaustion and excitement was overwhelming. He was in such a daze he had not even thought to disguise himself. He was wearing his full ceremonial dress, apart from his flame-shaped helmet which he had left in his chariot, back on the embankment.

"Isten?" he called, trying to shield his eyes from the midday sun. The light was flashing in the metal strands around the arch and the whole crumbling sandstone structure resembled a brazier, rippling with heat haze and dust clouds.

There was no reply, so he staggered on through the inferno, wiping the sweat from his face and wondering if he had lost his mind. Perhaps he had been hallucinating in the warehouse? Perhaps it was simply sleep deprivation that had conjured Isten's voice in his mind?

As he neared the arch, he saw that there was still a crumbling remnant of the stage, slumped and shattered, but bathed in enticing shadow. He clambered over the rubble and up into the gloom, breathing a sigh of relief at the drop in temperature. Someone had tried to build a kind of hut from old wooden crates and he leant against the wood, trying to steady his breathing as he looked around. After the glare of the amphitheatre, it was hard to see in the darkness beneath the arch.

Then he saw Isten. She was sitting right at the centre of the stage, cross-legged in the darkness, staring at him. He saw immediately that she had been telling the truth about one thing – she looked hours away from death. She was even more skeletal than before and her wild black hair was perched high on her head at an absurd angle. Her corpse-grey skin was covered in bloodstains and her clenched fists looked like they had been hammered repeatedly against a stone wall. Her eyes, sunk deep in bruise-dark pits, looked even more deranged than usual.

He crossed the stage, scowling at her. "Why didn't you speak up?" He knew he had no reason to be so angry with her, but he was enraged by the sensation of being in her thrall. She had summoned him and he had been unable to resist. This pathetic, wasted creature had power over him.

"I did," she replied, but her voice was a gravel-scrape whisper and he realized why he had not heard her.

"What happened to you?" he asked as he studied her blood-splattered leather armour and her emaciated limbs.

She shook her head. "It doesn't matter."

Again, he was outraged by her tone. He looked back across the terraces to make sure they were alone, then reached into his robes, resting his hand on one of his sedative pipes. She was an abomination. He had made a monster. She had to die.

She touched the mark he had left on her arm. "When you shared your sorcery with me–"

"Alchymia," he said. "It is called alchymia. And I passed it through your body, I did not share it with you. You were a conduit, nothing more. When we killed the Aroc Brothers you glimpsed a tiny shadow of what it means to master the Art. You're like an ape that's been handed a book. You might have seen the shape of it, the physicality, but you have no concept of its meaning."

She nodded wearily. "But, nevertheless, when you used me as your weapon, and when you transformed those weapons in Brauron, I felt something change in you as well as in me. You were as surprised as I was. And as excited. You were approaching the top of a ladder. A ladder you have been climbing for a long time." She leant forwards, her feverish eyes locked on his. "Tell me I'm wrong."

Alzen hesitated. For all of his anger and disgust, he could not help thinking of that moment of conjunction. She was right, his understanding had soared. By using her as his medium he had uncovered something profound. And her metaphor was unnervingly apt. He had often felt as though his journey to enlightenment was like climbing a ladder, with the final rung just out of reach.

"I know I'm right," she said. "You felt it too. Together, we reached a place you have never reached alone. By working through me, you almost crossed a final threshold." She grasped at a broken pillar and managed to stand, her legs trembling wildly. "What might happen if you tried it now, with my body right in front of you? What might happen if the contact was physical rather than mental?" Her words were slurred but full of passion. "Perhaps you can reach that final rung? Surely you want to find out?"

Alzen glanced back at the terraces again, tormented by doubt. With every word she made him surer that he had to kill her. A vulgar mind like hers had no place trying to grasp the secrets of the Art. But what if she was the key to his ascension? He was out of time. The number of killings had made no difference to his progress. In a couple of days he would be gone, his chance would be gone. The idea of doing what she wanted made him feel sick, but what if she was right?

Then he had a wonderful moment of clarity. Of course he could try. It would have no bearing on whether he killed her or not. He would simply try the experiment and then, whatever the result, he would show her the punishment for presuming to command her betters.

He relaxed and smiled, holding up his hands. "Forgive me, Isten. I haven't slept for days and it has robbed me of my manners. I'm behaving like a monster. You are clearly very ill. Why would I not help you?" He stepped closer. "If you think it might help, I will gladly shine a little of God's light into your soul."

Now that she had convinced him and he had stepped to her side, she looked suddenly unsure, backing away, as though she wanted to flee.

"What will you do?" she asked, wrapping her arms around her bony chest, staring.

"Just what you requested," he said, regaining his usual friendly tones. "I will simply do what I did before. I haven't prepared in advance, so I can't perform any grand transfigurations, as we did in Brauron or the palace in Gamala, but I have pushed my learning to the point where my flesh is charged, constantly, with Astral Light. If I pass a little through your skin, perhaps it will give you strength. Then we can go and find you some food and rest."

She nodded, still looking afraid, as she placed her hand in his.

He gently rolled up her sleeve, revealing the faded sigil on her bicep. His heart was kicking against his ribs as he cradled her filthy, bony arm and placed his palm against her skin. The darkness seemed to grow and the theatre fell away from his peripheral vision until all he could see was her ashen face.

He closed his eyes and turned his gaze inwards, searching for the currents of alchymia that now flowed constantly through his thoughts.

With unusual ease, he found a great confluence of holy flame, blazing in the darkness.

His breath stalled in his throat and a great sense of portent gripped him. He knew, suddenly, that Isten was right. This was the moment. He was about to ascend.

He willed the alchymia through his palm and his consciousness was carried along with it, flooding through capillaries and veins, rushing into her heart and mind.

The light blazed brighter, revealing a stark silhouette. It was a ladder. Isten's description had taken root in his mind. He saw his astral hands, reaching up to each rung, climbing higher into the light. With every rung, the light grew and along with it, his power. His muscles were aflame with rapture; glorious, limitless force surged through his chest, filling him with impossible vigour. He felt as though he could tear down the theatre with a thought. Or lift Athanor as though it were a leaf skeleton. He laughed, overwhelmed by the beauty of it. He was seeing the mind of God. He was becoming God. He was becoming the Ingenious.

As he reached for the final rung of the ladder, Alzen was weeping and laughing hysterically. He was so ecstatic that, for a moment, he did not notice the pain. Then it grew so intense that he had to pause, with only one hand on the last rung.

His mind was full of light, but his stomach was full of pain. Awful pain. So terrible it almost matched the glory of his ascension.

He ignored it. He could not stop now. He grasped the final rung with his other hand and hauled himself into the light. With a final lunge, he saw everything. The cosmos was revealed to him. He had achieved the impossible.

But, along with the revelation, came a rush of pain so intense that he fell back, dropping away from the light he had fought so hard to reach, and tumbled into darkness.

Alzen roared in agony and opened his eyes. He was lying on his back, looking up at the ruins of the proscenium arch.

The air was crimson. Blood was washing over him in

waves, lashing against his face, flooding his mouth and slapping down on the stage.

A huge shape was thrashing in the deluge.

Alzen tried to pull away from the pain, but something was locked around the lower half of his body, ripping it apart.

Then, with a savage roar, Mapourak's head broke through the fountain of blood, glaring at Alzen as it chewed on a glistening mass of organs and intestines. The lion's emerald hide was wet with gore.

Alzen groaned in horror as Mapourak shook the meat back and forth, as though wrestling a serpent, then gulped it down, growling and snorting. Then it lifted its enormous paws off Alzen and backed away.

As the blood flow lessened, Alzen saw golden shapes moving towards him through the darkness. He wept as he felt his life slipping away. He had won. After all these years he had achieved what the others never could. He could not die now.

"You have betrayed the Temple," said Seleucus, looming over Alzen. He waved at a group of phraters that had also emerged from the shadows at the back of the stage. "We all heard it from your own mouth. You have shared our secrets with this vulgar woman and you have committed the unimaginable crime of passing alchymia through common, mortal flesh." He waved at someone Alzen could not see. "If this woman had not come to us and revealed your apostasy; if she hadn't brought us here today to witness your crimes, who knows what damage could have been done."

Alzen tried to speak, tried to explain what he had achieved, but he was too feeble to move. Each breath he took was weaker than the last. His vision narrowed to a dark tunnel. All he could see was the Old King's metal-shrouded face.

"I only pray that by executing you I have saved your soul, Phrater Alzen."

Seleucus stooped over Alzen, bringing his mouth close so he could whisper in his ear. "Did you think I didn't know?" His eyes flashed. "Did you think I didn't know what you were doing?" He reached into Alzen's blood-soaked robes and plucked out the silver egg containing Coagulus. "I know what I gave you, Alzen. I gave you the rope to hang yourself."

Alzen tried to reply, but his next breath refused to come. Darkness flooded over him.

26

Isten dropped to her knees, staring at the bloody remains of Phrater Alzen. The monster had devoured him from the chest down, leaving little more than scraps of meat and a pool of blood. She felt as though she were in a dream. As Alzen had climbed the ladder towards the light, she had risen with him, tasting the infinite, feeling the untrammelled power. And from that glorious vision she had fallen to this horrific scene. The monster resembled a lion, but it was enormous and made entirely of green, faceted gemstones. It would have been beautiful if it were not so terrifying. As it padded towards her, its paws clanked on the ancient stage and its jaws opened, still trailing shreds of Alzen's stomach as it rocked from side to side, its savage gaze locked on her.

"Mapourak," said the golden giant, raising one of his hands.

The monster halted a few feet away from her, eyeing her with an eager snarl.

The giant waved the lion away and strode across the stage towards her, reaching out to take her hand.

She hesitated. All of the phraters she'd spoken to in the Temple District seemed strange and godlike, but the Old King was even more incredible. He reminded her of the Ignorant

Men, towering and gilded, with no trace of humanity.

She lacked the will to refuse him and placed her hand in his enormous grip.

He helped her up with surprising gentleness as the other phraters gathered round, their heads bowed, their faces hidden behind flame-shaped helmets.

Isten looked anxiously at the lion.

Seleucus shook his head. "You have done a great service to the Temple." His voice was like a hammer pounding iron, but he sounded genuinely grateful. "I have long known that Alzen was a canker at the heart of our fraternity, but I lacked proof. When you donned those yellow robes and breached the sanctity of our temples, you committed a crime, but you did it to halt a greater evil. You will not die today, Isten of Rukon."

Isten almost fell over. Whatever happened, she had expected death. She should have been overjoyed but, as the giant spoke, she realized something terrible. Alzen was dead. She could see his ravaged flesh lying just a few feet away from her. So why could she still feel his presence at the back of her skull? The numbing heat was still there. The sinister product of all his murders. If anything, it was even more noticeable. She grabbed her arm and rubbed the mark from her skin. Panic gripped her. The numbness remained.

The giant watched her in silence. Then he looked back at Alzen's corpse. "That man brought shame on the Temple." He seemed on the verge of saying more, then shook his head and turned to leave.

"You are free to go." He stepped down easily from the stage, his golden armour blazing as he walked out into the sunlit amphitheatre.

The other phraters followed, and after one last hungry look at Isten, so did the green lion.

Seleucus paused a few feet from the stage and looked back at her.

"I spared your life because you did me a good deed, Isten, but do not mistake my compassion for weakness. I will tolerate no false temples. Nor will I allow false creeds to preach hatred towards me and my brethren. I have removed your temple and scattered your followers. If they band together again, I will not be so forgiving. If I ever hear of the Exiles coming together, they will meet the same fate as Phrater Alzen. And so will you."

Isten could barely follow what he was saying. All she could think about was the alien presence at the back of her mind. How could it still be there now that Alzen was dead? She clawed at her scalp, drawing blood as her broken nails pierced the skin.

"Did you hear what I said?" asked the giant, taking a step back towards her.

"Yes," she gasped, feeling that she might pass out at any moment. "I understand."

Seleucus nodded. Then he waved some of the hiramites to Alzen's corpse. "Make sure no trace of that is left."

Then he turned and strode from the theatre.

Isten looked away as the soldiers scooped up Alzen's remains and slopped them into a crate.

Once the hiramites had left, she sat at the edge of the stage and cradled her head in her hands, feeling desperate and afraid. She had tricked Alzen so she could stop his murders, but she had also done it because she could not bear to feel his tainted presence in her skull any longer. "Get out," she hissed, pounding her palms against the side of her head.

She sat like that for several minutes, groaning and cursing, until she heard footsteps approaching the stage.

She looked up to see Brast rushing across the amphitheatre. His eyes were wide with shock.

"I saw what you did," he gasped as he reached the stage. He looked at the bloodstains on the stage. "Was he the one? The one you needed to get rid of?"

She nodded, but could not hide the desolation in her face.

"What's the matter?" demanded Brast. "You killed him. Or, you helped the Elect kill him." He shook his head in wonder. "How? How did you bring them here?"

"The chest you brought to me," she muttered. "There were laborator's robes in there. He gave them to me. I disguised myself and went into the Temple District."

"You went in? You're insane."

"I am," she said, with no trace of humour. "I knew," she corrected herself, "I *thought* they'd kill me, but I had to stop him. He was feeding on people. He was getting power by murdering addicts in the slums."

Brast sat down, staring at her. "But they didn't kill you. And now you're rid of him."

She shook her head, unable to explain. Then another horrible thought occurred to her. "The Old King said he had 'removed' the Alembeck. What does that mean? He said he had scattered the Exiles."

They both looked at each other with dawning horror.

"Quickly," said Brast, dropping down from the stage and reaching up to help Isten. "I'll help you walk."

27

It was painfully slow getting back to the Blacknells Road. Isten's legs could barely hold her and she kept halting to clutch her head, horrified by the numbness she could feel. It seemed to be growing, spreading through her mind.

It was mid-afternoon by the time they staggered out of an alleyway into the shadow of the Stump. As always, the huge building was resonating with the sounds of random drumbeats and drinking songs, but they did not pause to look at it, rushing on through the dust clouds, their eyes locked on the far end of the road.

The Marosa Library was still there, its spires and domes still intact, but at its side, where the Alembeck had always stood, there was an inferno of gold – spiralling tongues of metal had exploded from the ground, creating a forest of razor-sharp tendrils. There was no sign of the temple.

Isten and Brast staggered down the road, dazed expressions on their faces, joining the crowd that had gathered before the mass of golden threads. A few people recognized Isten, whispering as she approached, but she barged past them and gripped the blades at the edge of the web.

"Ignorant Men," said an old woman next to her. "They came an hour ago. It only took them only minutes to do this."

Isten stared at her. "What about the people inside?"

The old woman gave a comforting smile and gripped her arm. "They cleared out, a good hour before this happened. The hiramites came and ordered them to get their things and go. No one was left in there when…" The old woman hesitated, unsure how to describe what had happened. "When the Ignorant Men came."

Isten shook her head, peering through the dazzling glade. "You're wrong," she whispered, horrified. "I can hear someone. There's someone in there." There was a desperate scrabbling sound coming from right in the centre of the structure. "Someone's trapped."

"No. Don't worry." The old woman smiled and patted her arm. "It's just a mangy old fox. Look." She pointed through the mesh. "There."

"No," whispered Isten, shaking her head as she saw that the woman was right. The fox was bleeding and panicked, struggling desperately to free itself from the cage of blades that had enveloped it, powerless to escape. The animal was dozens of feet away from Isten, but she thrust her hand into the mesh as though she could help it.

Blood and skin fell from her arm as she struggled to reach into the metal.

"What are you doing?" cried Brast, hurrying to her side as the old woman backed away, shaking her head in confusion.

"Look!" cried Isten, pointing at the trapped animal.

"It's a fucking fox, Isten. A half-dead one by the looks of it. Get your arm out."

"It's *our* fox," she hissed, glaring at him.

He shook his head, confused, then nodded. "Oh, I see." He squeezed her shoulder. "That thing was ancient. I'm amazed it's lasted this long."

Isten groaned and let her head drop against the metal curls, closing her eyes, tormented by the sound of the fox's desperate struggle. "I can't help her," she said, speaking so quietly that even Brast could not hear.

Brast hugged her. "Isten, it could have been worse. That could have been Gombus, or Lorinc, or Puthnok."

She was too distraught to answer. How had she ever thought that she would be better off sober?

She allowed Brast to carefully extract her bloodied arm from the metal and lead her away from the crowd. As she stumbled after him, her hand in his, she felt Alzen's sorcery flooding through her thoughts, swelling and surging, rising like a river that had burst its banks.

28

Isten returned to the Blacknells Road each day, early in the morning, before the crowds arrived, and went to see the fox. She took scraps of food and hurled them through the bars, not leaving until something landed near enough for the animal to eat. She tried to throw water too, but it was useless. The dry, sun-baked earth soaked up the few droplets that landed near the fox. Several times, the fox looked directly at Isten. There was no fear in its eyes, only a savage, unbreakable will.

On the third morning, Isten arrived to find the fox dead, surrounded by a cloud of flies. Isten was still there hours later, slumped against the mesh, blistering in the heat, when Brast came looking for her. She was mute and confused as he led her home, unable to understand his questions.

They heard little word of the other Exiles. The hiramites' proclamation had been clear. Any gatherings, for any reason, would result in their immediate execution. Brast was worried that he might be breaking the law by sheltering Isten and he was visibly relieved when she stopped leaving the house and took to spending all her time in his bedroom, sleeping, or just lying on his bed, staring at the ceiling, clawing at her greasy tresses as though they were infested with lice.

For the first few weeks, Isten begged Brast to fetch her drink or anything else that could free her from her thoughts, but when he refused she was surprised to find that she didn't care. She didn't care about anything, for that matter. All she could think about was the grotesque interloper in her mind. The progeny of Alzen's murders, festering and seething, hideously vital, desperate to be unleashed. She let Brast bring her food and pretended to listen when he passed on rare scraps of news about the Exiles. There was no word of Gombus, and everyone else was being very careful to keep their heads down but, apparently, Puthnok had fulfilled her political destiny and become a firebrand. Despite the orders of the Elect, she had begun holding rallies, just like Isten's mother used to do back in Rukon. She was preaching against the Elect. Calling the people to action. Telling them that change was possible. That wealth could be shared and rulers could be elected. That revolution was within reach. That they outnumbered their masters ten to one. She was being protected by some of the Exiles and, before the hiramites arrived, she always managed to vanish, sheltered by her supporters. It amused Isten to think that Gombus had spent so many years trying to convince her to become a rallying cry, when timid little Puthnok was the one he really needed.

"They'll kill her," she said one evening, as Brast told her another story of Puthnok's trouble-making. She had not spoken for days.

He gave her an odd look and she realized how flat her voice had been, how uninterested she was in the disaster that was rushing towards Puthnok. The world felt unreal. Everyone Brast mentioned seemed like a ghost. Or one of the faded figures she had seen carved into the stage at the Kephali Theatre.

She shrugged. "She always wanted to be a martyr."

Brast lowered his gaze and began clearing away the plates. She sensed that he was becoming afraid of her. Even devotion has a limit, she realized.

One day, when Brast was out of the house, Isten ventured out with no clear idea where she was headed. She walked along the Saraca for a while, watching salvage crews and hovellers. Crowds of emaciated poor were working on the embankment and she wondered which of the families had been visited by Alzen to create the power she had so lusted after, still lusted after.

Her feet led her through dozens of winding streets and up spiralling walkways until she found herself, unexpectedly, outside the Rookery – the doss house where she had last seen Gombus. She went inside, squeezed her way up the stairs past the whores and tapped at his door. It was not properly shut and it opened to reveal an empty, litter-strewn room, devoid of furniture. There was a dusty old wine bottle on the floor and she picked it up, wondering if it was the one he shared with them on the night of Amoria's death.

"Where's Gombus?" she asked, looking back at one of the whores.

The woman gave her a wary look. "The old man?"

Isten nodded.

"He died, nearly a month ago." The whore narrowed her eyes. "You his friend?"

Isten was about to reply, then she simply shook her head and continued staring at the empty room. She felt no grief, nor any surprise. If anything, she felt a slight lightening of her spirit. With Gombus gone, there was no one to remember what had been promised in her name, no one to know how short she had fallen.

She put the bottle down and left the Rookery, taking a meandering route home. She went back to the river and stood for a long time at the end of a jetty, watching the poisoned, iridescent currents whirl past her through the gloom. As always, the corpses of plague victims were bobbing among the chemicals. It would be easy enough to join them, she thought – to plunge into the water and float away. Surely then, at the point of death, her mind would be her own once more. She laughed bitterly, realizing she was too much of a coward to kill herself. Then she turned away from the river and headed home.

It was dusk when she finally returned to Brast's house. He ushered her inside, checking that no one was watching.

"It's happened," he said, his eyes wide, as he stooped to light a lamp.

Isten dropped heavily into a chair. "What?"

His face was ashen. "They've caught Puthnok."

Isten felt a brief flicker of emotion, like the last ember of a fire.

"She was holding a rally behind the Stump. She might have got away with it but hundreds of people turned up." He shook his head. "People really believe in her, Isten. Not just Exiles – all sorts of people." He took a piece of paper from his robes, glancing back at the window, as though expecting to see someone watching him through the shutters. He held the paper out. There was smudgy, tiny text printed on both sides. "They've started printing extracts from her manifesto. People from across the city have been travelling to the Botanical Quarter to hear her."

Isten was not looking at Brast, or the paper. She was staring at the floorboards, remembering the sound of Puthnok's voice on the day she started preaching to the Exiles in the Alembeck Temple. She could see why people might follow her. There was no facade with Puthnok, just a simple, childish belief that things would be fair one day. "But she's been caught?"

Brast nodded, lowering the paper and sitting in a chair opposite Isten's. "They're going to make a spectacle of it. They want her to be an example of what happens to people who speak against the Elect. They're going to string her up in Verulum Square, with all the statues of dead phraters watching." He stared at the crumpled paper in his hand. "Poor thing."

"They're going to hang her?"

He nodded, turning the paper over in his hands. "Tomorrow night."

Isten knew she should feel something – panic, grief, anger, anything. Puthnok was her friend. They grew up together. But she just felt numb.

"I'm going," said Brast, speaking quietly.

"You want to watch?" Isten frowned. "Why?"

He looked at her with a mixture of embarrassment and defiance. "I can't help her, but I can at least bear witness. She may be a fool, but she's a brave fool, and she's probably the last honest soul left in this pit of a city." His eyes flashed, daring Isten to mock him. "I'm going to paint a picture of her."

She nodded.

"Will you come with me?" he said.
She shrugged. "If you want me to."

29

Puthnok had never been brave. She tried to pretend, sometimes, that she was like Isten, or like her brother had been, but she was not made that way. There were no lights in the cell, but a little moonlight was spilling down from a high, narrow window, and she could see her hands shaking as they gripped her knees. The hiramites were furious when they dragged her from the crowd; their voices contorted with rage as they hurled her to the ground and began to kick. There were bruises all over her body but she had managed to walk into the cell unaided so she guessed nothing was broken. She held her hand up into the shaft of light and the fingernail of her index finger flashed, iridescent, like the inside of a shell. The weazen, Tok, had given the nail to her as a gift, days ago, saying that she might soon be in need of a weapon. She'd refused at first, but the creature had seemed so wounded she relented and let him graft the blade to her finger, only vaguely listening as he explained how she could use it.

Thinking of Tok reminded her of all the other strange creatures that had come to hear her speak behind the Stump. She had never been more afraid than when she stepped out before them, but she had hidden it behind sure, confident tones, determined not to cloud her message with mumbled speech or cringing self-deprecation. For a moment, she remembered the crowd's fervour, how it rose as she spoke, ignited by the idea of change; then the soldiers came and the screaming began. How quickly hope can turn to panic.

There was a rattle of keys at the cell door and Puthnok backed away, stumbling under the weight of her shackles.

She blinked, blinded, as the door slammed open and the light of a mandrel-fire flooded into the cell.

Then the light was blocked as an enormous figure stooped and squeezed through the doorway.

Puthnok backed away until she was pressed against the cell wall. However afraid she had been before, it was nothing to the terror that gripped her as the door closed and she saw the figure that entered. It was a metal colossus, similar to the one that killed Amoria in the warehouse, but clad in even more complex spirals of metal tracery. There were tendrils of smoke coiling round the giant's helmet and he was gripping an ornate copper staff that must have been eight foot tall. As the giant approached her, Puthnok realized her mistake. He wasn't wearing a helmet – the mesh of glinting coils resting on his shoulders was his face. She could see human eyes staring at her through the wires, studying her like she was a peculiar insect.

She whispered a prayer and shook her head. "They told me…" Her voice was a ragged croak. She cleared her throat, trying to speak clearly. "They told me the execution was tomorrow night."

The golden giant continued staring at her in silence for a moment, then looked around the cell. He saw the stone slab that passed for a bed and sat down on it. Even seated, he was looking down at Puthnok.

"You're not what I expected," he said. His voice sounded like resonating metal – like the echo of a bell. "You don't look much like a revolutionary."

For a moment, Puthnok was unable to speak. She was shocked that this metal-clad monster could speak, and she was even more surprised that he seemed to want a conversation with her.

"Are you really Puthnok?" he said.

She nodded.

"You are the one who has been calling for the destruction of my order? You are the one who is trying to incite riots and rebellion." He sounded amused.

"*Your* order?" she whispered. "Who are you?"

"My name is Seleucus. I am your regent, Puthnok. I am the Old King. I am the lord of the Elect. I am the man you would like to see deposed."

Puthnok's fists clenched as her fear turned to rage.

Seleucus laughed. The sound was so loud and bright that Puthnok winced.

"You'd like to hurt me?" Seleucus shook his head, struggling to stifle his mirth. "You wretched little ingrate. You have no idea what I am; what I mean."

"Kill me," muttered Puthnok. "We have nothing to discuss."

Seleucus laughed again. "Oh, you're a delightful little creature, aren't you? I wish we could have met sooner. No, I'm not here to kill you. My duties are tiresome, it's true, but they do not extend to the murdering of paupers." He shifted slightly on the bunk and it cracked under his weight, scattering dust across the floor. "I came to make you an offer." He reached out, his long arm easily crossing the distance between them, and ran one of his cold, polished fingertips across her neck. "The noose can be a cruel way to die, Puthnok. Especially for someone as small as you. I'm afraid your neck will probably survive the fall. And then it will take quite a while for you to be strangled by the rope. You'll dance there for a long time, soiling yourself and sobbing as the crowds laugh at what a funny colour your face is turning. You might spend several minutes like that. Not a very dignified end, I'm afraid."

Puthnok wanted to be defiant, to sneer at him like Isten would do, but she was terrified, picturing the scene he was describing with horrible clarity.

"Unless…" said Seleucus, still stroking her neck.

"Unless what?" she whispered, too scared to move.

He took back his hand. "There will be a large crowd there tomorrow night. Executions are perennially popular. You will have a wonderful opportunity to atone."

"Atone?"

"To tell them, little Puthnok, how wrong you were. How wrong you are. How foolish you were to speak against us. Tell the crowds that you only said the things you did because you craved power. Tell them you regret your lies and beg them not to make the same mistakes you made."

Once more, Puthnok's fear was washed away by hate. "Never," she muttered. "You're here because you're afraid. You know I've started something."

The wry tone vanished from Seleucus's voice. "What do you think you've started?"

Puthnok flinched, unable to hide her fear, but then she raised her chin. "I've started an uprising. Killing me won't change anything. The people have opened their eyes." She waved at the network of gold that covered his armour. "You think you can hoard all this wealth while everyone else crawls in the shit, starving and bleeding while you hide in a palace, but it's all going to come crashing down around your ears. I saw it in their faces. They're your subjects no longer. This is the start of the end."

Seleucus rose from his seat and seemed on the verge of striking her.

Puthnok cowered, but the giant shook his head and sat down again, battling to keep his voice level. "What would you have us do?" he said. "Let the people choose their leaders? Who would that leader be, do you think? Who would be the leader that united everyone? Who's the person that would be chosen by the weazens and chosen by the aornos, and also by the ossops, and the krios and the hovellers. Who would they all agree on?" He laughed. "You?" He gripped the stone bunk and began crushing it as he spoke. "What do you think Athanor would become without us? Without fear. Without law. It would be a slaughterhouse. We've created a miracle here. This is the Great Work. Do you see? Athanor is the Great Work." He looked away, shaking his head, and he no longer seemed to be speaking to Puthnok. "Even some of my own fraternity have misunderstood, thinking that personal power is the goal, but it's not. The goal is Athanor. And it's beautiful." His voice grew rough with passion. "Athanor is not glorious because of its gold and its spires, it's glorious because of the people who live here; so many races, so many disparate souls, living alongside each other. No other civilization has ever achieved this.

Athanor has endured and grown and survived. We have created paradise, Puthnok. If you had even..."

Seleucus's words trailed off and he shook his head, seeming annoyed that he had said so much. "You can't understand, of course. Your kind never could. We let you into heaven and you want to tear it down. We give you a home and you want to change our laws – our way of life. Your kind believes only in destruction." He rose from the bench. "You had your chance and you've made your choice."

He was insane, realized Puthnok. He looked at teeming, starving masses, kept in line through terror and violence, and saw paradise. He was far more of a monster than she could ever have imagined. She massaged her shaven scalp, tormented by the idea that such a lunatic had so much power.

As Puthnok rubbed her head, something sharp scratched against her skin and she remembered the nail, the gift from Tok, a fragment of his own shell-like body, carrying all the violent, transformative power of his race. An idea occurred to her. She had spent her whole life surrounded by liars and she had always held herself to a higher standard, but now she wondered if it was time for a change. In her last moments, might a lie be excusable? Necessary, even?

"Wait," she muttered, sure that he would immediately see through her crude attempt at deceit.

He halted by the door, still stooped, and looked back at her.

"Perhaps I do understand," she said, loosening the fingernail in the way Tok had taught her. "It's true, I suppose. People would never agree on a leader. There would just be warring tribes. The city would be a mess."

"What are you doing?" he asked, quietly, his suspicion plain in his voice. "You don't believe that." He turned to face her. "This is fear talking, isn't it? You're afraid of a slow death." His voice brightened. "It's understandable. Why would you want to go like that, in agony? Swallow your pride. Say the things I want you to say, and I will give a signal to the executioner. He can make sure you die quickly and painlessly."

Seleucus sounded excited as he came back to lean over her. "Whatever you think of me, Puthnok, I would not break my word. If you repent before you die, I swear to you, on the Temple itself, that you will die in fraction of a second, of a broken neck, rather than hanging there for who knows how long, trying to breathe."

He was close enough. She had the nail in her palm. All she had to do was hurl it and he would die a horrible death.

Seleucus leant even closer. She could see his staring, eager eyes. She could kill him now.

And then what? She pictured the results of her murder. Another Curious Man would take his place. Another monster, indistinguishable from this one. A tyrant for a tyrant. And, in the process, she would make a monster of herself – just another liar, tricking and deceiving, saying things she didn't mean so she could wield power, like Isten. She would be a murderer. She would be like the Elect.

She dropped the nail to the floor and shook her head.

"You're right," she said, meeting his gaze with pride. "I don't believe it and I won't say it." She felt suddenly calm. "Let me die slowly, and with my soul intact."

His eyes widened. "You filthy little worm." He grabbed her by the throat and lifted her off her feet.

Puthnok gasped in horror as strands of metal exploded from the hand that was crushing her windpipe, whirling around her and skimming across her face.

"No," gasped Seleucus, hurling her against the wall and letting her slide to the floor.

Pain knifed through her and she curled up in a ball as he towered over her, his voice as savage as the hiramites who dragged her into the cell.

"Whatever game you're playing it won't work," he cried. "You'll die tomorrow, as planned, in front of everyone. And they'll laugh as you squirm. I'll tell the executioner to make it last. The pain will be horrific, Puthnok. I'll make sure of it."

Puthnok was winded, gasping for breath but, as Seleucus stormed from the cell, she was pleased to see that he was staggering with rage.

30

Verulum Square was almost as crowded as it had been for the Festival of Undying Light. There were no wicker statues and no one had painted their face, but there was still a hideously carnival-like atmosphere. There were dozens of hastily erected food stalls to cater for the crowds and the mandrel-fires had all been lit, shimmering across the faceless statues of Curious Men. There was a stark difference though. At the centre of the square a scaffold had been erected with a noose hung from the crossbeam. Gathered before the gallows, their upside-down faces leering in the gloom, were hundreds of hiramites, standing in motionless blocks, their falcatas drawn and raised in silent warning.

As Isten and Brast shoved their way through the crowd, Isten saw something even more surprising than the ranks of soldiers. At the far end of the square, at the feet of one of the statues, was a group of Curious Men, their pale, yellow robes gleaming in the twilight and at their head was the Old King himself, towering over the others with the Emerald Lion at his side. Isten had never heard of the regent attending any kind of public occasion.

"She's unnerved them," muttered Brast. "All this talk of revolution has worried them. Look," he said, pointing to some shapes behind the Old King, next to the phraters. They were large, copper braziers, propped up on metal tripods. "That's how they summon their power. Even with all those hiramites here, they're not taking any chances. Our little Puthnok has spooked them."

Isten nodded, but she was already regretting coming. Everywhere she looked she saw eager, excited faces – people shoving their way to the front, hoping to get a glimpse of the woman who had drawn the Elect from their temples. It was grotesque.

She was about to tell Brast she wanted to go when he grabbed her by the arm. "There she is!"

A murmur went through the crowd as Puthnok was brought out into the square. Her arms were shackled and her shaven head was covered in bruises and fresh cuts. She was still wearing her little round glasses, but one of the lenses had cracked. The hiramites shoved her forwards as though she was a dangerous fighter, despite the fact that she was barely five foot tall and looked more like a worried cleric. As always, she walked as though she was falling, tumbling forwards on her tiptoes, and the sight of her peculiar gait caused Isten to pause, tugging at an emotion she had almost forgotten. She allowed Brast to lead her back into the crowd.

The soldiers steered Puthnok up onto the scaffold where an elderly, regal-looking laborator was waiting to pronounce judgment. Next to him there was another hiramite. He was wearing a black leather mask.

Brast dragged Isten closer, and as they neared the rows of hiramites that were holding back the crowds, Isten saw Puthnok's face clearly for the first time.

Her breath caught in her throat. Puthnok did not look

scared. Or, at least, her fear was secondary. The main thing Isten saw in her eyes was defiance. She was unbroken. Unafraid. Prepared to die. It was the same furious determination Isten had seen in the eyes of the fox.

"Don't die for *this*," whispered Isten, surprised to find tears pricking at her eyes. "Don't die for Athanor."

Brast looked at her in shock. "What?"

She was not listening to him. As they pushed Puthnok towards the noose, the man in the black mask offered her a hood.

Puthnok shook her head and raised her chin, looking somehow taller than anyone else on the platform.

As they dropped the noose over Puthnok's head, Isten felt a dizzying rush of pride. It flooded her limbs with a vigour she had not felt for a long time. "Not for this," she whispered.

The hiramite in the black mask stepped forwards and tested the knot.

Then he stumbled, touching his chest.

Blood rushed through his fingers, and as he dropped to his knees, Isten realized there was a crossbow bolt sunk deep between his ribs.

Gasps of surprise and fear washed through the crowd.

The hiramites on the scaffold rushed to help the wounded man, while the ones lined up below looked to their captain for guidance.

"There!" cried someone in the crowd, and the captain ordered some of his men to break ranks and charge into the throng.

Screams rang out as the soldiers trampled and shoved their way into the mob.

Isten was shaking her head, still staring at Puthnok.

Another bolt sliced through the darkness, thudding into the chest of the old laborator. He was so frail that the impact kicked him from the scaffold and sent him pinwheeling back through the air. He landed on the flagstones with a crunch.

"Over here!" cried someone else, and soldiers rushed in that direction, eliciting more cries and leaving ragged holes in the rows of soldiers.

"They'll kill the lot of us," cried Brast, pulling Isten back the way they'd come, trying to lead her away from the scaffold.

She freed herself from his grip and pushed forwards into the tumult.

More bolts thudded into the figures on the scaffold, and those that still could began to scatter for cover, leaving Puthnok to stand alone in the moonlight, her head still trapped in the noose, her hands still shackled.

"We have to help her," said Isten, surprised by her own words.

Brast stared at her, horrified and incredulous. Then nodded, forcing himself, with obvious difficulty, to follow her towards the gallows.

The lines of hiramites were now in complete disarray and, as Isten approached them, she saw the reason for the random shots and the cries from the crowd. With carefully planned timing, the people standing near the broken lines of soldiers rushed forwards, howling and drawing weapons.

Isten laughed in shock. Lorinc was there, and Feyer and Korlath and Piros. Dozens of Exiles, openly defying the Old King's edict, smashing into the soldiers with a flurry of sword strikes and axe blows. Mixed in them were dozens more warriors – some of the headhunters Isten had hired and even some Aroc Brothers, all of them roaring as they tore through the reeling hiramites.

Puthnok's followers smashed through the soldiers with ease. Clearly, no one had really expected an organized, armed attack. The hiramites tried to fight back, but the Exiles ripped into them with such ferocity that they had to fall back, unable to do more than parry as they stumbled across the square. Swords clanged and flashed as the fight descended into chaos.

Half the people in the square were screaming and fighting to escape, struggling to reach the gates, but the other half stayed where they were, howling in approval.

Isten could not believe what she was seeing. Puthnok had stoked a fire. She had roused an anger that had lain dormant for thousands of years.

She remembered the dagger tucked in her jerkin and drew it out, rushing to join the battle with Brast following.

One of the hiramites stopped and stared at her, his shock visible through the upside-down eyeholes of his helmet.

"You!" he cried, drawing back his falcata and charging.

She sidestepped and lashed out with her knife.

The blade clanged against his helmet. The metal stopped the blade but she hit him with such force that his head rocked back on his shoulders and he stumbled away from her.

Brast rushed forwards and punched him in the stomach, doubling him over.

Another hiramite broke through the chaos and slammed into Brast, sending them both rolling across the flagstones.

Isten booted the soldier off Brast and lunged with her knife.

The hiramite parried, drew back his falcata to strike, then collapsed as Brast hacked him down with a savage flurry of blows.

The first hiramite barrelled into Isten, but she grabbed her knife in both hands and hammered it down between his shoulder blades. As they slammed to the ground, the soldier was already dead.

She shoved the corpse away and staggered to her feet.

Brast was breathless and pale, but he nodded at her and they both turned and sprinted towards the scaffold.

As she ran, Isten saw that the captain of the hiramites was trying to lead his men up the steps towards Puthnok. He'd clearly decided to finish the job the executioner had started. Lorinc and some of the headhunters had got there first though. They had blocked the staircase and were now battling furiously to stop the soldiers advancing.

Puthnok was watching the battle with a dazed expression on her face. It was clear that she had not expected this rescue attempt.

Isten reached the bottom of the steps just as some of the headhunters fought their way to the same point. They grinned in surprise at the sight of Isten, and together they launched themselves at the scrum of hiramites.

The soldiers lashed out with drilled, brutal precision, but the skulls embedded in the headhunters' flesh acted as a crude kind of armour. The shrunken heads crumpled and split under the flurry of blows but shielded the headhunters' flesh. The headhunters swung their axes, bellowing war cries as they cut the hiramites down.

Isten ducked and weaved as she ran, dodging axes and swords and bounding up the steps, kicking hiramites into the air as she ran past.

She had almost reached the platform when the hiramites' captain slammed her down onto the steps, his hand locked around her throat, his eyes blazing. "You?" he gasped, drawing back his sword to strike.

He slammed against her, vomiting hot blood as an axe whumped into his back.

Isten kicked him away and saw a headhunter looming over her. Dozens of faces grinned at her from his chest as he took her hand and hauled her to her feet.

She nodded in thanks and pounded up the final few steps.

Puthnok looked even more shocked as she saw Isten racing towards her.

Isten cut the rope and caught Puthnok as she staggered, racked by painful cramps.

Fighting raged all round them. Dozens of the combatants had followed Isten up onto the platform and figures were whirling around, stabbing and lunging.

"You came to save me?" Puthnok was shaking her head, looking from Isten's bloody face to the tumult around the scaffold. Hundreds more people had rushed to join the attack. There was a full-scale riot taking place. People were tearing down stalls and using the wood as clubs and stakes, attacking hiramites wherever they saw them. Some of the mandrel-fires had been kicked over, splashing chemicals across the other stalls and setting them alight. Fires were spreading quickly across the square.

Isten was as shocked as Puthnok by what was happening. "No," she replied, unable to lie to Puthnok. "I came to watch you die."

"But then you did this." Puthnok stared at her. "Gombus

knew. He was right about you. I never believed him but he knew."

A hiramite broke through the scrum and charged towards them.

Isten was ready. She dodged his sword thrust and hammered her knife into the back of his neck.

The soldier sprawled at her feet and, as he tried to rise, Isten booted him off the scaffold, sending him plummeting to the crowds below.

"Fuck! Them! All!" roared Lorinc, appearing at her side, laughing wildly, his face drenched in blood. He looked deranged. "Fuck 'em, fuck 'em, fuck 'em!"

He stood in front of Isten and Puthnok, and every time a hiramite tried to reach them, he tore into them like a wounded bear, ripping, hacking and punching until they were surrounded by a pile of bodies.

Others followed suit, forming a protective circle around Isten and Puthnok, fighting with shocking violence, determined to protect the two women as more hiramites battled up the steps onto the platform.

"Isten!" cried Puthnok, grabbing her arm and pointing across the crowds.

For a moment, Isten thought the flames had reached up into the night sky, forming a column of fire, but then she realized her mistake. The flames were being reflected by a towering colossus that was wading through the crowds. It was identical to the one that killed Amoria and the one she saw fighting headhunters in Brauron.

"An Ignorant Man," she whispered, as the giant automaton broke into a run, causing the ground to shudder as it pounded across the square. Its mane of metal coils was curling and growing as it ran, flashing in the firelight, adding to the impression that the giant was alight.

Behind it, at the back of the square, Isten could see the phraters, hunched over their braziers, hurling powders and oils, their golden masks lit from beneath as their sorcery blazed in the metal bowls. The Old King was watching calmly as the Ignorant Man ran towards Isten, leaning on his copper staff as though he were watching a boring play.

The crowds parted in terror as the giant passed, abandoning their protest and scattering through archways and alleys.

Even the hiramites faltered at the sight of the metal titan. They backed down the steps and left the Exiles alone on the scaffold as the Ignorant Man thundered towards them.

Isten thought of the dead fox, rigid and twisted in mounds of rubble. "No," she said quietly, looking down at Puthnok. "I won't let it happen."

The Ignorant Man extended its hand, fingers splayed, and the flagstones detonated, splitting into shards of gold. A glittering explosion engulfed the crowds. Screams cut through the night. People were ripped apart. Blood shimmered as body parts clanged across the square, half metal and half flesh, trailing wires and intestines.

The fighters around Puthnok fired a barrage of crossbow bolts and the giant's head jolted back, kicking up sparks and causing the Ignorant Man to stagger and raise its arm in a defensive gesture, as though swatting flies.

None of the bolts pierced its mask and, surrounded by dozens of screaming, wounded people, the Ignorant Man calmly raised its palm again, aiming it at the scaffold.

Isten could see the intricate circle engraved into the

giant's hand, glowing with heat.

Images streamed through her mind: Amoria, dead in the warehouse; the corpses in Brauron, piled on the riverbank; Alzen's terrified victims, weeping as he ripped their souls out. So much death. So much pain. All wrought by the Elect. Finally, she saw the Sisters of Solace – Naos, bidding her farewell in the library of Alabri House with the words: "The future is not fixed."

All those deaths. All those poor souls robbed to create Alzen's power. Their deaths could be worth something. For weeks, Isten had known what she carried. The monster coiled beneath her skull. She had tried to hide from the truth, but here it was, charging towards her across Verulum Square, preparing to murder every brave soul who had stood with Puthnok. The Elect had to be destroyed. And she had the power to do it.

Isten relaxed, allowing the flame at the back of her thoughts to erupt, billowing through her head. Light filled her eyes – the light she had stolen as Alzen died in the theatre, grasping at infinity.

She reached out with her right hand and her body convulsed, jolting as the light ripped through her palm, tearing the darkness open, crossing the heads of the crowd and slamming into the Ignorant Man.

It staggered, engulfed by a blaze of golden filaments.

The crowds below were bathed in brilliant light and Puthnok and the others backed away from Isten, lit up by the glare, shaking their heads in wonder as her body shuddered. The same metal threads that had engulfed the Ignorant Man were also erupting from Isten, surrounding her in a golden cocoon.

The crowds stared as the blast grew in brightness and ferocity, pummelling the Ignorant Man.

The giant staggered again, its hands raised in front of its face; then it fell, hitting the flagstones like a falling tower, shaking statues and throwing up a cloud of embers and dust.

Isten was barely aware of what was happening in the square. Her thoughts were already elsewhere. Her mind had leapt to a thousand places, racing across the city, tumbling down the Saraca, blazing through windows, roaring down streets, expanding, growing, engulfing Athanor's unmappable sprawl. She laughed. She could see everything. *Feel* everything. Her veins meshed with walkways and spires. She was becoming the city. It was orbiting her, turning in her wake, caught in her gravity.

The city shifted and strained at her touch, stretching and growing, like leaves kissed by the sun. As Isten's mind soared around the outer walls, she was flooded with joy and comprehension. She heard the city's heart beat and it was not, as she might have guessed, in the temples of the Elect. It was in a brothel, in the gardens of Alabri House, cradled by the Sisters of Solace. *They* were the soul of Athanor. And they had sent Alzen to her. They had foreseen this moment. They kept her alive for this. Her final reservations fell away and she focused her thoughts back on Verulum Square, revelling in her ferocious power.

The Ignorant Man was little more than a sparking heap of scrap, its back arched and one of its arms raised to the heavens in a silent plea.

Most of the crowds had reached the relative safety of the streets around the square, but they were still watching to see what happened next.

Back in her own flesh, Isten was shocked by the din that surrounded her. Her body was inside a tornado of metal strands. They were humming and clicking around her like insects, fluttering across her skin and buffeting her hair.

"Isten!" cried Puthnok. Her face was anguished and afraid. "What are you doing? What's happened to you?"

Isten was about to reply, when she saw movement on the far side of the square. The Curious Men were working furiously over their braziers. Plumes of smoke were rising into the darkness, filled with embers and flashes of light.

In a second, she understood, seeing easily into the minds of the phraters. They were summoning more Ignorant Men. The effort of producing so many was half-killing them. They cried out in pain as the columns of smoke took form, solidifying, becoming golden titans.

"Isten!" cried Puthnok again, sounding even more horrified, but Isten had no time to respond. The Ignorant Men were already running across the square, lights flashing at the joints of their armoured bodies. There were six of them and, as they ran, their weight split the flagstones and toppled the statues of the Elect watching over the tombs.

As she watched the statues fall, Isten remembered the corpses that were seated at their base, way beneath the ground in the catacombs – the bodies of Curious Men, preserved over centuries.

She smiled, realizing the perfect way to stop the attack. She plunged her thoughts down into the catacombs and into the dusty flesh of the corpses under the statues. Synapses flared and muscles twitched as Isten's power pulsed through the cadavers. All across the catacombs, the corpses of long-dead phraters rose from their seats, trailing shreds of skin as their eyelids rolled back from empty sockets.

Up on the surface of the square, the Ignorant Men slowed and halted, confused to see architecture coming to life around them. As Isten's will animated the corpses, they in turn roused the statues built in their likeness.

Isten was still laughing as she sent the crumbling fifty-foot statues lumbering across the square and smashing into the Ignorant Men.

The Ignorant Men punched and grappled with the statues, shedding chunks of marble and gold, filling the night with an apocalyptic din.

The phraters on the far side of the square staggered back from their braziers, smoke trailing from their masks as they collapsed, exhausted and shocked. Only Seleucus remained standing, watching the clashing giants with the same calm dispassion he had shown all evening.

As Isten's power continued to grow, more of the statues shrugged off centuries of dust and lurched into movement, pounding into the fray, slamming lichened fists into the Ignorant Men.

Isten enjoyed the irony of the scene for a while, but the energy jolting through her soon made it absurd to pretend this was a physical fight. She raised her arms and the square exploded: statues, giants, tombs and sepulchres; everything detonating at once, filling the air with metal and rock. The noise grew even louder and the figures next to Isten on the scaffold dropped to their knees, howling, their hands over their ears.

"Isten!" wailed Puthnok, trying to call her back from the apocalypse.

Isten's perception was now so heightened she could feel

every molecule of the inferno, every cell, warping and changing in the heat.

One by one, the phraters collapsed, crumbling like coals in a brazier, their robes erupting into flame and their helmets melting into their skulls.

Too late, the Old King decided to act, striding through the flames towards her. She could see his thoughts as clearly as her own. He was afraid and furious. He raised his staff and pointed it at her, his lion running after him, preparing to attack, but it was absurd. He was like a rat attacking a tornado.

Light flashed at the end of his staff and something spat through the air.

A shard of gold sank into her chest. It should have been enough to stop her heart, but it did no more damage than an insect bite.

She crushed him. Ending his reign with a casual swipe of her hand, flattening him with a golden tsunami, ripping him apart with razor-sharp beauty. Shock waves rippled through the air and smashed into the lion, shattering it, scattering shards of emerald through the crowd.

With the Elect lying mangled and crushed, Isten embraced the city, feeling its extremities as clearly as she could feel her blazing fingertips. She could mould it and reform it with a thought, casting streets into the sky and ripping buildings from the earth. Athanor was hers. As she reached out into the stars, she realized that she could send the city anywhere. Conjunction, the power hoarded by the Elect for all these centuries, was hers.

As the storm raged around her, Isten felt a moment of doubt. Her whole life she had been a disaster – ruining everything she touched. What kind of ruin would she wreak now? What would she do with this kind of power at her command?

Someone was screaming her name. With incredible difficulty, Isten managed to bring her gaze back to the scaffold.

Most of the Exiles were lying face down on the splintered wood, hands clamped over their heads as a metal tempest raged around them, but Puthnok was still on her knees, reaching through the tumult, tears streaming down her face, pleading with her to stop.

Isten walked towards her, carried on waves of metal, light bleeding from her eyes.

She grabbed Puthnok's hand.

Puthnok could barely look at her. She squinted into the glare, shielding her eyes as Isten leant closer.

"Help me," said Isten. She had intended her words to be a whisper, but the air shook with the force of them.

Puthnok shook her head, buffeted by shreds of metal, gasping for breath. "How?" she cried, hanging desperately onto Isten's hand as the storm continued to grow.

"You are the good in me." Isten's voice was a thunderclap. "Make me more than a weapon. Tell me what to do," she looked up at the metal-lashed sky. "Tell me what to do with this."

Puthnok stared at her with a mixture of terror and dawning recognition. "What *can* you do?"

"Anything!" laughed Isten.

Despite the violence of the storm, Puthnok's anguish started to fade. Clinging to Isten's hand, she managed to stand, staggering like she was on the deck of a listing ship.

"Can you take us home?"

Everything fell away: doubt, grief and guilt, transformed by an alchymia greater than anything Alzen could have imagined.

Isten embraced Puthnok, nodding and weeping with joy, flooding the city with light, hurling it into the void.

ACKNOWLEDGMENTS

Thanks to Marc, Penny and Nick at Angry Robot for all your support and guidance and for steering Athanor so skilfully onto the printed page. You are the nicest kind of angry and I've had great fun working with you.

Matt Keefe, you've probably learned your lesson (never ask Darius if he needs anything reading!) but your feedback on those early drafts was invaluable, as was your final edit, and I can't thank you enough for all your help and insight.

Nick Kyme, you had nothing whatsoever to do with this book. However… I would never have had the confidence to invent my own worlds without the help you gave me when I was writing about other people's.

Mum and dad, you filled my childhood with books and a love of stories, which is probably where all my problems began, so thanks for that.

Arthur and Joe, fruit of my loins, I would like to thank you for being a constant reminder that life is boundlessly wonderful and always worth fighting for.

Lastly, I'd like to thank my wife, Kathryn, for listening so patiently, reading so carefully, for being the most honest person I ever met, and for not kicking me in the balls when I said I'd like to be a full-time author.

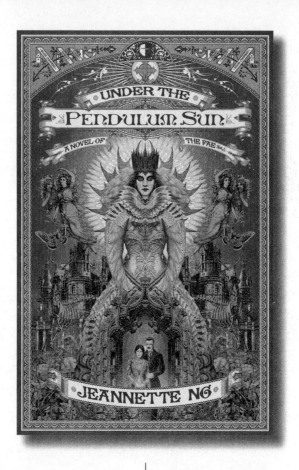

Two Victorian missionaries travel into darkest fairyland, to deliver their uplifting message to the godless magical beings who dwell there… at the risk of losing their own mortal souls.

Winner of the Syndney J Bounds Award, the British Fantasy Award for Best Newcomer

Shortlisted for the John W Campbell Award

UNDER THE PENDULUM SUN by Jeanette Ng • PAPERBACK & EBOOK
from all good stationers and book emporia